RETURN of The Part

by Mark Cunnington

To David

Best Wishes

Mark Cunnington

Trio Publishing

Also by Trio Publishing

The Syndicate
The Syndicate 2nd Edition
The Syndicate (R.I.P.) Part II

First published 2002

Published by Trio Publishing
50 Gillsman's Park
St. Leonards on Sea
East Sussex
TN38 0SW

ISBN 0 9537951 2 8

Copyright © Mark Cunnington 2002

All rights reserved. No part of this publication may be reproduced, stored or introduced into any type of retrieval system, or transmitted, in any form, or by any means without the prior written permission of the publisher.

This book is sold subject to the condition that it shall not, by way of trade or otherwise, be lent, re-sold, hired out or otherwise circulated without the publisher's prior consent in any form of binding or cover other than in which it is published and without a similar condition including this condition being imposed on the subsequent purchaser.

Printed and bound by Chandlers Printers Ltd
Bexhill-on-Sea, East Sussex

INTRODUCTION

Life can be very bewildering. Incidents can sometimes occur to unlucky or, depending on your viewpoint, fortunate individuals which are both unnerving and seemingly beyond all logical explanation. Of course ninety-nine point nine percent of the time there is a rational solution to the event involved no matter however bizarre it may seem on initial investigation. But what of the remaining point one of a percent? The following carp fishing tale undoubtedly fits into that small statistical range.

Our story continues from where we left it.

Chapter 1

"Dearly beloved," the vicar looked up from his bible and threw a sombre glance that was destined to be for my benefit, I was the only one present after all. "We are gathered here today to bid farewell to our close friend, Timothy Eugene Ramsbottom. Now Timothy was a dear…"

His words drifted in and out of my conscience as I surveyed the grim scene before me, my eyes moistening as I took in the whole sorry affair. This was so weird, so bizarre, it defied all comprehension, well, defied mine certainly. Directly in front of me there was the vicar, wearily going through the motions of repeating words he had uttered hundreds of times before, desperately trying to impart feeling into his voice and to show that he cared and felt what I should have felt. Before him lay the oversized coffin, inside which, lay the inert mass of molecules that passed for the person who had been my best friend. I shuddered involuntary, my stomach tightening, this wasn't a pleasant experience. At least whoever's job it was had made a good effort with the coffin, it looked substantial, well made and of good quality wood. Also there were no tacky, cheapskate brass handles on this particular death box, the beautiful Fuji DPS 20's in Gunsmoke with stainless collars were much more in keeping. The vicar wouldn't have understood them but at least the rod builder who had supplied them to the coffin makers had realised their significance.

To the left of the vicar, still mouthing words which my brain no longer listened to, was a cavernous mouth that had been freshly dug in Mother Earth. Gaping and ready to eventually swallow the morose oblong box, I presumed it had been excavated by a couple of grave diggers who, while shovelling for their wages, had cracked jokes and traded black-humoured observations, wholly untouched by what they were forming and by what would end up in it. The paradox of death, I thought, so crippling when close, so uninvolving when detached. I forgave both the gravediggers and the vicar, what else could I expect? I'd read headlines of hundreds dying and my thoughts of superficial concern, forgotten by the time I'd reached the sport pages, were no different. I suppose they were getting paid for it, but then again if money can't buy you love it was unlikely it would fair any better at trying to purchase grief.

Naturally there were exceptions to all this. There were the odd times when a huge swathe of the population got swept unto a burgeoning bandwagon of bereavement and mass hysteria. The death of certain heads of state, many of who were self-proclaimed deities, often caused such reactions from their respective submissive underlings. And what about Princess Di the 'People's Princess'? All those people crying and grizzling over a woman hardly any of them had ever met. What the hell was that all about? A melodramatic media. Self-indulgent weeping. Look at me, look how upset I am! Was it all for real? Did those people laying all those flowers really feel the same as if their mother or daughter or son had died? How could they? I hadn't felt like it at all, I'd felt nothing, yet Sophie had cried. Who knows? I'd have been willing to bet a few hundred quid they had soon forgotten their grief and hurt, unlike the loss of a true loved one. A tear shed after reading a depressing story of an operation on a small child gone hopelessly wrong and then on with life. Even September 11th, 2001 for all its shock-horror, live on television before your very eyes, Hollywood disaster movie for real, in your face impact only brought life into true perspective for a short while. That evening millions had tucked their children into bed afraid and worried but happy with their lot at being together and safe unlike so many tragic others. An event to change the world? In some ways yes but self-interest, greed and looking after number one soon returned, although maybe the Americans were truly moved forever by the unique experience of death on their collective doorstep.

Jesus, this whole thing was bringing some morbid thoughts into my head. I took comfort in the vision that the two spade wielders were probably waiting nearby for all the irrelevant chit-chat to end so they could backfill the mouth with its rank spoil in double quick time and sod off down the pub. Good luck to them. What a job. They couldn't possibly become involved, it would emotionally cripple them. I wouldn't have wanted it any different, not in this case, it would be so wrong.

Away from the centre of gloom things hardly got any better and looking further out from the stage, of which I was a leading player, despite my non-speaking part, there were the other nearby graves. Having walked by many of them to get to Rambo's final 'swim', I knew the majority of their headstones and plots were in various stages of disrepair and neglect. I gave myself a wry smile. Is this how it all ended? A series of clichéd platitudes, a broken body shoved underground or burnt and then forgotten? Perhaps all but the last, how could I ever forget Rambo and yet, was I enough? Surely there should be someone else? A father or mother? He was only a young man after all. Siblings? Friends? Where were they all? Briefly a rage burned brightly inside me, one of indignation and annoyance. It soon passed. I was getting carried away. I looked up to the sky and let my mind run with the clouds that moved briskly and effortlessly across their bright blue background. A south-westerly. I should be fishing. Hell! Rambo should be fishing! Should Rambo be fishing in Hell? I hoped not but again I had to chastise myself for the very thought. I was getting carried away big time.

I cast, nice pun, my mind back to the night Rambo had asked me to come in on bait with him all those years ago and how, consequently, the SS syndicate had revealed its true horror in gradual layers, like a putrid onion. Vividly I recalled the vision of Watt's tackle getting blown to fuck by one of Rambo's hand grenades, lobbed by my own fair - ok let's be objective here - foul hand. It all seemed so long ago, the jail sentence, the endless nights inside writing the truth about Watt and his cronies. What were they doing now? Whatever it was and although it hurt to admit it, it had to be better than what I was doing at this precise moment. It was unfair. As far as I knew, which I admit wasn't saying much, they were at least alive... and Rambo wasn't. I had to get that into my head. He was dead. Only the good die young, and Timothy Eugene Ramsbottom. He who had tried to make the world a better place with such vim, vigour and violence. Sure his last vocation had been flogging instruments of destruction to bitter, warped and twisted men so that they could go out and kill and maim others who didn't share their perception of 'better'. That I had to admit, but he had tried and if he hadn't sold them the gear someone else would have. Besides he'd always looked after me in my hour of need, what with buying me new Delkims during the TWTT madness, and, oh yes, paying my mortgage for me while I was, 'away'. I felt ashamed in a way that I could turn a blind eye to how Rambo had financed my mortgage but turn it I did. I pleaded guilty to being a member of the human race and all the shitty baggage that came with it.

But how things change. Out of the jail and then out of the blue the golden eagle had dumped on Sophie's mum in the form of a near two million pound lottery winning crap, of which just over an eighth had splattered our way. It had pebble-dashed the pair of us with a lifestyle of such fortitude and opulence, compared to our prior existence, that it was quite the most unreal moment of my life. Until now. Amazing, incredible etc. etc. and on the proceeds of a moment of chance I had taken him, the now deceased version, to Lac Fumant. Le Lac Fumant. The Smoking Lake. It was, still is, one of the most beautiful places on earth and for two weeks we had lived in a carp man's Eden and I had met Eve. Rebecca. Even on this darkest of days the recollection of her name and her form, so deeply ingrained in my mind's eye, brought a tingle to my very soul. Though if I was honest, not so much of a tingle as it had in the past, the passing of time and an incident over two years ago meant the voltage knob was getting cranked down.

During the months immediately after our return Rambo used to keep asking me about her, about what exactly went on in her room less than an hour after I had caught the mind-meld, fifty plus mirror that the others had so disbelievingly thought was just a figment of my accidentally drugged brain. Boy, I'd shown them. Yet when I stopped and really thought about it, the fact that I'd caught the fish and proved it to them, I often wondered if that too was a dream. Sometimes, even in the middle of the night, I would have to get up out of my and Sophie's bed, go down to the photo album and look at the shot of me with the fifty on the last Saturday morning, the one of our departure, in an act of strange self-verification. When he did ask I would tell him the secret of Rebecca and myself would go with me to my grave. How ironic, he'd beaten me to it, yet deep inside I was glad it was this way round rather than the other. What a terrible thought, nevertheless an honest one. Still, I was not thinking straight. He was dead, as far as the world was concerned.

"So you didn't then?" he would say.

"Didn't what?" I would respond.

"Shag her. If you had you'd tell me and brag about it to make me jealous," he reasoned.

"If I said I had, I could be lying, and if I said I hadn't, I could be lying then as well," I would say, muddying the water like a shoal of commons getting their heads down.

"Was she even there? Did you actually get to see her that night?" he might ask, varying the attack. I never told him one way or the other, I don't know why really. Perhaps, perversely, it was because he wanted to know so much and also because it became a running gag between us. It was one we both seemed to enjoy playing out again and again.

Rebecca. When we returned from holiday I was a mixed up man. I was carp-fished out and back with Sophie, but would constantly think of Rebecca. To go off at a slight tangent but still very relevant to my feelings, I remembered reading about an American golfer, Doug Sanders, I think his name was, who had apparently, golf not really being my game, missed a two foot putt to win one of the majors. He had then lost in the play-off and never again had the chance to win one of golf's big tournaments. This had all happened years ago, in the seventies, and here he was being interviewed in the nineties, as it was then and he was asked if he still thought about it much. 'Only every five minutes or so', he said. 'I'm getting over it now'. Or words pretty much to that effect. I knew what he meant. I had still thought of her umpteen times a day. I'd considered marking down in a book every time I did so but in the end I chickened out, afraid of how sad it would make me. Lac Fumant was history. And so was Rebecca. And now so was Rambo.

Moving on from my initial feelings about the Lac Fumant holiday, it was inevitable both Rambo and I would want to go again. From the initial return we both knew we wanted to go again. This was sound thinking but it all went a stage further when, through contact with the other participants of our two weeks of splendour, we decided to go for Lac Fumant Revisited. At this juncture I must tell you I had already received the telephone call from Pup, who I'd gone to see directly after coming home, about having some more bait made up. It had seemed insignificant at the time, other events were far more motivating and the pair of us had almost forgotten about it, but it was big time now all right. Oh yes! But more of that later.

If ever events proved there was no future in the past it was brought home with a jarring jolt to my already addled brain about two years ago, a year after the first trip. In our infinite wisdom we had decided to go back: Me, Rambo, Jap, Wim, Clint, Alistair, Paul, The Fatboys, Ian and of course Spunker in an attempt to try and recapture the moment. Like re-forming rock group dinosaurs and old school reunions have proved many a time, it's a recipe for disaster and we should have known better. We'd had our day and to try and seize it again was folly, not that we knew at the time, hindsight is a wonderful thing, but we should have known we couldn't possibly top the first time. The whole venture had 'anti-climax' written above it in bright, garish, surf-dude pink neon letters. I should have made do with the Lac Fumant video, which to me at least, was as priceless as a national heirloom and a whole lot more entertaining.

Things started to go wrong when firstly Ian and then Clint pulled out. A distraught Ian had phoned me to tell me Spunker had had an accident. In amongst tears he told me what had happened. Apparently the hound had been chasing a juggernaut on a dual carriageway near to his home… don't ask, I suppose he'd outgrown cars in a street, and somehow his jaws had locked onto the front wheel and he'd been dragged under the massive articulated lorry. Eyewitnesses told Ian that Spunker had gone around the front tyre like a canine Catherine wheel before his grip finally slackened and he fell under the speeding truck, only for all the other wheels to have a go at him. The driver apparently later commented that it seemed as if he'd hit a hundred yards of consecutive speed bumps. Spunker had died under the wheels of a lorry delivering forty tons of cat food and the vet informed an inconsolable Ian that his mutt had been run over a hundred and forty three times.

I remembered being somewhat flummoxed by Ian's call and wondered where he had got the one hundred and forty three. Did it matter? What sort of an anorak of a vet (it could only have been him, surely, the lorry driver would never have counted the bumps) would spend time finding that out? One that didn't have a lot of work on and needed to pad out the bill, I had reckoned. Mind you, it might have been a bit of an ice-breaker when trying to chat somebody up - by the way, my dog got run over one hundred and forty three times. Fancy coming back to my place for a coffee and a gawp at the vet's photos? I've got him mounted inside an oversized scrap book, it folds down pretty flat – perhaps Ian might need to do that now that his soul mate was a two dimensional dead dog. Anyway the top and bottom of it was that Ian was out of the trip, his life in tatters, much like the front tyre on the juggernaut, which at least bears testament to the lockjaw grip of the late King Slobberchops.

Rambo, however, had been unimpressed. "Wimp," he had sneered. "I always knew that dog was a big Jessie. One fifty I could have respect for but snuffing out to a measly one four three. Pathetic."

You see they never really got on but that's another story, The Syndicate (R.I.P.) Part II in fact.

A bit later Clint pulled out with severe arthritis. It seemed the gunslinger had seen better days and it was a good job he was an ex-gunslinger. I wondered guiltily about all the rain he had stood in during the time he'd lost his final gunfight with the Cypry Kid while me and Rambo had videoed him, pissing ourselves with laughter. Rambo, as unsympathetic as ever, had harsh words for him as well, saying it was more likely that the weekly drenching he received whilst working as a leaky plumber had caused his joints to swell. Whatever the reason, Clint wasn't coming either. The curse of Lac Fumant Revisited, I began to wonder?

Two days before we were set to embark the curse reared its ugly head again. Jap phoned to tell me Wim was seriously ill and had been violently struck down with hepatitis D. A virulent new form of the disease associated with an over-indulgence of drink, drugs and sex. These phone calls of doom were becoming commonplace so it was no surprise when I was informed that Jap was staying to look after his brother and help fix him, so he wouldn't be coming as well. Callously I thought that if Wim hadn't come so much and had so many fixes, they both could have made it. Whatever.

The whole episode was getting to have an air of desperation but I had consoled myself with the thoughts of the rest of the lads being at our carp fishing Mecca and of a certain young lady also being there. On arrival Lac Fumant was as beautiful as ever, of course, Bob was still the 'chief', but Rebecca had gone. Gone off to Australia with her new boyfriend. So much for me thinking she might want to see me. Her departure had been a spur of the moment thing. Bob himself only knew they were jetting off the day before we arrived. Due to this he'd had no chance to pass on the disappointment which was in store for me and for all the others as well, I suppose. I have to admit at the time I was gutted, but my rehabilitation about Rebecca had begun and I started to think of her less. About every ten minutes but the electrical tingle knob was definitely turned back a notch from that day on.

Apart from the amazing fact the fish didn't feed and I struggled all week to catch six twenties, a twenty-eight being the best fish of the week, the even more amazing fact concerned the Fatboys. Quite simply the Fatboys had made themselves thin. Despite me believing they carried their obesity with proud disdain and couldn't give a toss about what other people thought about them, this was clearly not the case. Maybe years of continual sarcasm, or deep self-loathing, though carefully concealed, or perhaps a sudden undeniable desire to get into a pair of trousers where the waist size was within a factor of one and a half times the leg measurement, had given them cause to diet. I had to admit that they had looked great but the very essence of their character, their jolly self-deprecating fatness, now gone, had robbed them of something innate.

There were no bankside fry-ups, no gut wobbling waddles to hit takes, not that there were many to hit, no red faced sweating at the merest hint of exertion or heat and no Saturday night get-togethers. It had seemed as if there was nothing of the original Fatboys left, it had all shrunk away in direct proportion to the amount of fat they had managed to lose. It was all mineral water (not even Diet Coke was good enough), fruit and small portions of everything and no lager. They even took it in turns to jog round the lake every morning while the other one minded the rods until it was his turn. Christ, they had even refused chocolate when I'd offered it. Although I knew their names they were strangers. Perhaps they were strangers to themselves, especially when they looked in a mirror, or looked at their cocks, from above. It must have been like seeing a long-lost friend, especially if they could now see their dicks when they were having a piddle. Whereas the carpet may have gained by not getting pissed on so much now the Thinboys had direct sight of fire, so to speak, the rest of us lost out. How dare they rob us of endless jokes and piss-taking! How dare they take away our favourite objects of ridicule! How dare they take away the characters that we had enjoyed laughing at and with! What a waste of a waist. It could be that was why they'd did it, the selfish gits. Yet in our hour of need we had adapted and took the piss out of them for being ex-fatties and inside, deep inside, they knew that we knew despite however stick thin they eventually became there would always be a fat bastard trying to burst out. They would have to manacle him until they died if they wanted to keep their new physical form. They were one cream cake away from him breaking free and causing a feeding frenzy that would put a shark to shame.

"I wonder what's happened to all the skin?" I'd asked Rambo.

Rambo had considered this and had a theory. "Well, boy, they probably look like one of those shar-pei dogs with their kit off or else it's all gathered around their backs and arses and held in place by a few bulldog clips and clothes pegs." He had held my eye with his and a raised index finger and had said knowingly. "Or they've had sections of it cut out and been re-stitched. There's probably a dinghy sailor with a spinnaker of human skin somewhere."

"Ergh, please! Anyway, doesn't human skin contract back?" I had argued. "You know, like in the case of pregnant women, leaving only the odd, slightly unappealing stretch mark. They'd have stretch marks the size of motorways," I had added, cracking up with laughter. "I don't know about carving unsightly scars across the countryside, their motorways would be carving an unsightly scar across their stomachs and arses."

Rambo had given me an old fashioned look. "Go and ask Alistair. He won't know but at least it'll use up a bit more time while he tells you he doesn't."

I'd known what he meant. The time between takes had seemed an eternity, a bit like one of Alistair's speeches in fact. Whereas the year before I'd turned my nose up at the endless supply of twenties, this time I'd have been more than happy to have a quick slug of alarm induced adrenalin from a mid-double. It just hadn't worked out to plan, even Virtual Paul seemed to be a well-rounded individual. He'd got a girlfriend, the poor cow, and had left virtual sex for the real thing, although I bet he was more adept at the button pushing type and still had moments of relapse. I could imagine her saying: 'Come on baby, push my buttons' and the daft sod jumping onto the game pad rather than onto her. Still, the very fact he had somehow managed to convince a real girl to go out with him was something in itself. No more Mr Cybergeek. Was nothing on that holiday sacred? Had nothing changed for the worse, from my selfish, self-interested point of view? In short, no.

On returning home, Rambo and I had felt deflated. What was this carp fishing lark all about? We had sampled the ultimate during the first holiday at Lac Fumant but second time around, apart from the visual beauty of the place, it had been mediocre.

We had then gone on to fish day ticket waters and club waters, found some better than others, but all were a little disappointing in some way or another. One week or even two weeks holiday fishing abroad now seemed too hit and miss. There were too many things that you couldn't control. The weather, the swim you fished and the company you had to keep during your stay and the actual place where you stayed. Sure we had hit the rainbow's pot of gold with Lac Fumant, but how many of them where there? Day ticket waters were invariably crowded, aesthetically unpleasing and had too many rules and regulations what with rig, bait and time constraints. Club waters scored better on these points but they rarely had the calibre of fish in them which both Rambo and myself felt as if we wanted to try for. We had talked at length about it directly after our return from Lac Fumant Revisited and although we still enjoyed our fishing on the various waters I mentioned, something wasn't quite right. Something was missing, a certain *je ne sais quoi*, well, not strictly true actually, I did know what and Rambo knew as well. I knew that he knew, he knew that I knew and we both knew that knowing what was required would freak me out.

Still, I was a big boy, although Sophie might laugh at the statement on at least two levels, and I realised I would have to do what needed to be done. Bullets have to be bitten, at some time or another. Billy Button bought a bitten bullet, if Billy Button bought a bitten bullet where's the bitten bullet, Billy Button bought? Rattling around my head like a marble in a biscuit tin, that's where. The answer was inescapable. The answer had made me quiver with trepidation. The answer was my personal taboo. The answer made me feel as if a cold clammy hand had wrapped tightly around my ankle and dragged me down into a swirling vortex of bad memories, bad vibes and bad Karma. And I mean 'bad' and not in the sense of good either. It was time, deep breath, calm… calm… for us to think about joining a… don't choke on the word… easy, boy… syndicate.

So, with the monumental decision having been made, we had set about finding a good one. It was a lot easier to say than to do and nothing we got wind of from our contacts seemed to be what we were looking for. Pup's phone call was still remembered but as time went on and nothing was heard, and he couldn't or wouldn't say anything else about the situation, it seemed as if that avenue would also be a dead end. Then, from nowhere in particular, totally out of the blue we got the nod, the pair of us, by all accounts, had made it to the top of the list. We were next in line for the all important interview, the only trouble being on the very day I'd received the strange telephone call it had been the day Rambo had died. Two weeks before we were due to meet the syndicate's owner, that day being today, Rambo, the complete shithead, decides to go and get himself killed and there's even more turmoil, angst and perplexity. As if I hadn't got enough grief trying to get my head around opting back into a syndicate after what happened the last time.

Grief. It was where this had all started and my mind wrenched itself away from its inward looking ramblings and focused on the vicar who had stopped talking and was staring at me as if I'd gone mad. Not far off. How long he'd been finished I couldn't say, but at last I came to, signalled him with the briefest of nods and went over to shake his cold, limp and bony hand. I gave him the slightest uplift of my tightly clamped lips, looked one last time at the coffin, turned on my heel and walked back the way I'd come from my car. Now what? How on earth was this going to work out? As I walked back through the other graves I thought I could hear the noise of frantic shovels and laughing coming from behind me. It could have been my imagination, I had no intention of turning around to look, so I pressed on, quickening my pace until by the time I was out of the cemetery and going up the road to where the car was parked, I was almost jogging.

I pressed the remote central locking key, heard the satisfying clunk, yanked open the driver's door, jumped in and slammed it shut. The car was hot from the trapped warmth of the sun's rays. This, combined with my recent exertions, made me start to sweat. I felt hot, sticky and uncomfortable, physically and mentally.

"At least that's over," I said to myself.

Suddenly a voice from the past spoke and made me jump like an arse-pokered cat. "What was it like seeing me get buried then, boy?"

"You!" I managed to half scream in a strangulated voice. "What the fuck are you doing here?"

The large body shrugged its massive shoulders. "I got bored hanging around in the pub so I broke in, no damage boy, pro job, and thought I'd wait here."

"Bloody hell, you nearly gave me a heart attack," I said, starting to relax a little. "I didn't see you in the car at all."

"I was laying down on the back seat. I thought I'd surprise you. Here! Imagine how much of a heart attack you'd have had if I was really dead? How about being perpetually haunted by an ex-carp angler, then?"

Rambo gave me a broad grin. He had his reasons for being officially dead. As I understood it most of them to do with avoiding paying money to someone or some government. It was all a bit much for me to take in, to be honest. A best mate faking his own death, me having to attend his burial service and in what, an hour and a half, an interview for the pair of us to get into the supposedly hottest syndicate in all England. Ho hum! Another ordinary day for a grenade throwing, prison sentence serving, lottery winning, hallucinogenic drug taking, inter species mind melding, fishery owner's daughter ogling, syndicate-psycho carp angler.

"Let's go," I said, cranking over the engine. "We don't want to be late."

Chapter 2

As I drove myself and the supposedly deceased Rambo to our appointment with the man who ran the syndicate, my mind, as was usual in the kind of circumstance I was about to become embroiled, was grinding over the facts with all the grace of a diesel cement mixer loaded with half a dozen engineering bricks. I imagined it to be making a similar sort of noise as well and was waiting for Rambo to ask me to turn the bloody thing off by way of a back-hander around the head. If only I could turn it off or run it out of diesel. I knew better. My capacity for mental rumination and navel gazing seemed insatiable and whatever the percentage of my brain that was involved in the actual driving of my car it couldn't have been enough. I was on autopilot in a car that never even had cruise control, or automatic transmission come to that. Laughably, in a world where the police prosecute motorists for eating a sandwich sitting at the lights, I looked a model driver as I motored on at legal limits with not so much as a word uttered to my passenger, both hands welded to the wheel my eyes straight ahead. Yet I wasn't in the car driving it, I was miles away, contemplating the possibilities around the corner, and I wasn't thinking pile-ups, lorries with spilt loads or wobbly old dears on push bikes either. I was thinking carp fishing syndicates. I was pretty convinced I really didn't want to be late but the nagging doubt tucked away in my head couldn't be denied its say. Brooding over syndicates seemed to be a forte of mine but in my defence, seeing as the last time I'd been in one I'd ended up in the gulag, I suppose it was understandable.

In short it all boiled down to agonizing over the thought that once again, if we came over as descent anglers and got the nod, I would be in one and faced with the possibility of all the shit which invariably associated itself with such a decision. Does history repeat itself? Can lightning strike twice? Once bitten twice shy? Nothing ventured, nothing gained? How long is a bit of string? And all those other enigmas wrapped up in conundrums and tucked into riddles.

I have to say here and now the feeling of chance and destiny guiding me along a path of fishing fortitude had somewhat left me from its fantastic peak at Lac Fumant. However, it had played a final, crucial role before seemingly disappearing altogether. This had been over two and a half years ago and was only now coming to fruition. Three years down the line from the French trip I was still looking for the next big carp fishing rush. Lac Fumant Revisited hadn't provided it, nor had the other places I'd mentioned earlier. I suppose it was inevitable that eventually it would come to this, joining a syndicate again, and it was equally inevitable I would feel like I did today. Between a rock and a hard place would cover it. I wanted all the things a syndicate could offer; exclusive fishing, quality venue, quality carp, accessibility, flexibility and freedom from fishing restrictions. What I didn't need were the things which had materialised in the last one; cliques, personality clashes, bitterness, jealousy, back-biting, financial rip-offs, stroke pulling, vast egos, conflict, violence and a total disintegration of all life beyond carp angling. Stick the pair of them on the balance scales and what have you got? Tough call, but I didn't want to be late so good old gravity must have managed to tug down the exclusive fishing etc. bundle a little more. Besides I was convinced I would never go to the lengths I had previously to catch carp. That *bête noire* was one I could control. Couldn't I?

My mind turned to how it had all come about. It had been Pup, the boiliemeister, who had put us onto the syndicate after returning from the original Lac Fumant holiday. Naturally I'd been back to see him with the picture of the fifty, which he immediately blue-tacked to the spot below the light switch in the 25mm plus room as promised, within days of our return. A bit gushing and egotistical, I know, but I'd defy most carp anglers not to start spreading the word of their own glory, particularly after what we'd caught on the trip. Besides I did need him to roll some more bait for me, so I had to go and see him in any case, honest!

He had been ecstatic on hearing the news that his pop-ups had been responsible for so many fish and doubly so when he was told the fifty had fallen to one. He had started clenching his fist, clad as usual in a surgeon's disposable rubber glove, punching the air and giving it the old 'yes' shout. In fact he had hissed out the final sibilant letter with such gusto I momentarily thought that someone had connected the compressed airline that he used for his sausage gun to his arsehole. He had even smacked a boilie up at the ceiling with the micrometer he used for his quality control tolerance measurements, similar to an overjoyed, match-winning tennis player. It was an eccentric performance but then he was an eccentric person. Anyone who turns their house into a boilie factory and collects old plastic bait packaging bags has to fall into that category.

Eventually, after he'd calmed down, I'd placed my order for more bait and, after having been enthusiastically shown the new rolling tables that did indeed have dimpled surfaces in order to indent boilies like a golf ball so you could slice or draw them from a throwing stick, I'd left. I'd returned a week later to once again have my nose's sensory perceptions blitzkrieged by the multitude of flavouring aromas that thundered around Pup's house and picked up the finished bait. The red boilies had a comfortingly familiar look to them. They said: 'I catch carp' in bold chunky letters. Only closer inspection had showed they all had pockmarked skin, like they had suffered from bad acne when they were younger. Pup's legendary pop-ups were still smooth and a hundred of them had gone into the back of the car as well. Once again I had said my goodbyes, hit him with a wedge of folding stuff that he never bothered to count and told him I'd be in touch as soon as my ammo was running low.

Two months later Big Chief Bob ran an advertising campaign for Lac Fumant using the photo of the double capture which Rambo and I'd had. It was the one of

Rambo's big forty and my beautiful fully scaled mirror. Apparently it had been this photo the latest syndicate leader had seen in Carpworld magazine and he had casually mentioned it during a totally unrelated conversation with Pup, who he had known for years. Pup had then told him he knew the pair of us personally, that he rolled bait for us and proceeded to vouch for our carp fishing prowess and character. For some reason the syndicate leader had said to Pup that the next time we were in to see him he could mention his water and ask if we were interested in going on the list. It was the last real piece of luck I felt had happened on the fate/fishing front. It had occurred a fair while ago now but it was by all accounts a huge slice of the fortune cake. The water involved was awesome. Allegedly.

Pup couldn't wait until he next saw me, instead he had phoned me that evening. This was the phone call I referred to earlier on. He had instantly launched himself into a brief speech of such reverence, respect and sheer deference about the syndicate water involved that it had initially both unnerved and exhilarated me at the same time. He had told me of its utmost secrecy, of how unique it was, that it was full of fantastic fish and how, if I said yes, Rambo and me could go on the waiting list. I had been momentarily chilled but it soon passed and I casually told him I would ask Rambo and get back to him later on. Rambo, unfazed as ever, had said 'Why not?', so I phoned Pup back a couple of days later and said we would like to go on the list. In deep emotive tones he said although we didn't realise it, the pair of us had just had a massive break. I thanked him very much but to be truthful, like I said earlier, it didn't seem so much of a deal then, what with Lac Fumant so prominent and the possibility of going back again being so intoxicating and exciting. It's hard to recognise that fact now but it does show the powerful grip Lac Fumant had on me at the time. Of the syndicate? Well, I knew it was secret, had great fish but had no more details other than it was unique. Ever heard anything along those lines before? Haven't we all, and what is the usual reality? Exactly! I'd soon stopped thinking about it.

Today it was a different story seeing as how our carp fishing had regressed, Fumant Revisited hadn't worked and other waters, whether club or day ticket, hadn't worked either. We needed something like Lac Fumant the first time, in this country and available 24/7. Perhaps the old adage about going abroad catching big fish then coming back and scratching around local waters for a few doubles had been right. Maybe the first Lac Fumant trip had set our sights so high we would never be truly happy again. When I had suggested this to Pup just recently he had merely said in hushed tones. 'You will be. If you get in, you will be'. I'd tried asking him more about it but he wouldn't say a thing only that I should wait until Rambo and me were contacted.

If my views on joining another syndicate were somewhat unclear, then they paled into insignificance compared to the facts concerning the new water. I'd been in the dark all that time ago and even today as we were driving to meet the man who ran it I still knew nothing extra. Things had come to a head two weeks ago; the day Rambo topped himself, when I'd had the strange phone call to ask if my friend and myself were still interested in joining a certain syndicate a certain bait roller had told us about. I'd had just enough gumption to confirm we were still up for it, after all what had we to lose at this stage? The voice said he'd be in touch again soon and the phone went dead. I'd felt as if I was playing a part in a spy movie. The call had been so out of the blue and the subject had been so dormant for such a long time I'd struggled to recall from memory the exact ins and outs of it. Now, suddenly, I was filled with a heady rush and immediately phoned Pup to ask a bit of background info. After all he had said, if I remembered rightly, I would have to wait until I was contacted and at last I had been. I'd pumped Pup more frantically than the world lilo inflating champion, more desperately than a porn star stud, in fact I'd pumped as hard as a shingle dredger and attempted to turn over as many stones, but he'd had none of it.

"You'll have to wait until you get another call from the man and get to see him face to face," he'd said.

"The syndicate owner?" I'd asked.

"Yep."

"What's his name?" I'd said.

"Can't tell you."

"Where about is the water?"

"Can't tell you."

"How big is it?"

"Nope."

"How big are the fish?"

"Nope."

"How many in the syndicate?"

"Nope."

"How much is it?"

"Nope."

"What sort of water is it?"

"Nope."

"Do you know anyone who actually fishes it?"

"Nope."

"What, no you don't know anyone who fishes it or no you won't tell me?" I'd asked, trying to clear up at least one point however irrelevant.

"Yep."

"Which one?"

"Nope."

"Fuck me," I'd said in frustration. "What can you tell me about the place?"

"Fuck all," said Pup, not in the least frustrated.

"Fuck all?"

"Fuck all."

"Fucking hell. Fuck all?"

"Fuck all."

"Why can't you tell me about it?" I'd said, a little sneakily.

"Nope."

I resigned myself to the inevitable. "I'll wait for him to ring me again then, shall I?"

"I should."

Defeated I'd hung up and proceeded to phone a dead friend to tell him the news. It was all a bit odd, really. For someone who was dead Rambo had sounded as if he was full of life and was pleased about the whole situation.

When the man phoned again to give me more details it got even odder. I'd picked up the phone and had been told it was the syndicate leader, that I had to be at such and such address at such and such a time on a certain day, and he'd hung up. Without hesitation I'd phoned up Rambo and relayed the news.

There was silence down the phone. "… Hmm. A bit awkward, boy. That's the day I'm getting myself buried."

"Well, you're not going to be there, are you?" I'd said somewhat exasperated. It was all very well Rambo killing himself off, it had to be realistic and God knows how that had been done, but I couldn't imagine him going to the lengths of being at his own funeral, in a box or otherwise. Surely the whole idea of killing himself was to stay alive, reap the benefit and have as few people as possible know the truth.

"No, but you are, boy," he'd replied. "You're the official grieving best friend."

Shit! And double shit! Could I pull that one out the bag? It was pointless asking for the day off, I knew my duty. "Do I get a tee-shirt and will there be anybody else there?" I'd asked.

"I doubt it. Everyone else I had something in common with is already dead, you know, little pieces dead. Anyway you'll be the only one there, no one else will know about it. I suppose you might get some old girl stand and mourn with you because she's nothing better to do with her sad life."

So it transpired that Rambo moved his burial service time to the earliest one of the morning or the 'grave yard slot' as I'd seen it, much to my amusement but not to Rambo's. This was a serious business. Death often can be, especially to the person concerned. Anyway once he was done and dust to dusted at an early hour we could go and see the syndicate man, which was about an hour and a half away by car, in comfortable time provided all went smoothly. Or rather by now it must be an hour away. I was back in the car and my reminiscing was over for the time being.

I turned to Rambo. "Do you...?"

"Welcome to the world of the living," he said, cutting me off. "Out of our little trance are we?" he added, as if talking to a small child.

I nodded. I had to try and clear up some of the things in my head, what with Rambo and this syndicate thing I was getting brain-boggled. I rushed into a hurried series of questions, trying to blurt them out as quickly as I could and unload them from my overburdened chest. "This killing yourself off business. What the bloody hell is it all about? Are you going to tell me now you've finally been laid to rest, or what? I mean, how on earth did you do it? Who else was involved? You must have had help from somebody somewhere and there must have…" I petered out partly due to the bemused look Rambo was giving me, which I caught sight of in the rear view mirror. (Never caught one of them, had linears and fully scaled). He had a half smile on his face and I suddenly felt a bit stupid.

I tried to explain. "It's crazy all this," I said, flinging a hand off the steering wheel. "You know when I was at the service I had to keep reminding myself you weren't really dead. At times I started getting carried away thinking you really were. It was so realistic, so confusing, I mean I had to pretend I thought that you were dead, even if I knew you weren't but there I was starting to think that you were..."

"That's because for all intents and purposes it was real. Is real," said Rambo cutting in again, before I disappeared up my own backside. "Timothy Eugene Ramsbottom is no more but Rambo lives on."

"Under a pseudonym with a new identity?" I asked.

"No, you don't understand, do you?"

I puffed out some air between my pursed lips. "That's an understatement. Here we are off to possibly join a clandestine syndicate where the only contact we've had is with a bloke who talks to me down the phone like he's a secret agent. The boilie freak who put our names forward won't tell us squat about it, either. I'm pooping my pants as to whether it's going to end up in tears like the last one and to top it all I'm taking my fellow prospective syndicate member along with me, who's my best mate, who happens to be officially dead… and buried. Too right I don't effing well understand."

"Does Sophie know about the syndicate?" enquired Rambo taking the conversation onto a theme I wasn't interested in developing.

"Don't ask."

"I just did."

"Did you do it because you owe lots of money?" It was the only answer I could think of.

"Will she go ape when she finds out?" said Rambo grinning.

I could play this game. "Are the Russian Mafia after you for an unpaid bill of well overdue AK 47's?"

"How are you going to break it to her if we get in?"

"What was in the coffin?"

"Does she know about Rebecca?"

"Who was in the coffin?"

"Did you really shag her on the night you caught the fifty?"

I couldn't play this game. My head dropped slightly and I remained silent. Rambo let out a yelp of triumph. Although he'd never get the answer to that question it was rather useful for blocking off any I might ask of him and for him winning stupid conversation games.

Rambo was in a generous mood and changed the tack of the conversation. "I guess I owe it to you to tell you the reasons why, boy, seeing as you're involved in it. You see I've been making money and enemies, the two sort of go hand in hand what with people being the jealous shits they are. Things started coming to a head with the people I was dealing with and also a friend of mine got wind of a, let's say, investigation into my business and…"

"Hold on," I said. "I thought you said all your friends were dead. I was the only one at the box backfill today, you know."

"Ok. 'B' list friend, acquaintance really. Like all the blokes I can call on to help me out or do me a favour, you know, like the ones who looked after you when you were doing time. They're not what I call real friends, not like the combat ones who risked their lives to help me, they're pretty much all dead. As well as that my parents died a long time ago and I was an only child. I was such a big son of a bitch my mum was in labour for a long time, complications set in and she died two days after my birth. My dad brought me up with help from the rest of the family, he never did remarry, and then the silly sod died aged 42 from a motorbike accident. I was just 16 and went straight in the army from school. My family was only a small one and since then they've all passed on."

"How come you're not dead like the rest of the army lads?" I enquired, avidly taking in all this stuff about Rambo's life. I'd never been told any of this before and had never dared ask.

Rambo grinned again as I looked into the mirror. "I am!"

"You know what I mean."

"Because I was the best," he answered. "I was the meanest motherfucker you could ever imagine. The best in terms of physical and mental capability with a massive inbuilt desire to survive coupled with the will to do whatever it took to achieve that survival. I've committed some truly gross acts to keep myself alive, believe me."

I did. "And now you've gone and got rid of yourself?"

"Yep. As I was saying things were coming to a head and it was time for me to sort it out. Basically I died abroad in an old Eastern Block country and then bribed a couple of people to get a suitable dead body labelled with a suitable death certificate. The hardest part was getting everything sorted out so I could officially get my body brought back into the UK to be buried over here. Much more believable that way. It took bribery on both financial and sexual levels, some brutal intimidation and meticulous planning but now I'm dead and only seven people know the truth. And you're one of them." Rambo waited for this little nugget of intelligence to sink in and then continued. "All in all this little façade has cost me plenty but not as much as if I'd stayed alive. Perhaps I could have ended up dead and poor." Rambo stopped and seemed to turn reflective, when he carried on it was in quieter tones. "You see I've been shitting on some mean bastards for quite a while now, surreptitiously ripping the piss out of them and taking their laundered money, the scumbags. As well as that a few governments were starting to take notice of the weapons I was supplying and who I was supplying them to. The time was right and it seemed a good career move to make, killing myself off that is."

"That's right, Elvis, Hendrix, Jim Morrison, James Dean, never did their careers any harm. Didn't do them a lot of good personally but their management could smile all the way to the bank." I said.

"That's right, boy. And seeing as I'm my management, I shall be laughing all the way to my Swiss bank. Different name of course, several different names in fact. No new identity as such, more identities. I'm retired at the age of 32 and I've more than enough money to last two lifetimes, provided I don't buy a new Porsche every year."

More questions were popping into my head and they had to be asked, now was the time. "So who do I tell you're still alive? What about Pup? What about the old syndicate members? If they knew you were alive and officially dead at the same time they'd shop you."

Rambo seemed unperturbed. "What you have to remember is right from the very start of all this mercenary stroke gun running lark is I've been using a different persona from my real one. I'm not daft. I knew one day I might like to simply melt away. Huh! Actually that's what had happened to the dead bloke who was me. Killed by a flame-thrower he was. Very convenient, similar stature but a lot of his skin was gone. Imagine the worst barbecue you've ever been to and think 'blacker and more burnt'. You get the picture?"

I nodded. Lovely.

"All those people who bought stuff off of me, they knew nothing of me or my background, nothing at all. The beauty of it is, this one group, the one I was really ripping off, actually think they've killed me because one of their bloke's was the one who torched me. Well, not me of course but the bloke I was paying to be me. To be on the safe side as soon as he did his flame throwing act I snuffed him out, you could say."

My brain boggled again. "Let me get this straight," I said desperately trying to grasp the implications of what I'd just been told. "You somehow managed to get someone to impersonate you and manipulated the situation so well you knew that your enemies - no, ex-business colleagues - would kill that person thinking it was you and you then in turn killed your supposed assassin. You then managed to bribe people to confirm the dead body was yourself, got it out of the country and over to the UK where you again bribed and threatened people to confirm the body was, I don't know, some fictitious person or..."

"No!" Rambo interjected. "Timothy Eugene Ramsbottom! Once I was in this country I wanted my true name to be the person who was killed. I was somebody else abroad so they never knew who I really was but for the purposes of the Government, Inland Revenue and Customs and Excise in the UK it had to be me."

"What about people like the old syndicate or Pup or all the other 'B' list friends?" I asked.

"They knew me but not as Timothy Eugene Ramsbottom. On my old SS membership form I was Wayne Thomas. They knew me as Rambo but that nickname was never used anywhere else in any other situation. As far as any of the authorities know I'm just not the same person and the photos they have of TER are ones which I had taken in disguise. It really is impossible for them to track me down. As for people like Pup there's no reason to mention it at all. What you've got to appreciate is I haven't just fallen on this idea, I've been planning it for over ten years now."

"What about travelling on a passport with a dodgy photo?" I said, seeking some loophole that Rambo had missed.

"I had several different passports, decent photos but different names," he informed me.

"How come then," I said thinking that I'd got a handle on him at last, "the authorities had wind of you?"

"Simple! Although I was stashing money away in Swiss bank accounts I still wanted to be making a fair bit of it and for it to show as some apparently unearned income. Then, when I killed myself off, that would be the end of it all there and then. If they pursue the dead man's account for whatever is in it then it will undoubtedly appease them and make them think they've got their share whereas in reality they've only scratched the surface."

"Wow!" I said as I grasped the shear cunning malevolence and the scope of Rambo's plan. As it all started to seep in I began to think about what he had told me. After a while I had to ask the question that troubled me most. "You could as a matter of fact give someone money to impersonate you in the knowledge that he was going to be killed?" I said with a tinge of disgust in my voice.

"The meanest motherfucker you could ever imagine," Rambo reminded me.

"And it's all worked out perfect?"

"Sure has, boy. The only thing that went wrong was when I stiffed the bloke who torched the other bloke, the one who I'd given the wedge of dollars to impersonate me, I was a bit slow in doing so. You see the wad of dollars had been burnt to fuck as well, if I'd have drilled him earlier I might have got nearly all my money back. Still, that's me being a bit picky I suppose and he wouldn't have been charcoaled so nicely."

Blimey! Or something like that. Again I started thinking it through. "Aren't you worried these people you were flogging the guns and stuff to will trace you back somehow? Couldn't one of the people you bribed drop you in it?"

"A small chance," Rambo conceded. "You see the group of scumbags who think they killed me are probably all dead by now. Somebody rather unkindly told their sworn rivals of their secret hideout and gave them a very good deal on the bazookas they would need to flush them away. Ha ha! I wonder who that was! The other individuals on the conspiracy side of things have been well paid and I've got a few keys to their skeleton cupboard. Skeleton keys, you could say. To the rest of my customers I've simply disappeared off the scene, happens all the time. I was only ripping off one bunch of crap."

"So now what?"

"A little carp fishing, I think, or even a lot. Don't you?"

"Yeah," I said, strangely enthused by hearing the sordid details of Rambo's master plan. If he could sort out all of what he had just told me then us getting past the upcoming interview should be a breeze. It was going to be a cakewalk, we'd impress this syndicate bloke and we'd be in. In the best syndicate in England, apparently. Then all I had to do was square it with Sophie. Perhaps Rambo would do that for me while I hid in the broom cupboard.

"One last thing," I asked him. "Now that you're out of the war game, any chance of dropping the camouflage gear?"

"Don't be stupid."

At least one thing wasn't about to be stood on its head and for that I was grateful.

Chapter 3

The door I had knocked on about ten seconds earlier opened, not fully, but just wide enough for a head to squeeze partially through the gap, held by an as yet unseen body. The pair of eyes in the head were set perhaps a little too deep and, if I was being especially unkind, a little too close together. The head looked Rambo and me up and down. The mouth, edged by thin, mean lips spoke.

"Matt and Rambo?"

"That's right," I said, as Rambo nodded his conformation.

"Come in," said the head and the door opened, the now visible body of the head held out an outstretched arm which beckoned us into the house. As we crossed the threshold the body and head which comprised the syndicate leader quickly moved the opposite way to us and went outside. Somewhat confused I turned to see him glance quickly up and down the road before he was satisfied with what he had or hadn't seen and followed us back indoors.

"Through the door to the right," said the leader.

Rambo and I walked through into what was once a dining room but had been converted into a makeshift office. The dining room table, which had been pushed hard against the wall and into the corner, had a phone, fax and answerphone on it and someone had apparently emptied, at random, about forty sheets of used A4 paper all over the top of it. In the diagonally opposed corner there was a computer with a screen, keyboard, scanner and printer which was housed on cheap, flat-pack computer furniture. It looked so flimsy I imagined one excited thump on the return key would bring the whole lot crashing to the floor. In front of the grotty little slide away draw where the keyboard rested was a swivel chair, one of the gas cylinder ones which give hours of entertainment by being able to be lowered and raised by the flick of a lever. In the middle of the room there were two proper chairs standing out like the proverbial spare pricks at a wedding. These had obviously been put in the room for the parking of two new prospective members' arses while undergoing interrogation.

"Sit down on the chairs," said the syndicate leader.

Dutifully we parked our bums and the syndicate man plonked his on the swivel chair and spun it around to face the pair of us. We looked at him and he at us. A vein throbbed slightly on the temple of the syndicate leader's head and he blinked more noticeably and frequently than would be desirable if you wanted to come across as a normal human being. His head turned quickly yet only slightly to the left and a hand came up to scratch the area of exposed neck the movement had revealed.

"You definitely weren't followed were you?" he asked earnestly.

I fought back an urge to guffaw at such a ludicrous question but the intensity of his close-set eyes rammed it back down my gullet. It might be he had good reason to ask. Maybe he had very good reason. I'd been party to the lengths people would go to catch carp, perhaps running the alleged best syndicate in Britain was like keeping a precious jewel safe from a seething legion of bandits, burglars, brigands, robbers, rapists and racketeers.

"We weren't followed," said Rambo easily. "If we had been I'd have noticed and sorted it there and then."

The syndicate leader's mouth twitched upwards in a half-leering smile and I could tell he'd homed in on Rambo's aura of authority about such matters. "Good. Good, now to business. I want you to read what I'm about to give you. Basically it's the rules of the syndicate and at the bottom is the required statutory deposit agreement. I'm afraid if you cannot agree to it then this interview will terminate immediately. You are very fortunate to have got this far and have only done so by me receiving a personal recommendation." His temple throbbed and then pulsed for good measure and he blinked four times in succession.

Good old Pup, I thought. The syndicate leader rummaged for the two correct pieces of paper on the dining room table while I, and undoubtedly Rambo, weighed up the pressured individual before us. He was, what, early forties? Something like that, thinning non-descript dark hair, tall, painfully skinny and what with his rather pointy nose coupled with the deep and close set eyes his face had a rodent quality about it. Rat-like, I suppose, facially, lanky physically and on the edge mentally. Oh well, been there, done that. People often say how relaxing fishing must be, those who don't go, that is. What do they know? FA that's what. Frustrating, boring, exhilarating, exasperating, uncomfortable, satisfying, addictive amongst many others but relaxing? Nah.

The bits of paper came and I was given two sheets of A4 stapled together. The first sheet was a list of fishery type rules which in their most basic form were; no guests, no dogs, no litter, no bent hooks, no barbed hooks, no lead core, no shock leaders, no fixed leads, no double hook rigs, no boats, no bait boats, no braid, no line under 15lb, no wanking in your bivvy (not really), no fires, no firearms, no blowing up of other people's equipment with hand grenades (not really again), no nuts, no keepnets, no sacking of fish for more than fifteen minutes which gave time to set up photographic equipment, no freshwater fish dead or alive to be brought onto site, no unattended rods and a maximum of three of them. An unattended rod was deemed to be one where an angler couldn't reach it within twenty seconds. Middle of the night, perhaps a can or two under the belt, an uncompromising bivvy door zip – it didn't bear thinking about. I made a mental note to begin practising sprint starts. The list went on; no reserving of swims, no continuous fishing in one swim for more than seven days, no fishing within one recognised swim of another angler without his consent and no fist fighting of large dogs that shouldn't be there in the first place and in any case were dead... as was the other protagonist, officially (not really on that one as well). All anglers must be in possession of the correct number of rod and line licenses. All items such as an unhooking mat, an adequate sized weigh sling and sack, a pair of forceps, a 50" landing net must all be dedicated for use on this water only. It added that your membership card for the syndicate must be carried at all times. The next bit was all the usual old boring rubbish about where to park, about shutting gates and the clubhouse building, general good conduct, respect for others and the countryside and so on. In bold letters at the bottom it stated that breaking any of the above rules meant instant dismissal from the syndicate with the loss of the annual fee but with the return of '1st deposit'. There were the usual disclaimers for the syndicate not being held responsible for damage to persons or property and the right for the adding to, deleting and amending of rules as it saw fit. So there! Stick that in your pipe and smoke it, pick the bones out of that and if you don't like it piss off, do not collect £200 when you pass Go and get on your bike. There was another separate section at the bottom of the page which said that all fish below twenty-five pounds must be put in the stock pond and registered in the stock pond log-book. It also stated that all forty pound plus captures must be reported to Michael Brown immediately and photos submitted as soon as practical. This last bit made my eyebrows get up to my hairline, bloody hell, how big were the fish in this place? My mind jumped back a few lines and I was soon wondering what the hell a '1st deposit' was when it was at home. I moved onto the second page and soon found out. This next page was all about the statutory deposit agreement and in bold letters the agreement was worded as such.

The Hamworthy Fishery Syndicate.

Hereinafter referred to as 'The Syndicate'.

I, the undersigned, accept that my initiation cheque for the sum of £2500 shall be held by The Syndicate's bankers until such time I decide to withdraw from The Syndicate, when it will be refunded in full but with no interest having been accrued. This sum shall be known as the '1st deposit'.

I, the undersigned, accept that should I breach any of the following points of contract written below I will forfeit my '1st deposit' and be immediately expelled from The Syndicate with no refund of the annual fee. Breach of such points of contact will be by the decision of Michael Brown alone and I accept his decision to be final and binding. Members will be granted one meeting with Michael Brown when under provisional expulsion where a definitive decision will be made with no further appeal.

Points of contract are as follows:

Anyone publicising fish catches in any form whatsoever will be in breach of contract.

Anyone caught attempting to move fish or suspected of trying to move fish or in suspected negotiation with third parties to move fish will be in breach of contract.

Anyone known to be informing third parties of details such as entry gate and clubhouse padlock combinations will be in breach of contract.

Anyone caught aiding non-members of The Syndicate in poaching will be in breach of contract.

Non-payment of annual fees, which are due on the 1st March, no later, will be in breach of contract.

Non-appearance at work parties (no mitigating circumstances whatsoever) will be in breach of contract.

Anyone caught mishandling fish and not taking adequate fish-care precautions will be in breach of contract.

Anyone caught in actions which undermine other anglers' basic rights to enjoyment and non-interference through poor conduct and anti-social behaviour will be in breach of contract.

Finally Michael Brown reserves the right to expel any member for reasons other than the above. A refund of '1st deposit' and a percentage return of the annual fee worked out on the remaining time span left of the annual fee will be made to the expelled member.

I added some more of my own, anyone caught breathing will be taken outside and shot and be in breach of contract. Anyone's face that doesn't fit will be given a huge boot up the arse to send him over the horizon.

"Is that all?" said Rambo with a touch of sarcasm mirroring my thoughts.

"That's all," twitched… Michael, I presumed. His vein throbbed for good measure. "Ideally I'd like you to not mention the place to anyone at all and just keep it totally to yourself but I have to be realistic."

"Are you Michael, then?" I asked.

"Yes," said Michael Brown, syndicate dictator, president, chancellor, general, judge, jury and anything else he felt like being. He blinked five times, like you do when England get knocked out of the World Cup or when you first saw ET but didn't want anyone to know you were welling up.

"How much is the annual fee? I asked.

"£1250," said Michael.

Holy fucking shit. The best part of four grand needed to be kissed goodbye just to get in this place and what did I know about it? I knew it was fucking expensive but apart from that and a name to the person who I'd spoken to briefly on the phone there was nothing else.

"What can you tell us about the fish and the actual water…" I started but Michael cut me off with a lifted finger. A trembling lifted finger, it had to be said, this guy was a bag of nerves.

"Like I said earlier, you have to sign the statutory deposit agreement before we go any further. This doesn't involve any money at this stage it simply means you recognise the need to abide by its implications if you get in. Which you haven't yet," he added, giving us both a going over with his beady and blinking eyes.

"What if we sign it and then decide, after you telling us more about it and giving us the nod, we don't want to join?" asked Rambo.

Michael gave us both a look of utter shock but then seemed to come to some inner comprehension and he winked at Rambo, least I think he did, it was hard to tell with all the extraordinary eyelid movement going on, and started to grin. His temple vein turned varicose in one second flat and the grin turned to a gentle chuckle, which quickly grew into a laugh and then into a frenzied, maniacal, convulsive fit of mad hysteria. Rambo and I watched bemused as his skinny body bent double and racked itself violently from the seemingly epileptic attack of laughter.

I leaned over to Rambo and whispered. "I bet he's in constant demand for TV sitcom audiences, don't you?"

"He's a bleeding head case," said Rambo knowingly and we both looked up to see if he'd popped a capillary and had blood oozing from his ears.

Finally his tickled funny bone was sated and Michael returned to abnormal, gave us a twitch and a few rapid blinks and shook his head. "Great! Cracking joke. I think I'm going to like you two," he gasped, trying to get some air back into his lungs.

Delkim transmitter on. Don't tell him you were serious, Rambo.

"It was a good one wasn't it?" smiled Rambo.

Good boy! Delkim transmitter off.

I was suddenly moved to a higher level of excitement by the tantalising prospect of what would soon be revealed to the pair of us. This was no act, this skinny, rat-faced bundle of raw nerve ends which passed as a human being was the real thing. Whatever burdens and stress came with the territory that comprised Hamworthy Fisheries, hereinafter known as The Syndicate, they must surely be there for a reason. This paranoid, nervy individual, seemingly under as much pressure as a doomed nuclear sub bottomed out in the Mariana Trench, could only be in such a state because of the quality of the water under his jurisdiction. Even if he was a natural worrier I couldn't see him being quite as far-gone as he was running a so-so fishery. No, what with the reverence Pup had put upon the place, this syndicate must be the dog's bollocks. The mutt's nuts. The hound's hangers. The canine's castanets. The pooch's pebbles etc. etc.

"We'll sign the '1st deposit' thing," I said. "Then you can tell us some more about the place."

Michael twitched his head and blinked. "You sign it and then you tell me more about yourself." And he thrust a wavering finger at myself. "And then yourself," he added, moving his oscillating digit towards Rambo.

I saw Rambo's eyes narrow and the muscles at the top of his jaw clenched and pushed out the edge of his cheeks slightly. I could tell he wasn't too keen on being talked to in this peremptory manner but such is the way of the 'Little Hitler'. I assumed it was all supply and demand to Michael, years of running something that people - mad carp anglers – desperately wanted to get into had given him the power of a dictator. Unfortunately such was his desire to keep control of that power and to protect what he had created he was forced to live on a knife's edge because people – mad carp anglers – might want to wrest it from his clammy grasp or steal part of it. Still, I reassured myself, I had no need to get sucked into the politics of it all. I'd just fish the place and enjoy it. In any case I might be reading too much into his jumpy disposition, he might have been a nervous wreck before Hamworthy Fisheries. Deep inside I bet he wasn't.

For the next hour Rambo and myself each waxed lyrical about our love for carp fishing, discreetly avoiding such taboo subjects as hand grenades, fraud, stroke pulling, full time swim hogging, jail sentences - in fact just about everything associated with the last syndicate we were in. We told him of the beauty of Lac Fumant and the fish we'd caught on the first trip but never mentioned the second one. We made it clear we were hoping his water would be as good if not even better. We bummed up the brilliance of Pup's bait, as we calculatingly thought they were friends. We understated, ok we never even mentioned, what an oddball we thought Pup was, living, literally, within a world of boilies, boilie ingredients, boilie flavours and boilie making paraphernalia. We hinted at our respective favourable financial positions, our innate respectability and how, despite the earlier mention of our love for carp fishing, we weren't driven to complete obsession. The type of complete obsession that can make an angler a pain in the arse. We pooh-poohed the notion of the seven-day rule ever affecting us, yet failed to mention that Rambo, now he was dead and on a sound fiscal footing, could fish away to his heart's delight ad infinitum. I also omitted to mention my lottery fortitude and although not being quite in the same class as Rambo, I had to do the odd little job as a now self-employed electrician to subsidise my existence, I had ample free time as well. On the other hand Rambo did manage to imply he was always ready and willing to sort out any trouble should it arrive in any shape or form. He stressed his 'commitment' to things once he was involved in them and his desire to see things were done correctly. It was amazing watching him, not once did he mention physical force or violence and yet in between the lines of his patter and by the sheer will of his personality, character and body language it was blatant where his talents lay. It must have sung out like a choir to Michael, the words being here was someone who was good to have on your side and to get him on your side, from Michael's perspective, all you had to do was let him, and me, in the syndicate. Rambo, bless his camouflaged socks, made it perfectly clear we were a twosome… but not in any sort of 'knobs up the arse' way, of course.

Michael listened and watched intently all the way through like a clued-up carp. He must have seen this sort of 'rig', if you get my drift, from others before us and have listened to some bullshit in his time. I wondered how acute his abilities to suss people out had become over the years and whether he would see through some of our, not lies, omissions, I suppose. It wasn't as if we were trying to make something of ourselves that we weren't, we simply didn't want to tell him the bad bits, that was all. Our line was one of a peripheral makeover, so despite my feelings of it going well, I was still apprehensive when he abruptly cut me off in mid sentence.

"Fine. I think I've heard enough," he said, rather too coldly for my liking. And then Rambo and myself sat there in silence while Michael blinked, twitched his head and scratched his neck as he had before.

    The wait seemed forever. The silence proverbially deafening. The tension mounted and inside, at that moment, I wanted it. I wanted the nod real bad despite my prior reservations and the fact that if I got what I wanted I was going to get stiffed for the best part of four K. It was a sum which brought about other difficult implications, ones I would have to circumnavigate later, yet I was undeterred by the cost. I desperately wanted to get in this over-priced syndicate, about which, as yet, I knew nothing in factual terms. The hype said it was worth it, would the reality? It suddenly dawned on me that we were the ones being manipulated, perhaps Michael was the one being economical with the truth. This sudden avenue of thought went cul-de-sac when Michael started to talk.

    "Ok. I've made my mind up. The pair of you are in. Let me tell you all about the syndicate."

    I straightened in my chair. A bolt of euphoria whizzed up my spine and embedded itself into my cerebral cortex. I shot a quick glance at Rambo but he was staring at Michael and never noticed my movement. He was gripped, I could tell, as gripped as I was.

    Michael carried on. "Back in 1984, through a series of events which needn't concern you, I became the owner of a site of land about an hour's drive from this house. This site covered some sixty acres and within the site there was an old gravel pit working that had been abandoned in the early sixties. The area of the working was, is, around twenty-nine acres. When it became mine it was virtually a barren water, totally untouched by any angling organisation and apart from a few eels and other bits, devoid of fish. In 1986 I stocked the water with the best quality carp I could find, I still have the relevant invoices should you wish to see them, and put in 180 carp between seven and ten pounds. There were three main strains, Italian, German and Belgium fish and I also managed to acquire a few original Leney fish. Over the coming years, as it later transpired, these fish started to pile on weight. Due to the events I mentioned earlier I was not in a position to have to worry about getting an income from the water, so for five years up until 1991 the fish were left to grow untouched by anglers. I was still fishing other waters and had told absolutely nobody else about the project I had started. In fact the person who supplied the fish, Gary and myself were the only people who knew what had gone into the water." Michael suddenly stopped, realising he was talking about people who Rambo and I didn't know. "Gary is somebody who is still a member and you'll get to meet him a bit later, by the way. He was a young boy in those days, mid-teens," he explained with a twitch.

    The fascinating thing I'd noticed during this introductory speech was all the while he was engrossed in telling us his story, I supposed it was his life story simply because I could tell the syndicate was his life, he hardly twitched or blinked. He was absorbed, staring into space and regurgitating the one big account of his time on

Earth. When he broke from his trance onto more mundane things, then his nervous habits returned.

He carried on. "Over that period of time Gary and myself fenced off the entire sixty acres, made a hardcore car park, dug the stock pond and built the wooden clubhouse including its toilets and shower facilities. We also put up gates on the original access road that, luckily enough, was still in good condition and made of sound concrete. This road had been put in by the gravel extract company and obviously had to be strong enough to take all the heavy lorries going to and from the site when it was being worked. It was one of the few things which didn't need a lot of attention but as you can imagine a phenomenal amount of work was put in by the pair of us over that period. The thing that spurred us on was the type of fishery we were creating; we considered it something special, yet in those early days we had no idea how special.

Although you might find it hard to credit we never fished for the carp once in those first five years, we simply left them alone while we got the whole place sorted out. Thinking back the amount of time and effort was extraordinary. There was so much to do. Apart from facilities like the car park, clubhouse, the site boundary and control of access there was also the access to the water. Much of it had become overgrown since the sixties and it all had to be cleared so that there was a track for vehicles around the pit perimeter. Then there was swim clearing, especially as much of the pit is tree lined. Many of those trees had been blown over in the big storm of '87 and some were in the water so they had to taken care of. Cutting up big trees with a chain saw from a boat is really hard graft believe me. I had to insist on doing it on my own, it was far too dangerous for the then young Gary to undertake. We still had to keep everything in check from one year to another because nobody was using the place and it was amazing how quickly things would grow and have to be constantly cut back. Nevertheless the pair of us did it and in '91 everything was as I wanted it. Gary and myself prepared ourselves to start fishing but before we did we spent a couple of months going over the water in a boat, feature finding and fish finding. The echo sounder revealed some amazing underwater features and to our amazement the fish showed up as being big as well. When we did start to catch them we were knocked back at what had happened to the carp. In those five years they had rocketed to mid to high twenties, not all of them but a very high percentage of the ones we caught. Apart from knowing numbers and approximate sizes I hadn't taken photos of the original stock, I didn't want to, I wanted them to be like new jewels when I saw them again and believe me they were. They were growing and growing and growing and it was evident the water was incredibly rich in naturals and this was sustaining the carp and pushing their weights up and up.

With the sure knowledge I had good fish in my water in '92 I set about starting up a syndicate. I filled the place instantly with friends and anglers I knew but during the next three or four years it did become a bit of a problem. Once friends become involved in something you run, where you have to dictate rules to them and when you have to get them to pay you substantial amounts of money it can become difficult. I'm a stickler for what I want, and I know exactly what I want for the fishery. After all I'd created it, I'd financed it, I'd done all the groundwork, with some help from Gary, but it was always my baby. I chose its direction and if people didn't like the direction they'd have to go... and of course some of them did. There are still a few original members, not many I admit, but some have stayed the distance. Some have moved away, financial circumstances have changed for others and some fell out with me and I had to get rid of them. It wasn't nice to fall out with friends so as the list of original mates got smaller and smaller I felt as if an alternative membership policy was needed. I decided to use respected people I knew to recommend anglers to me. Like Pup, of course. They knew the sort of person I would want and if they recommended someone to me, when a space came up, they would get an interview, like you have.

Anyway, all that is a little off what you want to hear about, you want hear about the fish. '94 saw the first thirty, '98 saw the first forty and when you two lucky people go to fish Hamworthy you will be sitting behind your three rods in the sure knowledge you are fishing for well over thirty documented forty pound fish. The largest fish to date is touching forty-nine pounds. This autumn we'll do a fifty and soon there'll be a shed full of them. Three to four years on and they'll be sixties. At the moment there are another sixty or seventy thirties and the rest are upper twenties. They're all young fish and still growing. Anything, as you no doubt read, that's below twenty-five pounds goes in the stock pond. The fish do breed and you will catch the odd growing fish that is a low double or single but I think a lot of the eggs and fry are eaten by the big fish so pasties aren't a major problem.

Anglers fishing for all these fish number twenty including myself, of which you are the latest two to join. There are twenty swims, although they have never been fully occupied at any one time. Because of this situation you'll find it a water where you can fish without any contact from other anglers. All the swims are isolated and have a lot of natural cover, I actually send out a catch report twice a year so anglers know what is getting caught. We have no catch log book as such, only the requirement to tell me of forty plus fish captures and to supply photos. When we go there a bit later I will show you every swim and answer any more questions you might have including tactics and features should you want me to tell you."

Michael paused and started to blink quickly. Rambo let out a low whistle. My heart was galloping like a Derby winner. Could all of what Michael had just told us be true? Never in my wildest dreams did I think there could possibly be a syndicate water of such quality within a couple of hours of my doorstep, give or take a few speeding points.

"Well then, boy. What do you say?" he said grinning at me. "Sounds like some sort of place." I nodded wholeheartedly. I should coco. Rambo turned his eyes to Michael. "I can well understand you wanting to keep it under wraps as much as possible, news of fish of such calibre is bound to get the scum crawling out of the woodwork."

"My only hope is the members are selfish enough to want to keep it to themselves," said Michael.

"I can't imagine anyone wanting to let a cat like this out of the bag," I said, apparently very naively by the withering look of disbelief from Michael.

I gave my brain a quick dig in the ribs with my elbow. Hadn't I learnt anything from previous experience? Still it was clear Michael's odd character wasn't an act, we hadn't been duped, this was the carp angling Mecca we'd hoped for and we were in, all I had to do was get the money. I pushed that detail way to the back of my puny mind and vainly tried to slip myself into Michael's bivvy slippers in an attempt to try and imagine the years of graft and toil that had gone into the making of his life's desire. Then I tried to imagine the feelings of insecurity, of paranoia even, that someone somewhere might be plotting to try and take parts of it away. Perhaps there might be individuals who didn't share his view of keeping it a joyous secret amongst a select few. Perhaps they might have darker ambitions; they might not care at all for the well being of his dream but would be quite happy to rip the lot of it asunder to promote whatever horrid plans they might harbour. It's one of life's big bummers, the more precious something is the bigger the fear of losing it or having it damaged. And by definition the more precious it is the more likely that some bastard somewhere would want to get their nasty mitts on it. I had some sympathy for the rat-like, blinking and twitching Michael. I could see his predicament but hoped he and this Gary had got it sorted. I wanted this place to run and run and with no aggro, but then I wondered if I was being naïve again. He'd had aggro, people had been asked to leave, our two places becoming available were evidence of that. There might even be hassle now. I didn't know it to be fact but even if it was the case I was still going to join. My thoughts were stopped by the sound of a knock at the door.

"That'll be Gary," said Michael getting up quickly from the computer chair. "He's got the new pictures of the bigger fish and he's going to come with us to the pit to help show you around."

Michael left the room while Rambo and myself grinned at each other like a couple of Cheshire cats. I could hear a muffled conversation and then Michael came back in.

"This is Gary, the person who has helped me most with Hamworthy," blinked Michael.

"Hi guys," said Gary, breezing in and immediately taking over the room with his presence.

Gary was clearly much younger than Michael, a full ten years at least and I have to admit he was one of the most striking looking men I'd ever set eyes on. He had film star looks, a bit Brad Pitt meets George Clooney, a tall powerful physique, though not quite in Rambo's league and a charismatic self-confidence that came from looking at physical perfection in the mirror.

He stood, both hands on hips, nodding apparent approval at Rambo and myself. Perfect white teeth shone from a bedazzling smile, his jet-black hair, thick and spiky, did not move an inch. "Mike tells me you're in," he said in an easy assured voice focusing his male model gaze on us and totally ignoring Michael. "Cool. Hey! Has he told you that the place is haunted yet?"

"Oh Gary," said Michael, his eyes going twenty to the dozen. Even his voice seemed to waver and become shaky. "Why do you insist on bringing up this silly old story in front of every new member?"

"Because it's true, that's why," said an unrepentant Gary.

Chapter 4

Michael's eyes fluttered for a few seconds, as had many a woman's in the company of Gary, I was willing to wager. "Did I forget to tell you?" asked Michael cutting an even more worried and rat-like figure now he could be compared to the Adonis standing next to him. Poor paranoid Michael. Cut him in half and you'd have a skinny piece of rock with the words 'overwrought' through 180 degrees clockwise at the top, 'distressed' through 180 degrees anti-clockwise at the bottom and through the middle a heaving bundle of writhing spinal nerve.

"You did," said Rambo. "The last thing I need is a dead carp angler who's still alive, to some extent or another, fishing on my water," he continued, shooting me a wry smile continuing his earlier joke from when he'd hidden on the back seat of the car.

Gary jumped in eagerly with an explanation. "A couple of the guys believe in it because they've had some far from sound experiences, the others are less convinced, simply because they haven't had a visit from the apparition. All the weird occurrences seem to have no logical explanation, much to the disgust of those unconvinced, but like I say a couple of us have been converted by things that go bump in the night. Of course we haven't got it on film or video to provide conclusive proof but I'm certain it exists. I doubt if it, whatever it is, is a dead carp angler, though," continued Gary, speaking directly to Rambo. "Perhaps it might be one of the workers from the gravel extraction days, apparently there was an accident and one of them did get killed. Personally I think it's more likely to be someone far more ancient, it might even be a she. I've never screwed a spectre, I've screwed just about every other type of woman there is but not one of those!"

Michael actually appeared to relax for a split second. It looked painful for him but he managed it. "Gary's had more women than he's had carp," he said with admiration and Gary flashed me a huge Hollywood grin.

"Been doing a lot blanking, then?" Rambo asked Gary, deadpan.

"Nah!" said Gary turning his handsome face towards Rambo. "I've had eighteen fish so far this year and I've had twenty-two women, not including repeat captures, if you see what I mean, or repeat shags come to that," said Gary seemingly unabashed by Rambo's none to subtle put down.

Shit! Was my first reaction, it was only April and he'd stuffed my lifetime's achievements into a cocked hat in four months and I'm not talking about the carp side of things. The cocky fucker. Of that there was no doubt. Film star good looks and what, within three minutes of him meeting us, he'd been bragging about his shagging. Here was someone playing the numbers game all right. Jealous? Possibly. Intimidated? Slightly. On what level? Ask me one on bait.

"Anyway, enough of ghosts and women," said Gary, presumably now he was satisfied he had impressed us two new members. "Let me show you these pictures I've got." Gary knelt down and started to unroll the large poster sized-piece of paper he'd been holding out onto the floor. "These are all the forties that have been caught up until now," he explained. "This is dead cool, believe me," he said, as he pinned down the corners of the poster with some heavy books Michael had passed him. I recognised all of the books, the ubiquitous 'Carp Fever', 'Redmire Pool', a Concise Oxford dictionary and 'The Trials of Life' by David Attenborough. Learn how to catch carp 80's style, have an in depth knowledge of one of carp fishing's most famous venues, understand and spell words and try to fathom the meaning of your own existence through the animal world. Or watch Sky TV (more rubbish than you could shake a remote controller at), East Enders, overrated celebrity chefs, moronic garden and house make-overs and contrived dominatrix quiz mistresses and just use the books as paperweights, stepping stones to things only very slightly out of your reach, table and chair levellers on very poor flooring or mozzie squashers (extra bonus points for every blood splat achieved).

"All the fish you see here have been painted in watercolours by Alan from photos given to him by the successful angler. The originals are much larger obviously, but he's then scanned those paintings, shrunk them down to a suitable size and had them printed on this poster with all the relevant information, including the carp's name. It's brilliant. Oh, I expect Michael also forgot to tell you should you catch a new forty for the syndicate it's an unwritten rule you can name the fish. We update the poster every ten new forties and as we had a rush through the twenties into the thirties this is the brand new one. Not even Michael has seen this one, I've literally just picked it up from Alan."

Gary looked at the poster, now fully unfurled on the floor, its four corners pinned by the heavy books. "Well cool. Well cool," he said shaking his head in clear veneration.

I posted an image of Gary looking down on a spread-eagled woman, wrists and ankles bound. Had he got to me or what?

The other three of us were soon on our hands and knees staring at the poster and it was 'well cool', it had to be said. My eyes perused the superb illustrations which were accompanied by small pieces of text that had been fastidiously placed on the poster. It was a professional looking piece of work and the intricate detail on each of the fish was superb. Each tiny painting, about the size of a 6" x 4" colour print was incredible. Scale patterns were picked out, colour and hue looked amazingly natural and somehow each fish seemed to have a lifelike feel of its own.

"Who's Alan?" I asked.

"He's one of the few originals left," said Gary. "He's an old boy, middle fifties, superb artist and a real carp anorak." Gary slapped the poster with the back of his hand. "This must have taken months of work but he loves doing it, ask him anything to do with carp fishing, he knows about it and if he doesn't he'll find out and then draw it for you. Top guy. Top guy."

"I think he should have illustrated both flanks of each carp," I said in a gently mocking voice.

"Actually, I think he has, but to cut down on space he's presented us with the most attractive side for markings," said Michael.

Gary started at the top left of the poster and pointed to the individual paintings. "This one's called Manuel, our first forty."

"Manuel?" queried Rambo.

"We could hardly call it Bazil could we?" said Gary laughing.

"Does it come from Barcelona?" I said just to prove I got the joke. No one answered.

"All my fish are English," said Michael stiffly. Ooops!

Gary carried on along the top line of fish with his index finger pointing to each painting as and when. "This one's called Pugwash as you can see, there's the capturer's name, the date and what weight she was. The next one's Pugwash's Mate and this one is The Black Pig. I went out with a girl who I used to call that, not to her face, mind you, but she was a big mamma. She used to squeeze so tight with her big thighs I used to think my bollocks were going to explode!"

I could see Rambo staring at Gary as if he was a space alien out of the corner of my eye but he made no comment and Gary was soon talking again. "All those fish were named by Sniffer, he and his fascination for cardboard cut-out cartoons have long gone."

"Apparently in the original books there was a character called Seaman Staines and Roger the Cabin Boy," I said.

This time Rambo did feel the need to chip in. "Urban myth, boy," he said. "Unlike our haunted pit ghost, which is more than likely a countryside one."

"You wait and see," said Gary, nodding and smiling at Rambo. "This last one on the top line is called Orion, can you see the three large scales down the flank?"

We all craned our necks to see. "See how the middle one is slightly offset, just like the three stars that make up Orion's belt."

"Patrick Moore's in the syndicate, then?" said Rambo sarcastically but with no malice.

"No! But Jim, who caught the fish as a first forty is a bit of an amateur astrologist, you'll recognise a few other of his names later on. The second line, let's see. The pale fish is called Moontan, this one is named Side Saddle, apparently the two vertical sets of scales here look like a pair of legs. Malc must have been on the wacky baccy, I think. These next two fish had got caught loads of times before they became forties so the names are pretty obvious. Meet Dopey and Toby, our resident mug fish and the final one is a classic Leney common called The Carving, such a deep, bronze fish. Beautiful! On the third line we have Trevor the Levor, a leather needless to say and next, this one with a red stain on its belly, is called Gorby. Get that?"

Rambo and myself nodded. "How about his one, then. See the ring of scales around the wrist of the tail? This fish is called Bilbo, know why?" Rambo shook his head and I was equally clueless.

"Lord of the Rings. Tolkien. One of the characters in that book," Gary explained. I was no wiser but took his word for it. I hadn't seen the film let alone read the book. "Next we have Flit Spin, Noel spoonerised a split fin which this carp has. Ah now, the next one's a good one, look at the large scales on this mirror."

Gary pointed and we all looked closer. "Huh! Looks just like the Olympic flag," I said in bemusement gawping at the five huge scales, a top line of three spaced out with two underneath more or less bang in the middle of the spaces. How unusual.

"That's right. He's called The Olympian, an amazing fish, Alan himself had this one at 41-6. Onto the fourth line. Penny Scale, you see that one scale near the tail? Next up, Beach Ball, short, fat and round, not unlike the guy who caught it, that was Mick, he's not in the syndicate now either. You see this next one, she's got a pelvic fin missing and she's called Minus One. This stunning looking fully scaled is called Page Three, for obvious reasons and this one which has got only one eye is called Cyclops. Now, from here on this is all new territory. All these next lot of fish are updates from the last poster. We've now got twelve new forties. By the time Alan had drawn the new lot of ten, two more had been caught. Basically he's been working on this all over the winter. Anyway here we go, new forty number one."

I glanced over to Michael whose eyes were now burning into the poster like Superman's when he's doing the red laser thing, his face was etched with agony and ecstasy. I could see his mind at work in the contortions of his face or at least what I presumed was going through his mind. Great news on the one hand, more big fish, his dream reaching even higher levels of achievement counterbalanced by greater prospects of someone trying to spoil his vision of the syndicate because of that achievement. And so on ad infinitum. I decided there and then he must have something wrong with him. Most people would revel in the upside of the situation he was in and not be dragged down by what might happen. His paranoia must be generic, or it was the syndicate from hell. It couldn't be though because he could blow people out. Why had our two places turned up? Christ! Stop it! I was nearly as bad!

Gary was talking again, he seemed good at talking, perhaps it was his assured demeanour. "Fifth line starts with this long, long common. It looks like a fucking missile so it's called Scud. This next fish is our biggest, touching fifty and you can see why."

And I could, the fish was an ugly looking thing with a disproportionate stomach bulging below it.

"Gut Bucket!" I read. "43lb 6ozs?"

"Yeah, it's been caught once more since and it's really stacking on the weight. Remember all these weights are the weights as recorded after going through the forty barrier for the first time. It's why they're all pretty much low to scraper forties but it's not what they weigh as they're swimming around at the moment, they're all bigger. This grey fish is The Italian Mirror, I caught it last autumn, it didn't fight one bit, I just wound it straight into the net, hence the name. The next fish is Hubble, our astrologist friend, Jim, again. This next one, Frankenstein, was caught by Rocky, he said it was a monster, hence the name. Talking of urban myths, or in this case misconceptions, it was the doctor who created the monster who was called Frankenstein not the monster itself. Splitting hairs I know. Rocky's a bit of a poseur, not a very sociable guy, I'm afraid, in fact he can be a bit of a nasty piece of work at times. He's a bit flash with all his gear, not that I'd tell him, he's as big as you Rambo and he likes camouflage gear as well. You two could almost be doubles. You could be twins!" Gary let out a laugh. "Rocky and Rambo."

"Rocky and Bullwinkle," said Michael.

"What are you on about?" asked Gary, a touch brusquely for my liking.

"Oh, some old cartoon thing I remember as a young kid and a film as well. Forget it."

"I think we already have," said Gary, turning his attention back to the poster. "Line six we have this mirror with the huge tail called The Paddle and this one, well, let me explain. The guy who caught this, Todd, only had a set of Avon scales with him at the time. You know the white, green, orange and other coloured things that go round four times, eight pounds each time, bottom out at thirty-two plus? So he weighs this fish and - bonk - right down to the bottom, he's no idea how much it weighs. He's got no idea full stop but there were are, that's neither here nor there. Anyway, luckily for him I happened to turn up just before he's going to put the fish back and so I got out my Reuben Heaton scales to weigh it at 42-9 and because of this Todd calls the fish Thirty Something. I ask you. This one's called Abba, they were on the radio when Dean got the take."

"Lucky it wasn't Napalm Death," said Rambo, dryly. "Or Spandeau Ballet."

"Spandeau Ballet?" I asked.

"I really fucking hated them," explained Rambo.

"This next carp is called Mint. Any offers?" queried Gary.

"In perfect nick?" I asked.

Gary shook his head. "Not that meaning."

"Caught on a Mint Imperial? A Tic-Tac? A bit of spearmint chewing gum? I know, caught on a day-glow white pop-up, heavily glugged in a mixture of toothpaste, Fox's glacier mints and Polo's," said Rambo adding. "It's the only descent bit of kit Fox make!"

"No! Caught after eight!" said Gary. And we all laughed, like you do. He pointed to the next one. "Lassie?"

"Caught in rrrrrrough weather!" growled Rambo.

"It was so bad you'd have had to have been barking mad to be fishing in it!" I said.

"It was raining cats and dogs, but more dogs than cats!" said Rambo

"The fish was the dog's bollocks! The mutt's nuts! The hound's hangers! The canine's castanets! The pooch's pebbles!" I said, wondering where on earth that lot came from.

"He didn't give himself a dog's chance of catching it!" said Rambo.
"He was dog tired when he caught it!" I suggested.
"It gave a real dog fight!" offered Rambo.
"He was like a dog with two tails when he caught it!" I added.
"He was in the dog house with his wife for going fishing for that session!" grinned Rambo.
"The rig he caught it on was a real dog's dinner!"
"No! The rig he caught it on was a real dog's breakfast!"
"It was caught during the dog days of summer!"
"He was wearing dog toothed trousers!"
"He'd just put out a fag and thrown down a dog end!"
"He'd just had a can of lager after getting blasted the night before to help settle his stomach, a hair of the dog that bit him!"
"It took a dog's age to land it!" I said, by now laughing out loud
"Put the bloody dictionary down guys and think bait," said Gary sounding miffed.
Sheepishly I put the Concise Oxford back on the top right corner of the poster, I'd seen the answer but wanted to keep going.
"Caught on dog food. Mad cow guts, soya flour, ground came last in the four-thirty at Kempton mixed 50/50 with Essential Products B5. That's five different bones to you," I said.
"Canine-8. It was caught on Canine-8!" chimed Rambo.
"Off the frigging top, not the bloody bottom," said Gary getting slightly exasperated.
"Caught on a dog biscuit," I said gently. "Lassie was a Pedigree Mixer freak."
"Yes! At last! Christ, are you two like that all the time?" said Gary. He was smiling but I could tell our little double act had peeved him slightly, I didn't know why.
"No, not often," I said and to change the subject I quickly pointed to the last two forty pounders on the poster. "What about the last two, then?"
"The last two, both winter forties incidentally, were caught by myself and Rocky. I called my one Amazon, sort of in honour of the amazing woman I'd had three nights earlier and Rocky had his fish on Boxing Day and he called it Tyson. He'd fished from Christmas Eve through until New Years Day and it was the only take he had."
Wouldn't it be a bit of a dull old world if we were all the same, I thought. There was Gary, self-appointed shagmeister, scrolling through a list of unobtainable women, to the likes of most blokes and then there was Rocky, sad, flash bastard in camouflage kit fishing all the Christmas period. What a way to carry on. How one-dimensional could you possibly get? I had all the questions because I'd asked them about myself, but crucially, I have to admit, not at the time I was doing it. Only after, when I'd seen the light, had I thought about it and it was a bit late then.

"So there you are then guys, it's an awesome list and it's going to get even more so. I say we have a quick cuppa and then we can go down to the pit and I'll show you around and you can see for yourselves where these beasts live," said Gary.

Rambo nodded and I did as well. "Get the kettle on then, Michael," said Gary.

Michael gave a synchronised nod and blink and left the room. "He won't make old bones," Gary confided to the two of us when Michael had gone out to the kitchen. "The guy's a stress heart attack waiting to happen. Control freak, you see. He won't let go, he won't delegate or trust anyone, not even me, to help run his precious syndicate and take some of the pressure off him. I mean what does the guy think I'm going to do? I've been involved as long as he has and I'm his best friend but he won't let me help. It's a shame but that's the way it is, he's silly, one day he's going to pay for it with some real uncool health problems."

I nodded but said nothing and Rambo didn't even nod. Michael came back with four mugs and we drank our tea and chatted about this and that and then wasted no more time in getting into Gary's car and setting off to the pit. Rambo and myself sat in the back, Michael sat in the passenger seat while Gary drove and talked. The pair of them had an odd sort of relationship. You would have thought, if you didn't know any better, it was Gary who ran the syndicate and Michael was the second string of the pair. Michael seemed slightly in awe of Gary and never had anything other than praise for him, whether it was for his fishing or for his fornicating. Despite that, from what Gary had said earlier, Michael's admiration didn't extend to letting Gary wield any real power within the syndicate, which seemed strange. Gary, on the other hand, although he talked of the wonder of the fishery we were about to see, was often a bit curt with Michael. What did I care? We were off to my new syndicate and a skip full of whackers, long time friends often have peculiar mannerisms.

The trip to the gravel pit soon passed, Gary was full of stories about the place, people past and present although he refused to elaborate on any of the ghost stories. He said he had promised the sceptics within the syndicate he wouldn't tell any tales to new members in case it subliminally influenced them in any way. We would have to wait for our own personal visitation should it ever come and it did seem as if the vast percentage thought it wouldn't. I was more hopeful of a visitation from large lumps of carp than of lurking loathsome phantoms. Ghost carp? Well, if they were in there and above thirty, I wouldn't say no.

For the rest of the afternoon we were shown around our 4K investment. Looking at it and knowing what was swimming in the wet part of it, it looked like money well spent. The access road had run for at least a mile until we'd arrived at the main entrance gates. To me it was something akin to cruising down a huge driveway to a massive stately home that oozed class and splendour. I hadn't been disappointed, the whole aura and feel of the place seemed magnificent. The gate was chained shut with combination padlocks, which we weren't allowed to see, the combination that is, not the padlock. It was Michael who told us that until our cheques were written and cleared we couldn't be party to such details.

"No offence guys," said Gary.

"None taken," said Rambo, lying.

The clubhouse was a fine wooden structure with toilets, a couple of showers, bait freezer, all the usual stuff you'd expect at somewhere top notch. After a pretty superficial viewing it was onto the walk around the perimeter of the pit, having crossed the car park - or was it a carp ark - with only two other vehicles in it, it being adjacent to the clubhouse.

As we set off in a clockwise direction my first feeling was one of remoteness. The isolation was extreme. Prior to the actual access road we had spent a good fifteen minutes winding down seemingly endless country lanes barely wide enough for two cars to pass and after coming off of a 'B' road. We were in the back of beyond all right and the whole sixty acres was very mature, natural and in the middle of nowhere. As much as possible had been left untouched for nearly forty years since the gravel extraction had finished and it showed by not showing, if you get my drift. To the pit's north end there was an even older wood, it had been there for hundreds and hundreds of years and this wood alone constituted nearly twenty acres of Michael's super sixty. Apparently this wood hadn't been touched in living memory, the gravel extract company certainly hadn't ventured into it and to popular knowledge nor had anyone else for a very long time.

The pit's perimeter walk was in fact a track that was wide enough for you to take your car around. This meant you could simply drive around to your swim, drop off your gear, complete the circle by car, park up and walk back to your swim. Depending on which swim you chose you had anything from a few yards to thirty or so to the water's edge from the track. It was very convenient as it eliminated the need for donkey work or sherpas, there was to be no more lugging of gear for anything other than a short distance. You could even move onto fish by car should you be inclined to bust all your gear down into small enough pieces to get it in the back of a motor. I realised my one last chance of keeping any semblance of physical fitness had disappeared for as long as I stayed in the syndicate. Today we were walking it but I couldn't see me ever having to do it again with gear on my back.

The car park and clubhouse were at the southern end of the pit so we walked up the west side seeing as we were going clockwise. We stopped at every swim, but I was amazed at how little we did stop and how far we walked to get to the next one. Gary and Michael pointed out various good spots to fish towards and told Rambo and myself of any features and places where the big fish had been caught. Compared to what I'd been used to of late it all seemed so spacious. Twenty blokes fishing twenty-nine acres, twenty-nine acres set in over sixty acres, no wonder it seemed a hike between them. On some of the day ticket waters we'd recently fished if you so much as stepped outside your bivvy and tripped over one of the guide-ropes you could easily find yourself sitting on the lap of the bloke in the next swim, or with a Delkim rammed up your left nostril. It was evident even if you were fishing on this pit together, as a pair, you were still very much alone. There would be no casual saunters up the bank for a chat and cuppa, especially with regards to the rules for attending your rods. Having a social isn't quite the same if you have to wind in, is it? Bloody carp anglers. I blame telecom workers for converting the first Optonics myself. The originals were so pathetic you had to put your bedchair around the wrong way, so your back was to the water, just so you could hear them. More than four foot away... not a peep registered, then all of a sudden you get an upgrade with a telephone speaker bolted on the front and we'd all gone Aboriginal. Walkabout. Now with receivers you can hear your alarms in the next county, still, they wouldn't be much use on this water, what with the prospect of four grand down the tubes.

Further up the west side the ancient wood started to appear and by the time we turned along the top northern bank – the pit was virtually a rounded off square, there were no little bays or arms at all apart from a couple of small points to the south that only went out fifteen or so yards – it was thick and dense and only yards from the perimeter track. The trees look gnarled and weathered, their spacing dense and congested. Despite it being a bright day the wood looked very dark and forbidding only a little vegetation grew at the bottom of the trees because the sunlight couldn't break through the mass of twisted and entwined branches. I'd never seen a wood like it to be honest, it looked old and it gave off a sort of ancient emanation. All the trees looked twisted and contorted, almost as if they had grown in pain and the texture of their bark, so dark and rutted and heavily weathered added to the strange overall effect. The wood consisted of mainly oaks, beeches and horse chestnut trees but it was the large oaks that caught my eye, seemingly spaced out at random amongst the other trees, made more evident by their huge size. I have to say I thought it was a creepy wood, not one you'd imagine children would want to run and play in but I kept my irrational fear to myself. Was it irrational? Not with what Gary had said about the pit being haunted, the dope didn't need to elaborate with detailed anecdote, the seed he'd sewn was more than ample, what with the possibility of it being nourished with fertile imagination.

I'd been somewhat distracted by my arboretum angst from what Gary and Michael had been telling me about the pit and I joined in again to hear Gary harp on about the gravel bar that ran parallel to the north bank at about 70 yards range between the two islands. In the next swim one of the syndicate members was fishing but we didn't stop to visit him and left him in peace. Halfway down the east side the old wood faded out and was gone and my head was beginning to ache with carp info overload. There is only so much you can take in when being shown around somewhere over a few hours. The bombardment of gravel bars, drop offs, plateaux, margin hot spots and all the other wonderful features like weed beds that would soon grow, weed beds that were there two seasons ago but didn't grow last year but might grow this year soon begin to lose any significance simply because my poor old brain couldn't cope.

The features I was most struck by were the three islands the pit had. All were a good size and reachable from the bank without the use of a banned bait boat. And easy to remember! Since Lac Fumant and the fifty mind-meld mirror, island margins held a fascination for me and I was planning on fishing a swim that gave me a cast at one on my first outing. This would mean fishing the north bank for two of the islands or a swim further down the east bank for the third one. In any case I was sure Rambo and myself would go around the place together again and put some game plan together. If there was one thing I have learned during the period from spotty adolescent carper until now was that it pays to disregard a lot of the unwritten rules of a venue. You know the ones that say: 'They never get caught on top here, mate', or: 'You need to put in lots of bait'. 'Don't use too much bait'. 'Never spod'. 'Always spod'. 'They don't like marker floats' and the wonderful: 'You've got to put it on a sixpence'. All those kind of carping grapevine rumours that may, or may not, depending on the talents of the person making the comments, lead you astray. I'm telling you, until you can prove or disprove it yourself never take it as gospel... and you can take that as gospel!

We passed the other member fishing the east bank swim to the island, left him to his own little world, passed the stock pond and eventually completed the three hundred and sixty degrees and returned to the car park. Time was now pressing on and Gary had a later engagement so it was back in the car, a return to Michael's house to be on the end of a severe warning from him to send in our membership money to him within seven days. We nodded, there then followed a round of hand shaking and at last, feeling totally knackered, I was in my car with Rambo with a chance to speak my mind.

"What do you think, then?" I asked.

"Impressive place, very impressive fish, not so sure about the two members we've met but... fuck them, I'm up for it. I fancy catching a few new forties," said Rambo grinning. "I'll tell you though, boy, the old wood has something about it, not sure what, but it has something."

"It was a bit off putting, almost frightening," I readily agreed, pleased even Rambo had noticed what I had felt. "Even if Hollywood Gary hadn't mentioned the pit being haunted, I'd have still viewed the wood with trepidation." I paused and laughed at Rambo. "You're not sure what the wood has about it because you don't understand fear," I said.

"Believe me, boy," said Rambo earnestly, "I understand fear more than you'll ever realise. It just so happens I don't suffer from it."

"It might be scary," I told him, getting dragged back into practicalities, "but it won't be any more scary than when I have to tell Sophie I'm back in a syndicate again. She'll go ballistic."

"Like Watt's bivvy?"

"Yeah! And when I tell her it's nearly four grand for the pleasure I might end up in a similar state."

Chapter 5

They, whoever 'they' are, say there is a time and a place for everything. Personally I was unconvinced. Informing Sophie I was about to enlist in a syndicate and the cost of doing so seemed to have no place whatsoever in the four dimensional world in which we lived. In reality this was total bollocks because if I didn't get my cheque off to Michael on time I'd lose out so really the subject's place had a very strict definition, time-wise. If anything the time constraint agitated the situation, it increased the pressure on broaching the subject at the right juncture and that juncture seemed oh so elusive within the window I had. Besides, Sophie herself seemed unusually on edge of late, it was crazy watching her because although it hadn't registered to begin with, now I had my burden to off-load, her behaviour made more sense. The tension during mundane conversation, the inability to relax, the slight suppression of appetite were all traits she'd started and now I was following. The kernel of understanding got larger and it dawned on me, being the dumb male I was, a full two weeks after she'd started acting this way, that her behaviour meant *she* had something to tell *me*. She was on edge because something was bothering her, like joining the syndicate was bothering me.

I'd been in a position to know I was definitely in provided I got the cheque off in time for three days now, double provided I could tell her and she didn't kill me. Once that obstacle was cleared and she concurred (I hoped) I could sort the dosh from our joint account and all would be hunky-dory. Since I'd needed to tell her about all this my mannerisms had mimicked hers and I could now see things for what they were. Before, oblivious, now in the same boat, blindingly obvious. What if she said no? What would Rambo think about that? What would I think? The hole was simply too black to even think about at this stage, just popping the question was bad enough, let alone worrying about the answer I didn't want

Mealtimes were quite a laugh, in a non-funny way. What with her feminine intuition, or however you want to label it, I suspected she now realised I wanted to tell her something. So there we were, two - in the eyes of the law anyway - adults, both weighted with the need to impart information to a partner, who, for God's sake, had shared the best part of their adult life in each other's company. Communication breakdown. A severed telephone cable. Postmen on strike, no stamps, no writing paper and a biro that didn't work. Email server down. A voice box buggered by laryngitis. Lips hidden by a morning paper. Boxing gloves on Braille reading fingers. Pathetic. It never did seem to be the right time, for either of us. We sat and picked at cold food, avoiding the moment because the moment never came because we were avoiding it.

I wondered what on earth could be so heavy to cause her to feel like she did. Perhaps she thought the same. Perhaps she was going to leave me. Perhaps she was getting shagged by a male Olympic gymnast, or, at a stretch, or more likely the splits, by a woman. Perhaps some woman had tapped into her until now hidden latent lesbianism and my knee-jerk reaction was; can I watch? Your wife or partner leaving you for another woman, think about it once you get past the male fantasy crap. One normally looks like a steelworker in a boiler suit for a start and where does it put your machismo? Is it the ultimate male put down? She's more of a man than you'll ever be. Pass the cyanide capsule or sneak in and fit dud batteries when no one's looking. Surely it couldn't be that. What the bloody hell was it?

One mealtime I was thinking about the question when I looked up to see her staring at me and the concern that had to be the answer to it was written all over her face. My mouth dried instantly but I managed to hold her eye. The colour drained from her face, her eyes welled with tears and I felt my whole body sag under the expectation of the ensuing onslaught of both her revelation and mine. Whose world was about to be rocked the most? I would soon know, this was the moment. 'They' were right after all.

"Oh, Matthew," she cried tearfully. Then, steeling herself with a deep breath, she blurted. "There's something I must tell you. It's been worrying me for weeks but I didn't have the courage." Her voice rose in hysteria and like a dam wall bursting she suddenly screamed. "Oh my God! What are you going to say about it?"

Shell-shocked, I replied with the only words I could think of, the ones I'd been dry running for the last three days. The words were dry all right. "I've got something to tell you as well," I said gravely, the words like dust in my mouth. "It's pretty heavy, so don't be cross. Please don't be cross," I pleaded.

"Whatever it is isn't as important as what I've got to tell you," she said, getting up to rip off about six pieces of kitchen towel to dab her wet cheeks.

"What I'm about to tell you might put a strain on our relationship," I said, trying to prepare her but at the same time slightly put out by her previous assumption. She must be confused, I reasoned, in this state she might go ape. I had no notion as to what she might say or do after all the grief a syndicate had caused the two of us last time.

Sophie wasn't about to be outdone. "What I'm going to tell you will certainly put a strain on our relationship, there's no question of that. The biggest strain possible," she said, and she blew her nose. My dad's better than your dad. You've got an elephant? Well I've got a box to put it in.

I had got up from my chair to go over and put my arm around her but her words of strained one-upmanship sandbagged me and I staggered, reeling from them, back onto the chair. Holy fucking shit. What the fucking bloody hell was going on? She wasn't confused, I'd got it all wrong, she was certain. Positive. Convinced. 100% plus VAT.

"So whatever my thing is, you don't think it can top yours?" I asked.

She shook her head and started crying again but this time she was laughing as well. I was really confused. I was now very frightened as well.

I sat slumped in the chair. "Go on, then. You first, let's get the big one out of the way," I said weakly.

Sophie shook her head again. "No. You go first."

I swallowed and not wanting to go into a Harry Hill dialogue routine I capitulated and said my party piece. "Rambo and I are going to join a carp fishing syndicate," I began, keenly watching her face for signs of a reaction. "It's a really nice place with loads of big fish but it is a bit expensive. Pup, you know, the boilie bloke I told you about? He was the one who told us about it and we just said ok, we'd go on the list, you know, nothing ventured etc. and then we came to the top of the list, we had an interview and we've had a look round and we both liked it… and… and… we're in, as long as I pay up soon." I added tamely as a look of deep concern passed over Sophie's face. It hadn't come out quite as eloquently as I'd hoped but at least it was out of the bag. Like a great big scabby, flea-ridden, mangy tom-cat.

"Oh, Matthew!" she started and I could see raw emotion start to take over her body. The tissues she held up to her face were held with fingers that trembled more than Michael's. "Oh, Matthew!" she said again in a tiny voice that reverberated because her whole body was beginning to shake. I'd never, ever, seen her so emotional even on the day I'd been sentenced to jail. "Oh, Matthew! Things are going to be so different."

And she came and sat on my lap placing her left arm around my neck. I'd lost all comprehension, I had no idea what her secret was, so I hugged her, this woman who was the true love of my life and I could feel her body quivering as if she had been submerged in cold water for some considerable time.

"What is it?" I asked quietly.

"Oh, Matthew!" she started but then paused and moved her head back so we had eye contact. I was sucked into her red, tear-blurred eyes and she started to laugh and cry at the same time again. I shook my head with tiny, jerky movements, a stupid half-cocked smile on my face and lifted my shoulders in an imperceptible shrug. What was it? What was this thing?

"Oh, Matthew! I'm pregnant!" she cried. "We're going to have a baby! You're going to be a daddy!"

It was like a string of Chinese crackers going off inside my brain. Bang! Pregnant?!! Bang! She was on the pill. Bang! A dad? Me?! Bang! Real responsibility. Bang! Babies cost money! Bang! Less fishing time. Bang! Fishing costs money. Bang! Conflict of interest! Bang! A boy or a girl? Bang! Cots. Bang! Nappies. Bang! Sleepless nights. Bang! Less fishing time. Bang! A dad? Bang! Conflict of interest! Bang! Pregnant! Bang! A dad! Me! Bang! Baby things. Bang! Less fishing time. Bang! Conflict of interest! Bang! Babies cost money! Bang! Less fishing time. Bang! A boy or a girl? Bang! Cots. Bang! Nappies. Bang! Sleepless nights. Bang! Conflict of interest! Bang! Less fishing time. Bang! Pregnant?!! Bang!

She was on the pill. Bang! Conflict of interest! Bang! Conflict of interest! Bang! Conflict of interest! Bang! Conflict of interest! Abort! Abort! Abort! Cerebral overload! Abort! Abort! A string of looped Chinese crackers that could repair themselves and explode again.

"Well?" she said, no doubt looking at my blank, dazed expression. If I hadn't been sitting down I'd have said you could have knocked me down with a feather. Actually that would have sliced me in half. If I'd have been standing up you could have knocked me down with the draught of a wrist rotated helicopter rig. "What do you think? Are you pleased?" The last question was virtually begging to be answered in the affirmative and I knew it was the crux of all her worries. This baby was unplanned and as having children had never been on our agenda, up until this moment of course, she had no idea of how I would feel.

"Are you?" I asked, dipping a toe in the water. I was too numb to have any feelings at this precise juncture, it was simply too unexpected for me to rationalise.

"I think so," she said dabbing her eyes again but she was much calmer now her secret was out. "I've always wanted to have kids, but I've always thought it would happen in the future, not now, I wasn't worried about having them now because I thought we could always have them later on. It was a massive shock to find out I was pregnant and I was so frightened you might not want a baby yet I couldn't bring myself to tell you. You've always wanted to be a dad, haven't you?"

"I think so," I answered honestly. "I haven't really thought much about it. Like you, it was something that would happen at some indeterminate point in the future, not something which was going to happen to me now. I mean, how did it happen?"

Sophie gave my hand a squeeze. "You see when a man and a lady love each other very much a little baby starts growing in the mummy's tummy..."

"You know what I mean," I said, squeezing her hand back, only much harder for her cheek. "You've been on the pill for ages haven't you..." and then a dark thought entered my head "...you didn't stop taking it, did you?"

She shook her head vehemently. "No. No! Of course not. Nothing's a hundred percent certain when it comes to contraception."

She was spot on. There I was planning a season of hard fishing on a new syndicate water and now it was more than likely I'd be up for decorating the spare, sorry, baby's bedroom. I toyed with the notion of suing the pill manufacturer and my barrister standing up in court and saying: 'M'lud the plaintiff wishes to add the following to his list of costs caused by this unexpected pregnancy, namely that of his loss of personal liberty and fishing time for the next umpteen years and those, sir, are priceless'.

Me a dad. Bloody hell. I sometimes wondered if I'd grown up enough to have left school let alone be entrusted to bring a child into the world.

Sophie grabbed me back around my neck and hugged me, planting a kiss on my cheek. "So what do you think then, dad to be? Are you happy?"

I smiled. "Yeah, I think so. I haven't really got my head around it yet, it's a bit too much to take in at the moment. Crikey! Me a dad. And you a mum. Do you think we'll cope?"

Sophie snuggled up to me, she was back to her old self now her nervous tension had been uncorked. "Yes. We'll cope. We've been through some tough times and survived, we're a strong pair and we're better off than most. What with the money we've got behind us we can give our child a good start in life."

I looked down at the floor. Some of my firecrackers were coming into reality already.

"What is it?" asked Sophie, picking up on my discomfort.

"Does that mean I can't join the syndicate?" I asked.

"How much is it?"

"Nearly four thousand," I said feeling that now I was having to justify it, it did seem a gross amount of money. Set back, but undaunted, I tried to claw back at the stark reality of the costs. "You see it's not quite as bad as it sounds, two and a half of it doesn't ever get cashed in not unless you get chucked out for bad behaviour. The syndicate keep it in their coffers and pay it back should you ever leave. Apart from that it's only £1250 a year, plus the loss of interest on the two and a half, I suppose." The adage of stopping digging when you're already in a hole seemed most apt.

"So you get your two and a half grand back if you don't blow anybody up with a hand grenade, or don't die while still a member, provided, of course, the syndicate owner hasn't already embezzled it in the first place. Apart from that it's only around a hundred pound a month. Honestly, Matthew! Are all you carp anglers so dim? You spend thousands on tackle, you spend thousands on places to fish, thousands on bait, all to catch a fish that's nearly as stupid as the men who try and catch it… And then you throw it back. No, you spend thousands on photographic gear to take photos of the damn carp and then you throw it back."

I thought thousands on bait was pushing it a bit but then some of the boilie backfill gang might do it, talking annually, and technically I didn't blow anyone up, only their gear but overall she was about right. "At least I don't piss it up the wall and chase other women," I said half-heartedly.

"Some of them do, while they're fishing. You've told me,"

I had. What was I thinking? Not of an extra mouth and all the associated paraphernalia when I had told her, that's for sure. I'd never mentioned Rebecca, thank Christ.

"Is that a no, then?"

"No. I know how much you like going but our lives are going to be different once the baby's born. You won't want to go fishing as much once the baby's around, you'll want to spend time with him or her. They'll be things to get ready as well, the baby's bedroom, stuff to buy, you won't be able to go just when you want, you'll have to fit fishing around life, not life around fishing. It can never be like it was the last time, Matthew. You have to realise. It can never, ever be like that again."

"I wouldn't want it to be. I was in the grip of madness, I haven't been like it since have I?" It was hardly likely I'd have been standing there speaking to her if I had.

"Not as bad but you've been to France, twice, you go whenever you like with Rambo, you've hardly worked a full week since you came out of prison, you bought all the new gear with our windfall and now you want to spend that kind of money. What with my wages and the private electrical jobs you've done, not that you've done many, we haven't dug into the lottery money mum gave us and that's the way it's got to stay. I don't want to work once the baby's born, my place is to look after him or her. I don't want us to have a nanny, I want to be a proper mum. I've been giving it a lot of thought, as soon as the pregnancy test showed positive I knew I wanted to do it the way I consider to be right. But, and it's a big but, we'll lose my money if I do. We'll be over sixteen thousand pounds a year worse off. It's an awful lot of money. You'll have to start trying to build up your electrical business to compensate because we don't want to start eating into our nest egg. I'm sure mum will help out because she's so rich but that's not the point. We've got to pull our weight otherwise we're just sponging and I couldn't bear to think we could be so inclined."

"So no, then?"

"No. If you want to join, you earn the money and you pay for it all. We've got just over seven months until there's going to be three of us, there's the house to sort out, you'll have to start thinking about how you're going to get your business up and running and then there'll be all the new things we need to buy, trips to the hospital for scans, antenatal classes and other things I haven't even thought of."

"I've got to send the cheque off within a day," I pleaded. "I won't be able to earn it in time."

Sophie was cross. "For God's sake, Matthew. What's more important to you? Me carrying your child or you blowing thousands on a carp fishing syndicate?"

Who could tell? Gut instinct at that moment was for the four grand to get into Hamworthy. What a terrible, terrible admission. It rattled me to my core, the old demons were back. Or were they? This thing, this child, this recently fertilized egg which had attached itself to her womb excited and scared the shit out of me at the same time. Why did it have to happen now? If it wasn't for the syndicate the conflict wouldn't be so strong but I realised the rest would be. A man at last. Forget leaving school, forget choosing a vocation, forget leaving home, forget finding a partner, forget mortgages and hire purchase, this was the real deal. The biggest most awesome charge, that of raising a child. And if you blew it, well you only had to look around at all the fucked up kids, fucked up by useless parents who were more interested in their own self-absorption whether materialistic or hedonistic. Children left to their own devices of computer games, watching videos and junk TV and then fed on crap fast food by parents too tired, in both senses of the word, to try. There were children trying to grapple with broken families, different dads, one for the week and one for the weekend and a succession of changing circumstances and surroundings. No wonder they struggled. And there I was, on stand-by for a call up in less than eight months time, worried about going fishing. Perhaps it was the shock of the moment but my head was scared by what I was going to lose and unable to grasp what I was going to gain because I had no impression or feeling for an unborn child. It was all right for her, she was so emotionally in tune, what with it growing inside her. Me? Becoming a dad seemed an almost abstract concept, my only feeling for the child was an orgasm six weeks ago.

"You are," I mumbled, ashamed to be lying. "I don't have to choose though, do I? Can't I have both?"

Sophie smiled and her anger passed. "No. You're right. You don't have to choose. I'm being a bit hard on you. I was as shocked and frightened as you are now when I first knew but I've had longer to come to terms with it. It's getting used to the thought of sacrificing some of the things we take for granted. It was why I was so frightened to tell you, it would have been different if we had been trying for kids but out of the blue like it was, I wasn't sure how you'd re-act." Sophie let out a little sigh. "The going out, spending money on leisure activities and clothes, being answerable to only our own selfish needs will all have to change. We're going to be a proper family and once the little one is born it will be different, but we'll adapt, we'll cope with the extra demands. Other people do, so why shouldn't we?"

I smiled and nodded, yet from what I saw of it, and I'll be the first to admit I hadn't exactly looked hard because it held no interest for me, there seemed to be a bloody lot out there not coping. I could think of loads of carp anglers whose marriages were dashed on the rocks of long session hours and obsession. And what about people like Rambo who never seemed to have partners? Did they choose not to have one or was it they couldn't get one because of their habit? There ought to be a law against going carp fishing and having a relationship, other than one with the inside of a bivvy. I had to stop, I was getting carried away again, like I usually did in such circumstances. On reflection there must be thousands of carpers who held down good jobs, had a happy family life, who put all their obligations into a structured, sensible life-style, it's just they couldn't possibly get to go carping as much as they wanted to. Surely it was impossible? Like oil and water, a family and carp fishing couldn't possibly mix. Something had to give, something would suffer whether through lack of funding or lack of time commitment. Perhaps in a year or two's time I'd have a better idea but at this moment, having had the deed of fatherhood emotionally dumped on me barely ten minutes earlier, I was convinced it was a non-runner. And it wasn't just carp fishing, it was football, golf, cars, drinking, womanising - write your own list of interests - that clashed with happy families. It was serious stuff and I was afraid of it all. What if it was born and I had no feelings for it all? What if it was born and I resented it because of all the extra onus it placed on me and all the time it took away? What if it was born and I loved it so much I wanted to spend every waking hour with it and never go fishing again? Yeah, right, stranger things have happened but I couldn't think of any. Fuck. I had less than eight months left, I'd worry about it when the little blighter was born and in the meantime I'd try and make the most of the time I had left. I could always leave her and the kid. I'd actually thought it but could I ever be so callous? This was a major deal. Less than eight months left.

"We'll cope," I said. "So can I draw the money out and pay it back later?"

Sophie gave me a hard stare. "How old are you?"

"Fifteen?" I ventured.

"Don't flatter yourself. Twelve, at a push. You take the money if you promise to pay it all back before the birth. Promise."

"Promise." I could always ponce it off Rambo.

That evening I wrote out the cheque and first thing in the morning I rushed down to the post office to send it off to Michael via 'guaranteed next day delivery'. Once I'd got that out of the way I stopped and felt guilty at what I'd done. Was I suffering from the syndicate syndrome all over again? Yesterday I'd been told the most important news of my whole life and all I was worried about was how it would affect me getting hold of the money to get in the syndicate and how it would affect the time I had to fish the syndicate. Perhaps it was a case of post coitus depression or some such masculine scourge. Having enjoyed the joyous sensation of shooting my seed I was now suffering the consequence of it starting to grow, in a supposedly egg-free, oestrogen-enhanced environment, I might add. Sperm surprise. Spunk shock. Come consternation. I put it down to agitation and a backlash against the real or imagined hurdles becoming a father would put in front of me. Maybe this wasn't to do with the syndicate but all to do with my impending change of status and all it encompassed. I hoped so. Less than eight months left to sort it out and get my head together.

The rest of the day was spent tentatively putting some ideas together about how I could get into more electrical work. Sophie had been right, since coming out of clink I'd only done jobs as and when they had come in. I hadn't actively advertised but had started off doing very simple little jobs for friends of a friend, a few power points, extra lights, that kind of thing which had given me back some confidence and earned me a few quid. What with the fortuitous lottery bonus plus Sophie staying at work and earning decent money I'd had an easy time of it, picking and choosing work and refusing anything sounding a bit tricky or too much hassle. The clear route seemed to be staying self-employed, I couldn't see me ever being able to cope with being on someone's payroll what with all the restraints. No, being a free agent would be ok as long as I could get the work in, do it in a professional manner and get paid. When I put my mind to it I was a decent sparks but doing proper work rather than little 'justers' would be different. The psychological wall of dealing directly with clients, pricing, getting materials and then getting paid would be a far different cry from when I'd been buffered by the office staff, a foreman and the management of a firm. I'd have to get my head around that as well.

The following day I had a call from Michael. He was as terse as usual on the phone. "Matthew?"

"Yes," I assured the voice.

"Michael here from the syndicate. I've got your cheque and seeing as it's a building society cheque I can confirm you are officially in the syndicate from today. I'll forward you all the necessary paperwork tomorrow. You'll see there is a work party in a week's time. If you're not there you know what the penalty will be. Goodbye."

The smarmy git.

Chapter 6

The trip Rambo and myself made to the syndicate water for our obligatory work party seemed a lot less involved than the one we had made previously. The seemingly endless detours down narrow, winding lanes were simply missing The route we had both received along with our membership card was much more direct and straightforward. It hadn't been rocket science to suss out we had been around the sun to meet the moon on our first trip. This, presumably, was to disorientate the pair of us so we couldn't find the place very easily on our own without the instructions that had come only after our wedge had gone the other way. I'd remarked to Rambo that it would have been easier to blindfold us, if a tad less subtle. This action of typical paranoia must have been of Michael's making, his bitter little mind had still considered us to be possible impostors despite our recommendation from one of his 'reliable sources' i.e. Pup. Mind you, both Rambo and myself thought it a little futile, after all if you were keen enough to go to those lengths it seemed likely you would find the water eventually as all you would need would be an Ordnance Survey map. Perhaps the reason was to wage a real or imagined psychological war on us, to keep us on our toes, to try and impress on us what a big deal it was to be in the syndicate. Big Brother, or rather Blinking Michael, is watching you, albeit in intermittent flickerorama vision.

Despite the new route the feeling of isolation was still very much apparent as we made our way down the mile long track to the set of gates that fronted the only means of vehicular access to the water. Vast tracts of land spread away to the horizon either side of the track and it was only the sight of a car park full of motors and a small herd of aimless carp anglers standing by them which brought civilisation back to mind. The gates were already open so I drove the Escort van through them and parked at the back of the other cars. Last in, first out.

The conversation on the way had not been about carp, it had not been about the syndicate, it had not been about parting with eight thousand pound between us, good as, and here we were on a work party before we had even had chance to fish the bloody place. We hadn't babbled about bait. We hadn't tête-à-têted about tactics. We hadn't spoken about swims. We hadn't even rabbitted on about rigs. Firstly, we had talked about how I'd managed to get Sophie to let me join and then about the shock news of her pregnancy. Rambo, who had been drinking a can of Coca Cola at the time of this revelation, had snorted a good percentage of his last mouthful down his nose and spat the rest out onto his camouflage trousers. Apart from it being a direct reversal of what you might be expected to do with a line of coke and the conciliatory fact that the stain would never show on his combats, I could tell the news had touched a nerve.

"She's what?" he'd choked, wiping the last droplets of the sickly, sugary drink that symbolises decadent, materialistic, consumerist Western democracy onto the back of his hand and then flicking them onto the floor pan.

"If we break down on a nest of red ants you'll be eaten alive," I'd said sarcastically, peeved at his re-action.

"She was on the pill, wasn't she?" he'd said.

"That's more or less what I asked," I'd admitted.

"Did she stop taking it to get sprogged-up?"

"That's more or less what I asked as well," I'd said, getting a little excited.

"Bit of a conflict of interest between lots of carp fishing and becoming a new dad," Rambo had pointed out in a serious voice.

"That's more or less what I'd thought," I'd said, with even more sarcasm, seeing as it was so obvious.

"Less time..." Rambo had started.

"I know," I'd interjected, somewhat annoyed.

"Less money..."

"I know," I'd said a bit louder.

"More responsibility..."

"I know," I'd said, louder still, now really irritated by Rambo's regurgitation of my very own perceptions.

"More..."

There was a flapping of wings as I'd launched myself off the handle. "I fucking know! Are you sucking the fucking thoughts out of my fucking head?" I'd screamed, spittle flying off my speeding lips.

Silence. I'd never spoken to Rambo like that before. Few had, I'd wagered. Even less had done so and stayed alive.

Rambo was benevolent and understanding and didn't slit my throat. "Whoa! Easy, boy. Easy! I can understand you're in shock," Rambo had said and then he'd muttered more under his breath while shaking his head as if he really was deeply sorry for me. "What a time for it to happen. Just when you get into a place like this..."

"I know," I'd sighed with heavy resignation, my temper spent.

"I expect she wants to pack in work, doesn't she?"

"Too right," I'd said with a flick of the head and roll of the eyes.

"I expect she wants you to sort out the spare bedroom?"

"Too right she does."

"I expect she wants you to work more to compensate for her packing her job in?"

"Too bloody right. It's exactly what she wants."

"You're in an awkward situation what with all the money you've got originally coming from her mum. If it was yours you could argue the toss on stronger grounds," said Rambo, grabbing the mechanics of my situation in one.

"Tell me about it," I'd said.

Rambo had pulled an almighty grimace. "What a time for it to happen to you," he reiterated. "What bad luck. You're really going to be falling between two stools if you're not careful. Whatever happens you'll definitely be clearing a few of them up."

I'd nodded and then not really understanding I'd asked. "What?"

"Stools. Shitty nappies," Rambo had explained.

I nodded, now with true comprehension. "Too fucking right."

Rambo had paused and looked across at me from the passenger seat, his right-angled gaze burning into my left temple. "It is yours, isn't it?"

I'd looked over at Rambo. It was the one original thing he'd said. My heart melted a little. It was mine, I had the utmost faith and belief in that. My child. My child. My heart, completely thawed, skipped a little beat and something inside me stirred. My child, I'd done it to her and now she was carrying my child while I was carrying a chip on my shoulder about what it was going to take away from me. I wondered what it would give me back but it being just over seven months away it was too abstract an idea for me to get a handle on it.

"Yeah. It's mine all right." I'd confirmed positively, and after a while I'd added. "How come you seem to know so much about it?"

Rambo had exuded an air of world-weariness. "It's the oldest trick in the book for a woman to get herself pregnant in order to try and tie a bloke down. I've seen it so many times, boy, so many, many times. It never works, it just causes resentment all round. I've even had it happen to me."

"Really?" I'd said, taken aback. "What did you do?"

"I baled out, boy. I upped sticks and left. The bitch tried to pull one on me and I left her to it."

"Did she have the baby?" I'd asked, fascinated by another revelation from Rambo's past.

"I don't know," he'd said, matter of fact. "I was gone, boy. Out of there fast. What she did with it after trying to trap me with it was up to her, I wanted nothing more to do with her."

Rambo had gone silent and seemed slightly lost in a world of memories. "Don't you ever wonder what happened, whether she had the baby or not and where it might be now if she did?" I'd asked.

Rambo had stared straight ahead, looking out of the car's windscreen at some distant point further down the road. Finally he answered. "Sometimes I do," yet he'd said it in a way that hinted he didn't want to talk about it anymore, so I hadn't. I'd pushed my luck once with my tirade at him and I wasn't going to do it again.

After the shock horror revelation headlines we'd settled back into the topic of how I was going to try and build up the electrical business, how I was going to try and blitz the things I had to do and how I was going to make the most of my last seven months of... freedom? It sounded the wrong word but not to Rambo, I could tell.

The journey passed and the last part of the conversation had turned to finding the pit and comments on the journey compared to the last time and, quicker than we thought, we had come to the track, driven down it and seen the others.

"Well, I suppose we better get out and greet our fellow syndicate members," I said. "Wouldn't it be funny if Watt turned out to be in it?"

"Not really, boy..." Rambo's attention wandered and his voice tailed off and I saw he was clocking somebody. I followed his eye line half expecting to see Watt but instead saw a large figure all decked out in the latest designer camouflage gear. The type of gear where the camouflage pattern consists of very realistic leaves or reeds and not just patches of greens and browns. The figure had a matching cap and gloves and looked more ready for a catwalk rather than a work party. "... Look at that cunt," sneered Rambo. "What a total arsehole."

Just then a pick-up came down the track and pulled up alongside ours, inside it was Michael and Hollywood Gary.

"Hi, guys," said Gary leaping out of the car, giving a charisma enhanced smile. "All ready for the social event of the year? All twenty members together, like one big widespread happy family re-uniting at Christmas, squabbling over the TV remote and remembering they can't stand the sight of each other. Well cool."

"What do you mean?" I asked.

"Well, what with the lay out of the pit, the rules about not fishing adjacent swims, the fact that it isn't over-pressured because of the costs involved people don't get to mingle too much. Jesus, you've got to work full time to be able to afford the fishing in the first place. The amount of people and the amount of room, nobody really gets to know anybody that well. Most people join in as individuals, in fact it's very rare for a pair of mates to get the nod, so the spread-out family analogy is pretty cool. Sure, me and Michael know all the names but I bet none of the others could go through all twenty very easily." Gary sidled up to me and whispered in my ear. "Anyway between me and you old Mike there likes it that way, less chance of anyone getting friendly and posing a threat to his little dictatorship. Divide and conquer, all that sort of stuff." Gary gave me an exaggerated wink, a nudge in the shoulder and a toothpaste ad smile. "It'll all change when he keels over with a heart attack."

The rat-like Michael was soon out of the pick-up as well. Ignoring Rambo and myself almost completely, apart from the vaguest of nods, he strolled over to the others and started barking out orders while his eyes flickered like a humming-bird's wings.

"Right everybody, gather round. I'm going to split you into groups of five today and give each group a specific task."

His words had an immediate galvanising effect on the herd of listless carp anglers who snapped out of their torpor, rushed towards their leader whilst metamorphosing into a flock of forelock tugging, fawning, grovelling, servile, wannabe-led sheep. If ever a group of anglers were shit scared of losing their place and their '1st deposit', this lot were it.

Michael carried on issuing orders. You could tell he'd done it before and was rather good at it. "Alan, Matt, Rambo and Darren, group one. Gary, Jim, Dean, and Ron group two. Jez, Grant, Gordon and John, group three. Noel, Malcolm, Todd and Keith, group four and myself, Rocky, David and Steve, group five. My group will give the clubhouse a thorough clean and sort out some of the equipment you others will need. Gary and Jim come with me and get a couple of strimmers, Dean come and get the sacks and rakes to clear up what the strimmers cut down. Same goes for Jez and Grant, two strimmers for your group, Gordon, you get sacks and rakes. Noel and Malcolm come and get the bow saws and the secateurs for your group, Alan and Darren you get out the two Yardman mowers and a couple of wheel barrows for our new members Matt and Rambo. Put all the heavy equipment into the pick-up and I'll drop it off as and when."

It was pandemonium as people who were not quite sure who they were with and what they were supposed to do wandered around trying to look as if they did know who they were with and what they were supposed to do while the older hands who did know who they were with and what they were meant to get and where they had to get it from started to get things sorted. Eventually all the gear was with the right people, put in the back of the pick-up and little groups started to make their way off around the track that circumnavigated the pit. I'd heard Michael tell a few people where to go and what he wanted doing but Rambo and myself hadn't a clue what was required of us until an older man in his late fifties came up to the pair of us. He'd already parked up two lawnmowers, which someone else had put in the pick-up and this time he and a young lad in his early twenties had both put wheelbarrows next to the mowers.

The eldest man, a pleasant looking bloke with a neatly trimmed grey beard came up to me and offered out his hand.

"Good morning young man, you must be Matthew… and to you as well, Rambo, is it?" he said to Rambo moving on to shake his hand in turn. "I'm Alan, and this young upstart is Darren," he continued, gesturing towards the ex-wheelbarrow touting lad behind him.

"You're the one who does the paintings of the carp for the poster aren't you?" I said, pretty sure I'd remembered Gary had said it was an Alan who was the artist.

"That's right," said Alan smiling. "Have you seen the new poster already?"

"Yeah," I said enthusiastically. "We were actually having our interview when Gary brought it over. I think he'd only just collected it from you, it was very impressive. The paintings of the fish were brilliant, you're a very good artist."

"Why thank you. Very nice of you to say so." Alan looked around to see we were the last group to make a move and Michael jumping into the pick-up and starting it up. "Um, look, shall we show willing and make our way to where his lordship wants us to go? I'm afraid it's always a bit confusing to begin with on these days but once we get on our way we'll have time to chat during the day and get to know each other." He gave Rambo and me a brief nod and smile as if to help us concur with what he was saying and the pair of us both agreed. Alan didn't even so much as look at Darren as he walked off towards the track that ran around the pit and the disappearing tailgate of the laden pick-up. "As senior member of both this syndicate and life in general I hope you'll let me organise you chaps and get you to do the more physical work. We'll try and make a good show early on because I know what it's like with you boys. After all, one boy's a boy, two boys are half a boy and three boys are no boys at all."

"I won't argue with you," I said.

"Me neither," said Rambo. "Especially as I haven't got a clue what you're on about."

Alan stopped, turned and walked up to Rambo and looked him in the eye for what seemed an eternity. Rambo held the older man's stare with casual ease, looking down on him from his seven or eight inches of height advantage with a smile.

"You're a real soldier aren't you, son? said Alan, eventually. He'd said it seriously, dead straight with no hint of humour.

"I was," said Rambo.

Alan laughed and slapped Rambo on the upper arm. "Ha! I thought so! I can tell these things. An artist's eye, you see! An artist's eye! You're not a fake like others I could mention. Come, let's go." He turned and walked a few paces and then swung around to look back at me. "And you son, you strike me as having a talent, one you might not even be aware of. I see in you the ability to... enough! Let's go."

The old boy was a nutter, an eccentric nutter. All carp anglers are nutters but not all nutters are carp anglers. How was that for talent in the homespun philosophy department? Useless, that's what. Rambo and I followed Alan and Darren walked a few places behind us. Rambo upped his pace to get alongside Alan and I did likewise to get alongside him so all three of us were abreast, with Alan in the middle.

"So, have we spent our money well, then?" asked Rambo.

Alan let out a nasal, two tone laugh. "On the whole, I'd have to say you have. If you're half sensible anglers you'll catch a lot of big fish, that's for certain. It is one of the best syndicates in the country, if not the best. I don't think any rational carp angler could argue with that, but then, how many rational carp anglers are there? Rational carp angler, an oxymoron perhaps?" he laughed again, but this time to his self, as if he was pleased with his play on words. "As you have no doubt seen and are seeing again this very morning, the surroundings are most pleasant. Very conducive towards painting, I might add. The solitude, the unspoilt natural beauty, even the light seems to have an enhancing effect on the majesty of this place. It really is a pleasure to simply sit and look, let alone sit and look and fish, and catch, and catch big fish. No, truly you are lucky to be in here. Some of the members are a little below par compared to the setting but that's because I'm getting an old fogy and don't suffer fools gladly. Especially young fools. By young I mean anyone under forty. You see I have this reverse ageist policy whereby I, as an old carp angler, take it upon myself to be especially critical about the young supposedly up and coming carp angler. Like Darren for instance," he added lowering his voice and continued in hushed tones. "The lad has only been fishing for ten minutes and he's a desperate wannabe. My artist's eye has told me he's out to catch fish and publicise them, the bait, the rod, the reel, the line, the buzzer, the rig even the boilie-stop if he thinks it will ingratiate himself with some manufacturer who will help him achieve his aims. And his aims are to become a professional carp angler, simple as that. He wants to be a consultant, doesn't matter who with, he wants to be a writer and he wants to be sponsored. I think he'll try to catch a good number of forties and then hawk his story around all and sundry for takers. He is a very clever young man, to have managed to get in this syndicate with such an agenda and to fool Michael is testament to his intelligence. I'm afraid I don't have much time for him. He's a typical young carp angler. A 'Smash', as I like to call such people, add water and you have an instant carp angler, as opposed to adding water and getting instant mash potato. Do you remember the funny little tin can Martians from the ad? I mean the young disown the old, criticise their ideals and standards and I reciprocate and do the same to them. And why not?"

"There isn't a lot of aggro though, is there?" I asked, wondering how Alan could surmise all what he had just said and Michael apparently couldn't. Darren wouldn't have told him his game plan and I remembered how uncomfortable I'd felt under Michael's fluttering gaze during the interview when we were being a little conservative with the truth. Still, we had got away with it and escaped undetected and had been offered our places. Perhaps it was his artist's eye working overtime and a large dollop of spite or personal dislike of Darren. I cooled towards Alan, despite his painting skills, for slagging off another member within a few minutes of meeting us seemed rather unnecessary.

"No. No, none at all. Generally speaking you don't actually come into contact with the other members often. None of us come from shared backgrounds, a strategic move of Michael's, I'm sure. What with the way the swims are and the harsh rules about attending rods and swim occupation, of which I agree whole-heartedly, we mainly come and go as individuals. We meet on these occasions and share a few tales and perhaps some have helped each other out in terms of relating fish captures and movements, there's no log book for fish caught you see. Gary is very close to Michael because of their long involvement, or should I say Michael is very close to Gary, I'm not too sure about Gary's motives at times. A funny lad and a bit too good looking to have developed a rounded personality, I'd say. He's so used to women and men being bedazzled by his looks that I'm sure he's had it too easy. He's never had to try and impress anybody with his real self, his appearance is usually enough and I think he's lacking something because of it. A very personal observation, I'm afraid, you're probably thinking I'm a cantankerous old fool and maybe you'd be right." Alan looked at us both turning his head left and then right but neither Rambo nor myself said a word. Alan continued on another tack. "To be frank if you want to carp fish this pit properly social fishing is very difficult. I think I'm right in saying you two are the first 'pair', so to speak, to be admitted. You must have had very good references."

"What happened to the two we replaced?" I asked.

"They left of their own accord. By chance I do know their story and I'll tell you it later."

Alan put down his shutters and marched on and Rambo and myself exchanged glances but again said nothing. Was he mischief making by letting us in on what he knew or just spreading rumour. We were young carpers by his definition so why take us into his confidence?

For the rest of the day we worked hard at our allotted chores, of which ours was to mow the grass in each swim. Mow the grass. Not to pick up the shit left by other anglers and society in general and fill forty-four dustbin liners with plastic bags, tins, discarded tackle, old copies of Carp-Talk, new copies of Big Carp/Advanced Carp/Carpworld (delete as appropriate), bike frames, broken washing machines, ex-joyridden cars (both torched and untorched), supermarket trolleys, roadkill (squirrels, foxes and badgers), hypodermic needles (HIV positive and those containing fish oil) but to mow the grass. No bedding of a permanent set of buzz bars into six inches of concrete or whacking down gypsum reject and hoisting a six foot sign with: 'Peg 8, do not fish beyond the roped-off limits of your swim' splashed all over it. No wading through a sea of mud and looking across to the next swim, three yards away, at a carp angler up to his neck in mud saying: 'Don't come over here, mate. I'm standing on a fucking horse'. None of those, we had to mow the grass and very nice it was too.

Rambo and myself did the business with the petrol rotary mowers which had a back roller so we could still make the stripes so beloved of cylinder machine jockeys. We chucked the cuttings into the wheelbarrows which Alan and Darren then shifted to another spot for later collection by the pick-up which in turn were taken back to a giant grass cutting pile where it was left to biodegrade into quality real estate for worms. Perhaps one day the son of Darren would say, or perhaps even Darren himself would say: 'What's a worm, then?' Who was I kidding? I was only about nine years older than him, yet strangely I could feel myself turning against this ambitious carp angling whippersnapper, despite the good chance it might not be true. Rumour, gossip, person rivalry, jealousy. Ah, the cruelties and anomalies of the carp fishing hierarchy. What is the magic formula to define superstardom? (Time taken x weight) ÷ by citizenship on passport of carp + ($\sqrt{}$all trade tie-ins + articles published per month) + ego rating (On a scale of 1-10, 1 = shy and retiring, 10 = Napoleon meets average film star/model) = perceived importance of capture. By the capturer. The rest? Some think sad bastard, others bow down in worship.

We had started in the first swim you would come to by walking clockwise as we had on our other visit and we gradually worked our way around the west side of the pit. During the day we came across some of the others beavering away at their tasks, trimming back trees, strimming some of the denser light vegetation that a mower couldn't touch and other similar chores. I was struck at how well organised it seemed to be despite the earlier chaos. Michael had known exactly what needed to be done, had the equipment to do it and the organisation skills to get us plebs to do it. Nervous nutter, yes, but his time running the syndicate had honed his delegation and co-ordination attributes of mundane tasks.

By midday we were around to the north-east corner by the old wood and I wistfully looked out at the tree-lined island directly in front of me as I mowed the unworn grass. The noise of the mowers meant it was impossible for me to speak to Rambo and I was cocooned in my own little world of thoughts and engine noise. I made my mind up there and then that when I came to the pit for my first fish I would try and get in this swim.

The din from our mowers only stopped for re-filling of petrol and emptying the grass collection box. The mowers operated on a 'dead man's handle' system so as soon as you let go of the large handle that ran underneath the hooped tubular push bar the engine cut out. Even with the reach of an orang-utan you'd have been hard pushed to have had your hand sliced off by the spinning blade, rotating less than a foot from the grass cutting's escape chute. When we happened to coincide either of these two events simultaneously, the re-filling or box emptying, we heard the sound of strimmers and chainsaws. The place seemed alive with diligent work party carp anglers, all slaving away, trying to impress their mad leader and not get on the wrong side of him. With Michael, you could be out on your ear in the blink of an eye and there were plenty of them.

Soon after we had moved down one more swim Michael turned up with burger and chips for all of us, a can each of chilled soft drink for thirsty workers and more unleaded petrol for thirsty Briggs and Stratton engines. He'd cooked the food in the clubhouse, wrapped it up and had sped around the track in the pick-up, dispensing fast food and cans from the driver's window, usually thrown, to the nearest recipient. At least he hadn't chucked 5 litres worth of unleaded at us, Darren had taken it out of the back of the pick-up. The four of us parked our arses on our respective bit of work party kits and began to eat and I promptly burnt my arm on the mower exhaust.

"You want to watch that, boy. It might be hot," said Rambo spotting my sudden lurch as the nerve ends in my arm told my brain to move it, the arm specifically, like yesterday.

"Didn't hurt," I lied, pushing the cold drink can against the affected area and making sshhh steam noise.

"Pain," said Alan. "The body's defence mechanism against further damage or injury. Do fish feel pain, I wonder?"

I looked at Rambo and he looked at me and then I looked at Darren.

"Take no notice," said Darren. I think it was the first words he had said all day. "He's always putting out little comments like that. I've been in his work party for the last two years and he always comes out with something similar. Usually to new members as well."

"I was simply enquiring," said Alan.

"Why ask what you can't answer?" retorted Darren.

"Mankind would have never achieved scientific advancement with that mindset, son."

"Look, if I ever come back as a fish, I'll let you know somehow. All right, *dad*?" Darren replied sarcastically.

"Reincarnation into a different species. An interesting concept. How will you tell me, Darren?"

"I'll regurgitate boilies into your sack after you've caught me, you'll have to read the signs though."

"Like tea leaves?" said Alan.

"Like tea leaves."

Although it was superficially good-natured I felt a slight air of antagonism between the two of them, especially after Alan's comments about young carpers and his off-hand attitude to Darren, so I decided to change the subject.

"What about the story of the two blokes whose places we've taken?" I said.

"Ah yes!" Alan exclaimed. "Yes, I was going to tell you about it, wasn't I? They were both in our last two work parties, nice enough fellows. One was a chap in his early thirties, a journalist for a local newspaper, the other was much older, around my years and he was a carpet fitter, if I remember correctly. I can't say I saw them on the pit at any time other than the two work parties but on the first work party they both commented about having experienced some strange occurrences. Unlike you they had been in the syndicate for several months, one of them almost six prior to their first work party and had fished quite a few times."

"What sort of strange experiences?" asked Rambo as he munched on the burger.

"Paranormal experiences," replied Alan. "Ghosts, if you'd prefer. Both those anglers were convinced that the pit was haunted and were sufficiently scared not to renew their memberships."

"Bollocks!" scoffed Darren. "They were a couple of Noddies who caught fuck all and pulled off because they couldn't stand spending a fortune on blanking and didn't have the bottle to admit it. So they fell back onto all this 'haunted' crap as an excuse, the one every new member hears about when they join, usually from Gary."

Alan looked at both Rambo and myself.

"Fair comment, boy," said Rambo to Darren. "It was the first thing Gary said to us once he knew we had joined."

"S'right," I confirmed.

"I mean how did all this shit start?" asked Darren gaining in confidence. "Which current member has had anything odd happen to them? I reckon it all started with Gary. God knows why, he's the one who's always on about it. Tell me who else ever says anything about it apart from when they're brown-nosing Gary to try and get in more with Michael? It's pathetic. Name me one other person who's had one of your so called 'paranormal experiences'?"

Alan looked a little shamefaced. "I don't think there is anyone else. You could be quite correct my son, out of the present set I'm the only one. However, I do think you'll find Michael is actually rather irritated by the whole thing."

"That's true as well, he seemed quite upset when Gary mentioned it to us, although it's hard to tell when Michael's upset, what with him being a bag of nerves," I chipped in.

"Well there you go then, dad," said Darren.

"Gary does seem to enjoy upsetting Michael with his repeated comments concerning the ghost. It's true he does exaggerate about how many people claim to have had an experience and I don't know why he does it, to be frank. I still believe in the ghost, I know what I experienced. What puzzles me is why it has apparently, if everyone is telling the truth, only happened to me. All I can suggest is possibly some of us are more prone to seeing the other side or to being contacted by the other side," said Alan.

"Oh yeah?" said Rambo. "On the other hand it might be your 'artist's eye' causing you all the trouble."

I laughed but Alan was staring at me as I did so and I stopped almost straight away.

Chapter 7

"Anyway, look, I'd better go, when are you going again? Are you? Right, I'll see what I can do. Well done anyway, cracking start, mate. Cheers."

I put the phone down and noticed the mixed emotions of hearing about a good friend having some big fish when I couldn't be there. The jammy git. Rambo, first visit, 48-hour session and the swine catches a couple of thirties plus a twenty-nine common while I'm trying to get my head, my work, my upcoming fatherhood and my first trip to the syndicate sorted, without, I'd just like to mention, not upsetting Sophie so much so it threw her into an early miscarriage. Fortunately the only miscarriage so far was one of justice, of all the times for her to get pregnant and it had to be now. I kept thinking of Rambo's glum face while we had been in the car on the way to the work party, how he had shook his head and said how unlucky I was to have this extra burden thrust upon me, when the only thing I should have been having to worry about was how I was going to catch my first forty. Then he'd proceeded to tell me he'd been the victim of an unwanted pregnancy and had simply left the girl involved to it. The only mitigating circumstances being she had got herself up the duff, as we lads so eloquently put it, on purpose, or so he said. I had fleetingly thought about leaving Sophie on my initial finding out of her pregnancy, but who was I kidding? I was morally trapped by how she had stayed by me during the first syndicate crisis. I owed that girl, besides I really loved her… it was just bloody inconsiderate of her to get her womb all in a twist and for things to go pear shaped. Now there was another thing… What if she lost her figure and I didn't fancy her afterwards? What if she went all mumsy on me and started dressing in floral prints and cardigans? What if she got stretch marks like I imagined the ex-Fatboys had? We men suffer, I can tell you, and what with her soon to become a raging sea of hormones with a beached whale on the shore chucked in for good measure I felt the need to go carping. That minute.

Sophie was out around her mum's when I felt the compelling need to go. The baby and all its manifestations, my new business and all its hassles plus the fact Rambo had caught some fish put my head into pressure cooker mode. I had to go, I simply had to go before I freaked. I felt like a mad, caged animal, trapped by the bars of guilt and moral obligation, slowly being crushed by a descending ceiling of thick concrete that was my impending responsibility. Well, I still had the key to the door for the best part of seven months but after that, who really knew if I'd ever have it again, or perhaps more pertinently, how often I could get it? Bollocks to it and sod the consequences, I'd only go for twenty-four hours. It wouldn't hurt. The decision was made. I went and put the gear in the van. Those bars of guilt and moral obligation still bent a little when worked on with the crowbar of delusion and the even more powerful gorilla bar of self-interest. I left a note on the kitchen table explaining I was going to see somebody concerning some work and then afterwards was going to do a quick overnighter.

Driving to the pit it all came flooding back to me how it used to be in times long ago. It was like revisiting an old friend. Going back to before Lac Fumant and the lottery win and the SS Syndicate full time battle to an era when I was a wage slave, stuck in a remorseless nine to five, five days a week grind, the feeling of release and sensation I was now experiencing was like it had been then. I'd all but forgotten the impression of escape, the awareness that I was leaving the mundane and banal behind and was slipping into a world where I could escape the shackles of normal life and abscond into the cloistered world of carp fishing. It felt good, I'd touched base camp, and I'd got back to my roots. Here was the reason why we all did it, a joyous wave of euphoria swept me, my gear and my van along the road in an ever-increasing state of excitement as the possibilities of what might happen and what I might catch burnt brightly in my head. Nothing could touch me while I was at the pit, perhaps a bit of a naïve thought what with the double-edged sword, the mobile phone hanging onto me, but that April morning I believed it. I would forget my worries, or at least postpone them until my brief session was over. I'd had it too easy of late, fishing virtually when I wanted, with no real pressures to worry about. I'd lost sight of one of the most important aspects about going fishing and it was nothing to do with catching fish. I knew, however, if the session went badly and I was driving back the other way heading into what I was now leaving I'd have a totally different set of feelings to the ones I had now. I could remember that happening years ago as well.

Honesty told me I was a self-indulgent fool, compared to most my situation was still easy. People would kill to be in my situation, baby on the way or no baby on the way but it still didn't make it any easier. I'd been scarred for life by previous events and my venture into the new and unknown was daunting. That was my excuse and I was sticking to it.

The car park was empty, what a glorious sight. My heart beat a little faster and after re-locking the gates behind me I drove the van around to the swim that I had set my heart on fishing while I had been mowing during the work party. Despite me knowing exactly where Rambo had picked up his fish, the small point in the south-east corner, I wanted to start in the far north-east corner of the pit. The swim there gave me a comfortable cast to the largest of the pit's islands. As I stood in the swim, my back to the old woods, I estimated the cast to be around the sixty to seventy yard mark, well within my capabilities despite me being one of the bait boat crew.

Luckily all my tackle conformed to the syndicate laws, regarding main line breaking strain, lack of shock leaders and rigs being only semi-fixed via my favourite method of silicon pushed half over a swivel. Due to this there was no need to for me to worry about setting up, all I had to do was get the gear out and into play after tying on three new hooklengths which I had already prepared, in Blue Peter fashion, earlier on. This had been on my last session on another water which must have been getting on for four weeks ago. No time to lose. With all my gear out of the van I jumped back in and drove around the pit's perimeter heading back to the car park. I passed the stock pond on my left and as the car park came into sight I saw another motor had arrived in the short period between me arriving and dropping my stuff off. It could have only been ten minutes or so but the car's driver was re-locking the main gates having only a few seconds before opened them and driven his car through. I vaguely recognised him but couldn't put a name to him, he wasn't in our work party and we had all drifted off at the end of the day without mixing.

I parked the van, got out and locked it up only to see the other car coming towards me and pull up alongside. The driver's side window came down and the vaguely recognisable face opened its mouth.

"All right, then, mate?"

"Yeah. You?"

The face nodded. "You're one of the new blokes aren't you? You and that other big bloke in the camo gear. That right?"

"That's right," I assured him. "I'm Matt and my friend is called Rambo."

I saw his face curl into a smile. I suppose I could forgive him and his thoughts, undoubtedly laughing at the Stallone parallels, but he hadn't the benefit of having seen the awesome Rambo in action. The uppercut on Spunker, freeze-framed by the bolt of lightning, was an indelible mark on my memory. If he had seen the fist fight he wouldn't have been laughing. The tosser. I suddenly decided I couldn't forgive him.

"I'm Grant," I shook the hand that was thrust out of the car's window. "Where are you going to fish?"

"I'm going into the far north-east corner, the swim directly in front of the biggest island."

Grant pulled a face as if to say it wouldn't have been his first choice. "I'm going to be fishing the south-west point, it's normally a better bet at this time of the year. It's produced some good fish for me over the years."

For some reason I suddenly thought it was a good time of the year for Sophie to be pregnant with seven months left. What if she'd have fallen pregnant in October with all the winter ahead rather than the optimum months I had? What a bummer that would have been.

My reply was distracted and sounded so. "Yeah... right."

Grant's face clouded for an instant but he was soon away again. "You see if you want to do well at this place you really have to find the spots. Even though I know this place like the back of my hand I'll be doing a spot of feature finding to begin with, with the old braid, you know? A little bit of silt, or a little bit of clear gravel, find it and you'll be in doing the business. I'm field testing a bait for a well known company, I can't say too much because it's all a bit hush-hush at the moment."

I lifted my eyebrows in an 'oh really' expression and said nothing although I was tempted to say that if it was hush-hush why the fuck tell me and then tell me he couldn't tell me.

"Obviously I can't publicise results openly but it'll give them a pretty good insight. They were desperate to get me working with them, what with me being on such a prolific water like this." I nodded again. "The swim where you're going to fish has got a bar running across it about forty yards out. I'd pop a couple on that and one in the margin if I were you. The island itself is very snaggy in terms of casting tight. The branches are growing well out into the pit. For some reason Michael won't let anyone go out in a boat and cut them back, he wants them to remain really natural."

"Does it get busy here at all?" I asked.

Grant seemed thrown by my disregard for his opinions. "Not really. The most I've ever seen on here is about a dozen, usually it's three or four, sometimes six. We've no full timers or time bandits because Michael would have them out. It doesn't matter so much anyway, what with the pit's layout and size. I've come here to fish not to socialise, to have those lumps out."

"Darren and Alan were in our work party, they seemed all right," I said innocently. "Michael's a bit of a weird one, though..."

"Alan can be a funny old sod, he comes on all mystical and occult at times. He's been in a long time and thinks we should all bow down to him because of it. He's a good artist and knows a lot of about carp fishing, not about how to catch fish but all the trivia stuff from the past. He wouldn't know a pivoting stiff hair rig if it hooked him in the bottom lip. And he's always on about this non-existent ghost of ours. What a load of shit that all is! I don't know much about Darren, I've never even spoken to the bloke or met him on the bank or in a work party. Michael's Michael, a bit jumpy to say the least. He's always been a bit like it but I reckon he's got worse over the years. It's probably the pressure of keeping this place under wraps as much as he can. I've even heard rumours from old members that he's threatened to have them beaten up if they start blabbing about the place too much. Another odd thing is he doesn't really fish it that much, I'd be down here nearly every day if it were my water. When he does come he only fishes for a short while, I can't remember him ever doing a night in the time I've been a member. He's got no family, he's a total loner, if he didn't have this place he'd have nothing. Mind you I'd swap him for what I've got to own this syndicate."

"Beat people up?" I said in a disbelieving voice.

"So others have said. Ask me when I'm out. I thinks it's sour grapes from those who've got the elbow or couldn't get to grips with the place. It's not mega-hard but you've got to know what you're at if you want to pick up the good fish."

I nodded yet again. "How far out did you say that gravel bar was?" I thought I'd better pander to his ego.

"About forty yards, I've got the distances written down in my book, I usually pace it out and then clip up and tape up for future reference. Can't go wrong then, even in the dark I'm spot on. What bait you on?"

"My own," I answered.

Grant gave me a clandestine look and touched his nose with his right index finger. "Fishmeals," he said and gave me a wink and pulled away a little too quickly, the gravel spitting out from under his front wheels.

"I wouldn't know a pivoting stiff hair rig if I saw one either, not unless it was accompanied by a two thousand word article," I muttered under my breath. "Fishmeals? A red herring or perhaps he's trying to make my rowing boat catch a monster crab." I gave myself a rueful smile. Still, the bit about the island being snaggy might be useful and a bit of background on the other members, even if taken with a pinch of subjective salt, hadn't gone amiss.

Two hours later I was all set, bivvy up, rods out, kettle boiling and three baits strategically placed. Two out by the island margins and one in the close margin. Grant could shove his forty-yard gravel bar up his arse, sideways. He had been right about the island though, closer inspection through my binoculars had shown just how far the trees on the island had grown out over the water. Even if I hit a perfect cast I would still be approximately six yards out from the island's edge, most of the time it would be further than that. The only good thing was the bottom seemed clear enough, I'd had a little cast around, if there were any underwater snags they were tucked away directly underneath the growing branches. I'd still have to get my act together if I had a take, otherwise I could see any carp that was worth its salt and was keeping up with what it was expected to do by reading all the latest (and earliest) carp articles, would be straight in them.

My first cuppa on my new syndicate water felt good, I swallowed the tea and drank in the whole atmosphere of the place. The early afternoon sunshine was pleasantly warm for the end of April, bordering on being hot in fact, and the view from my bedchair was lovely. I could look out over the water to the large island right in front of me and away to the right was the other slightly smaller one. These two were pretty much equidistant from the northern bank and also a similar distance off of their respective west and east banks, something in the order of 130 yards. Whatever it was it would have been too far for a caster of my standing to have reached the side of either island from any bank other than the north one. There was a huge expanse of water between the two islands and from my swim I could look all the way down to the southern end of the pit and see the south-west point, where Grant was fishing. Behind my island was the third island, sitting virtually central between the north and south banks, which again was about seventy to eighty yards off the east bank. This island sat in the one slight feature of the pit in terms of its perimeter. The pit's edge wrapped around this island and went out to form the south-east point, where Rambo had been successful on his first trip, it then turned due south again, back parallel with the north bank before forming the other mini-feature. This feature, where Grant was, formed the other point, the westerly one and from then on the bank ran predictably straight up towards the north bank. I could see from Grant's point right up to the edge of the island that was to my right, it was a big stretch of bank but it would have been hard to have spotted any anglers should they have been there. The banks, as Michael intended, were full of vegetation, cover and trees. Even if the pit was busy the solitude was still preserved, what with the ruling of no fishing in the adjacent swim it meant the closest anyone could get to me was a minimum of a hundred yards. It was great, it's not that I'm anti-social or anything but other carp anglers, who needs them? Apart from going in for fish for you, taking photos, lending you small items of tackle, giving you tips, making you tea, having a natter, getting fish and chips, landing carp and lending you books (strictly illegal - M.C) what have carp anglers ever done for you? Kept you company? Company? Pah! Shut up!

My bivvy was pitched on the beautifully mown grass that was fresh, clean and springy and was tucked behind a large bush which grew down to the water's edge and marked the eastern edge of the swim. I had only six yards or so of open area, where my three rods were parked, before more vegetation started on the other side. Some other members of the work party had trimmed it all back neat and tidy after we had come through with the mowers. It really was idyllic, all I had to do was catch something and I was confident I would. Rambo's success meant our bait was still a winner, as I had known it would be. He'd also had one of the fish on a Pup pop-up and I had one on the left hand rod that was cast to the island. I threw the dregs of the tea onto the ground and turned back towards my bivvy and for the first time, what with my adrenalin rush in setting up and getting sorted, my gaze fell upon the old wood. If the pit was beauty personified, a quick one eighty produced a totally different scenario, one way you had light, this way you had dark. The pit exuded nature's splendour, the wood nature's dark and ruthless side. The old trees looked even more bitter and twisted than I remembered from before. They looked ancient, unfriendly, intimidating and a feeling of disquiet ran through my body. I told myself to stop being so idiotic and promptly remembered even Rambo had agreed there was a spooky aura to the wood. I put my cup back in my bivvy. What was it Alan had said about rational carp anglers? Whatever it was he was right, I was being totally irrational. I was a grown man and we were talking about trees, for heaven's sake. I parked my bum back on my bedchair thinking how very alone I was. It had seemed so great until I had reminded myself of the old wood and now it was a little disconcerting.

Over the next hour the sun shone on my south facing body and warmed me through and I soon forgot about the wood as I willed my indicators to signal my all important first take. A huge fish crashing out over my pop-up rod heightened my sense of expectancy. Did I feel under pressure to succeed first time out? The honest answer was yes. All the money I'd spent to get in the syndicate, the fact Rambo had caught, the added fact I had virtually sneaked off without Sophie knowing and a genuine desire to prove my worth as a carp angler, although to whom I wasn't exactly sure, all put me under the cosh. It had better be worth it, was the message and it was loud and clear.

Gradually the sun lost its strength as the afternoon passed and the sweatshirt I had taken off a few hours earlier was put back on. A few minutes after I had a couple of bleeps on the right hand close margin rod. I had looked quick enough and noticed the rod tip had knocked. Fish in the swim? Almost certainly. Fish on my bait? Highly likely. Forthcoming forty? Adding up the pit's head of carp and dividing by the number of forty pounders gave you the odds on that one. I wasn't fussed; a take and a carp on the bank to get me on the scoreboard would be good enough. Nothing else materialised for half an hour and then the very essence of carp fishing, a period of hours of waiting, sitting on hands, observing, doing nothing and then kapow! The right hand rod's line was whisked off the reel by an unknown carp and the Delkim told me in it's own rather histrionic fashion, that, hey! It was happening on this one over here. I struck into the fish and after a fairly straightforward scrap lasting some five or so minutes my first Hamworthy carp was safely in the net. The fish wasn't a monster but it was a beautiful mirror and looked a twenty. Subsequent weighing proved this to be so, my first fish at 23-9 and I was well happy.

As I lowered the carp, still in the weigh sling, onto my unhooking mat, I saw another big fish crash out by the island again. The fish I'd already caught, if I stuck to the rules, should go into the stock pond and seeing as the rules also said that fish couldn't be sacked for more than ten minutes or so, I was now in a dilemma. Taking the fish around to the stock pond meant I would have to wind in and I definitely didn't want to do that. I decided to do what any self-respecting carp angler would do. I took the 23 down to the water's edge and put her back, no one would have seen me and if by some million to one chance they had I'd just say it was over 25 and that would be the end of it. I re-baited the successful rod, cast out and set about making myself something to eat.

Dusk came and despite more fish activity out by the island all my buzzers remained mute. I was convinced one of the longer-range rods was going to rattle off at any minute but it didn't happen. Dusk turned to dark, the bedchair went inside the bivvy and the sleeping bag went on top of it. By ten I was all snuggled up inside the bag with the mosquito netting of my Apotheosis zipped up to offer a little bit of protection from the cool night air. It was a cloudless night and the stars were out and it had turned decidedly chilly compared to the earlier warmth of the day. I listened to some owls calling from the direction of the old wood, I couldn't say they particularly affected me, but the little gnawing feeling of apprehension staved off my tiredness and kept me awake. Eventually, at what time I wasn't sure, it must have been very late, I drifted off to sleep.

Abruptly I woke up. It was if an unseen arm of tremendous power had dipped itself up to its bicep into my tank of sleep and had yanked me out with incredible force and violence back into the conscious world. Disorientated, physically shaking, both from cold and shock I listened for the high-pitched tone of an angry alarm. There wasn't one. Frantically I looked for the Delkim receiver box to spot a red, yellow, green or blue light, convinced some electrical gremlin had silenced the take that had awoken me. There wasn't one. Whatever had woken me up, it wasn't a carp.

By now I was shaking uncontrollably and felt incredibly cold. I looked up at the bivvy's ceiling and it seemed bright enough to be almost dawn. I peered at my watch. Two a.m. I pulled back the sleeping bag, unzipped the mozzie door and with great trepidation I stooped out through the flap. Outside it was ridiculously bright. I looked up into the sky to see a fantastically luminous full moon and looked down to see my very own moonlight shadow. The power of the resplendent full moon blotted out all the stars and I stared up at it for ages until my neck started to ache. Everything was bathed in moonbeams. I gazed out into the pit and studied the huge reflection of the moon on the water and was reminded of the night in France and my drug trip when I had watched the moon's watery image then. An owl's call made me spin towards the old wood and for some reason I felt compelled to go towards it.

With both of my arms wrapped around my body in a vain attempt to trap some warmth and control my violent shuddering I inched slowly up from the swim, over the track that ran around the pit where I had driven the van earlier, to the very edge of the wood. It looked bizarre. The different lighting characteristics of the moon compared to the sun seemed to cast a surreal spell on the trees. The branches that looked so contorted by day looked even more forbidding now, what with the varying degrees of light, semi-shadow and dark shadow which fell upon them. Grotesque patterns, whether real or imagined, formed in front of my eyes and then shifted and were gone before another heaving, writhing mass of branches would transmogrify into something even more unspeakable. I stood, unable to move, transfixed in a huddled convulsion as branches turned to snakes, snakes into deformed faces, deformed faces into wondrous beasts, wondrous beasts into branches.

I felt, or heard, I'm not sure which, a wind spring up from somewhere deep within the wood. It whooshed through the woods careering one way then the other like a demented slalom skier forcing the ageing branches out of its way. Some were unable to stand its power and due to their stiffness and brittleness they broke with sharp cracks of gunfire. The shots became louder and louder, the whooshing more intense. Then, the wind was directly in front of me, bending, barging, bursting, breaking and bludgeoning thick thigh-sized branches like they were twigs as it made straight towards me. I could see it. I could actually *see* the wind. It was like a tunnel of shimmering heat haze gradually getting wider and wider as it homed in on me. And then it hit me. Like a jet stream of freezing air it buffeted me and pounded my flesh, not only from the front but all around me, even the soles of my feet were pummelled. A hissing, sibilant scream started in my head. It was louder than any buzzer, louder than any concert, louder than Concorde, louder than anything I could imagine. Still the wind raged around my body and the sound raved inside my head. I put both the palms of my hands up to my ears and pushed them together as hard as I could to try and stop the insufferable noise and to try and hold my head together and stop it exploding.

Unpredictably and in an instant emotion and thought flooded me, not mine but someone else's. It was like being an empty vessel and then getting filled by a crashing tidal wave. Friendship. A close friendship turned to deceit, a nasty deceit and with it came hurt, deep hurt and a wounded soul. A reprieve. An apology and the prospect of reconciliation, all hope rekindled and perhaps the chance to re-create what was lost. A meeting. Gradual realisation, this was deceit again but this time a terrible cruel and calculating deceit. Pain. Excruciating pain. Utter disbelief. More pain and vile suffering, physical mutilation, gaping wounds. Blood, hot sticky blood, flowing and flowing and flowing. Repeated blows. Thud. Thud. Thud. Dulled pain and perception, all life ebbing away. Profound sorrow. A life too short, so much not accomplished. Bitterness at the loss of all life's opportunities. Darkness. Death approaching. Hateful blows still raining down. And then a sudden burst, a flash of pure willpower to light the dark. Justice and revenge! An overriding wish for justice and for the truth to be known by someone. Justice and revenge. Death at last, almost a release from such torment and agony… but no rest. Justice and revenge from the afterlife. Help. Help. Help. Frustration. Acute frustration. Help.

The hissing escaped from my head and I span around with the force of it leaving my body and sank to my knees. The shimmering haze of wind seemed to fly out into the pit and disappear through the trees of the island where my baits were. I stayed kneeling, retching and vomiting the remains of the meal I had cooked myself the previous evening. Saliva ran profusely from my mouth. My stomach contracted again, sweat soaked my body and I heaved and puked my stomach empty. Even after the most drunken of nights or after any sickness bug I had never vomited like I did then. I spat yellow bile from my mouth. The feeling of nausea finally left me and I literally crawled back to my bivvy, wet with perspiration from the effort of throwing up and with abdominal muscles sore and cramped. I dragged myself back onto the bedchair and curled myself up into the foetus position. Drained of energy I pulled the sleeping bag up to my shoulder. I'd met the ghost of the syndicate or rather it had come to meet me. My last thoughts were to pray I wouldn't get a take and, exhausted, I fell asleep.

Chapter 8

Something was bugging me, so I pulled the sleeping bag over the top of my head which was marginally better, but the feeling of discomfort was still with me. I rolled over. That didn't work either. I turned onto my back and forced my legs out straight, my trainers pushing deep into the bottom of the bag. I stretched my arms and yawned, no, the nagging thing was still there. I surfaced slowly out of my tank of sleep, my stomach feeling hollow and tender. Dededededededededededededededededededededededededede! That sound seemed familiar. Dededededededededededededededededededededededededede! I groaned. There was no God, or if there was he wasn't listening to what I'd asked him. A take! The very last thing I needed. I dragged myself out of the bag and stumbled down to my rods, the left one of which was responsible for all the racket. I cursed Pup's pop-up for its effectiveness. I felt as weak as a kitten, so weak I was a fortnight as the old cliché goes and I rather creakily hit the run. The rod bowled over with the heavy resistance of what felt like a hefty carp. I didn't need all this. Why couldn't it be a scamp of a common, or better still a line bite? I was clutching at straws.

Hanging on grimly to my Harrison Ballista Slim I felt like shit. The mother of all hangovers. Weak, weary, wan, wobbly, wasted, washed out, worn out, wilted, withered, unwell and unwilling. I had a stomach that had been kicked by a vicious mob of donkeys, a head that had been used as a football by a team whose manager still concurred with the long ball, kick and rush, kick it up in the air and when it comes down kick it back up again style and a mouth that tasted as if I'd spent the entire night indulging an unshowered, steroid-enhanced, Eastern block female shot putter, who had spent all day pumping weights, in wanton cunnilingus. I was as rough as a bear's arse. A bear's arse where all the skin and fur had been sliced off and replaced by a grafted sheet of durable silicon embedded with flint chips, broken glass, industrial diamonds, masonry nails and shards of angle grinder wheels.

It wasn't a magic moment. I should have been up on the rush of euphoria, high on the slug of adrenaline, supremely alert on the Pavlov's dog-like response to my buzzer. I should have been but I wasn't. I was flatter than a week old can of opened Pepsi, flatter than a punctured tyre, flatter than a remote control car's battery owned by an obsessive kid who, like me at that moment, couldn't be re-charged. I was as flat as a pancake on a piece of four inch thick carbon steel sheeting being run over by a steam roller driven by the entire cast of 'The Fat Club' TV programme. I was a wretched creature, I was more wretched… but you can see what I'm getting at.

I made little impact on the tussling carp. We were only a couple of minutes into proceedings but I could have gladly chucked the rod into the water and walked away, well, crawled away, from the contest. I imagined what I was experiencing was something like being six hours into a marlin fight with a broken harness, in 40 degrees of heat with raging sea-sickness. I had no nausea now, only a body suffering from the after-effects of it. By now, due to my sloth in hitting the take, the carp was way down to my left. I'd been lucky in the sense that it had bolted that way, away from the snags off the island. This lump hadn't read any mags. I tried to pump and wind but it was hard going, the butt which I had tucked into my belt line for extra control and leverage, was pushing on my most delicate area and hurt like hell yet gradually I managed to put some line back on the reel. Very slowly I turned the tables and started to win, inch by agonising inch I pulled the carp back up from the left until, at last, I had the fish rolling and boiling directly in front of me. By the amount of water it was shifting I could tell it was a hefty beast. It broke surface and I caught sight of a broad back with a clutch of large scales. A mirror and a big one.

It was time for the end game. With a face contorted and grimacing I managed to manoeuvre the landing net into position despite it feeling like it had a solid cast iron handle rather than a carbon one. The massive 50" net was virtually impossible for me to wield in my weakened state and I was only to well aware I would have to play the fish right out if I wasn't going to make a pig's ear of landing it. Without going into the prolonged anguish of the most arduous of fights I managed, in the end, to get the fish over the net and lift it enough to sink the big mirror into its mesh. Blowing like an old man, and definitely feeling like one, I stood and tried to summon enough energy for one last lift. With rod and landing net handle in left hand and my right hand gathering in the net mesh a foot from the spreader block, I bent my knees and ... hup! Bugger all happened. No hup! No even a hint of hup. I was both hupless and hopeless. What a state to get in. The fish was simply too heavy and I was too weak to get the bloody thing out of the water. If it wasn't so farcical I'd have laughed or cried, or both but that would have tweaked my guts even more, so I did neither.

I put the rod down but held onto the landing net handle and looked down into the clear water at what I'd caught. It was a big fish. If asked to put my life on its weight I'd have said high thirty possible forty, whatever, she was a beauty. She might even be a new forty for all I knew. What to name it if it was? Caught on the morning after the haunting before, so: The Ghost, The Apparition, The Spectre, The Phantom, The Spook, The Wraith... no, I was going to keep the visitation close to my chest. This was all very hypothetic seeing as I couldn't even get the carp out of the water, let alone set up my photographic gear and hold it while I snapped it. By the time I got my strength back the poor girl might have dropped back in weight to a mid twenty. What was I going to do? I know it sounds melodramatic and completely absurd but I felt so awful, so weak and so abused by what had happened to me I felt tears well in my eyes. It wasn't only the physical discomfort but also the mental anguish I felt as well. I mean, how many times do you get emotionally possessed, raped even, by a spirit from the afterlife? I sat and gently sucked in air through pursed lips and tried to gather my wits about me wondering if I could work a way out of my predicament.

Failing that, I'd have to sit it out and hope something would turn up. After ten minutes, which I'd spent trying to work a way out and had failed miserably, something or rather someone did turn up.

"What've you caught then, boy?"

I looked up from my position of apparent meditation. Rambo! Thank God! The cavalry at last.

"In there," I said, nodding down to the water, a feeling of relief washing over me now my mucker was here to bail me out... again, like he always seemed to.

Rambo came down to the water's edge and peered into the landing net. "Fuck me! That's a tidy old fish you've got there, boy! I was only asking a general question, I didn't realise you were sitting there with one in the net." Rambo looked about him. "I never even noticed you didn't have three rods out," he admitted. "What on earth are you doing sitting there like that?"

"What on earth indeed," I sighed, looking up at him. "I'm feeling pretty bad actually, I don't know how I managed to land the fish considering the mess I'm in. I honestly can't lift the sodding thing out of the water, I'm so weak."

Rambo looked at me with a furrowed brow. "Christ!" he exclaimed in genuine shock now that he could see my face. "You do look like shit! What the hell happened?"

"Go on, guess," I tempted him.

"Food poisoning?"

I shook my head gingerly.

"Twenty pints of lager?"

"You know I don't drink much," I said.

"Exactly!" he countered. "... I know. Bad drug trip."

"Wrong story," I pointed out feebly.

"Gastroenteritis? Cholera? Yellow fever? Hmm, not enough mozzies yet so I guess malaria's out of the question as well?"

"They're all out of the question," I told him.

Rambo shrugged his huge powerful shoulders. Every time I saw him do that I expected his camouflage jacket to rip and without his skin turning green. "I'm stumped. Come on then, let's hear it."

"You're not going to believe it," I warned him.

"Give it a go while I sort this carp out for you."

"Before I do, one question from me. What are you doing here?"

"You're never going to believe this either," said Rambo lifting the carp and landing net onto my unhooking mat. "I'm actually here to do a spot of carp fishing, six day's worth, to be precise. I saw your van in the car park and thought I'd have a little walk around to see where you were and how you were doing. You know, see if I could spot a few fish. There, I bet your story isn't as mad as that."

"How could it be," I said, playing along to Rambo's gentle sarcasm while managing to stand upright and move over to my carp.

Rambo had unwrapped the folds of the net's mesh to reveal the true beauty of the carp and we both looked down in awe at the remarkable mirror. She was a forty all right, a good forty.

"I've seen this one before," said Rambo. "It was on the poster at Michael's. Look at the scales." Rambo pointed a finger at the clutch of distinctive scales that were four or so inches down from the start of the dorsal fin. I remembered too, as soon as Rambo had pointed out the five scales.

"It's The Olympian, isn't it?" I said. The pattern of the scales left nothing to choice, it was her all right.

"Got to be," said Rambo. "Let's weigh her."

While Rambo zeroed in the Reuben's on the weigh sling I told him about the earlier mirror, what it had weighed and how I broke one of the syndicate rules because of the fish that were crashing out over the bait The Olympian had eventually taken, albeit hours and hours afterwards.

"Let me guess where that bait was cast…uh… not out to the margin island, by any chance?" said Rambo with false seriousness.

It was my turn to shrug. "It worked at Lac Fumant for the fifty…"

"Eventually!" said Rambo, piss taking again as he gently tucked The Olympian into the weigh sling and lifted up the scales with a weigh bar.

"What's the damage?" I asked.

"To you, boy, forty-eight pounds and eleven ounces. Want to do it and check?"

I flapped a droopy hand at him. "No way. I'm shot."

48-11. An English personal best by a mile. What a stonker of a carp but in my depleted condition it meant little, in a few days I could thrill at the capture but not now.

"Photos? enquired Rambo.

I declined. "Seeing as how I'm breaking rules like they're going out of style let's sack her, or rather you sack her, you make me a cuppa and I'll tell you what made me into the state I'm in."

Rambo rolled his eyes in a 'bloody hell you don't want much do you?' fashion and then did exactly as I asked.

"Put the back of my chair up for me," I whimpered.

"Jesus! There!"

I climbed on the bedchair and put my sleeping bag over my legs. Rambo handed me the mug of tea and I took a few tiny sips.

"Ohh that's nice," I said, not solely about the tea but my general state of comfort. Rambo sat on the groundsheet the other side of the mozzie flap with his legs drawn up to his chest, his huge forearms resting on his knees sipping at his mug.

"You ready?"

Rambo sighed and then laughed. "I guess so. We've had a few scrapes while we've been carp fishing so I reckon we just add this one to the list. It'll have to be pretty good to beat your spying on Jennifer and Mike's sex session…"

"Yours and Spunker's fist fight…"

"You blowing Watt's bivvy to smithereens…"

"You stringing Spunker up in his own bivvy…"

"You and Rebecca…"

"No comment. The Lac Fumant video with the Cowboy getting gunned down in all that rain."

"The Lac Fumant video with you out on your bedchair," said Rambo nodding pointedly, "but weirdest of all is you and that drug trip and mind-melding with a fifty-five mirror and then catching it. Spooky."

Something clicked in my head. Something Alan said. I gave a little involuntary shiver, frightened of what it meant. "Perhaps you've just hit the nail on the head," I said sombrely.

Over the next half hour I told Rambo everything I could remember about the incident. I was expecting him to butt in and to start taking the piss big time. I thought he'd ridicule me and call me all the names under the sun, but he didn't. He sat, sipped his tea and listened intently, he asked no questions, never interrupted me once until I'd finished. The only thing I could add was that whatever it was had no malice towards me, its anger was directed at something or somebody else. I tried to explain to Rambo that the ghost, I was pretty convinced it was the ghost, couldn't talk to me in words but only in general feelings and thoughts. The emotions I had experienced were so powerful my body clearly couldn't handle them, they were raw, violent and terrifying. The only one to have left me slightly confused was I had felt acute frustration at the end, just before it had left me, but I wasn't sure if this was its frustration at not being able to fulfil its own wishes, its revenge, or frustration at its inability to tell me exactly what it wanted. In basic terms my reading of the happening was the ghost, when alive, had been badly let down by somebody but had then been offered the chance to make up only to be tricked again, lured if you like, to a place, the old wood, where the other person killed him or her. It was right at the death of the then living ghost when something odd had happened and the sudden bright surge could have signalled the end of a mortal life and the beginning of an afterlife. I was no expert on the occult or spiritualism but surely this type of thing could only happen in exceptional circumstances or they'd be a fucking lot of ghosts around. Or there were but only a few of them could reach back over to the land of the living and only a few in the land of the living could hear them when they did. I wasn't too sure why the trees had transmogrified before I'd seen the wind, or rather the ghost, and could only guess that they were a portent of it coming. Another idea was they had somehow become ingrained with the violence of the foul murder but it was only an idea that I liked because of the pun on the word 'ingrained' and I stretched it further thinking perhaps the trees were cross, then they'd be crossed-grained.

Rambo was no fool, he ignored my rambling theories and he picked up on my earlier comment concerning his one about the mind-meld. "So you think that you're some sort of medium, then?"

"Exactly." I said, impressed with how he was taking this all in. "Perhaps my mind-meld, although drug induced, woke up some latent ability I'd always had but never realised or never had call to be used. Perhaps the ghost knew I could feel him and could communicate with me. Maybe he couldn't reach any of the others because they didn't have... I don't know what, whatever it is a ghost needs to communicate with a living person. You know the more I talk about it the madder it seems. You see Alan said something to me on the work party day. Do you remember when he said you were a real soldier and went on about his artist's eye?"

"Yeah."

"He said I looked like I may have a talent I might not be aware of but then didn't say anything else. He also said something later on like 'some are more prone to reaching over to the other side', or something similar, and he was the only one who'd had a paranormal experience. Do you remember?"

"Yeah," said Rambo again.

"Perhaps the old boy has got some special ability to see into people, his 'artist's eye' as he calls it, that's why he's seen or felt the ghost as well. I'll have to try and have a word with him, not tell him about this straight away but just bring a similar subject up in casual conversation. I've got to get to the bottom of it or it will bother me forever." I paused and considered how stupid this must all be sounding. It was ok for me, having experienced it but what about Rambo having to listen to it all with an undoubted cynical and sceptical appraisal. I'd have given myself short shrift if I'd been listening. "Do you think I'm full of shit?" I said embarrassed.

"Boy, if you were full of shit I wouldn't have ever asked you to come in on bait with me all those years ago. I wouldn't be sitting here listening to the tallest of all angling stories all the way through if I thought you were full of shit. We've been through a lot together like we said earlier but this is... well, this is another dimension isn't it?"

I nodded. It was. It was beyond all reasonable grounds. I'd heard rumours on the carping grapevine of haunted waters, of anglers noticing or hearing odd things at night but hadn't taken them seriously until now. If you asked a thousand carp anglers about weird things going bump in the night what answers would you get? Who would admit to having encountered eerie happenings? How many would own up to having seen or heard or felt something which didn't seem quite right? Who would admit to having been frightened? How many had night fished on their own? And how many had always gone with a mate? And had kept a light on all night because they were bothered by being in the dark on their own? Who would answer truthfully about those things? Who would admit to having a baseball bat under the bedchair? More for tackle thieves than ghosts and ghouls but there was another side to it even if that side was unspoken or kept in denial. I'd seen the other side, been touched by it and it had given me the fright of a lifetime. If other carpers ever got to read my story would it ring alarm bells with them even if their experiences were, and surely they were, much less obvious than mine? Sleep tight in your bivvies lads, somebody will hear your screams, even I might hear your screams. And if you do die of fright then you can return and haunt the rest of us to get your own back. Come to think of it, that could be what was happening already.

Rambo stood up purposefully, his mind apparently made up, the time for listening over, and he walked out of the bivvy. He turned and looked back at me on the bedchair. "You saw something, boy, or perhaps you thought you saw something. Whatever it was, was real enough to you. I've seen blokes shaken up by death, bad wounds or by being under constant fire and they all looked as bad as what you did earlier. Combat neurosis they call it. There are a few things that can back up your story," and he pointed towards the old wood, "so I'm going to take a look over there for those broken branches."

"Wait for me," I said. "I want to find out if I'm a raving head case as well."

I crept of the bedchair and followed Rambo up to the track. I felt a little better now having drunk my tea and some of my strength had returned. I only felt about sixty-eight walking behind Rambo rather than the one hundred and eight of earlier. My mind started to wander and to wonder. What if there were no signs? Could it have been possible to imagine it all? It seemed inconceivable and I hoped Rambo would find some tangible evidence.

Much to my disgust and relief the outpourings of my stomach were highly visible on the neatly mown grass of the track.

"Exhibit 'A'," I said. "One pile of cold puke." Despite my attempt at humour the sight of it turned my stomach and momentarily I felt queasy again.

"So straight in that way was where it came from," said Rambo nodding into the wood.

"At the end, yes, to begin with it was switchbacking to and fro deeper into the wood but the last bit, where I could actually see the wind heat haze was straight out in front…" My words tailed off. My line of sight to where I could remember the wind coming from was now filled with a large branch, almost severed, hanging down by the last bit of bark, parallel with the tree's trunk. It was only a few yards into the wood.

"Look!" I said gesticulating towards it. "The branch!"

Rambo had spotted it. "I'll go and take a closer look." He strode forward for a few steps and then turned back to me. "Are you coming?"

I shook my head. "I'll wait here, I don't want to break any more rules. I've still got two rods out."

"Of course," said Rambo grinning and he marched off.

The wood looked menacing as I watched him inspect the offending branch and go deeper into it. It was surprising how small a distance he had to go before I couldn't see him at all such was the density and darkness of the wood. Soon I couldn't even hear him and a strange silence descended over the trees. I tried to remember how large Michael had said the wood was but I couldn't recollect, had he said ten acres or twenty or had he even mentioned it at all? I also asked myself how long ago it was any human, one who was alive that is, last ventured into it. And whether they came out in the same state.

A good half hour passed. I started to get a bit edgy and wanted to call out but stopped myself from doing so. What was he doing? I peered deeper into the woods but I couldn't see into it for trees. Another twenty minutes passed and I was starting to get genuinely concerned. I walked to the very edge of the wood and actually went in level with the first tree and then a few feet passed it.

Rather ridiculously I put my right hand edgeways up to my mouth. "Rambo!" I hissed in a whisper. "Where are you?"

Something touched my shoulder and I nearly leapt to the top of the tree. "Right behind you!"

"For fuck's sake!" I declared, my heart pounding. "Don't do that to me. Are you trying to kill me off, or what?"

"Your rods *are* quite nice," admitted Rambo.

"Well? Find anything?"

"Let's go back to your bivvy," said Rambo. "You might get another take." The pair of us walked back in silence.

"Well?" I asked again.

"Most peculiar," said Rambo. "In fact I would say it was so peculiar that if you could bottle it and sell it as real ale you could call it 'Olde Peculiar'."

"You didn't find anything did you?" I said both convinced and disappointed.

"Apart from the one broken branch?" Rambo reminded me.

"Apart from the one broken branch," I corrected myself. "That had broken weeks or even months ago."

"It was a fresh break and for ten or so yards behind it in a dead straight line there were more freshly broken branches," said Rambo.

My flesh began to creep and goose bumps came out all over me. "Really?" I asked, sure Rambo would say: 'Of course not you dork, I'm winding you up'. But he didn't.

"Yeah. And when I got to a certain point the line of destruction veered off left, then right, and so on. Exactly as you described but the force being imparted on the branches weakened as I followed the trail deeper back into the woods and it became harder and harder to track. Eventually I couldn't find any signs of anything so I had a good rummage around in that vicinity. The area where, as far as I could tell, the force would have started or if you like where the ghost materialised." Fascinated and partly filled with dread I hung onto Rambo's every word like a drowning man might hang on to a piece of passing flotsam.

"Did you find anything?" I demanded, intrigued by what he might have found.

"It was dark in there, boy, but I always carry my mini Maglite and I scoured the ground as best I could, pushing all the leaves away and sifting through the twigs and other crud."

"And?"

Rambo held out his two hands and spread his fingers. "Fuck all! Not a snifter. Seven days hard fishing in a swimming pool."

Rambo had drawn a blank but still. "So it all fits in with what I said, then?"

"As unbelievable as it seems, and believe me I don't believe in unbelievable things, money and physical violence are my twin gods, I have to accept you were… not sure of the correct word, so let's say… 'contacted' by a spirit, spectre, ghost, whatever you'd like to call it. Who it was, why it did and for what reason I cannot say."

I thought I knew some of the answers, not all, but the ones I did were all vague. "Who? No idea. Why? Presumably because I was receptive and could hear it. For what reason? To help with its revenge, it must think I can help, why it thinks that I haven't a clue not unless it can only contact a very small number of us. You know, an 'any port in a storm' type of syndrome," I explained to Rambo. I shook my head in amazement. "Bloody hell, I don't need this, I've got seven months left before my first child is due to be born, I'm under instructions from Sophie to get my arse into gear…"

"And bang out a few more," interjected Rambo.

I ignored the jibe. "… And sort out my electrical business, the baby stuff, placate her rising hormones and rising weight and now I've got to ponce about with getting plagued by a poltergeist, albeit a platonic one."

"It wasn't exactly harmless was it?" said Rambo.

"True it shook me up, the contact and all that, but it wasn't trying to hurt me, it was trying to get me to help it."

"If it can make you throw your guts up simply by contacting you, why doesn't it just go around to whoever it wants revenge on and scare the bastard to death?" said Rambo.

I had no answer and pulled a face. "Search me, I mean do they sell ghost reference books in WH Smith? Ghosts for Dummies. Which Ghost. The A-Z of British Ghosts. Or magazines? Loaded… with Ghosts. Ghostworld. Performance Ghosts. Make your own Ghost… the start of this fascinating monthly magazine tells how to summon up your own ghost and comes with a superb binder to collect all the issues. Part two comes free with part one at the reduced price of just £1.99. How would I know? I'm no expert on the rules, ask me an easy one on quantum physics." As an afterthought I said. "Are we really having this conversation?"

"It'll all come out in the wash," said Rambo confidently.

"What will?"

"The vomit on your sweatshirt. Come on, boy, let's get The Olympian out of the sack and take some photos. I expect she needs to do her daily training regime and then I need to get my gear sorted and start fishing. You might have seven months until your life changes forever but I've only got seven days until I've got to pack up for this session."

"My life has already changed forever," I said.

And so it had. I summoned up enough strength to hold the magnificent Olympian and get some photos and then Rambo departed back to the car park to get his vehicle and tackle having decided to fish the same swim as he had last time. Once my forty was safely back in the water I started to pack up. It was a slow laborious task feeling as poorly as I did but I felt I couldn't ask Rambo for any more help as he was clearly itching to get his baits in the water. Besides, I did feel a bit better, and at least Rambo had proved I wasn't going clinically insane by finding the route of the wind. I laughed to myself. How ironic. If I wasn't clinically insane then the world was, this was the make believe world of films, of television programmes, of books. Ghosts didn't exist in the world of carp fishing, ghosts didn't exist full stop, did they? You heard rumour and gossip but what of it? There were plenty out there capable of exaggeration and spinning a yarn.

Going carp fishing had introduced me to many pleasures and to new exhilarating experiences and equally some awful ones as well. It had broadened my horizons, made me go to places, like jail for instance, made me do things, made me deal with and meet different people which I wouldn't have done had I not fished. It had made me scheme and toil to find the time and money to go. It had made me cheat, lie and suffer. It had made me happy, euphoric and exulted. It had put me up, knocked me down, embraced me to the point of suffocation and then released me and pandered to me like a mother to a favourite son. In short it had been a massive driving force through a good percentage of my life, sometimes more than others but for all the strange events it had afforded me none could surpass the visit of The Ghost of The Syndicate. The questions the event threw up, if you pardon the pun, were huge and ones which great minds had grappled with since time immemorial. Life after death. A parallel universe of dead souls. Their universe crossing into ours with inter-reaction. Clairvoyance, mediums, ouija boards, séances, talking to the dead, heaven, hell, God, the Devil, human existence, reincarnation, which buzzers to use. No, not the last one but come on. To become a player in all that lot due to the possible awakening of a talent by the mistaken passing of an incorrect tablet by one Dutch brother to a slightly pissed, cunt-struck carp angler away from home on a two week fishing holiday as paid for by a lottery winning mother-in-law etc was, how shall I put it? Daunting. The haunting was daunting. But I wouldn't go jaunting about and flaunting the haunting in case it turned out to be me at the end of a taunting. No sir, I'd keep my cards close to my chest and just suck it and see.

I slammed the van door shut behind me having just locked the pit's entrance gate. No. I wouldn't tell Sophie about this, not in her state, she'd probably miscarriage on the spot. The whole episode would have to be another thing for me to tuck into my festering brain and mull over. Jesus H Christ. Was there enough frigging room? The way things were going it was just as likely he'd pop round and tell me.

Chapter 9

Back in my other existence away from the syndicate another delicious, well quite the opposite actually, irony had reared its horrid head. Having had the most awful of times during my visitation I had to suffer Sophie going through the same thing. She too had something inside her that was causing her to throw up but in this instance it was far more commonplace. Every day I had to hear her retching and being ill into the toilet, a vessel that seemed to be able to magnify the event, and every guttural call and spit brought my still vivid memory back even closer. Her bouts of morning sickness made me feel ill and the pair of us came to dread them with equal vigour. Sophie would complain about how awful they made her feel and I was every inch the sympathetic partner. I knew exactly what her morning sickness made her feel like and I could empathise to the nth degree. It also reminded me of an expression someone had told me about years earlier concerning motion sickness, or as was the case in this little anecdote, seasickness. The person involved was hurling and chucking over the boat and another person, who had good sea legs was telling him about the two stages of seasickness. Stage one was when you felt so ill you were afraid you were going to die and stage two, where the unwell person was at, was when you were frightened you *weren't* going to die. How true it was, how very true. And yet my heightened sensibilities seemed to be appreciated by Sophie as I mopped her perspiring brow when the nausea passed. It gave her support in her moments of discomfort because I could identify so exactly with the way she was feeling.

"You're only remembering the last time you got drunk," she had said, teasing and not meaning it.

"Blimey, I haven't got that good a memory. It must be at least five years ago," I'd reminded her.

"What else could it be? You don't get many sickness bugs and I can't think of a single time you've had a stomach upset since I've known you."

"And with your cooking," I'd teased her. "Strong constitution you see." Bless her, if I'd have told her the truth the baby would have popped out there and then.

It was after one bout of morning sickness when Sophie had told me that the day before her mum had promised to give us some more money, after the baby was born, as a gift to the child. I'd had to stop myself saying how pleased I was because I might be needing some new reels soon. She was on my case straight away. Perhaps her changing body had rendered her psychic? I was up shit creek if it had. Imagine every innermost thought laid bare? The murder rate would go up wouldn't it?

She'd explained quite curtly. "What I don't want is for the money to be used by us to pay for things we could pay for if you were working hard. I don't want the financial situation used as an excuse for you to go fishing more than you usually would, it wouldn't be fair. I'll be working up until I take my eighteen weeks of statutory maternity pay, I think the earliest I can leave is fifteen weeks before my expected week of confinement. I'll have to check, and then I'll leave to look after the baby. I'll be showing mum that I'm doing my bit and you have to as well. Her help will be the icing on the cake and enable us to give our child the best there is." Damn the girl's moral principles, I'd thought. What with the money, however much it was, plus the two hundred odd thousand in the bank I'd reckoned I shouldn't really have to worry about proper work at all. I was wrong, I'd got away with it up until her pregnancy but the goalposts had shifted. "Besides," she'd continued, "I think we'll probably start to think about moving house soon, especially if we're going to have any more kids. This place won't be big enough for four of us."

"Let me get to grips with having one," I'd snapped. "Before we start a bloody football team." Gloomily I could see she had it all mapped out in her organised, honest, non-manipulative mind. It was this honesty and decency which had first attracted me to her, ok that and her looks and body, ok her body, her looks and then the other stuff, but now it was a tiny bit wearing seeing as it was depriving me of easy street and easy fishing in the near future. Really I couldn't complain, like she'd said, I'd had a good run of it and I was lucky in having that. I could see rather than the money being a buffer for me to live my life in carp fishing indulgence, our windfall was going into security, property and stability for our forthcoming family. Oh well, I'd have to get used to it, at least it had allowed me to get into the syndicate and I grudgingly had to admit that her stance was the most responsible.

Over the time since we'd received the money I had considered going into the carp fishing world in a commercial sense, like owning a tackle shop or my own water but I'd known what the answer would have been if I'd suggested it and I didn't have the gall to ask. It all hinged on the fact that originally the money had come from her mum and prior to it I'd ended up in prison because of carp fishing. Yet despite all this she'd waited for me to be released from jail and had stuck by me even after all I'd put her through and she had still let me start up again and let me blow a not inconsiderable sum on gear and Lac Fumant. I had to keep reminding myself of this when I felt cornered by the prospect of becoming a dad. She was special, a very special person. Yet, the commitment required by fatherhood frightened me, more than the ghost did. How wrong was that? I tried to talk myself around it but the feelings were there and I couldn't stop them.

A week or so after my first session, which incidentally I'd got away with, no grief from Sophie at all, I received my very own poster from Michael. It was exactly the same as the one Hollywood Gary had brought around on the day of our initial interview. I gazed at the remarkable painting Alan had done of The Olympian and was reminded he himself had caught the fish as a first forty but at over seven pounds lighter a few years back. As I inspected the painting I felt an increasing urge to go back and try to catch some more of the magnificent fish that were residing in the pit. I also felt an urge to talk to Alan about my encounter with the ghost, it wouldn't be hard to do because his address, phone number and email address were all on the bottom of the poster should anyone want to commission him for any painting work. Why, I only had to phone him up on the pretence of talking about a shared fish capture, informing him how big it was, where I'd caught it, or that I wanted him to do some painting work, the baby's bedroom, Sistine Chapel only with carp touching fins and I could work the conversation around to what I really wanted to talk about. I ruminated. All I had to do was pick up the phone. I couldn't bring myself to do it.

I had a few jobs I'd got lined up, nothing too taxing, a few extra power points and a couple of electric showers and I had also managed to draw up a list of people to contact about doing some work for them in the future. Builders, plumbers, conservatory suppliers, those types of people, but my mind wasn't really in it, how could it be? I forced myself to do it as a means towards an end and realised this was how it had used to be, how it was for ninety-nine percent of carp anglers. It was called real life and making a living but in truth I was still playing at it compared to the rest. Before the baby had taken root inside Sophie I'd had the perfect carp fishing arrangement, no financial worries, an easy going partner who was happy I was going so long as I kept it in moderation, which I had, unlike years ago. Now, though, the baby had tipped the scales by increasing the burden on Sophie, increasing the burden on our money and by increasing the burden on my free time. At the moment, seeing as the blighter hadn't been born and Sophie wasn't too incapacitated, I wasn't suffering unduly but I could see it would change more after the birth and that was the stark reality of it.

I'd read in some of Sophie's pregnancy books that parents were often ambivalent towards the birth of a child, apparently it was quite normal to have mixed feelings and going through pregnancy was a phase of emotional growth. It didn't actually cite loss of carp fishing time but you could tell by reading in between the lines it was what they meant. I was still unable to grasp the concept of what positive impact a baby might have on my life. I saw it all negatively, I saw all the things I'd have to do that would stop me from doing what I wanted. There was no other side, not yet, I was too detached from it all despite my empathy with Sophie's morning sickness. I hoped it would come but what if it didn't? Would my feelings turn to real resentment? What a total shithead that would make me. I hoped my feelings would change because I wanted them to be real and not contrived. Perhaps, eventually, I too would gain emotional growth but in the mean time I'd have to settle for being an emotional pygmy, stunted by my own self-interest. I wanted to be a good dad, but at the moment I wanted other things more.

What should have concerned me greatly but wasn't, was the contact at the pit. The revelation would have crippled weaker men but somehow over the ensuing fortnight since it had happened I seemed to take it onboard better than I could possibly have hoped. Why this was seemed hard to explain, perhaps my springs were fully compressed with the weight of being in a syndicate, becoming a father and having to consider adapting my ways from the wonderfully free and unstressed existence I'd enjoyed since a week after coming out of clink. I had no fear of going back to the pit, I desperately wanted to go back, to get in some more carping time before the baby was born and also to see if I could find out more and then help the ghost.

'Help the ghost'. I laughed at the concept of such a notion firstly because I didn't have a clue as to how to go about it and secondly to talk about something so conceptual in such practical terms seemed a massive contradiction. At best something might turn up, like the way Rambo had when the forty was stuck in the net. That carp might as well have weighed forty tons, for all the impression I'd made upon it but I'd got out of trouble by pure luck and chance and that appeared my only hope. At night, over the period I mentioned, as I lay in bed, I tried to grapple with the implications of the big questions my visitation raised but they were well beyond my mental capacity. Did everyone who'd ever died become a ghost? Was it only those that came to an especially violent end who did? What happened to those that didn't become ghosts, did their souls go straight to heaven or hell? Would Rambo eventually meet the souls of all the people he'd killed, including the one he'd paid to be himself and conspired to have killed by an assassin who he in turn had then killed? It'd make for a nice cosy chat wouldn't it? There were too many questions, and remarkably for someone who had churned over the ins and outs of far less complicated scenarios, my head gave up and didn't waste any time on it. Problems I could grasp and perhaps come to conclusions, whether right or wrong, I'd go for, but something like this? No way. It was way, way out of my league and I settled for the fact it had happened. Undeniably there was something after death for some and I did seem to have some small ability to be able to be in contact with it. The feeling of chance and wondering which way fate and the chain of life would go, so strong when I'd stood outside the door of Rebecca's bedroom, was back with me again. It was, if anything, even more exciting now than it had been then and seeing as I was now over the initial shock and had come to terms with it I felt uncannily empowered by it. What was I destined to find out? Surely I would find something? If a spirit from the afterlife had singled me out then there must be a reason. The reason could be a desperate ghost clutching at straws. I hoped it wasn't the case.

By the middle of May I'd paid my dues enough to confidently ask Sophie for a decent session at the pit. I'd earned some money, put out a few feelers to the businesses I'd mentioned and had even made a tentative start on the baby's bedroom. It reminded me how much I detested decorating but at least I'd started. Her morning sickness had eased slightly now she was nearly twelve weeks gone and we were due to go to our first antenatal clinic - I couldn't wait - on the Friday. It was still impossible to tell by looking at her that she was pregnant but she was spending longer in the toilet, not because of throwing up but because she was becoming slightly constipated. I thanked my lucky stars I was born a male, loaded the van and grasped my window of opportunity, three days, with both hands. I was off fishing while Sophie was off to work whilst carrying my child that had taken me about ten minutes of humping to produce some eighty days ago. Do men have the best bit of the deal, or what? It wasn't a question that needed answering, it certainly wasn't a question that needed asking, not unless you fancied a boot in the crotch. If men were women we'd ask for gas and air during the conception, let alone the birth.

Any feeling of guilt evaporated during the journey and once again I was wrapped up in the release of carp fishing. Stop the world, I want to get off and go fishing. I'd phoned Rambo up on the Monday morning of my departure to tell him when I was going only to find the bastard was already there. He was following a loose one week on, one week off policy and would be at the pit for two of my three days. I hadn't spoken to him since the visitation so we had a lot of catching up to do on what Rambo had caught and other dealings concerning the syndicate. Firstly, Rambo had caught plenty of fish. He was getting a fish a day with an average weight of over thirty pounds and he'd had his first forty. Not a new one but one of the so-called mug fish, the one called Toby. He was fishing his favoured point as he had done every visit - if it ain't broke don't fix it - and he'd been visited by Michael several times on both of his week long sessions. The only other members he'd bumped into on various separate occasions were Darren and a chap called Noel, who I remembered had been the bloke who named the forty, Flit Spin. However, these weren't the only anglers around and Rambo had spotted some other syndicate members from his south-east point swim. His swim was right opposite, although some seventy yards away, from the stock pond and it was here he'd seen other members returning smaller fish. Rambo wasn't too sure who was who but he had recognised Rocky in his catwalk camouflage suit and Darren amongst others. By the amount of activity around the stock pond it was clear everyone was having a few of the smaller fish. Michael had told Rambo during one of his impromptu visits that all the fish in the stock pond were eventually sold on to other syndicates and clubs.

Rambo had said that despite there being at least six or seven other members fishing it was only by virtue of the fact he was near to the stock pond and was keeping his very keen surveillance skills on a high state of alert he'd noticed the other anglers. The pit was great for solace, even when there were people around, as we'd realised and as others had told us. Rambo felt that if it hadn't been for the chance meetings with the three anglers and if he hadn't been next to the stock pond he could easily have thought he was all alone. I'd asked him why he'd bothered to try and keep tabs on things and he'd explained that despite not having any creepy goings on whatsoever his very reliable other sixth sense had kicked in. Rambo's sixth sense was sniffing out trouble. You didn't live a life like he had, and to the point, still be living it, without the keen awareness of 'something going on'. It was a hunch, if you like, and I was more than happy to agree if he had an inkling of trouble there was a good chance it would materialise. Only not as violently as the ghost.

"Drop your stuff off in your swim, boy, come round for a cuppa and we'll have a chat," he told me on the Monday morning as I spoke to him from home, and it was exactly what I intended to do. I drove too fast and too dangerously to carve ten minutes off my journey time but it seemed vital I did so. Obviously it wasn't vital, it made no difference whatsoever but when you're gripped the right foot pushes down a bit harder.

Before I called in on my old mucker I dropped my gear off in my island swim. My island swim. I'd been in the syndicate five minutes, fished it once and it was my island swim. It's funny how you see things like that, I'd have been quite put out had someone been in it. I then parked my van in the car park and walked anti-clockwise around to Rambo. If you'd have drawn a line due north from his swim then you would have virtually bisected mine, the distance between them being at least six hundred yards. (I hope all these Imperial measurements are not pissing off any carp fishing Europhiles, if they are... tough).

"Three cars in the car park, excluding ours," I said as I jerked my thumb over my shoulder and walked into Rambo's swim.

"Rocky, Darren and Noel," said Rambo turning his head around and looking over the top of his bedchair. "I think Michael's gone, he doesn't exactly clock up the hours, or at least so he says, a day session here and there, that's all. I haven't seen any sign of Hollywood, though. I don't think he's been around. Anyway, enough. How are you going then, boy? What about Sophie? How is she?"

I was pleased he'd started to call Gary, Hollywood, my nickname for him. It might have been unfair on him, he'd been more than pleasant to us, but it seemed a good nickname for my part. Superficially beautiful, shallow, self-absorbed, tacky and driven by casual sex, greed and money? I couldn't lay the last two on him but I was happy to go with the rest while turning a numb brain to what I might nickname myself considering my failings on the parenthood theme. It was possible I was being too harsh on him.

"I'm fine, thanks. Sophie's all right. She's been a bit sick in the mornings but she's over it now. Everything seems to be going according to plan."

Rambo poured scalding water into an already tea-bagged mug. His kettle had an uncanny knack of being perpetually at boiling point. "Got your head around being a daddy, yet?" he asked looking up at me through wafts of steam.

I puffed out my cheeks and shoved out some air. "Not really. I'm having ambivalent feelings and I'm waiting for my phase of emotional growth."

Rambo handed me the mug. "The only phase you're likely to get in touch with, being an electrician, is three phase and 415volts worth of it and it'll kill you. Maybe becoming a parent will do the same."

"Nice joke," I said. "Had anything since I phoned?"

"No. The main feeding times are definitely early morning and late evening, but you've a good chance of getting one out in the middle of the night. Poltergeists permitting, of course. I haven't had a fish out in the middle of the day. What's the time now?" Rambo looked at his watch. "Nearly twelve, I'll give it until three and then recast and re-bait for this evening and the night." Rambo shoved a chocolate digestive in his face and thrust the half eaten packet towards me. "Where are you going to fish?"

I teased one out of the limp remains of the cylindrical wrapping and sipped my tea. "Same place as before."

Rambo raised his eyebrows and slightly cocked his head. "Not worried about another visit?"

I shook my head and smiled. "No. I don't think I'll get another one. It'll leave me to it now, I reckon."

Rambo let out a snort. "It's fucking weird. You know, I've never ever considered anything like there being life after death but possibly there is something after all. Have you thought about it?"

"Yeah. And I gave up. It's too much to handle, I'm going with the flow on this one."

Rambo gave another snort, only this time it was one of derision. "A bit unlike you isn't it, boy? You could worry for England."

"My worry cache is being used up elsewhere."

I could tell Rambo was unconvinced, he probably thought it was a case of macho posing on my behalf. "Have you any idea how old this ghost is?" he asked.

"No. None at all really. I didn't give it any thought," I said, a bit caught out by Rambo's question.

"You should," said Rambo gravely. "You see if you're right in saying someone was brutally murdered and because of it this spirit evolved as the person died, then when it happened is really important."

"I'm not with you. How could you possibly find that out?" I asked.

"If you say the ghost wants your help, doesn't that tell you something?"

I shrugged. I was beginning to feel like the most stupid boy in the class being coaxed along by the patient teacher.

Rambo continued. "Look, if the ghost was murdered a hundred years ago the person who did it would be dead themselves. What could you do? Dig them up and tell their bones how naughty they'd been." I saw Rambo's drift and felt a tingle of excitement run up my spine as if someone was using it as a xylophone but hitting my vertebrates with feathers instead of little wooden hammers. "If the ghost wants you to help get justice and revenge it must mean the murderer is still alive and that you're in a position to get to know this person, and even more incredulously, you might already know them!"

"Fucking hell! It's not someone you've already bumped off is it?" I said as the clear reasoning of Rambo's words hit through to me.

Rambo waved a chomped digestive at me. "I've already thought about that. And as far as I'm aware that isn't the case. Not unless it flew in on a plane or made one hell of a journey. As you said, what are the rules on ghosts and say… their travel arrangements? Do they need a passport to travel? What about inter-continental haunting? Have they got a union or codes of practise? Fuck knows? I'm sticking to the notion that whoever got stiffed, got stiffed in the old woods within the last fifty or so years, give or take. All the ghost stories I've ever heard about, ones concerning old buildings, waters and such like, the spirits are usually residential. You don't seem to get them jetting in from away."

I looked deeply at Rambo. "You've been thinking about this a lot haven't you?"

Rambo turned away from my gaze. "Yes. Yes I have. I'll level with you boy, this has made me think more than anything else in my entire life. I've dealt in death, more than you'll ever know or want to know but I've never thought about it like this. I'm not frightened, it's just it's opened up a whole new angle on things and it's one I'd prefer closed. And the best way I've found to close any issue is to resolve it and the best way for that to happen is for you to help the ghost. I can't believe I'm saying these things and if it wasn't for the fact it happened to you and I found physical evidence to back up your story…" Rambo's voiced tailed off. "I'm grappling with things I know cannot happen. I can't even go back on my old adage of 'when in doubt kill it'. The fucking thing's already dead! We've got to work it out, that's all I know but how? Don't ask me how we go about it, I haven't got a clue."

"Don't worry," I said. "Something will turn up."

"I bloody well hope so. It's too fucking odd, boy, for my liking. Too fucking odd."

I nodded. I had two lives. One was concerned with a dead thing which had somehow been reborn into an apparition, the other was concerned with an unborn thing which was alive in Sophie's womb. I changed the subject.

"What about this notion of yours? This hunch of something going on?"

For once Rambo looked less than sure of himself. "Oh, perhaps it's me getting a bit side-tracked by this episode of yours. What can I say? It seemed to me Darren was asking too many questions about how long I was going to stay here and how much I would be fishing this coming season. If I stop and think hard I suppose it was all fairly innocuous. I bumped into him in the clubhouse, we didn't talk for long and he didn't pump me, it'd be too obvious. It was a feeling I had, that's all. I might be way off though."

"I doubt it, mate," I said. "You know what these syndicates can be like."

By two I was all set up in my swim looking out over to the island. I'd left Rambo once his chocolate digestives had run out preparing for the ensuing feeding spell. I'd walked around to my swim, not seeing a soul, either in a living body or without one and had set up my gear with speed and expectancy. That was over now and it was back to the old waiting game. The sun shone out from behind the odd cloud and warmed my face due to my south facing aspect, like it had on my other session. It was a nice spot although the old woods weren't far from my back. I was still a little put off by them even if I was unconcerned about the ghost. They still seemed to have a malevolence all of their own. They simply looked scary, end of story.

I couldn't see Rambo's swim from where I was because of the island and I had no idea where the others were fishing apart from knowing they were not either side of me. I'd checked those two swims so as not to contravene the rules. I was alone with my thoughts, for all intents and purposes I could imagine having the pit all to myself. I wondered what it would be like to own a place like this, whether it would be worth the aggro of trying to keep a bunch of avid carp anglers in check. I considered if you had enough money you could minus them right out of the equation and fish it alone or with the odd friend. I had an odd friend, Timothy Eugene Ramsbottom, or whatever name he was going under now he'd killed that particular persona off. He probably said the same about me, I was willing to bet, and he'd have the greater foundation to stake such a claim.

Syndicates, like kids – who'd have them? – well I was in line, much like my leads, for both categories and I asked myself which would end up giving me the most grief. An unfair question seeing as my first child hadn't even been born. I'd have to give it ten more years and have a think about it then. Rambo's latest hunch didn't faze me but it would have done at the very onset when the thought of rejoining a syndicate had filled me with trepidation. Hah! Those cerebral meanderings had long been superseded. I suppose it did back up the theory that if you had a sore finger a good hard punch on the nose made you forget about it.

I sat in solitude for a couple of hours, absorbing my surroundings and gradually getting more and more excited at the prospect of the upcoming feeding time. I diligently scoured the water for carp movement although I very much doubted if I would have had the will power to move one of my three rods from their carefully positioned marks. I lit my stove and started heating up my kettle. It was on the point of boiling when a voice from behind spoke to me.

"Hello, Matthew. I timed that right, I'll have a cup."

I recognised the voice and looked back towards the woods to see Michael. His skinny body, topped by his rat-like face shifted nervously across the grass.

"All right, Michael? I think I can spare you a cup. Sugar?"

Michael nodded quickly and with a jerky movement. "Two."

I handed him the mug of tea and watched in slight fascination as his bony fingers clasped the mug and as if by magic it immediately started to oscillate. I watched the surface of the tea quiver as the mug which contained it was twitched and fluttered by Michael's jittery arm. Contradictory Michael. Nervy, paranoid and yet brusque at times and quite domineering when he was ordering syndicate members about. I wondered what he was like away from the syndicate, in other aspects of his life and then remembered someone had told me it was his life and there was nothing else.

Michael didn't touch his tea, instead he was looking at me with his beady eyes. "Have you seen Tom Watt, lately?"

Chapter 10

I was tempted to say: 'Who?' but I would have probably looked more foolish than I supposed I looked already. I don't think I quite let the mug of tea in my right hand slip so the hot liquid poured over the lip, it must have been touch and go, and I did manage to rally myself before Michael had the chance to reach over to me and push up my bottom jaw so my lips touched.

"Wow! I haven't heard that name for a long time… from somebody else that is," I admitted.

Michael's face twisted into a sneering grin while his eyes flicked up and down like a 1970's black and white portable television in a poor reception area. "I don't suppose you have," he said coldly.

I was expecting to get the boot there and then, dismissed from the syndicate on my second session with no second chance and without a second glance. Goodbye ghost, goodbye forties, goodbye £2500 and when Sophie found out, Goodnight Vienna. Michael had clearly found out about the SS syndicate, the one we had so conspicuously failed to mention in our interview. I guessed it meant Rambo would be for the chop as well.

"You've found out about all that nonsense, then?" I said a little uncomfortably.

Michael sneered again, the vein in his temple pulsed. "I've always known, right from the time I investigated you when Pup put your names forward. Although the SS was a very small syndicate and very inconsequential compared to the one you're in now I found out about it. You see you don't get into my syndicate lightly and I have a lot of contacts in the fishing world. You might not think anyone outside the circle of your old syndicate cares much about what happened, possibly they don't, but people talk to other people concerning various things. Never underestimate the grapevine, especially when it comes to carp fishing, you'd be surprised at how much you can find out about people if you know who to talk to… and offer them an incentive to do so."

I was dumbfounded. My gob was smacked. "So you know about our long session, the hand grenade business and me going to jail?"

Michael looked like a smug rat, one that had found its own detached sewer with all the filth it could eat. "Yes," he confirmed.

"What else do you know about me?" I asked, intrigued that someone had gone to the trouble to bone up on my life story. Fame at last or more likely infamy. A little disturbingly I asked myself if he knew what had happened between Rebecca and me? Impossible! No one knew. Naturally if anyone got to hear of the circumstances they could have a guess at what happened, call it how they saw it –

I then had a hideous thought - not unless he'd managed to bribe Rebecca! Bloody hell!!

"I know you went to Lac Fumant twice but I wasn't really bothered after I found out about you and Watt trying to outdo each other," said Michael nonchalantly.

I was both confused and relieved he hadn't dug deeper. "So how come you let me and Rambo in if you knew there had been so much trouble with us in our last syndicate?"

Michael took a slug of tea and laughed. "You've got it the wrong way round. That's why you got in. No pair has ever made it into my syndicate before, you and Rambo have set an almighty precedent. You see I don't like pairs. Pairs are two mates and people getting into little groups cause a lot more trouble than individuals, as you well know. I can't keep everyone as an individual after they've joined, anglers are bound to team up, but I can make sure they are all on their own to begin with, if you see what I mean? It isn't easy running a place like this, trying to keep it under wraps as much as possible, it's very hard. The power of the grapevine will win in the end, especially if you have individuals after glory. God knows what will happen when someone has a British record carp out of here. It'll happen one day and the lid will be blown off for good. At the moment most of the members want to keep it to themselves, fish for their own satisfaction and not shout it to the world but it gets harder to encourage that mentality as the fish get bigger." Michael pointed a trembling finger at me. "That's another reason why you got in."

Now I was even more confused. "So we're not going to get kicked out?"

"Have you broken any rules?" asked Michael, his beady eyes narrowing even more and turning them into little slits.

"No," I lied with indignation.

"Well there you are." Michael looked out towards the island and scanned the water. "Let me explain," he said. "I shan't tell you who told me of your exploits with Tom Watt, naturally I remember reading *his* account of it all in Carpworld, the arrogant bastard."

"So you knew him!" I said and was suddenly transported back in time to the days of Tom's handsome face, his cronies and his subtle superiority. The vision of the smoke drifting across the small water which had been my home for nigh-on nine months after I'd blown his bivvy to bits also resurfaced. I laughed inwardly. It was a great memory, nostalgic almost, looking back on the horror written all over his face after I'd mocked him in the free-for-all melee at the disintegration of both the syndicate and his tackle. Having said that, it was only a great memory in isolation when I disregarded the personal cost of the affair as a whole.

"Knew him and detested him," confirmed Michael, his thin lips looking cruel and vicious. "You don't have to know why or when but simply take it as read, anyone who gave Tom Watt problems went up in my estimation greatly. I'd also heard about Rambo from the same sources and to be truthful I found it hard to accept that someone could be so awesome but having seen him you get the feeling he can be when he wants to be." Michael paused for a second or two. "Pup had spoken highly of you and explained your previous syndicate shenanigans were only done to combat a monstrous ego and stroke pulling. So I thought to myself, I could do with somebody like you two around."

"Rambo can be awesome," I assured Michael answering the first bit of his little speech. "You wouldn't credit the things I've seen him do and they only revolve around carp fishing. As to the other side of his life, well, that's even more remarkable." He's dead for a start, I thought but I had no fear of Michael unearthing that little secret. "What did you mean by you could do with someone like us two being around?" I added.

"At your interview, when you were busy telling me everything apart from the things you didn't want to…"

"Was it that obvious?" I said cutting in.

"Not that obvious," said Michael. "I knew you were hiding up the past and I had to laugh to myself when Rambo hinted he would sort out any trouble if it occurred. Even so, without knowing what I did I'd have still felt you were giving me a little bit of bullshit. I've interviewed a lot of carp anglers who were bursting to get into my syndicate and I've got a nose for anglers being economical with the truth."

You can say that again, with a nose like a sniffer rodent, I thought but I only said sheepishly "I did wonder at the time."

Michael started up again in answer to my original question. "As I was saying, Rambo made it clear he would help if there was any sort of trouble and that was the other reason for letting the pair of you in. 'A' - for fighting against Watt and 'B' - for helping me out with any possible trouble in the future."

"Is there trouble, then?" I asked. It looked like Rambo's hunch was right.

Michael's demeanour turned even stranger and he looked quickly to his left and right as if expecting someone to come leaping out of the undergrowth. "You've got wind of trouble?" he asked anxiously. "What have you heard? What have you seen? Who was it?" he blurted.

"No! You mentioned trouble," I said trying to get a grip of the situation.

"What sort of trouble?" said Michael who was getting more and more agitated.

I felt my head spin. I wasn't going to tell him of Rambo's hunch or about the ghost, I'd simply used his words and asked an innocuous question. "No! No!" I pleaded. "You're getting the wrong end of the stick. You mentioned the possibility of trouble and it being handy to have someone like Rambo around to deal with it and I only asked if there was trouble. Not that I'd seen or noticed any."

Michael stopped and blinked about ten times in as many seconds, filled his skinny rib cage with air, making him a 36" chest at most, and blew it out down his large pointy nose.

"Thank God," he said, cocking his head to one side and scratching his neck. "I'm always thinking something is about to go off. I've been thinking it virtually every day since I started the syndicate. Negative, I know but that's the way it is when you run something on your own. Let me explain my reasons, I can see that the pressure is going to increase in this and the coming seasons as more and more anglers are likely to catch forties so in effect you, and particularly Rambo, were to be my little extra insurance package. Another thing is my personal life has changed lately and I can't get to the pit so much as I used to, especially at night, so basically all I'm asking is for you and Rambo to keep an eye out for me. I had reckoned both of you would be fishing here a fair bit so you would be an ideal extra couple of pairs of eyes for me." Michael paused and I grudgingly thought that I wouldn't be here as much as *I'd* reckoned, let alone anyone else. "The other thing is because you're new, you haven't any ties with the others and hopefully you'll want to keep the place as it is for as long as you can. By keeping an eye on the pit you'll be helping yourselves and me out. I'll do the dirty work when it comes to getting rid of anyone who has misbehaved, should it ever get that far. I've become used to the awkwardness associated with such things so you won't be directly involved in the more unpleasant details."

"We'll look out for you," I said simply.

Michael nodded. "Thanks. If you turn up anything I'll show my appreciation by reducing your subs or something similar. The main thing is I don't want you to tell anyone else, it'll only cause aggravation, especially you both being new members. Some of the others will get jealous."

"Not even Holly... Gary?" I said surprised.

Michael shook his head vehemently. "No. Gary has been a rock concerning this place, without his help I don't suppose I would have ever succeeded like I have. But things do change and even he's not fishing as much as he used to. Despite his interest and success with women he's always found time to make carping his number one passion but lately that has altered."

"Oh," I uttered indifferently.

Michael's eyes fluttered but in a slightly more feverish manner than usual. "Yes, he told me a month ago he'd met a couple of stunning looking, lap dancing, ex-international gymnasts, who were also bisexual nymphomaniacs and it'd been the most fantastic three in a bed sex he'd ever experienced. Due to it being an ongoing affair carp fishing was now coming second."

My mind boggled. Who was coming first and third? The permutations of going to bed with a couple of bisexual women were mind blowing. I tried to grapple with the complexities of who might feasibly be doing what to whom while the other one was doing something or other to either one of the others, perhaps even both, or even to themselves. The endless possibilities of sexual deviance, especially when coupled (ha-ha) with sex toys seemed circular. He could be... while one of the girls were... while the other one... or the two girls would individually... while he... or perhaps both the girls would... while he... or he and one of the girls could... while the other one... or they all could... while they all watched each other and, even more seductively, the girls could execute every single one of the moves hanging upside down while doing the splits, still cavorting and arching and shimmying their perfect bodies in a climatic visual performance of erotic, sensual magnitude. I could see the attraction in it.

Two women in bed together at the same time. That alone would be the ultimate achievement, let alone with all the extra trimmings Hollywood had in the deal. It was another situation, like the ghost, which was beyond my sphere of reference and likely to ever be so. As a man though, you just had to think through the mechanics of it and pitifully I picked on the analogy of getting two runs at once. Which one do you pick on first? The better-looking run? How could you tell what was going to be on the end of it? Do you concentrate on hitting one take and seeing it out to the end and run the risk of losing the other one? What about trying to do both at once, a little twiddle on one rod, put it down, pick up the other, a little wind on the other reel, put it down, back to the first one, I mean, would it work? At least in fishing if you went the full distance with one rod you could try the other but with sex, not unless you were on something, that wasn't going to happen. In half an hour, yes, but that was hardly any good. On the bleak side two runs at once was likely to get you so excited you might pick one rod up and… pop! The hook was ejaculated and everyone was left embarrassed and unsatisfied. Another idea was to admit defeat and call for a mate to come round at the onset and hit the other rod. It wasn't the answer. For a start do they really count if you don't land them? Even if you did cast out and set the trap. The other thing was when your mate pulled his one out it might be bigger than yours. Maybe help of another kind was needed and, like your buzzers, new batteries were sure not to let you down. Fluky, bloody Hollywood had it to perfection with the girls willing to get to grips with each other and take some of the heat off of him… and think of the visual bonus! The jammy, sodding git!

"Go on, tell me one of their father's owns a brewery and the other one gets Ferrari's to road test," I said.

"Who'd give a toss if they did?" asked Michael.

"True. Lucky old Gary, eh? Still, I'll expect we'll all get a blow-job by blow-job account of the goings-on eventually. He seems to revel in telling you about that type of thing. I know he'll ram it down my throat about how he rammed it down both of theirs, in the end it'll be boring listening to his boring and I know I'll get the hump over repeatedly hearing about his repeated humping…" I stopped, I didn't want to alienate myself too much by having a pop at Michael's best mate and he was giving me a funny look. "How come you haven't mentioned all this stuff about Watt and the SS to Rambo? He's told me that you've seen him several times before?" I queried, diverting the conversation.

Michael was upfront and candid. "You seemed more approachable. I was less sure of how Rambo would react and it was you who featured the more prominently in my source's report." He glanced at his watch. "Look, I'm going to push off now, have a word with Rambo and square it with him. As I said, I can be very generous to those who help me, you won't lose out on the deal. Ok?"

"Fair enough, Michael, I'll see you later," I said, and seemingly satisfied he turned and walked off. I followed the sight of his scrawny, narrow shoulders and wondered when it was he'd last managed to eat a solid meal. Could it be he was so thin because he'd had fifteen years of appetite suppression caused by stress? I'd had it for a few days when I'd worried about telling Sophie about the cost of, and the entry into, the new syndicate, while she'd worried about informing me of her up the duff, bun in the oven, in the club, one up the spout, in the family way, expectant, with child, condition. It wasn't nice and I felt sorry for him.

The poor sod didn't have a lot going for him physically but it was a dead cert whatever he did have had been ravished by trying the keep the syndicate on a steady footing. Sure, he was autocratic and dictatorial but you had to be. Most good managers are strong and stand by their convictions and if you go into a position of trying to be friends with everyone you'll probably get pissed on. People, and especially carp anglers, don't say: 'He's a nice bloke we won't muck him about', they're more likely to say: 'He's as weak as dishwasher, let's do what we like'. It was a sad reflection on carpers but society was the same. You only had to look at law and order, minus a real deterrent and the chance of getting caught, add a load of liberal elite thinking which rejected individual responsibility and you had a soaring crime rate. Start dishing out a bit of serious shit to the scumbags who were the perpetrators and you might start making a few of them have second thoughts. But no, we couldn't do that. Welfare state? Disability pay? Unemployment benefit? All fantastic ideals and ones to uphold but so prone to the worst of human nature, the lazy, cheating, something for nothing, lead swinging, dependency traits which sadly made the genuine all get tarred with the same brush.

Perhaps I'd judged Michael too harshly. It was easy to rip the piss and mock his nervous afflictions and easy to be scornful about his unattractive physical attributes. I was positive Grant was right about Michael; I bet he had no life outside the syndicate, no wife or family (how hypocritical was I?), no other interests. His little tale of something cropping up and keeping him away from the pit was probably a white lie to hide the sad state of his life. He went home to an empty house mainly because he ran the best carp fishing syndicate in England. He'd never metamorphose into another Hollywood but he might have eaten better, kept himself better and totally rid himself of his horrid nerves had he not done so.

I asked myself how Michael coped with having such a good-looking best mate, who at this very moment was probably indulging in some explicit sexual act with two staggeringly pliable women? Hollywood spoke glibly of hundreds of women he'd bedded over the years but when had Michael last been indulged with some female company without paying for it? There. Even in my head I was cutting him down. The poor bastard, all to run a syndicate for us lot to be in. Without him it wouldn't exist. I don't suppose it had to be the way it was but I could easily comprehend how you could get sucked into it being so. Michael had lots of fishing contacts and I expect he had a few friends but the syndicate had probably lost him more and created some real enemies. Even his main mate, Hollywood, who seemed to be the only one he wasn't dictatorial towards, was rude to his face and talked him down behind his back. I'd decided I'd try and help Michael because like him and Pup I'd been there and didn't want to go back. Well, perhaps only a little way, which was probably a bit further than having a child would allow. The other thing was I had found another person who hated Tom Watt. It was only fair his pleasure in knowing I had despised Watt should be reciprocated.

As soon as Michael was gone I phoned Rambo up on my mobile to inform him what Michael had told me. Rambo was quite taken aback and like me pondered on the subject of who was the most likely source of his facts. It couldn't have been someone who was friendly with Watt, or you wouldn't have imagined so, but the rest of the original syndicate all seemed as plausible as each other. Maybe one of those had spoken to someone else who had spoken to someone else who… and so on. In the end we decided it didn't matter but we were both a bit nonplussed at the notion that events all those years ago had contributed to our passage into the present day syndicate. What goes around comes around and in this case it was true.

I told Rambo about Hollywood and the long period of silence that ensued after me relating his good fortune was followed by Rambo asking if I was winding him up. I assured him I was only winding him up if it turned out Michael was winding me up but my assessment of it was Michael had told me the truth as far as he was aware. Rambo suggested it might be a case of Hollywood winding Michael up, or taking things a step further, perhaps Hollywood had himself been wound up by the girls in question. I had to agree this might possibly be so; I had no means of verification so far down the line. Rambo submitted his final feelings on the matter and they were he'd believe it when he saw it. I told him that I'd be more than happy to see it and just hoped and prayed Hollywood had the foresight to get it all down on 8mm videotape. I did call into question the slight illogical discrepancy in Rambo's attitude, pointing out to him he was quite happy to accept my story of the ghost, yet felt unable to do the same for Hollywood's nights of three in a bed lust and lechery. Rambo finally admitted his qualms over the couple of quims under Hollywood's quilt were motivated purely by jealousy, and, like me, deep down, he knew it would be true.

Finally I told him about Michael suggesting we might like to become an extra couple of sets of eyes for him on the jiggery-pockery front. I said Michael had hinted at some sort of pecuniary reward should we turn up anything and I was more than happy to go along with it since he still loathed Watt as much as we had. Rambo concurred and asked if I'd told Michael anything about the ghost or his own hunch, to which I answered in the negative, saying I wasn't going to mention it to anybody for the moment. Rambo then went on to say he'd have to ring off now because his middle rod had a rip-roaring run on it and he'd phone back if it happened to be a forty.

I pressed the red button on my phone and gesticulated aggressively at my three mute buzzers. "Come on then, you useless bastards! Get on with it!"

The three of them ignored me and said nothing. Rambo never phoned and the late afternoon passed into evening and evening into dusk. Inside my bivvy I wasn't quite so cock-sure about being left alone by the ghost and a nagging apprehension set in my stomach. I didn't want to go through it all again. As it turned out my original thoughts were correct, I had an undisturbed night, not the least bothered by either ghosts, carp runs or stunning looking, lap dancing, ex-international gymnasts, who were also bisexual nymphomaniacs.

The session got into gear the next morning. At last some carp felt like feeding out by the island margin where two of my baits had been parked for the best part of eighteen hours. The first was a super fully scaled mirror that nudged my Reuben Heaton scales a smidgen past a complete circle, 31-2 and a fish which had to be photographed. Usually in this sort of instance I would have loped off down to where Rambo was fishing and got him to come up and wield the camera for me. That was out of the question this time, so, being a law-abiding member of the syndicate, when it suited me, I sacked the fish and set up my photographic gear.

The Canon Eos 500 went onto the tripod and was set up with its lens pointing towards a strategically placed unhooking mat. The mat had been placed out of shadow and to the fore of a nice leafy background. I had no junk in the background of my photos, at least when I had the wit to remember. I put an adjustable bankstick to the side of the mat and I knelt down in fish holding pose and checked the top of the bankstick was a few inches above my head. I then went back to the camera, pushed in the jack plug of the remote switch and framed the bankstick and mat. I'd had the lead of the remote switch lengthened from its original and useless few inches to one of around fifteen foot, which meant I could hold a fish and snap myself. Thanks to this I could run the cable out to a position alongside the mat all ready for later. I auto-focused on the bankstick so that it was roughly right (the button on the remote would focus and release the shutter when needed), checked the framing again and then removed the bankstick. Now all I had to do was go and get my photographic partner, get her out of the sack on the unhooking mat and hold her while pushing the remote's button. Pushing the button with a slimy right hand that was also required to grip hold of a carp's anal fin was the trickiest part of the manoeuvre, especially if the carp was misbehaving and being generally awkward. If this was the case the right hand had to produce some seriously contorted dexterity, a bit similar, I'd always imagined, to the fretwork antics of the average angst-ridden lead guitarist.

Apart from this the only other consideration to take place was what sort of demeanour to put on for the camera. Carp, being carp, tend to always go for the wide-eyed look of vacancy and to be honest they do lack the quality we humans call 'character'. Not even the most avid of carping head cases, on drugs or otherwise, could lay claim to seriously implying carp had character. You could tell one from another, by its markings, and there were certain fish that got caught more than others and from specific areas more than others but you couldn't call it character. They're fish. Take a picture of one and capture the moment of capture and you've got a fish on fishmonger's slab. Inanimate, a cold unblinking eye, gob either open or shut, usually depending on whether the angler holding it had stuck a finger in it and that was about it. The size and bulk might be impressive but nobody looked upon the photo of a fish and said: 'Ah, look at the expression on its face'. Therefore the onus on character falls heavily upon the angler. It is he who has to impart his personality into the photo to compensate for the lack of it from the carp. Fortunately there are lots of ways to do this, that's why carp trophy shots are so varied and so endlessly interesting and absorbing. For a start you can either kneel down or squat down, or, this is a brilliant one, squat on one leg while you kneel on the other. Of course if you're feeling radical you can change leg within this structure as well. Next you can either hold the carp with its head to the left or to the right and you can either smile or look fucking miserable. Now, if you want to smile, the happy smiley face is always direct to lens. You can look fucking miserable to lens but it doesn't really work. If you want to bring over the sheer trauma of being a super-serious, fuck me I put some hours in for this one, mega-pro, big-time, I can cast four hundred yards and go in for fish in the middle of January because my bait boat has an attachment so it can double as an ice-breaker carpmeister... look down at the carp and look fucking miserable. Not at the camera. *Not* at the camera, ok? I can't stress that strongly enough. If you look at the camera on that sort of pose you lose credibility points, big style, because you haven't any.

Once, due to the myriad of poses mentioned, I took it upon myself, on a long session a few years ago, to actually work out how many different types of carp angling trophy shots there were. Obviously I couldn't account for every subtle nuance, even though I had a calculator with me and the session had lasted a week. I decided to group things together where they made no discernable difference to the overall concept of the photo and by doing this I came to the conclusion there were two. One is where you successfully hold a carp and take a trophy shot. Two is where it flaps just as you or your mate presses the button. In that photo you come out with a face like a bulldog chewing a wasp with a one ton weight tied to its bollocks via a slipknot with the other end attached to a heavily laden skateboard rolling down a slight incline and the carp gets its underbelly in focus like a starship in Return of the Jedi.

Anyway, I got a number one of the thirty fully scaled and still had forty-eight hours to go. It wouldn't go too quick, it was two whole days. Imagine being made to sit in a field on a chair for two days. It'd last a lifetime.

Chapter 11

"Yes, your blood pressure is fine," said the nurse. She gently pulled the Velcro fixing apart on the black material she had wrapped around Sophie's upper arm and gathered it along with the gauge, tube and rubber bulb into a neat arrangement and put it away. "I hope you've remembered your urine sample for me," she asked kindly of Sophie.

Sophie nodded and took a small container out of her bag and gave it to the nurse. "There you are," she said.

"Good. Now in a minute I'm going to take some blood for testing, it'll involve me putting a needle into your arm and syringing some out. It's very routine," she gave Sophie an assuring smile, "and it won't hurt at all."

The nurse busied herself with the syringe and attached a needle after opening the sterile packaging. "When is the baby due?"

"November. The middle of November," Sophie replied.

"Is it your first one," the nurse enquired further.

Sophie nodded with a girlish grin. "Yes. My first child and still another 27 weeks until he or she is born. It's all so new and exciting but it still seems a long way away."

The nurse smiled warmly and turned her attention to me. "It'll flash by, don't worry, and in no time at all you'll have a newborn baby."

The paradox of time. It had fairly whistled by for me during my three-day session at the syndicate and was likely to carry on at a similar rate until I was lumbered with fatherhood. For Sophie it would be dawdling along, a never ending expanse of time like a vast ocean to be crossed before her day came and yet the same period would be like stepping over a brook for myself. Lumbered with fatherhood. I wasn't exactly covering myself in glory over this dad thing. The problem being the syndicate was even more interesting than it was originally and my heart begged for me to be there. My brain, while trying to temper my heart, was kidding itself, if the truth be told, and every minute I was away from the syndicate was spent trying to work out the quickest method of getting back there without my head getting bitten off.

It wasn't simply the three thirties I'd caught on the last session or the prospect of naming a new forty or of even catching the first fifty from the water that was so enthralling. It was the chilling buzz of the ghost's visitation and the unsolved murder with the who, what with, why, when and what for questions attached which added so much more. As Rambo had said, a new dimension and he was so correct. There was also Michael's offer to the pair of us coupled with Rambo's hunch and, on my part at least, a desire to repay his trust in us by letting us join. This desire was manifested by a feeling of slight guilt I felt about the way I'd judged Michael and because there was a bond between the three of us, it being that we had all, at one time or another, hated Watt.

I wanted to unearth trouble and be the one, with Rambo, who told Michael about it. I wanted to solve the mystery of the ghost and help its tortured soul to be laid to rest. I also wanted to catch a new forty and revel in the atmosphere of my new syndicate as much as I could. Extra time fishing went hand in glove with increasing the probability of being able to sort out all the other items on my wish list.

I wanted it all. What I didn't want was any electrical work, any decorating, or anything appertaining to the baby, whether shopping for clothes, cots, baby seats, toys, you name it, which involved my input. I wasn't interested in it. It was that grim. I had, however, learnt my lesson from the past. Although not interested in all of those things, I forced myself to do a modicum of them to buy myself more time fishing and to not be the truly dreadfully obsessed person I was when I had learnt to hate Watt. Some might say I was still pretty dreadful at the moment but the child in Sophie's womb still failed to have any positive pull on me. On the other hand the yearning to be at the syndicate was pulling like Hollywood at a nightclub, like a nitro-dragster on the strip, like an F1-11 climbing in the sky. The pit was a giant electro-magnet and I was a single iron filing. The compass in my head, so vulnerable to the magnet, always pointed towards the pit.

It wasn't easy keeping up the pretence but I owed it to Sophie. I told myself I would have the riddles of the syndicate solved by the end of the summer and with the weather having turned colder by the time of the birth I'd be in a much better state to come to grips with being a good father as opposed to being a crap prospective one. I chose not to consider the prospect of being unable to unravel the mysteries before me or of the greenhouse effect giving us another ridiculously mild winter or of what would happen the following spring.

"There. All done," said the nurse holding up the crimson liquid in the glass container.

I stared at it. How bright it was and such a powerful colour as well. It was the colour of life, pulsing through our bodies and every now and then coming out of it in some degree or another. I thought of the rest of Sophie's blood coursing around the placenta and feeding the tiny but growing nugget which had stuck itself to her insides. I thought about how much of it Rambo must have seen in his time as battered and blown-up bodies had been punctured by various hard and sharp metallic objects. Then I moved onto the ghost and the sickening blows that had rained down on it as I'd experienced its pain and the feel of hot, sticky blood oozing out of its body and with it life itself ebbing away. Bloody hell. And undoubtedly the last two notions in my head were exactly that.

"Ok, all done," said the nurse. "We'll see you again in four weeks for your scan and your first peek at the baby."

It was on one morning, a few days after the visit to the antenatal clinic, when I was attempting to get some more decorating done in the baby's room, a certain deceased person called on me. It wasn't the ghost who wafted up the stairs it was another dead person, which in its way was nearly as unnerving. I'd heard the doorbell ring but hadn't heard any voices after Sophie had opened the door. She had called up the stairs.

"Matt! There's someone here to see you! He's coming up, ok?"

"Right ho!" I had shouted as I carried on sandpapering the window board. I had no idea who it was but assumed it was my dad, popping in to see how I was getting on.

"All right, boy," said the voice. Its owner surveyed the scene in front of it. "You'd make a good painter and decorator... cry!"

It was Rambo, in ex-army boots, camouflage trousers, olive coloured tee shirt and camouflage jacket. I wondered what his suggestions on the colour scheme might be? A dash of brown here, a daub of green there, some khaki everywhere. I didn't bother to ask.

"Hello, mate!" I said caught slightly on the hop. Rambo hardly ever popped by. In all the time I'd known him the only occasion he had ever come to my house was when he had stayed the night before our early morning departure to Lac Fumant and a sneaky visit while Sophie was out soon after my release from clink. My pulse quickened, something must be up.

"To what do I owe the pleasure of this pleasant surprise?" I asked and then suddenly twigged it. "You've caught a forty haven't you, you jammy sod?" I snapped my fingers and left my index finger pointing at him, horizontal style, as a new revelation hit me. "A new forty!"

"Funny you should say that," said Rambo grinning from ear to ear. "I suppose you *could* call it a new forty," he continued in exaggerated fashion, "but it wouldn't be a *very* accurate statement because it was only a *forty* on the way..." Rambo looked down into my curious eyes and gave me a massive double eyebrow lift, "... to becoming a *fifty!*"

"What!" I said. Gormless to the power of three.

"A fifty. Fifty pounds. A new fifty. Never been caught at forty, just ploughed through the bait and naturals and got caught by me at over fifty. Fifty pounds and nine, count them right there, boy, ounces. Pit record, thank you very much, caught on one of those fucking Pup pop-ups."

"You bastard!" I said with real feeling. "You jammy, sodding bastard. You're luckier than bloody Hollywood." Rambo lifted his eyebrows again and moved his head backwards while tucking in his chin. "Ok. Strike that from the record, but even so. What are you going to call it? It's a new forty so you have the right to call it whatever you want?"

Rambo shot me a flashing grin. "I thought it should be a name that reflected the glory of the fish and one which encapsulated its awe-inspiring rate of growth. I didn't want a name to humanise a wild creature. I didn't want a name to belittle it. I didn't want one that made reference to its physical form but above all I didn't want one which epitomised the low grade, poorly educated, idle mentality of the crass carp-naming sub-culture."

"Very worthy of you. So?" I could see where this one was going.

"So I called it, Steroid. Anabolic Steroid to give it its full name and the nickname is Bulkbomb, that being the colloquial phrase for the said synthetic steroid hormone."

"Ah! What else. How charming," I said and then paused. "Still, not as big as my one on the pop-ups," I reminded him.

"French fish!" Rambo teased. "Mine's made in England, born and breed!"

"How do you know?" I said, joining in the game.

"Michael said so," Rambo replied like a little boy in the playground.

"Michael's said a lot of things, are all of them true?"

Rambo ignored my question. "English fish, boy. Better, harder to catch, worth at least four of your ten-a-penny, fifty-a-chuck, easy-peasy, not-worth-a-light, any Noddy can catch one, French crap."

"Say's who?" I asked with mock belligerence.

"Everyone!" said Rambo stridently.

"Everyone?" I queried.

"Everyone who thinks that English fish are better, harder to catch, worth at least four, ten-a-penny, fish-a-chuck, easy-peasy, not-worth-a-light, any Noddy can catch one, French crap."

"Well, they would do," I protested. "Carp are carp, mate. You can't differentiate between one country and another and say one country's carp are easier to catch than another country's."

"You can," said Rambo. "Generally speaking if you had to catch a forty pounder in a week and could either fish in England or France, where would you fish?"

"France," I answered.

It was Rambo's turn to point an index finger. "Exactly. Because they're easier to catch."

"No!" I said firmly. "No, no, no. Because there are more of them in France, which makes it more likely, through chance, you'd catch one. Not because they're inherently easier to catch. That would depend on the water itself, how much pressure the carp had seen, how many of them there were and how big the water was. Carp aren't indigenous to this country, statement of fact, so how have they become so clever by being in this country, for what ever length of time it may be, when its lineage is foreign."

"The English weather makes them more intelligent. By being exposed to English weather and subsequently by being immersed in English rainwater they've become more intelligent," said Rambo fighting back laughter.

"You're grasping," I told him.

"English fish are better and harder to catch," said Rambo.

"You're repeating yourself," I reminded him.

"English fish are better and harder to catch," said Rambo again. "They mean more than French fish."

"Is that an echo I can hear?" I asked, cocking a hand to my ear. "And I'll tell you what, when I caught that French fifty it meant everything to me. Fuck what anybody else thought about it."

Rambo winked. "Touché, boy. Touché."

For the rest of the day we drank tea and talked about Rambo's latest capture and got on with the decorating. It was Rambo's suggestion and I didn't hesitate in saying yes. Typical of everything he did Rambo was brilliant at rubbing down and quick with it. His powerful arm worked the sandpaper into a blur and he whizzed round the skirting board and both sides of the door in half the time I would have taken. I'd already emulsioned the ceiling and coving white and the lining wallpaper in two pastel colours with dividing border, suitable for either sex, so it was undercoat time for the woodwork. Forget Rambo, come in Rambobrant the well-known painter. Rambo's cutting in showed a steady hand and fine hand/eye co-ordination and again he was very quick. There's rough and slow and there's quick and neat, the two opposite ends of the spectrum and Rambo was up in the violet end of neatness.

At lunch Sophie brought up some sandwiches and mugs of tea and looked approvingly at what we'd done. "It looks nice, Matthew, it's really coming on. Once we've sorted out the carpet, curtains and baby things it will look lovely. You've certainly done a lot this morning. You don't fancy coming round to help him every day do you, Rambo?"

Rambo laughed. "Well you never know, I might help him do some electrical work as well if he asks nicely."

Both Sophie and I were taken aback. "Really?" I exclaimed.

Rambo nodded. "Yeah. I don't mind giving you a hand on some jobs. I don't need the money, but if I help you'll get them done quicker and earn a few quid more."

"If you help Rambo, he'll pay you," said Sophie in a very heartfelt tone. "You've already helped us more than we could ever hope to repay you, in fact we never did, not for all the time you paid our mortgage while…" Sophie struggled for a word to call me, "… silly, there, was in jail."

Rambo looked unconcerned. "He paid for the Lac Fumant trip and as I said at the time it's all water under the bridge. I'll help him provided, and I hope you don't mind me saying this Sophie, you let him come fishing with me for the time I save on the job. I don't want payment, just a little extra fishing time with my mate."

Sophie looked a little bit shocked. I felt shocked but rather more than a paltry little bit. What on earth was Rambo playing at? This was very dangerous territory, if it didn't come off it could make things even more difficult for me.

"Well, I… I'm at a loss for words," she started. " Gosh! You'd do that so he could go fishing with you?" she asked incredulously.

Rambo nodded once again. "This season will be the boy's last fling before becoming a dad," he said easily. "Why, only the other day he was saying once the baby's born he'd have a different set of priorities in his life. Matt said he couldn't see himself wanting to go fishing quite so much because he'd want to spend more time with the baby, didn't you?" Rambo looked over at me and I gave a laugh, trying desperately not to make it appear too self-conscious and forced. Rambo continued. "Underneath it all he's pretty excited I can tell you, he keeps on about it all the time, wondering what it'll be like to be a dad, not that I know, never having been one you see." Rambo looked reflective while I was treading water in treacle trying to get a handle on what he was saying. "To begin with he was a bit unsure but now he's really looking forward to it. 'A new phase in my life', he calls it. I didn't think carp fishing would ever be knocked off its podium but once the two of you are three, or four, he's mentioned the possibility of twins, I reckon it will be. I don't suppose he's said as much to you, what with us men being men and keeping all that sort of stuff zipped up inside us."

The cunning whelp, I got his drift. A slight over-egging of the pudding with the bit about the twins but not bad. Would she go for it? My heart thudded.

Sophie wasn't quite dumbstruck but not far. Her face broke into a huge smile and she melted. "Matthew! Rambo's right, you haven't said anything to me. Do you really feel that way now?"

I looked at her and smiled and gave her a dorky shrug of my shoulders and she rushed over and hugged me. I hugged her back tightly and as I did I could feel the slight bump of her stomach push into mine. It was the first time I'd noticed it and a wave of guilt swept over me as I played my part in Rambo's artful treachery. That's not to say the wave of guilt could wash away the lighthouse of hope and saviour, with its beaming torch lighting the way towards more carping time. No sir. I wanted to pull it off but I did get a pang of self-reproach.

The pair of us separated. "Go on with the pair of you," she said. "I'm not that daft to believe he's been quite so star-struck as you say, Rambo."

Rambo turned over his hand and showed an upturned palm. "A little over the top," he said, crinkling up his nose, "but he's changed and so will his situation, so I'd like to help him make the most of this summer and autumn if it's all right by you."

Bizarre! Here was a man who had killed umpteen people, including himself, tip-toeing around a young pregnant woman, telling her what she wanted to hear, in a schoolboy farce that bordered on: 'Can he come out and play with me today, madam?'

"As long as the bedroom's ready..." Sophie started.

"We'll finish it tomorrow," said Rambo quickly.

"... And he pays the syndicate fees out of what he earns..." she continued.

"No sweat," promised Rambo. "I've actually got some work to do for some mates, they'll be good earners as well."

"...And... so long as he isn't stuck at the gravel pit when I go into labour," Sophie said, with her tongue in her cheek.

"Hmm," said Rambo. "I can't guarantee that!"

Sophie laughed. "You men! You're completely mad!" She stopped laughing and shook her head. Her long, straight black hair flowed from side to side and her body language, she had both of her fists propped on her hips and her legs were astride, was positive and self-confident. She looked flushed from the laughing and as I gazed at her I really noticed, now that she was well and truly over her morning sickness, how gorgeous she looked. As the small baby inside blossomed so did she. She was more like a woman now, whereas before I had her marked down as a mere girl. She looked radiant, her hair appeared even more lustrous of late and her complexion looked glowing and full of life, as if it mirrored her condition. The very tiny bump only hinted at it but now her breasts were more full than they had been and soon any casual observer would see she was pregnant. Pregnant with my child. Not only did she look absolutely ravishing but there were all the other parts to her that were not simply physical beauty. Her kindness, her honesty, her high morality and her ability to put up with a tosser like me who had put her through the grinder time and time again. The carp fishing grinder. And with the aid of my mate I was about to dupe her once again, admittedly in a much smaller way, so I could carry on grinding. I was overcome with guilt again and a large amount of self-disgust, it was like carrying out adultery only the other woman was carp angling.

Hadn't I thought about all the ruined lives of countless children when Sophie had originally told me of her pregnancy? Hadn't I been quick to condemn their hapless, hopeless parents and yet what was I up to? Hastily I told myself I wasn't a parent yet and could still redeem myself even if I went along with Rambo's ploy because I knew, deep down inside, it was impossible for me to deny it and not want to do it. Despite my guilt, despite my love for Sophie and despite the fact I was aiming to pull the wool over her eyes again I had to do it. She might possibly even understand, given I wasn't singularly driven by catching carp this time, because the visitation by the ghost was enough to intrigue anyone. If it ever got resolved I'd tell her but not now, not at this time. I had until the birth of a new life to discover the truth about one so violently taken away. And if I didn't? Perhaps I'd have to let it go but inside I felt confident. I'd pulled it off under pressure and within a time scale at Lac Fumant, so why couldn't I do it again?

"Is it all right, then," I asked.

"Yes, it's all right," said Sophie, letting out a sigh of resignation. "Why did I ever fall in love with someone who loves fishing so much?"

"There are worse things," I said meekly.

"I know. You could have been a drug dealer and ended up in prison, rather than being a carp angler who ended up in prison," said Sophie sarcastically. "I expect there are women equally fed up at being golf widows or football widows or boozing widows. I wonder how all those men would feel if their women spent as much time out or away from home?"

"It'd suit me," said Rambo. "All the time they were out, I could go fishing!"

Sophie gave a rueful grin and went over and jabbed her finger in Rambo's solar plexus. "Ow!" he muttered, tenderly rubbing the spot.

"Promise me, *no* hand grenades, you big lummox!"

"I promise," said Rambo.

"Good, because I'm holding *you* responsible for the welfare of *him*," said Sophie pointing at me. With that she turned around and strutted out of the bedroom. As she left I caught sight of a huge smile on her face.

"Feisty!" said Rambo. "Is she like that in bed?"

"Never you mind," I told him. "Did she really hurt you when she jabbed her finger in your guts?"

Rambo laughed. "You can't hurt anyone doing that. Look."

In a flash Rambo jabbed me in my solar plexus. I felt the wind rush out of me and I doubled up in agony. "I see what you mean," I gasped. "How could I have suggested anything so laughable?" Eventually I straightened up and got my breath back. "Are you serious about what you said to Sophie, you know about helping me out and doing some work for some friends?"

"Too right, boy," said Rambo and then his face clouded a little. "You didn't mind me setting out the plan did you? It worked a dream, provided it's what you want, and I was sure it was otherwise I wouldn't have done it."

"Yeah, it's cleared the way to get there a lot more," I said gratefully, not wanting to show my initial reservations and guilt, not now I'd squared it in my head anyway.

"It'll be a whole lot more," Rambo said mysteriously.

"What do you mean," I asked.

Rambo explained. "Well, all these jobs for my mates don't exist, but they do, if you see what I mean and funnily enough they're all a long way away and we'll have to stay in digs to do them economically. Not that we'll be working, we'll be fishing. We can say we'll be working for a week here and a week there but we won't, we'll be fishing for a week here and a week there."

It sounded great but I saw a snag. "What about the money we're supposed to be earning from all this work?"

"I'm not earning any, I'm working for nothing, remember? You'll be the one who's earning."

"Ok," I said, a bit frustrated at Rambo's pedantic stance. "So what about the money *I'm* supposed to be earning?"

Rambo gave a throwaway gesture with his hand. "Oh, I'll pay you the money."

"What?"

"Look, Matt," said Rambo completely deadpan. "I've got more money than I'll ever need now I've killed myself and got everything financially sound and if it costs me a few grand to get you fishing this year then I'm not fussed one bit."

"Wow!" I said slowly, perturbed at both the offer and the fact he'd called me 'Matt' rather than 'boy'. "I don't know if I can take money after what happened before, besides we're not exactly hard up after the lottery win."

Rambo put up a hand to shut me up. "Only the other day I got 100k come in on the insurance payout for my own death. I'm flush, don't even worry about it."

I considered what Rambo had said and my mind diverted to a tangent. "How come you've never bought your own water?"

"When I'm older, I think," Rambo mused. "I'm in a position now to consider it as a viable option but that hasn't been the situation until the last few months. If I did do it I'd want to build the thing from scratch and that takes time. In the meantime I'd still want to be fishing a quality venue, somewhere like we are at the moment. The answer is to fish other places and start up your own as a sideline and see how it develops. Now, are you up for it or not? I'll pay you the money in cash and you can make out false invoices to make it look even more realistic. I'm sure Sophie won't give a monkey's where the money's coming from once it starts rolling in."

"Sure," I said. He didn't know Sophie that well. She'd have been mortified to know the truth. I'd have to play it very carefully to make sure it all looked legit and still make the effort to be with her when she really wanted me there. "Here! Did you tell Michael about the new forty... I mean, fifty?"

"Yeah, I gave him a ring. He wasn't his usual self and I did detect a slight softening from his abrupt line, especially when I told him I was happy with the offer he'd made to you about keeping an eye on things."

I looked down at the floor and hesitated at asking my next question. It had to be asked because I'd only thought of it a few minutes ago. "Rambo?"

"What?"

"Can I ask you something? Be honest. Why are you going to so much trouble to get me to the pit? It's not solely for my wonderful company or as a final fling before I depart into the black mire known as 'family life', is it?"

Rambo shook his head. "No. It's not that selfless of me, but I guess you've sussed that out. To be honest my hunch hasn't proved to be correct so far but your thing with the ghost, well... I don't know what to make of it. I went in those old woods and I followed the line of the broken branches from the one you showed me, the snapped twigs, the displaced leaves, I followed them right back to the place where it seemed to have started. When I got there I searched and searched in those fallen leaves for a fair while and found nothing. If there was anything to be found there I would have found it. That type of thing has been part and parcel of all my working life, a mistake made, a clue missed could mean the difference between life and death, yet I found nothing." Rambo rubbed the stubble on the end of his large square jaw. "I haven't got whatever it is you've got. You don't know what it is, so I'm as sure as hell certain I don't. I would never have caught the mind-meld mirror, the ghost would never have visited me but I can help you pin down in this reality whatever clues come into your head, wherever the fuck it is they come in from.

Like I said to you before, this whole episode has got to me, this life after death thing, and as I also said, I'd like to resolve it. I won't do it on my own, or rather I can't do it on my own, but if I can help you get to the pit as much as possible the pair of us might. Something cruel happened in that wood, one fact we can be positive of, but apart from that it's all a big mystery. One I haven't a single clue or suggestion towards solving."

"To be honest, mate, I haven't much of an idea either," I admitted. "We'll get to the pit as much as we can and see what turns up. Not very scientific, I know, but it's worked for me before."

Rambo gave a tiny smile. "Something's turned up already," he said.

I felt my flesh creep and the hairs on the back of my neck tingled. I felt goose bumps on my bare arms down from where my tee-shirt sleeves ended. "What has?" I hissed.

"After I caught the fifty I felt as if I needed to calm down a bit so I reeled in my rods and went around the pit for a walk. I went up to the north end, to the swim where you had the visitation and had a nose around. Nobody was fishing the top bank because I checked in all the swims, then I went to see if I could spot the first broken branch you had showed me from the track. It was still there, hanging down from the last bit of bark and I thought to myself I might have missed something when I'd looked in the leaves the time before." Rambo fixed me with his hard, cold eyes. "So I went and looked again."

"What did you find?" The words barely came out.

Rambo looked away as if he was bitter. "Fuck all. I was stupid to think someone as good as myself would make a mistake." His eyes turned back on me and his huge fist reached out and grabbed a scruff of my shirt and he pulled me closer to him. "And then I noticed it," he said, his lips pulled tight over his top teeth.

"What was it?" I croaked as my legs began to shake.

It wasn't a thing," said Rambo, whose face was so close to mine I could feel his hot breath. "'It', was something was different."

"Different?" I whispered hoarsely. "What do you mean something was different?"

Rambo slackened his grip on my shirt a little. "Something was different from when I'd left it. I'm not sure what it was that was different, all I can is say that something was different."

"Meaning?" I asked.

Rambo yanked me back towards him with such velocity I felt as if I was on a switchback fairground ride. Our noses were an inch apart. "Meaning, somebody else has been back there. Somebody who may have noticed the branch and found their way to the spot by chance, or more likely," Rambo squeezed my shirt so hard that some of my chest hairs were ripped out, "somebody was returning to the scene of the crime. That somebody being the murderer of the person who is now the ghost."

Chapter 12

"Why do they do that?" I asked Rambo as the pair of us sped to the pit in a van not laden with electrical tools and materials but carp fishing equipment.

"Do what?"

"Why do murderers return to the scene of the crime?"

Rambo gave the nicety some consideration. "I don't know. I've never gone back to a place where I've stiffed someone, but then killing someone in a war zone is hardly murder. Not unless you're one of those non-confrontational pacifists."

"It could be a common misconception," I theorised. "It might only happen in movies and books and not in real life. A detective might know, one who investigates murders, I expect there's a grim pattern to it all, like there is to many things involving us humans."

"I know in most cases of homicide the person who gets killed is usually either related to the murderer or at least knows him," said Rambo. "Getting bumped off by a complete stranger is relatively rare. Not that you'd be impressed with a statistic like that if you were minding your own business, doing a bit of carping, and some maniac comes along and blows you away with a Magnum."

"Our ghost knew his killer. I wish we did," I replied sincerely.

"Me too," agreed Rambo. "You see what bothers me is the problem of whether it's a current member of the syndicate, an old member of the syndicate or someone utterly detached from it. You would think the chances of a person who wasn't a member coming back to check up on an event which happened God knows how many years ago were slim. On the other hand it's a pretty good place to knock someone off and hide a body. There might have been a time between the gravel pit workings stopping and Michael starting up the fishing when hardly a soul would have ever visited the place. If it were an old syndicate member he's taking an almighty risk coming back, surely it wouldn't be worth it? It's more likely the killer noticed the one broken branch and it set the alarm bells ringing and he, I doubt if there are any females involved, couldn't stop themselves from going in to have a look. I bet it put the shits up him when he saw my investigation all marked out on the ground."

"You say that," I said, "but if there was nothing there to be found because the area was clean, even you didn't find anything, why would they worry about it? Why would a broken branch a few yards into the wood point to anybody finding something...?"

"At least fifty yards away," Rambo answered,

"Exactly! Fifty yards away. You see what I mean? Another thing is, could they come in a back way? Possibly if they came in from the north side of the old wood they'd have no fear of being detected by anglers or anyone else. The broken branch might not have entered into the equation one iota."

"Good point," conceded Rambo.

"Disregarding the killer," I continued. "What about the victim? He's even more elusive. How on earth would you begin to find out about him? Search old records for missing persons from this part of the country? What records though? Old newspapers going back how long? Police records?" I snorted. "But I don't think you'll be too keen on pursuing that course of action."

Rambo laughed. "Not really. I'm ninety-nine percent sure I've covered all my tracks but I don't want the police to start sniffing around either of us." Rambo let out a laugh. "What could you tell them? No tangible evidence whatsoever and only your very unbelievable and highly unlikely visit from the ghost. We'd get scoffed out the station most probably but if they did take an interest it could open a nasty can of worms, ruin the fishing, scare off the carp and the killer. No, this one is down to us. Me and my muscle and you with your… whatever the fuck it is that can reach over to ghosts and huge mirror carp."

So there it was. Not much to ask was it? Solve a carp syndicate murder before my first child popped out, or was dragged with sterilized forceps into the world. At least with Rambo's ruse working a treat on Sophie we did have a good deal more time at our disposal. The pair of us had finished the baby's bedroom the following day as promised and, on Rambo's suggestion, we had carried on and decorated the whole of the upstairs landing, the stairwell and the hallway downstairs. We had worked like Trojans, in fact it reminded me of the time the pair of us had mixed up bait in Rambo's flat all those years ago. In those long distance days I had worked myself into a frazzle so as to try and keep up with the unknown man mountain along side me and not wimp out on him. Now it was the bond of friendship and shared goals which drove me onward and the decorating ceased to be a chore and became a means to an ends.

Our relationship had changed since those days when I was physically afraid of him. Much had happened since then, most of it bordering on the amazing and unlikely, but this was the zenith of weirdness. The two of us decorating my house, firstly to accommodate my first born, secondly to appease the woman I loved, thirdly to manipulate her into letting me go fishing, fourthly to catch big carp, fifthly to prove Rambo's hunch, sixthly to help put the ghost's soul to rest and finally to find the murderer and solve the syndicate's dark secret. If indeed it was the syndicate's dark secret and not somebody else's and it just happened to take place on our little bit of the world.

Belting along in the van we were supposedly on a job for one of Rambo's 'mates', guess for how long? Bearing in mind the longest session you could fish for was a week. No, wrong, nine days! Let me explain. Rambo's idea was to turn up, bivvy up, fish for seven days, pack up, sod off, sneak back, bivvy up again, this time deep in the old wood and keep an eye on things for the remaining couple of days.

"Bivvy up in the old wood?" I'd exclaimed, in wide-eyed horror. "Fuck that!"

Rambo had seemed unflustered. "We'll be all right, boy," he'd said. "Besides you didn't seem overly concerned at going back and fishing in the swim where the ghost came to see you."

"The ghost wasn't out to get me, only to make contact with me. You haven't seen tree branches change into snakes, gargoyle faces and hideous beasts," I'd told him. "The old wood seems evil of its own accord."

Rambo had shrugged. "Whatever. Look, boy, if there's anything going on it isn't going to happen when anyone's around. All we can hope to do is be there when others think we aren't and hope nobody else comes along. Then, if we're very lucky, we might see something we shouldn't, if you get my drift."

I wasn't convinced. It was a long shot, even if we stayed for two whole days the chances of us being around when an occurrence, whatever it was likely to constitute, happened was very slim. Still, my life seemed to be a series of long shots when you analysed it so perhaps fate would pull it out of the hat for me again. It crossed my mind while on the subject, the possibility of one day continuing my memoirs from the end of my first attempt to set the record straight about Watt and Co. So much had happened it was plausible it would entertain someone somewhere if I could get it down on paper. Huh! Like I had time. I only did the first part because I was in clink. Still, if this affair went tits up and I found myself back in there again I could at least set about doing it then. Sophie could come and visit me with my as yet unseen child. I let it go. It was clear that the prospect of bivvying up in the old wood, even with Rambo alongside me, was making me go a bit mental.

"How are we going to get into the old wood without being seen?" I asked wearily. I could see there was no way out of it, Rambo had made up his mind.

"I bought an Ordnance Survey map so it should be simple enough to find our way in from the north end. I'm not sure how far the land Michael owns stretches so we might have to do a spot of trespassing. The other thing is we'll have to park up out of sight and well away from the area so a nice little yomp looks on the cards as well."

Rapture! Bivvied up in the wood from hell and a gut buster of a hike to make for the pleasure of it. At least I'd seven whole days fishing before having to worry about it and, looking on the very positive side, we might find some clues during that period. Then we wouldn't have to bivvy up in the wood. Williams, I told myself, you'll end up bivvied up in the woods.

The journey to the pit was uneventful and so was the setting up. Getting the rods into play was no more noteworthy than usual and the whole session had an air of utter normality about it. As a bonus, at least on the fishing front, we had the pit to ourselves and the first three days epitomised every reason why you would pay the big money we had to get into it. Fishing in my swim up by the island I saw no one apart from Rambo and I only saw him once a day. Likewise he was unpestered down in his favoured south-east point swim and the carp, well the carp played ball, like they often do at this time of the year, it being the back end of May. Four thirties to me and five of them to Rambo along with another six fish between us all weighing in around the upper twenty mark. For three days it really was superb fishing.

I couldn't believe we were all alone on the pit, I would have thought that the place would have been crawling with anglers but it wasn't. In the end I marked it down to Michael's shrewdness in choosing syndicate members and being able to suss them out. He had clearly chosen his twenty members well, successfully managing to somehow judge their personal situations, finances, carp time budget so as not to create an overly busy water. Full timers and sponsored anglers never stood a chance of getting in and because of that it made it better for all those who were. The peace and solitude were all encompassing, I was in my own little world in my head and my head was in another little world which comprised the pit. As I soaked up the atmosphere and the sense of being so far away from the rest of civilisation, a bit of an illusion seeing as we were actually in Kent, I came to an obvious conclusion. It was a very good place to commit murder, what with so much space, so few humans and so much cover, it had to be said. And I said it to myself time and time again during those large gaps of inactivity involved in carp fishing.

I churned the happening over and over, trying to get a fresh angle on it but to little or no avail. The nuts and bolts of it were that there had been a murder in the old wood which was both brutal and thuggish. For some reason a burning spirit or soul had been created at the time of physical death which was bent on justice and revenge. I had been contacted, somehow and by some inexplicable means, and all the raw emotion of the murder had been transferred from it to me and then it had gone, whooshing over the pit after asking for my help. Rambo had traced the trail of damage from the ghost's shimmering haze of wind back through the old wood and he'd scoured the wood's floor, perusing the fallen foliage for any hint of the dark deed. He hadn't found any. It was only on his second return that he had noticed it. The 'it', as he explained, being something was different, intimating a person unknown, possibly the murderer, had returned to the scene of the crime. Who else other than the murderer would have had cause to look there? Had they been warned of something afoot by the broken branch? The affirmative to both these last two questions seemed the most likely. To be truthful I was at a loss to see how Rambo could know something was different when he couldn't tell me exactly what it was. It didn't seem to make much sense, but Rambo being Rambo, and this sort of thing falling within his sphere of expertise, I took it as fact.

With no recourse to police records or other documents it did seem to be a cul-de-sac situation but as I'd mentioned before I had my faith in something turning up. Regularly through those first three days something did, to the call of the buzzer, another thirty or high twenty and due to them I wallowed in my carping decadence. Yet with nobody else around and nothing new to go on concerning the syndicate's possible dark secret no headway was made in that department. I hadn't expected otherwise. Thoughts of carp and evil wrong doings occupied my time and to my eternal shame the only time I considered Sophie and the baby inside her was when I made the bogus phone calls asking how she was and told her how our 'job' was going.

On the fourth day things began to change as at last some other anglers started to show. I was having my 'bathroom break' in the clubhouse around eleven each morning. This was the latest I could hold back my regular morning bowel movements without cacking my pants and compromising the chance of a take. The feeding spell seemed to have a vague sort of ten o'clock end and while the odd pick up occurred around this time, holding on for another hour meant you felt it was safe enough to reel in without blowing an opportunity. As I left the clubhouse after freshening up I heard a car come down the track and to my surprise it tooted me. The driver got out of his car and unlocked the gate and I could see it was Alan, the syndicate's artist.

Alan beckoned me over and after asking me where I was fishing offered me a lift back to my swim as he intended to fish a few swims around further clockwise from where I was. I agreed, I could always nip and see Rambo a bit later, and Alan was someone who I felt could shed a little more light on my visitation. I had no intention of telling him what had happened to me but I was very interested in finding out what his unusual experience had been like. We chit-chatted about various things and I told him about my first forty and Rambo's fifty and how he'd soon have to start up a fifties poster. He seemed genuinely pleased we had caught some great fish and was quite shocked by Rambo's out of the blue, straight from a thirty, fifty. He asked what Rambo had named the fish and I told him. If he was unimpressed he hid it from me very well. He said it'd be interesting to track down the most recent photo of Rambo's fish prior to his capture to see how much weight it had put on and in what sort of time. I agreed and on his insistence jumped in to his car.

Once he'd driven me to my swim I asked him to come and have a cuppa with me before he started to set up. Alan seemed enthusiastic enough and pulled his car tight over to one side of the track and turned the engine off. We walked the few yards down to my gear and I put on the kettle.

Alan scratched his neatly trimmed grey beard and not for the first time since he'd tooted me did I feel that he was keen to ask me something. "So, young man? Are you enjoying all this?" Alan waved his arm theatrically, it was a question but not the one he wanted to ask I was certain.

"Too right," I said. "Great surroundings, super fish and hardly anybody about."

"Not even a ghost?" asked Alan. That was the question.

I shook my head and hoped I could dupe his 'artist's eye'. "Not even a ghost. But I must admit the old wood can set your mind wandering off on a scary path."

"Yes," said Alan both a bit distracted and disappointed.

It was my turn to move. "Why do you have this fascination with the ghost when no one else thinks it even exists?" I asked.

Alan looked slightly annoyed. "Others may be sure of its non-existence but as someone who has experienced it I say to them – don't deny what you can't understand. The world is full of things we don't, as individuals, understand and yet we accept them and believe in them. Do you understand how gravity works? How atoms cling together to make your body? How electricity flows down a wire and makes an electric motor turn?"

"No," I said, "but I can see it with my own eyes, or at least the effect of it. Milk? Sugar?"

"Milk only, thank you. Yes, a fair point I admit."

I passed Alan his mug of tea. "So what did you experience, then?"

"It only happened once," said Alan, his eyes narrowing as he focused his attention on recalling the incident. "Oddly enough it was on the very first night I fished here."

"Christ!" I said. "How long ago was that?" In my mind I was slightly agog it had happened to Alan on his first night as it had for me.

"Why... almost ten years ago." Alan's furrowed brow cleared as he was sidetracked. "Ten years. Time has an odd habit of catching you out and making you think less of it has passed than really has."

"Hmm. So what happened?" I said and immediately kicked myself for my indecent haste. I didn't want to give anything away, Alan could be the murderer for a start. I laughed inwardly. Not really the type; but what type are the type? In any case the ghost wouldn't have visited him for help but that just brought up the question of why the ghost didn't have a go at the person who killed him. Perhaps he was already dead? But then who went back to the area in the old wood which Rambo had raked around and why had the ghost asked for help?

"I was asleep. The whole affair is indelibly inked onto my memory and I suddenly awoke and felt cold. I can remember feeling as if I had been torn from my sleep and, strangely drawn, I left my bed and my bivvy and went outside. It was a foul night, dark, no moonlight, windy with squally showers but suddenly the wind increased and started to batter me. I can recall a horrid sibilant hissing as well, I remember thinking my head was going to explode from it. Quite peculiar and unique I can assure you. Soon after I had a wave of what I can only describe as differing emotions come over me, but only vague hints of despair and pain. It was something akin to hearing snippets of conversation from a person alongside you, yet never gleaning the true meaning or even the slightest gist of what they were trying to communicate to you. Most frustrating. It only lasted for a few seconds and then whatever it was left me." Alan looked up at me and I swore for a second he was close to tears. "Do you know what the overriding impression it left me with was?"

"No," I said, smitten with what he was telling me.

"That I'd somehow failed a test, that I'd been a failure and not lived up to expectations," said Alan gravely.

"What do you mean?" I asked.

"I'd let the ghost down. That's what I felt, my son. It'd come to me to be heard and I hadn't the skill or innate ability to hear it."

I tried to look sceptical. "It's some story," I said trying to keep my comments nondescript.

Alan looked at me hard. "You see, son, every time we have someone new join I wonder if they will be visited on their first night like I was and I cling desperately to the hope that if they are they will be a better listener, for want of an expression, than I was. For ten years I've been waiting for someone else to join and solve the riddle for me because I know I am incapable of doing it myself. I think of it every wakening hour, you know. In a way it was the most significant moment of my life."

"I used to think of a girl like that," I said. "I don't think about her so much now. Other things have taken her place."

"You may have a very salient point again, young man. Sadly nothing has taken the place of my encounter and to use a rather tired pun, the whole event still haunts me." Alan shifted his weight onto his other leg and drank some tea. "Do you know, I really did think it might be you who might get a visit?"

"Me!" I exclaimed. "Why me?"

"My artist's eye." Alan turned away and I saw his shoulders sag a little. "More wishful thinking on my behalf, perhaps. It can cloud judgement, you know, irrational hope. I'm simply another irrational carp angler."

"It might happen to me later on," I offered.

"No, I think not, young man. I'm convinced our ghost knows if you can hear and he's so despairing of his situation he'll make contact the moment he can. That means your first night or not at all."

"So who is he?" I asked.

Alan gave an empty gesture. "I have no idea. I've spent many, many hours trying to find out by searching various public documents but I've been unable to forward any worthwhile suggestions. There was a death here before Michael owned the water, an industrial accident when one unfortunate worker was killed during the gravel extraction days. I even went to visit the widow, who, despite her grief was rather complimentary to the company her husband had been employed by. The accident was almost solely down to negligence and bad work practice by her husband. The company had looked after her by paying a more than generous lump sum and a lifelong pension and somehow it seemed impossible to consider he was our restless soul."

"What about the wood?" I persisted. "That's even older. How come it looks so… so…" I was lost for words.

"So full of malice and pain?" Alan suggested. I nodded. "I think it's more down to our human phobias than anything. It does look an unusual wood, granted, but perhaps it's how it's intended to be. Some things are beautiful and aesthetically pleasing, others are not. Trees usually are, it's true, but by some freak of nature this wood isn't. It could be the soil, a specific small mutation in the genetic material of the trees, I don't honestly know. All I do know is it looks odd to human eyes and our imaginations do the rest."

I wanted to ask Alan his theory on trees morphing while in the presence of a ghost but thought it a bit risky. "Have you ever been in the old woods?"

Alan shook his head and gave his odd little two-tone laugh. "No! For all I've said I haven't. I mean, why would I want to go in there for a start?"

You tell me, mate, I thought. "Oh, no reason, I know I wouldn't fancy having to sleep a night in it."

"Yet you'll happily do it many times a few yards away. If the bogeyman's in the woods he's quite capable of coming out of them and cutting your throat. Human phobias, you see and we're back to our irrationality once again." Alan handed me my mug back. It was still half full. "I must get on, young man, thank you for the tea, I expect I might see you before you pack in. When are you leaving?"

"In three days time."

"Good luck," said Alan.

"You too," I reciprocated.

And Alan left, his interest in me now gone because, as far as he was concerned, I'd been unmolested by the ghost. I went and sat down on my bedchair and thought through what he'd said to me. I was amazed at how alike both his and my experiences were and his explanation of his inability to read the ghost's emotions seemed spot on. He hadn't suffered like I had and he'd been left soon after first contact. The weather conditions of his night were the complete opposite to mine and on these two points only did his story significantly differ from mine. A small notion I'd had about the full moon being significant had been blasted away, perhaps I'd watched too many clichéd horror movies with too many clichéd human phobias. This was all very well but it did rely on one assumption, it being the old git was telling me the truth.

I busied myself with rebaiting my three rods. During the process I was sidetracked by the conversation with Alan getting replayed by the Dolby Pro cassette recorder in my head to the extent that I impaled myself on a baiting needle. Swearing profusely I now had the implement dangling from my skin with the curved end well embedded in the fleshy bit between my thumb and forefinger knuckle. A constant stream of blood ran down my hand and back up my arm as I lifted the palm of my left hand to survey the damage. Very gingerly I eased it out by turning the curved point around the small opening in my hand. It hurt like hell but I was relieved I had long ago disposed of my old barbed baiting needles. One of those would have been serious grief. I cleaned the wound with a disposable antiseptic wipe and put on a waterproof plaster and carried on where I'd left off. By the time I was ready to cast out the last rod Rambo bowled up with a look of excitement on his face.

"All right, then, boy?" he asked.

"Apart from skewering myself with a baiting needle," I said, holding up the damaged hand to show him, "I'm fine."

Rambo gave a small wince. "Must pay more attention in class."

"You're right there," I admitted. "Anything happening down your end?"

"Nothing last night, I had a scraper twenty this morning first thing which I put in the stock pond. You?"

"A high twenty at around six this morning and I bumped into Alan in the car park when I was going down for a dump."

"What did he have to say for himself? Anything?"

I told Rambo the whole little story while I got him to catapult out some freebies for me. Holding the catty was uncomfortable for me because the handle sat right on the spot where the baiting needle had stuck in. It had been bad enough casting.

"Interesting," said Rambo. "But is it as interesting as this?" Rambo pulled out a piece of what looked like catapult elastic and shoved it under my nose.

I gave him a questioning look. "Are you being serious? Or taking the piss?"

"Look at it!" said Rambo.

"It's a foot away from my nose," I informed him. "I'm looking at it all right. You're holding it between two fingers and it looks like a decent sized worm only it's not a worm it's catapult elastic. Green catapult elastic."

Like an eloquent barrister Rambo turned on his heel and put his hands up to his chest as if he was holding onto an imaginary pair of coat lapels, the green piece of elastic still in his right hand. "Tell me, Mr Williams, when was the last time you saw 'exhibit A', a piece of *green* catapult elastic of *this* sort of length. Please note the emphasise on the colour and dimensions."

"Never," I answered honestly.

"How about a piece of elastic of *any* colour of such length?" Rambo insisted.

I shrugged. "Bloody hell! I don't know, it's too short for a catty... never, I guess."

"So are you suggesting it has been cut to this size on purpose?" implied Rambo.

"I suppose so, but I've never seen a piece of that length," I assured him.

Rambo turned stern. "Come, come, Mr Williams. A carp angler of your standing and years of experience. *Never!*"

I wrinkled my nose. "Give me a clue."

QC Rambo lightened up. "Ok. Think riggy. Think; launching yourself off a tall structure and not wanting to die."

I had it. "A bungee rig! Christ! How long is it since anyone's used one of those?"

"Quite so, Mr Williams. Superseded by the power gum shock resistant fine line rig, circa 1990, I wouldn't hesitate to say as late as the mid '80's. With a couple of swivels superglued in either end and then whipped tight around the barrel with Black Spider braid, we are talking a long time ago. It was the rig for presenting lighter than may be suitable hooklengths. The cushioning effect of the elastic allegedly compensating for a lack of line strength." Rambo walked up to me and towered above me, eyes burning into mine, his hands still tugging his imaginary lapels. "As you well know, Mr Williams, the bungee rig was also used for, shall we say, more sinister motives."

"I'm sure I don't know what you're talking about," I said, and I didn't.

Rambo exploded into a vision of outrage and fury. "I put it to you, Mr Williams, that you know only too well what I'm talking about! This," he held the piece of elastic in front of my face and waved it violently, "sickening piece of filth, when tied to several yards of line and baited with a boilie is a weapon of the criminal mind."

"I don't know what…" I said.

Rambo ploughed over the top of my feeble protestations. "Once thrown in a likely margin and the elasticised end tethered by a metal spike of some description and cleverly concealed with bankside vegetation it becomes a lay-line. In short, Mr Williams, it becomes a hidden fish trapping device!" Rambo paused for a second to give extra emphasis. "Which in turn becomes a fish stealing aid!"

The game of charades was over. "Blimey!" I said. "Do you think that's what it was used for?"

"Not this one, obviously. This must have fallen out of someone's kit."

"A bit tenuous isn't it?" I ventured.

Rambo cocked his head to one side. "Sure is, boy, but it's the best I've got so far to back up my hunch."

Chapter 13

"Do you think the van will be all right?" I'd asked, deeply concerned. "There's a hell of a lot of fishing stuff in there and it could all get nicked while we're gone."

Rambo had puffed out his cheeks. "I know, but what's the alternative?"

"I'm onto that one. We drive back to a car hire garage, leave the van all safe and secure there, and come back in a hire car. It even eradicates the slim chance of someone who's a member spotting the van in the vicinity of the pit, wherever we eventually decide to leave it," I'd explained.

Rambo had gone for it and now we were using a Nissan Micra instead of my Escort 1.8 Turbo diesel to help in our cunning plan. The only trouble being that Micras were not designed with carp anglers and carp tackle in mind, especially hulking great Goliaths like Rambo and their directly proportional rucksacks. The boot, with only two rucksacks in it, one admittedly well oversized, was at bursting point. When we'd loaded up at the hire garage the pair of us had to jump up and down on them repeatedly to pummel them flat enough to get the hatch down. We had re-created the tired sitcom scene of packing the holiday suitcases only the language, which had accompanied it, was hardly conducive to early evening viewing. After that debacle I'd had to insert Rambo into the passenger seat with the aid of a gorilla bar and had told him not to breathe too deeply unless he wanted to pop the door off its hinges. After I'd issued this warning I'd noticed the car had listed to port so to be on the safe side I'd quickly jumped in the driver's side to counter balance it in case the whole lot keeled over.

The car was weenie. All through the journey back to somewhere adjacent to the pit I had to keep saying to Rambo. "It's no good, I can't understand you when you talk with your kneecap in your mouth."

Rambo had written me a note, it said. "Why have we slowed down?" It was poorly written, probably because his head had kept on hitting the roof every time we went over a bump and had jolted his writing arm.

"Either a couple of flies have become stowaways or it's because we've lost the tow we were getting from that starling when it flew past us," I'd answered.

Actually that's not fair, the Micra was quite nippy, sixteen valves and so on but it was tiny. Not as small as I've exaggerated but looking across at Rambo, all bent arms and legs, struggling to control the origami conundrum known as an Ordnance Survey map, it only needed a little embellishment to take it to the next slightly absurd level.

Rambo, his head bobbing and jolting over the map, guided me to where he wanted us to be and told me to park anywhere in the narrow little lane we found ourselves.

"This'll do," he said.

Rambo shoehorned himself out and I got out the driver's side at the same time. The pair of us turned and faced each other across the car's roof, which only came up to the middle of Rambo's thigh.

"We might as well take the car with us," he said. "I'll put it in my back pocket. It's not a lot bigger than my radio and it's got one in it."

"Get off the tree branch, you're not fooling anyone, you know," I said.

Rambo got down. This time he leant on the roof. "Why would anyone want to make a car so small, so red and so ugly?"

"So it does sixty miles to the oily rag and no fucker wants to steal it," I replied.

Rambo looked wistfully up the lane. "I hope you're right or we'll have a long walk back. I'll tell you what, if some kid's lost a roller skate he'll have this away so that he's got a pair again."

I walked to the back of the car; it took two strides. "It's not that bad," I said, chastising him as I heaved at the plugged rucksacks in the boot. "My granddad used to drive a bubble car, now *that* was tiny…"

"They're not coming out, it's the back wheels lifting off the ground giving you the impression they're coming out," said Rambo mockingly.

I soldiered on. "… Three wheels, two at the front, one at the rear. The whole front was the door; literally you opened up the whole front and sat in it. You'd be lucky to survive a head on collision with a large insect." My rucksack came free and I swung it onto my back. "Christ! This feels heavy, what's in it?"

"*On* it," said Rambo. "There's a Nissan Micra *on* it."

"It was the cheapest," I told him.

"I know," said Rambo, jabbing his thumb in his chest. "I paid for it."

"Well, what are you complaining about, then?"

Rambo swung his rucksack onto his back. "Has anyone ever told you camouflage looks good on you?"

I looked down at the uniform Rambo had insisted I wore. "No."

"And they're not likely too, either," he said, trying to keep a straight face.

"I suppose the regulation black face paint comes later, does it?" I said haughtily.

Rambo laughed. "It wouldn't be the same without it."

I juggled the rucksack's straps so they felt what I jokingly referred to in my mind as 'comfortable'. "Which way, then, supreme leader?"

Rambo flicked open a compass, consulted the now A5 sized Ordnance map, wetted his entire index finger, held it up to the wind and pointed. "That way."

Before he could stride off I grabbed his rucksack with my left hand. "Oi!" I said authoritatively. "Don't go too fast, will you. I'm not as young and fit as I used to be."

"None of us are as young as we used to be, boy, and I doubt if you were ever fit," said Rambo.

"Fit to drop, then?" I suggested.

"Definitely. Let's go and hope the effort is worth it."

I fell in behind Rambo and got used to following the huge bobbing rucksack, which apparently seemed filled with helium, while mine remained resolutely filled with lead.

As we marched back in a vaguely southern direction, heading towards the old wood, a full three miles away, I ran through the seven-day session we had completed earlier in the day. After my chat with Alan the fishing had become less productive and I'd only landed two more fish but both were cracking low thirties, one of which was a true leather. Rambo had caught only one more but had spotted Rocky turning up in his haute couture camouflage outfit yesterday morning and desperate wannabe Darren in the evening. A desperate wannabe according to ailing Alan the second best ghost psychic in the syndicate. That I knew of. Neither of the last two had bothered to introduce themselves. They had picked their swims, set up in them and gone about their carp fishing business unaware of our intention of spying on them and anyone else who happened to bowl up in the meantime.

As I started to flag, a good thirty yards from the Micra, I seriously questioned the lucidity of what we were embarking upon. What on earth did Rambo expect to achieve? Did he really expect us to see fish stealing skulduggery taking place, if there was any going on in the first instance? At the moment his hunch or theory was all held in place by a single thread of catapult elastic. It was the only shred of physical evidence to supplement his gut feeling and due to the nature of it I thought I could safely say he was stretching things a bit too far. Still, as I'd remarked to myself before, you couldn't afford to disregard somebody of Rambo's standing. And the pair of us did have a healthy track record when it came to the sharp end of proceedings similar to the ones we were embroiling ourselves in. Perhaps we would come up with something to titillate Michael's paranoia, but if we did, strict dictionary definition would demand that it would cease to be paranoia at all. Where would that leave poor old Michael? What's worse, having delusions of persecution or finding out they're real? And while I was ruminating on Michael, where was he? I'd have expected to have seen him at least once in full week's session. I hadn't seen him since the visit when he had confronted me about Watt. Perhaps he was at home wanking himself daft as he got himself absorbed into an imaginary world of Hollywood and the two girls. What if Hollywood had tired of them and passed them on to Michael? A very dubious concept, true, but it might have been a case of the female attention killing him off. I smiled ruefully to myself and licked a salty upper lip, if the walk didn't kill me off a couple of night's bivvied up in the old wood should do the trick. Despite what Alan had said about it only being one of nature's ugly woods and nothing more sinister.

I was into my stride now and although I lacked the effortless power of the Terminator in front of me I was holding my own. Just. For the first mile and a bit we cut across grassy meadows and then we followed the line of a small chalk stream, which happily we didn't need to cross. The stream diverted off sharply to the east after a half mile or so but we kept on going south aiming for the extreme northern edge of the old wood, roughly in line with the back of the swim I had vacated hours earlier. We stopped for a rest, well, Rambo stopped to let me have a rest and he showed me where we were on the map and where we were aiming for. The area of wood that lay directly behind my vacated swim was the deepest section of the wood, a distance of approximately eight hundred yards from its start at the track around the pit to where we were going to meet it. As it curved away both to the east and west it reduced in width and petered out, still up to the track but much further down the sides of the pit. On the map the wood was indicated as being nicely crescent shaped, similar to the classic depiction of the moon in children's nursery rhyme books. How bland it looked on paper, a small splodge of light green with cute little non-coniferous tree motifs within it. It should have had the skull and cross bones sign indicating weird morphing wood and the letters RG alongside indicating 'resident ghost'. These Ordnance Survey maps were crap and I told Rambo the same.

"I don't suppose the Ordnance boys were as gifted as you. Think how lucky you are," he said.

I rolled my eyes sarcastically. "Mmm, that's right."

"Come on, then, the quicker we get there the quicker the trees can strangle us in our sleep." It was Rambo's turn to roll his eyes.

We started off again and after climbing a small undulation we were faced with a large dense hedge coming into view. It was a hawthorn hedge, or at least I reckoned it was not being especially clued up on shrubs, and was very dense and spiky. Whatever its true name was made little difference, we couldn't get through it, couldn't get over it and we couldn't get under it.

"We'll have to go around it," I stated with massive insight.

"Nice one, Einstein," said Rambo. "Any particular way you fancy going around it?"

"Don't they show hedges on that poxy map of yours?" I asked in frustration, borne out of tiredness and the prospect of even further to walk.

Rambo stared at his map. "Oh yeah!" he said in mock surprise. "Blast! I never noticed that blue line running across there... nope, hold on, as you were, I've got the map upside down, that's the M20." And he slapped me across the top of the head with it, the map, not the M20, but only playfully because my skull never fractured.

"Come on, Sherpa Tenzing," said Rambo as he started off following the line of the hedge.

"You haven't by any chance got a donkey in that rucksack, have you?" I called to him.

"I've got a camel," said Rambo earnestly, "but I'm saving him for the way back in case we have a heat wave and all this lot turns to sand."

The hedge detour took us an extra half an hour and after another fifteen minutes steady walking the old wood eventually loomed in front of us. The last stretch to the wood was on a gradual decline and although I was less than over enthusiastic to be walking straight into it I was glad of the easy terrain. I was feeling fairly knackered by now and my mouth hung open and I spat out phlegm regularly as my lungs tried to clear themselves and take on more oxygen. I looked down at my wristwatch. It was nearly six o'clock so we had enough time to set up in the woods before darkness fell and heat up something to eat. I was gagging for a cuppa as well.

The wood itself had been fenced off and this was clearly the boundary to Michael's Hamworthy Estate and the one he and Gary had erected all those years ago. Fortunately it was an all-wood affair comprising posts with horizontal timbers and was a cinch to climb even for someone as tired as myself. We both straddled the fence after stepping up onto the first rail and eased ourselves back down to the ground.

"Not far now, boy," Rambo said softly as we entered into the wood. "We'll go in about three hundred or so yards, find ourselves a decent spot and set up camp. Once we've had a bite to eat, a drink and a little rest we can get our heads around what nocturnal activity we're going to indulge in."

"Ok," I wheezed and let fly with another globule.

Rambo went into the wood first and I followed him. I was an old wood virgin. It was my first time whereas he'd been in a couple of times before and I wasn't sure what to expect, not in terms of the wood itself, but how I was going to feel about it. The vision of the ghost's wind whistling through the trees and the way the branches changed into snakes, faces and beasts was so momentous it was clearly going with me to my grave. I just hoped I wasn't walking into that very grave right there and then.

As I went in behind Rambo it was instantly darker, very gloomy and the atmosphere felt claustrophobic and clinging. It wasn't only the tight proximity and denseness of the trees contributing to this but also the stifled air. Ironically there wasn't a breath of wind within the wood such was the shielding effect of the trees and the cracking and rustling of our footsteps as we walked over rotten branches and fallen leaves seemed to reverberate in an oddly muffled, insular way. I looked up and around myself as we picked our way through the old beech, horse chestnut and oak trees and spotted something I'd missed before. Although the oaks, the large ones were dotted seemingly at random, and the chestnut trees looked gnarled and sinister the beeches had a rather smoother trunk in comparison and were far less intimidating. There were fewer beech trees than the other two types and it was because of this fact I hadn't noticed them so readily. The beech trees looked normal. Had Alan been right? Was the appearance of the others down to a natural abnormality and was it then a case of man's imagination coming to the same eerie conclusion? I'd still seen what I'd seen as regards the ghost's wind changing them but I felt a tad less apprehensive.

Suddenly Rambo stopped. I'd been so engrossed in my own thoughts I nearly bumped into the back of him.

"This is far enough, we're in about three fifty yards. Let's see if we can find a couple of clear spots to put the bivvies."

"Ah, the old 'finding the clear spots' routine," I said.

The two of us mooched up and down and soon Rambo found a spot right alongside a huge oak tree where we had room to put up both bivvies virtually side by side.

"Are we going to tie a bit of string around this tree and run it out behind us so we can find our way back to it?" I asked.

Rambo gave me a snap of his fingers. "Nice idea. Maybe we'll leave a series of bright orange boards shaped into arrows as well."

"Seriously, though, it isn't going to be easy finding our way back here in the pitch black, is it?" I said. I had visions of us stumbling around in the dark, hopelessly lost and me going slowly round the twist and emerging, eventually into the daylight, a gibbering wreck.

"Leave it to me, boy, just leave it to me," Rambo reassured. "Right! Let's get organised, get the bivvies up, have a bite and a cuppa and then we'll crack on."

An hour and a half later we'd done as Rambo suggested. It seemed odd to have so little amount of gear in my bivvy, minimalist in fact, but the long walk and the nature of this 'session' had dictated what we had taken with us. A bivvy each, a sleeping bag each, a stove between us, some food, drinks and Rambo's special bag of goodies. Rambo had carried the stove, food and goodies while I'd contended with only a bag and bivvy in my rucksack. Despite this I still felt desperately tired from the hike. My legs were all wobbly and although I'd had some hot food and a sit down the prospect of even more gallivanting around was slightly dispiriting. Still, if we wanted to crack the mystery of the syndicate it had to be done.

"What time have you had most of your takes during the night," asked Rambo as he smeared my face in blackout paint.

I considered the question. "I've had a few around midnight and a few more dotted through the night willy-nilly," I said.

"Keep still," said Rambo roughly pulling my head into place by my hair. "I would say midnight as the banker hour from my experiences as well. What we'll do is aim to get tucked up somewhere near to where Darren and Rocky are fishing for that time. I reckon they'll be fairly close to each other. Whereabouts I'm not sure, they might have moved down to where I was fishing, we'll have to see. Ok?"

I nodded. Whether Rambo could see that I nodded or not I wasn't too sure because he had turned his torch off and I was blacker than a boilie glugged in soot. I checked my pocket for my Maglite. I didn't want to be without a torch tonight. Eventually the time passed and with an ETA for the witching hour the pair of us left. Here we go again, I thought, not prebaiting or aiming to string up giant rottweilers but spying on fellow carpers.

I followed Rambo through the wood. How he knew which way to go defied me but we came out onto the pit's perimeter track unmolested. It was a dark night. Looking upwards, now free from the obscuring properties of the trees' branches and their newly growing leaves, I could see no stars. Blanket cloud was above me and I prayed it wasn't rain bearing, getting drenched into the bargain wasn't a prospect I was keen on at all.

We carefully made our way down the eastern side of the pit heading towards the point where Rambo had fished his earlier session, the one that was fairly close to the stock pond. At every swim Rambo would motion me to wait on the track and he would glide into the swim without so much as sound and check out its occupancy rating. When he returned from the swim two up from the south-east point swim, the one actually closest to the stock pond, he whispered in my ear that it was 'with bivvy'. The phrase caused a link in my head and I wondered how Sophie was 'with child'. My child. Do dads get involved in this sort of chicanery I asked myself? Of course. Men never really grow up. It's only the lack of physical ability which tones them down in their latter years.

Rambo said he knew who was in the swim. "It's that prick, Rocky," he whispered. "The cunt's got one of those new Viper TT Chameleon camouflaged bivvies."

"You don't like him, do you?" I hissed. "I can tell."

The whites of Rambo's eyes widened. Underneath the blackout paint I knew his face was as black as thunder. Black on black. I could see it being more a case of camouflage on camouflage violence. "Not especially. I've never even spoken to the bloke and I hate him."

"We all make assumptions like that," I said quietly.

"But not everyone ends up doing something despicable about it," said Rambo, the malevolence in his voice radiating in volumes despite the low setting.

"Are you going to?"

"As soon as I get a reason, I'll flatten the bastard," menaced Rambo.

"He's a big bloke," I said. "He might be well-hard for all you know." I didn't know why I said it, perhaps it was how I would have viewed things but to Rambo it was almost an insult. One so stupid it didn't even deserve an answer. There was silence, continued silence, a little bit more silence and still some more silence. "Ok," I said. "Point taken. Daft thing to say. We get something on him and then you flatten the bastard."

"And his poxy designer camouflage outfit," added Rambo.

"And his poxy designer camouflage outfit," I conceded. Like it made a difference what I said.

We skirted around the sleeping Rocky and the thought uppermost in my mind was designer camo sleeping bags. Did anyone make one? Someone made the luggage but I wasn't so certain about the bag. Not even Rambo had one of those, well not a designer one obviously, but he didn't even have a conventionally camouflaged one. I was convinced I'd seen one advertised with the camo bit on the inside and plain green on the outside, which seemed a bit cart before the horse. It only had to be a matter of time and with that thought I looked at my watch. Eleven o'clock as good as damn. There was no one in the next swim but the one after the south-east point swim where Rambo had fished was occupied, presumably by Darren. He must have moved into it once Rambo had packed up. Rambo told me to wait behind a large bush to the side of the stock pond while he legged it up to the car park to see how many cars where in there. In a matter of a few minutes he was back.

"Only two cars," he said. "That's a result. It means they've the opportunity to play. Now we want them to have a result so we can see what the score is." Rambo paused for a few seconds. "Come with me. While I was fishing down here I found a nice little hidey hole for us to tuck ourselves."

We quickly moved around to the other side of the stock pond and embedded ourselves in the undergrowth beneath a young tree. The tree was only a few yards off the track, Rocky's bivvy at most twenty-five yards away and with Darren seventy yards further towards the car park we were in a good position to notice should either of them move or do anything together. As I lay there next to Rambo I wondered how long he had in mind for us to stay, it wasn't uncomfortable at the moment but give it an hour or so and it would be. And there was the boredom factor of being in the pitch black with nothing to say or do but wait. And don't say: 'A bit like carp fishing, then?' because it wasn't. We were fishing, fishing for clues, only we didn't know if there were any in this particular water.

I must have dropped off because the first thing I could recall was being elbowed in the ribs and then hearing the distinctive noise of an angler scrambling from his bivvy to the accompaniment of the one-noter, fortissimo, in F, scale of C major. The designer camo clotheshorse was in. We listened to the aural saga of Rocky playing his carp and no doubt Rambo's mind's eye visualised the scene as mine did as we both strained to hear the soundtrack. The clunk of a big pit reel baitrunner conversion being snapped into gear, the faint noises of physical exertion and five minutes later another buzzer beeping and an Anglo-Saxon curse all wafted through the night air and down our auditory canals. The other buzzer note must have meant the hooked carp had picked up another line. Then another beep but of a different tone sounded. Rocky was dipping his other rod to make sure it didn't happen again. After, the scream of a clutch could be heard as the carp made a powerful lunge close to the bank. As much as I knew that Rambo loathed Rocky I knew he was pulling like hell for him to land the carp. In other circumstances it would have been oh so very different. Finally we heard an exultant: 'Yes', as the carp was netted and more general pandemonium as Rocky undoubtedly shifted the carp to his unhooking mat, found his torch or put on his head beam and unhooked her. I heard a rummage. Weigh sling being found. I heard a click. Scales coming out of pouch? Most likely. Then another: 'Yes', a big fish presumably. Now we came to the crux of the matter.

Rocky came walking towards us, a small torchlight shining on the ground in front of him and I felt my heart rate quicken. What if I should sneeze? Forget that, pal, I couldn't, end of story. Rocky carried on towards Darren and was soon out of earshot.

"The moment of truth has arrived, boy. If it doesn't happen now I'll have to admit it's unlikely to ever happen," said Rambo gently. My heart pounded some more and for good measure gave an odd little flutter, or was it one of my intercostal muscles starting to cramp? Whatever, like sneezing, now was not an ideal time to die from a heart attack, not that there ever is I would imagine. My heart rate soon became of secondary importance as I heard returning voices and I tried desperately to discern the words being spoken. Again I caught glimpses of a flickering torchlight as it came into my very limited field of view.

"… On, then?"

"The middle one. Belting take! It hammered away, caused me all sorts of grief 'til I got it under control, it picked up one of the other lines at one stage but I got it sorted."

"Have you phoned him, yet?"

"No, not yet. I'll give him a bell now."

I heard the sound of mobile phone digits being pressed and then as the two anglers walked within feet of us the pair of them stopped.

The second voice, the one who had caught the fish, namely Rocky, bawled into the mobile. "Wake up you lazy tart, I've had a big one! Get your arse out of bed and get down here now!" All went quite as, I supposed, the stunned individual on the receiving end of Rocky's wonderful news collected their wits about them, wiped the sleep from their eyes and answered back. Rocky was soon shooting his mouth off again answering a string of questions. "About ten minutes ago… thirty-eight-ten, one of the fully scaled… I know, right result… just me and Dazza… yeah, that's right. The two new geezers pissed off this morning… yeah, I don't know how they got let in… the big one's a bit of a monkey, shit camo gear… Dazza's met them on a work party… eh? Well, let him know later on… see you in a bit… yep, keep the mobile on… by the stock pond but we'll walk down… ok, mate. Cheers." The phone beeped again. "Twenty minutes," said the same voice that'd had the telephone conversation.

"Make me a tea, then," said the other, who was clearly Darren.

The two wandered off to Rocky's swim and had their tea while Rambo and I stayed flat out under the tree. It seemed blatantly evident what was going to happen and our wildest hopes had been realised. These two scheming halfwits were nicking fish. My mind raced. What was the going rate for a near forty, British passport bearing, fully scaled mirror? Three grand? Four? More? I didn't really have an inkling, but however much it was it was easy money if you were set up and organised. Two fishing, another on stand-by with a van all set up to collect any fish and, having heard Rocky mention telling someone in the morning, a buyer ready with the readies. Who was the person with the van? Another syndicate member? It was hard to tell even with the reference to us. I knew who the monkey would be when Rambo confronted Rocky. Voices stopped my reasoning.

"I'll just check the stock pond." It was Darren speaking and I heard his footfalls and body motion go to the opposite side of the stock pond to where we were. I seriously wanted to shuffle my body around to try and make out what he was doing but both Rambo and myself had backed ourselves into our hole and so were facing the wrong way. I couldn't risk moving so I made do with listening.

Darren let out a laugh of delight. "All right! I've got one! Doing the business or what? Get a landing net and another sack, Rocky."

"Nice one, Dazza."

I heard Rocky run back to his swim to get the net and come running back. "Any good?" he asked as he got to where Darren was.

"It's been on a while and it's knackered. Bungeed right out, mate! Here we go."

I heard the fish being lifted from the water while I mentally doffed my hat to Rambo. He'd been spot-on concerning the bungee lay-line. The pair of conniving bastards were lay-line fishing the stock pond while no one else was around. From a fish nicking point of view it made obvious sense. Firstly the pond was probably pretty well populated with carp as I couldn't see Michael draining and taking them out more than twice a year. Secondly the fish were undoubtedly hungry and struggling for food in such a tiny pond and could be prone to getting hooked on single boilies. Why singles, I suddenly thought, the pair of them might have even been baiting it up. Cheeky sods! Thirdly there was little or no chance of being caught, or at least there wouldn't be not unless Williams and Ramsbottom (deceased) were on your case. I mentally laughed at the idea of Rambo being a ghost and fishing in a white two-piece suit while I flirted with his widowed wife. Don't mention ghosts.

Rocky let out a low whistle. "Got to be a low twenty. Nice brace! The old kiddie will be happy! Put it in the sack and then back in the water and hold this one as well. I expect Alan'll phone soon."

My ears nearly popped off my head. 'Old kiddie'! 'Alan'! It was the last name I expected to hear. Five minutes later Rocky's mobile rang. "Yeah, still ok, pal. We'll walk up now we've got another one... I know... Dazza had it from the stock pond... Cheers."

I heard the two of them lift out a sack each while mumbling self-praise and congratulations to each other. They started to walk off and I wondered what our next move was but elected to do nothing until Rambo gave the orders. As soon as they were well out of earshot Rambo started to crawl out of the hole and I did likewise.

"What now?" I whispered.

"I'm going down to the car park and deck the fucking lot of them. Once I've done that I'll ring Michael and see what he wants to do from there. You walk down half-way and I'll give you a shout when they're all unconscious," said Rambo. It was all very matter of fact.

"Umm... what if...?" I started my brain whirring in a false neutral.

"See you later, boy. I'm going to enjoy this, I'll give him fucking monkey, all right."

And he was gone. I followed as I was told but I was so flabbergasted by hearing the name of Alan and the likely bloodshed about to ensue due to Rambo's instantly dispatched violence I barely knew what I was doing. Car headlights snapped me out of my stupor and I watched them stop at the gate after they had trundled down the access track, while it was opened. The car drove in and the white headlights turned to red taillights as it turned around and then the lights went out. An irony, I thought, seeing as a few humans' lights were going to go out as well. At any second I was waiting to hear either the dull thud of physical contact or Rambo's call to say it was over and the culprits were down, out and bloodied. I heard neither. Ten minutes passed. Then, to my consummate astonishment I saw red lights again and heard an engine start up. The red lights moved and continued moving up the track and they were gone! This wasn't right! What was happening? Frantically I wondered if the impossible had taken place. Had Rocky flattened Rambo? Was I all alone? I'd never get back to the bivvies alone. What if Rocky now knew about me and was at this very instant pounding up the track to hideously smash my face into a bloody, mushy pulp. Sorry Sophie, I tripped over at work.

Shit! I stood in the pitch black and felt a wave of pure terror and panic come over me. Indecision and indecisiveness paralysed me and I realised how utterly inept I was at this sort of thing without Rambo around to help. Out of nowhere a hand grabbed my clothes and I flinched, expecting a crushing fist to come pulverising into my cringing face.

"Come on, boy, back to base."

It was Rambo. Thank God it was Rambo. I turned and got pushed hard between the shoulder blades. "Walk quickly," said the voice behind me. "I'll tell you what happened when we get up the top end of the pit."

I did as I was told and played out a hundred scenarios in my head on the way, none of them any more feasible than the other. We reached the top end of the pit without mishap. I stopped.

"What happened?"

Rambo breathed out a sigh. "I made a decision. I hope it was the right one but it was spur of the moment, flying by the seat of my pants stuff, I can tell you. I was all in position as the car came to the gate and I was just about to take Darren out as it turned and reversed in, but then I stopped."

"Why?" I asked intrigued.

"Because it was a pick-up."

"A pick-up?" I said.

"Michael's pick-up," said Rambo. "And the Alan driving it wasn't our grey bearded artist Alan."

"Are you sure?" I asked incredulously.

"Positive. I decided it went a little bit deeper than what we've found out tonight so I did nothing. Sometimes doing nothing is a lot harder than doing something," said Rambo with feeling.

"I bet. You were dying to smack Rocky, weren't you?"

"An understatement. Come on, let's go and get some sleep and in the morning I think we'll head for home. We need to think this over and not do anything rash. All right, boy."

"Yeah."

Rambo gave me a friendly slap on the upper arm that would hurt in the morning when I woke up. Despite reservations and despite not having a chair I slept soundly in my bivvy in the woods, such was my state of physical exhaustion. And, rather oddly, when I awoke my one resounding thought was that I was going to be the father of a baby girl. A baby girl called Amy.

Chapter 14

The nurse squeezed a tube of transparent gel onto Sophie's slightly distended belly and rubbed the hand held scanner across it like a painter spreading out a thick dollop of paint. Her movements slowed and she carefully adjusted her hand position while studying the TV monitor to the side of her. A white quadrant had appeared on the monotone screen and as she found the correct angle for the ultrasound scanner an eerie image appeared within it.

"There were are," the nurse exclaimed quietly. "There's your baby. Can you see all right, Sophie?"

Sophie, who was lying flat on her back, had her left hand under her head to ease the strain on her neck as she peered across at the screen. "Oh yes! Can you see it, Matthew?"

I sat and gawped at the tiny screen. "Sort of. I'm not too sure what's what though. Is that the head?" The image wasn't clear and seemed to shift and change constantly.

The nurse pointed. "That's the head, there's the main body and can you see the two little legs folded up?"

Now that she'd pointed them out I could, with a little imagination, see that they were legs. "Where are her arms?"

The nurse looked at me in mild surprise and I realised what I'd said. "We can't see them very well at the moment, maybe in a minute the baby will move and we might."

"You said: 'Her arms'," said Sophie.

I kicked myself. I wasn't going to mention it in case it opened up some awkward questions but it had slipped out in the moment. The trouble was I'd never been so sure of anything in my life and the complete belief had simply manifested itself in my words. It was a girl. And at some stage in the indeterminate future it would be decided upon that she should be called Amy, but not by me. How did I know? Ask me one on ghosts. The two seemed inextricably linked. Life and death, birth and demise, the circle was endless and had been since the start of creation, whatever that'd entailed. From somewhere, God knows where - if he existed, I hadn't received any inside info on that one – I'd found the ability to see and contact, or rather be contacted by, forms, for want of a better word, residing in the voids in between. The voids that sat astride life and death, the areas from beyond the grave and within the womb. A lightning bolt of diverse thought rocketed into my head. The grave. Where was the grave of the ghost? Not in the old wood but the ghost had shot out into the pit and something somebody had said suddenly niggled my brain but I couldn't put my finger on it or remember what it was.

My mind was jangled off the subject. "Matthew!" Sophie persisted. "You said: 'Her arms'?"

"It's a hunch," I said rather lamely, copying Rambo. "I woke up one morning when we were away doing the London job and had this feeling we were going to have a baby girl." I started to sweat and my cheeks felt they must be the colour of crimson. It was bloody hot in the hospital but my lies were the real stokers of my internal fire.

"Can you tell whether he's right?" Sophie asked the nurse curiously.

The nurse smiled and moved the ultrasound scanner around. "Are you sure you both want to know? I can usually get it right most times at sixteen weeks."

"It's up to you, Soph," I said and in a moment of devil-may-care I added. "I already know. Girl. Definite."

"Are you that sure?" Sophie asked. I nodded. I saw it ticking over in her mind. "It won't hurt to know," she said finally. "In fact it'll be a help towards buying the baby clothes and toys." She looked at the nurse who'd been studying the monitor closely. "Is he right?"

The nurse smiled. "I can't see any dangly bits so I'm pretty sure he's right as well!"

I stood up and took a mock bow. "Thank you. Thank you. The world's greatest psychic, one who specialises in the fifty-fifty, toss of a coin scenario." The two women laughed and I'd got away with it.

The nurse carried on making various measurements of the baby, its head, limbs, body and also a specific area at the base of the neck. She explained this was to check for deformities, growth rate and the neck measurements were to detect spina bifida and Downs syndrome. I hadn't considered the possibility of having an abnormal child but when I asked her what the odds were of a Downs syndrome child for someone of Sophie's age I was shocked to find it was something like one in a thousand. Was that all? In that case what were the odds of any given person dying on any given day? It'd vary with age but I bet it put winning the lottery into perspective. It wasn't millions to one but a few thousand to one, more like and it was much the same for an unborn child. Life was a lottery but the odds were worse, or to put it correctly, they were better for it being worse, whereas the lottery's were worse for it being better. A lot worse but don't waste your breath telling Sophie's mum.

If nature worked perfectly, say 99% of the time, if indeed it was that competent, it still meant suffering and heartbreak for one in a hundred to one varying degree or another. I tried to imagine how complex the process was of a fertilized egg dividing and dividing into a fully formed but very tiny baby, all within sixteen weeks. I couldn't and in that instant I had a second revelation. It struck me as being a wonder, a process that had been repeated billions of times and yet each time it was unique. It was the wonder of life and of you and your partner's own personal creation. I was moved unlike I had been before.

I sat and stared at the, it had to be said, ghostly image on the screen and was swallowed into a new world. Had this little thing, in some impossible way, been able to contact me? Or had her sex and name come to me via a third party as I slept in the old woods a couple of weeks earlier, the third party being the ghost? I was touched in a way I hadn't been before as I looked at the tiny female life I'd helped create and I hoped she didn't know of my earlier reactions. How could I have been so callous and cold to put carp fishing before her? To see her as something that was going to take away rather than give? Ok, so reality said it wouldn't be Disneyland or saccharine US family TV unreality but even so. She was precious. She was ours for we alone had made her. I'd be there for her and carp fishing would still be there for me. My new man emotions faded. They were here to stay but it didn't mean I wasn't going to gun it to the birth, fish hard and try to solve the ever-deepening riddle of the syndicate. When she was truly with us then I'd take it from there and divide time as needs be. My worries and consternation concerning my carping/fatherhood conflicts were eased and replaced with worries about her being safely born and free from medical problems. Maybe I was growing up? It was strange it had come to me in a giant mental stride. I had always thought it would have been a slow insidious type of thing. I'd always imagined it would be a case of me one day analysing my life and realising I'd matured yet the process had been so slow I'd barely noticed it. A bit like a long-lost friend commenting on your changed physical appearance and attitude which, because you had lived with it every day, was not apparent to you. However I read it, it was one of those 'Eureka!' moments.

We asked for a picture of the scan and the nurse cleverly caught one of the baby looking straight into the scanner. Again the remarkably ghost-like eyes looked out into mine, it was uncanny. I took the photo and put it in my wallet, she would come everywhere with me even when I was lying to her mother about what I was doing. That night I wrote 'Amy' on a piece of paper, dated it, popped it in an envelope and melted some candle wax across the seal. I gave it to Sophie and made her swear on her mother's life she wouldn't open it until after our little girl was born.

"How did you know it was a girl?" she enquired after she had promised and understood I was adamant on saying no more about it.

"I don't know," I replied in all honesty. "It came to me overnight but it's no big deal, like I said, I had two chances. Right or wrong."

Sophie screwed up her face. "Nice though," she said and snuggled up to me. It was and I was grateful of the experience.

The month of June saw Sophie get bigger and bustier while the syndicate pit got busier. I was fascinated by Sophie's enhanced chest and the hormone's within her, which had made her so radiant, now made her ravishing. And wanting to be ravished. Her body, now decidedly different, was a sexual thrill to both of us and as much as I enjoyed touching and caressing it her response to it was totally reciprocated. All her responses seemed heightened and she seemed in a permanent state of instant arousal, which titillated my ego and my self-perceived prowess. It was easy to see why Hollywood rated himself so highly. The constant stream of attractive women queuing at his bed must have made it hard for him to keep his feet on the floor. Mind you, now he had the couple of stunning looking, lap dancing, ex-international gymnasts, who were also bisexual nymphomaniacs I couldn't see his feet being on the floor. At ninety degrees to it possibly, or equally, dangling eight foot beneath a chandelier. I was willing to bet he had more friction burns on his body than a piss-poor, naked skateboarder attempting tricks on astro-turf. Who cared, I was more than happy with my lot even if I was mindful it wouldn't last and Sophie would surely lose her heightened state as she became more swollen and heavy.

Rambo and I continued to work a fair few sessions at the pit and after each session he would give me a large wad of ready cash for payment of the 'work' we had completed. This money I then waved under Sophie's nose when I returned home and told her the great white lie over its true origination. I must admit I felt guilty receiving it and then guilty lying to Sophie over it but heroically I managed to accept the money and tell the porkies in order to keep up our frequent visits to the syndicate pit. After each session we would always go home via Rambo's place so I could wash away the evidence of my fishing and to put my gear in his flat. Even Sophie could tell the difference between a power drill and a rod holdall and a drum of cable and a reel of 15lb Big Game line.

On our first trip back after kipping in the old woods we had tried to fathom out the significance of Michael's pick-up being the vehicle to transport the stolen fish. It was very odd. I even wondered if it was a ruse to test us out, a little plot by Michael to see if we were capable of helping him keep an eye on things. It didn't make any sense if it was the case and it was far too elaborate to even contemplate it being true. Rambo and I were stumped and what had looked like a break-through now seemed a dead end. We ran through differing story lines; one implicating Michael in the stealing of his own fish, one of his pick-up being stolen and then put back without his knowledge and yet another of the pick-up being a duplicate.

"These are fish thieves we're talking about, not the fucking Mysterons," Rambo had said.

"Captain Rambo, indestructible…" I'd sung and we'd laughed to hide our frustrations.

Our major problem was the pit getting more angling attention and stopping the likelihood of more shenanigans taking place, not knowing any of the others sufficiently well to glean information from them and the nature of Michael's cunningly hand picked syndicate. When we had been in Watt's syndicate it was very close knit and everyone knew everyone else, except, ironically enough, the loner called Rambo. True it was cliquey but we all knew each other's names and a bit about each other. Secondly the water was small enough and the layout such that you could watch other people and what they got up to. Membership had remained unaltered for the last five or six years and there had been only ten of us, most coming from the local area. On this pit, however, there were twenty virtual strangers, some long standing members but many fairly new ones, their joining times all staggered. Apart from the one work party, again another of Michael's strategies, we never hardly met. Swims were isolated, rules were strict and not conducive to socials or very long stays and the members themselves came from where? I hadn't a clue. Some might travel for hundreds of miles and all on their own. Not unless someone made the specific effort to come and see you or bumped into you on the way to and from the car park or clubhouse anglers hardly mixed. Darren and Rocky were a pair but for odious reasons and Rambo and myself were a pair. We had been a pair before joining, something so peculiar that Rocky had even mentioned it while speaking to someone about coming to collect some nicked fish. It was virtually certain Darren and Rocky hadn't been a pair and I nagged myself to think of a catalyst, which could have possibly brought them together. It was all very unusual and I wondered if there was another syndicate like it anywhere else in the country. I doubted it. Michael had made it so but where the hell was he? He hadn't been seen for three weeks, at least not by us and somehow it didn't seem right.

Eventually a tiny piece of the mystery did fall into place when Michael turned up in my swim when Rambo and myself were a day into a three-day session during the third week of June.

"Hello, Matthew."

I recognised the voice and swung my legs over the side of my bedchair to see the rat-like face and skinny body from where the voice had emanated. The vision I saw made me double take. My words stalled on the starting grid and were at last bumped started by my embarrassment in not wanting to give Michael the impression I'd noticed anything wrong.

"… Hello there, Michael."

I was going to ask how he was but it was a stupid question because I could see how he was. He was terrible and looked like death popped in a microwave and put on a number one reheat. His face looked pale and wan and his beady little eyes had lost their sparkle, even his sharp rodent-like noise looked blunt and lifeless and as for his body, it looked even worse. Michael was skinny at best, a walk around in the shower to get wet job, for sure, but he'd lost even more weight. Although it wasn't nice to compare him to such things Michael looked as if he'd walked off a black and white Nazi newsreel depicting the glories of Auschwitz. Even more gaunt and angular than before his body looked on the point of collapse, a bag of bones would have looked overweight if it had been put alongside him.

Michael sensed my unease at his appearance. His eyes still fluttered and blinked but he seemed to have lost his nervous energy, he looked drained of life force. "I'm afraid I haven't been very well," he explained.

I waited for a more forthcoming explanation but none was offered so I felt duty bound not to ask. "Oh, right," I said trying to pitch the right level of concern. Not too little so I appeared disinterested and not too much because, if truth were told, I thought Michael looked as if he was going to die and I assumed the last thing he needed was any implication of that. "You do look a bit peaky."

He nodded and I wondered if his scraggy neck would snap with the strain. "What about Rambo's fifty, what a fantastic fish?" he said trying to summon up enthusiasm despite his discomfort.

I agreed. "Sure was. He was made up with it. Do any of the others know yet? You know, has the word got around?"

Michael's whole body twitched. Would his rib cage take it? "Not unless you've told anybody I wouldn't have thought it has. I usually send out a fish catch report, as I mentioned when you had the interview to join, twice a year. The only people I've told are Noel and Gary. I told Noel when he phoned in to say he'd had a new forty and it simply lead the conversation into Rambo's fish. I don't think Noel would say much to anyone, he's quite single-minded about his carp fishing and not unless he can see the benefit in an action he rarely does it. He'd think spreading news of a fifty would most likely make the pit busier and make it harder for him to get the right swim. I also mentioned it in passing to Gary who's been around to see me several times. Gary's been very supportive, as usual, while I've been ill, but he hasn't been fishing here at all, what with the girls wearing him out."

"That's still a runner is it?" I asked unable to show disinterest in the subject.

"Very much so. I think it's now the longest relationship Gary's ever had," Michael said.

"Come on, how long?" I asked fearing a ridiculous answer. I wasn't disappointed.

"His previous longest fling was two months and it's longer than that now," Michael answered.

Two months. Hollywood was the ultimate serial monogamist, happily hopping from one sexual encounter to another and never looking back. I had to admit the two girls must be something else to hold his interest for so long and to stop him going fishing. I tried to say something pithy and wise but ended up muttering. "He's a lad."

Michael's attitude changed slightly and he looked furtively either way and hushed his voice although it was all rather half-hearted and lacked his usual drive and intensity. "Any developments to report? Have you spotted anything odd at all?"

This was the crunch question, the one Rambo and myself knew would eventually come. And we both knew it would be me who would be asked it. Michael seemed reluctant to speak directly to Rambo concerning such matters and the onus on what to divulge appeared destined to always fall upon myself. In fact the question had taken much longer to be asked than I'd imagined because of Michael's strange, debilitating mysterious illness, which had kept him away from the pit's banks. What did I say? I was still undecided as I'd been all the times I'd played out this very meeting within the confines of my thick skull. How much to give away? How much to hold back? Rambo had told me to do whatever I thought was the right thing when the situation cropped up and that was exactly what I did.

"Nope. Nothing obvious," I said and then went slightly onto the offensive. "Why are you so concerned with all this, Michael? I mean you can chuck anyone out at any time, so what's the problem? I don't quite understand why you asked Rambo and myself for help. It's not as if you haven't managed up until now. You seem to have done all right on your own so far."

Michael looked a little put out. It was an effort for him to defend himself, I could see it plainly enough, but gamely he tried to put the record straight. "I explained the reasons why before, nothing's changed. You two've got a good track record on trouble. I told you I couldn't get here as much as I used to, although at the time I wasn't expecting this illness problem to make it quite so chronic. The size of the fish are getting bigger, consequently the grapevine will have more reason for finding out, especially as Rambo has now contributed to the situation by catching our first fifty and I felt as if I needed help to control it all. That's it in a nutshell."

I looked at Michael's shallow, weedy chest heaving. His animated response had taken a lot out of him and if anything, he looked even more ill than he had when I first set eyes on him a few minutes earlier. He was clearly very sick even now. "So this isn't some elaborate charade to test us, then?"

Michael's brow furrowed. "No, no, not at all. I trust you two more than a few others in the syndicate at the moment. You see every time I've dismissed someone from here I've always had a genuine reason. I can honestly say I've never thrown anybody out over a personality clash… Do you mind if I sit down, I'm feeling a little weak?" I got up off my chair and offered him my place. "…If I'm to run this syndicate to the standards I want I need some help, it's as simple as that."

"Why not ask Gary?"

Michael looked up from the bedchair. He had his forearms crossed and resting across his thighs. With his hollow cheeks and concentration camp limbs I envisaged him as the skull and cross bones. "Gary's done too much already. More than any best friend deserves to have to do." Michael looked down at his toes, head bowed. "Gary would like to run this place and one day, maybe sooner than both he and I imagine, he will. I've always kept him away from the nasty day to day running of things, much to his dislike and slight annoyance I think, but I've always thought it the right thing to do, for his own fishing pleasure as much as anything. As soon as you have to get involved in the nitty-gritty, day to day chores it does take the edge off the pleasure of being here, I can assure you. He's contributed in other ways, especially at the outset, offering his time and enthusiasm and when his day comes he'll realise why I let him enjoy the fishing side of it while I took the other pressures because, as I've said, the latter definitely takes the edge off the former."

Sympathy for Michael filled my thoughts. I'd got it partly wrong, his problems couldn't be all stress and syndicate related, a good percentage of them must have been a medical condition the poor sod had been born with. His words were unambiguous. His time on planet earth was numbered due to his terrible ailment, whatever it was, and when he died, Gary would take over the running of the syndicate. Now, whether that was good or bad news for the rest of us £1250 a year, £2500 '1st deposit' paying members was hard to fathom at this specific juncture but I made a mental note not to be so scathing towards

Hollywood's sexual anecdotes. And never to call him, 'Hollywood', either, well, not to his face or to the face of anyone I didn't trust. That pretty much made it exactly the same situation as it was now, I'd call him 'Hollywood' to Rambo. I was rambling.

I wondered whether Hollywood knew all this, somehow I doubted it, but in the back of his mind the thought must have occurred. I could vaguely remember a little whinge he'd had when Rambo and myself had first met him concerning Michael's lack of delegating. It was clear he wanted to help out even more than he was allowed by control freak Michael, and as best friends often do, he'd become agitated with him. I wished I could remember the thing which had niggled me at the hospital when I'd suddenly thought about the ghost's grave but for the life of me I couldn't, like I couldn't every time I tried. What I did suddenly think of was the relationship between Michael and Hollywood and for the first time I wondered if Michael's appearance was due to him having AIDS. Was Michael gay? Had he always had a crush on the gorgeous Hollywood, right from the time he was a teenager and they had first met? Was it a hidden one-way love never likely to be returned in a zillion years by the outrageously heterosexual Hollywood? Not being a fully paid up member of the politically correct union some of my sympathy evaporated but I decided I was clutching at straws. He didn't come across as being like that and surely there would have been a rumour from someone somewhere, like Darren, at the work party. Besides AIDS hardly explained the symptoms of the trembling hands, fluttering eyelids and overall nervousness. It seemed I must be barking up the wrong tree but I filed the thought for later should any extra gen support the idea.

It all ended up meaning I didn't know what to say. "Sorry, Michael, I only wanted to get it absolutely straight in my head," I ended up muttering by way of an apology for putting him through more aggro than he needed.

Michael gave me a low wattage smile. "That's ok. It must seem a bit odd from your point of view."

"Not as odd as fishing a water with a resident ghost!" I joked.

Michael's body jolted as if an invisible and silent bullet had hit it. His head turned and looked at me while his nearest shoulder to me twitched and gyrated. "Have you seen the ghost? I mean... those silly old stories keep cropping up from time to time, I can't understand why people keep bringing the subject up."

"Have *you*?" I countered holding his eye.

Michael looked at me, eyelids dancing, and then turned away. "No."

As much as I knew the sex of my unborn baby girl and her name to be, I could see Michael was lying. Why the denial? Why the façade of discrediting? Why, whenever I found out or sussed out something new, did it raise more questions and never seem to supply any answers?

Michael was still facing away from me and his voice was barely audible. "Have you seen it, Matthew?" He said trying to turn the tables once again.

I didn't answer, I was furiously struggling with argument and counter argument within my head as to what to tell him. Michael's head turned back to face me. "Tell me the truth, Matthew, have you seen a ghost on this water?"

I wavered and then it was out. "I've seen something, what exactly, I'm not sure. I suppose it could have been a ghost if you were prone to making those sorts of assumptions and believe in those sorts of things. To be honest it happened so quickly and was over so soon it could have been my own imagination," I said, not being honest at all. "I felt a chill in the air when I got out of my sleeping bag to check on a single beep, a rush of wind like a body speeding by me and," I threw open my hands in an empty gesture, "that was it. Goodnight Mr Ghost, if it was he or she. Ms Ghost, perhaps!"

Michael gave a dull smile. "It was probably your imagination. I can remember waking up with the shakes and feeling cold when a buzzer goes, what with getting out of a toasty bag and then feeling the cold night air. I expect you didn't put on any extra clothes before you went out and it might have been a clear, cold night."

I nodded. "I didn't put any extra clothes on and it was a full moon, I can remember that."

"There you are. A disorientated carp angler, half asleep, suffering a temperature drop of at least 20°C. There's normally a rational explanation," said Michael.

Even for irrational carp anglers, I thought. The phrase made me think of Alan and my denial to him of any knowledge of the ghost. Still, I was on safe ground, there was no way Michael would tell Alan what I'd just told him. "You might be right," I admitted. "Who can say?

At that moment my mobile phone rang and I went inside my bivvy and took it out from the inside pocket and answered it. "Hello."

"Hello, boy, only me. How's it going?" said Rambo.

"Yeah, all right. How about you?"

"Fine. Is Michael with you?" Rambo asked.

"Yeah, that's right. Why's that then?" I said trying not to arouse Michael's interest in the conversation and not wanting to seem scheming or rude by walking off.

Rambo's voice continued. "I went back to the clubhouse to have a crap and saw his pick-up, that's all, and I guessed he'd make a bee-line for you. Anyway I'm not phoning because of that, I just wanted to know if he was with you and whether you could find out something from him. You see when I was coming back out of the clubhouse dickhead Rocky was coming the other way. I gave him a look like a summons and the cheeky sod said something to the effect that he'd heard I'd managed to fluke out the pit's first fifty. I'll tell you, boy, I was close to re-arranging his face on a permanent basis but I kept my cool, said he was right and left it. Now, the thing is, you know about it and Michael knows about it. How come the camouflage clotheshorse knows about it? Ask Michael, not directly of course, use your forked tongue, the one you use to tell Sophie how hard you've been working, if he's told anyone about the fifty. It might help tie in a few people together if you see what I mean."

I was frantically thinking on my feet. "He's here with me, he's been pretty ill I'm afraid but he's on the mend now, that's why we haven't seen him around. Ok. Yep. Will do, mate," I said and turned off the phone and stared into mid-air. I already had a partial answer, Michael had been ill and the only person he'd told was Hollywood and this Noel bloke, the one who was prone to the occasional spoonerism. Hollywood hadn't been fishing as far as we knew and according to Michael, Noel would have kept it under his hat. Someone was creating a smokescreen and acting out of character, or at least it seemed that way. I couldn't for the life of me see Hollywood wanting to nick fish from a water he'd helped create and which was destined to be his one day even if he was not one hundred percent certain of this last bombshell. Had Noel spoken about the fifty to Rocky, or Darren, or somewhere else. Perhaps when receiving a delivery of stolen fish? Rocky had made a big mistake, a big, big, big mistake in trying to taunt Rambo and unveiling a hidden connection. There was still one more connection to be made. I had to go for it.

"That was Rambo. He noticed your pick-up when he visited the club house and was wondering how you were and where you'd been and... well you heard what I said... he sends his regards." I paused for a second before continuing. "Here... this is something I've been meaning to ask you, what made you get a pick-up for a fishing vehicle? It's not the safest way to carry tackle around is it?"

Michael shrugged his bony shoulders. "It's useful enough for carting stuff around, especially at the work party but as you say it's not ideal for tackle. You can't leave it for five minutes if you've got tools or tackle in the back. I remember I had a strimmer stolen from it once when I was filling up with diesel."

I attempted informal indifferent insouciance but my heart upped its tempo. "Does anyone ever borrow it from you?"

Michael gave a glum shake of his skull bone with one layer of skin. "Not really. In fact it's been at a garage having some work done on it for well over a month or so. I took it in just before I was taken ill and I only got it back a few days ago."

"What garage do you use? Are they any good?" I said trying to keep things going after Michael's disappointing answer. "It's always handy to know a good garage especially if I have some trouble in this neck of the wood, you know, where I don't know the area so well."

"Broughton Motors. They're off the A290 by Pean Hill," said Michael who was very uninterested in this whole line of questioning.

At least it wasn't where we'd hired the dreaded Micra but it still meant more bloody questions to ask, the most immediate being; how implicated was Noel by the mere fact he'd possibly spoken to Rocky about Rambo's fifty? Hollywood was in the frame but you couldn't count him, Michael wouldn't be willing to leave his proudest achievement to him if he didn't consider him to be a true friend and to be beyond reproach. Either way I was treading water in a swimming pool of deviousness and nefarious actions. Would I ever get to the bottom of it? And if I did, would I be able to get back up to the surface without drowning? Time to slip on the aqualung of astute deduction and avoid the diving boots of acute corruption... by catching the bastards and shopping them!

Chapter 15

The feeding spell had passed over an hour ago, the rods had been wound in and I'd popped along to see my mate, as you do, to let him make me a cuppa. Subsequently I sat in unashamed luxury, my arse parked on a well-padded bedchair, sipping a Rambo-made, PG Tips special in a mug the size of a kiddie's sandcastle bucket, without the castled rim. The tea would spill all over your lap. The summer sun was hot, and so it should be as well, since we were now well into the month of August. The time since I'd spoken to the sickly Michael had whizzed by and the progress we had made in trying to determine the mastermind behind the fish thieves and the whereabouts of the ghost's grave could be summed up in two words. Fuck all. And it wasn't for the want of trying either. On average we had fished a session of three to four days every ten days, we had kept our eyes peeled and had even gone to the extent of winding in on many nights, thus depriving ourselves of action, and having a prowl around, all to no avail. On three occasions we had cut our session short because Darren and Rocky alone, had been on the pit with us. We'd gone through the charade of packing up, of going to the hire garage and getting the same Nissan Micra, of squeezing into the damn thing, of parking it up, of hiking into the old woods, of bivvying up and then sneaking off around the pit to spy on the two fish thieves. And what had they done? Fuck all. On the first outing two other members had turned up while we were gone so it was game over and a complete waste of effort before we'd even started. On the other two times Darren had lay lined the stock pond but had blanked, as had his rods, and, much to mine and Rambo's anguish, so had the camouflage clotheshorse. They'd caught fuck all, the useless gits, and so had fuck all to steal. It all went to underline how fortunate we'd been to catch them at it on our very first go. Beginner's luck? Hardly so considering Rambo's perfect planning but it made the pair of us realise what a tricky task we'd undertaken.

As to the main players in our tiny little world of carp fishing syndicates? Well, Michael was non-existent, Hollywood was conspicuous by his absence and Noel, you see Noel didn't seem to fish the same slots as us even though we'd tried virtually every permutation in terms of different days of the week. We tried Monday to Wednesday. We tried Wednesday to Friday. We tried Friday to Monday but it made no difference, so, in keeping with the general trend we saw fuck all of Noel.

During this period I'd speculated on what the ghost might be making of my efforts to help him. I presumed it was able to see into our world but how much of it was open to its ghostly gaze, I wasn't sure. What did it do with itself when it wasn't out manifesting itself to slightly psychic carp anglers? It had a lot of time on its hands seeing as it had only popped out to say: 'Boo!' to Alan, and myself and if my intuition was correct, to Michael. Three people in how many years? It was hardly overworking itself, but who could guess at the restraining parameters it was under? I expected there were a set of rules. Something akin to our laws of physics which governed the structure of our universe, for spectres and it could have been these that placed the ghost under unfathomable constraints. Where did it go during the vast periods of inactivity? Back into the remains of its dead body? Where was the body? Where was the grave? I was beginning to think it was a watery one. After all the ghost had shot out over the pit and I could see the attraction of dumping a dead body plus large concrete weight in the middle of twenty-nine acres of water so long as nobody foul-hooked it! What a gruesome catch, worse than a three pound snotty in the middle of the night! This did presume the ghost was killed after the pit was dug but was this the case? When all was said and done I decided I knew fuck all about ghosts and fuck all about my specific one, which wasn't strictly true, but it did cover my general feelings of dissatisfaction.

Rambo had taken a visit to Broughton Motors, hoping to uncover the other Alan, the unrecognised pick-up driver, as we assumed the vehicle had been used on the fish stealing night while it was there being repaired, or rather, had been repaired. To go along with the rest of our recent efforts Rambo, naturally enough, didn't find him, nor find any reference to him when he made discreet enquiries. At the end of the day, to drop into football player parlance, the significance of the involvement of the pick-up was lost on me. Had it been used in previous raids, if there were any? How would it have been known that it was in the garage? Who would have known it was there? Was someone trying to be extra clever by rubbing salt in Michael's wounds and if so what was the point? If he found out it was shit against the fan time, the whole point was not to be found out, so why bother with the added insult? I'd covered the angle of it giving extra cover to the driver by it being a known vehicle, but even that had no credence. What could be less worrying than a chance sighting of the syndicate owner's car going on route either to or from the pit? Usually nothing, but at least two people had said Michael didn't ever fish at night, so far from the pick-up giving cover it might have aroused suspicion. Why did Michael never fish at night? Because of the ghost? Because of his condition? What was the other thing someone had said which I felt sure had a significant bearing on the situation? I still couldn't remember. What did it all mean? What sense could I make out of it? Not a lot I was ashamed to say and my brain reeled and addled like it had so many times in the past over other matters. Yet for all the bizarre states of affairs, mad personalities and desperate scenarios that the pursuit of carp fishing had lead me to, this one was by far the weirdest of the lot.

If success in all the above departments was decidedly iffy, then on the carp catching front, at least, things were awesome. I'd now had ten thirties and three more forties, all existing poster members and all well up on their listed weights. In fact when I'd hooked and landed Page 3 I was convinced I too had matched Rambo and caught my very first English fifty. The fully scaled mirror was a magnificent creature and had thumped the Reuben's down to a mind-boggling 49-14. It was by far and away the most fantastic looking carp I'd ever seen let alone ever caught and the fact it couldn't quite manage to get gravity to winch it through the half-century barrier made no difference whatsoever. Apart from me wishing it had managed to get gravity to winch it through the half-century barrier so that I could say I'd caught an English fifty. It was a sad little eye opener on my brainwashed mentality and I rightly chastised myself while Rambo teased me mercilessly for not being able to catch a 'pukka', 'keeping it real', English fifty as he had earlier.

"You wait until we find out that Michael's fish, although he bought them as being home-grown, were actually imported by a buyer further down the chain," I'd said.

Rambo had laughed and so had I. Putting out a list of meritocracy for carp fishing, whether on angling ability or specific carp status, was as sad as it got. We were going great guns but had spent nearly four grand for the pleasure of getting at the size of fish we had in front of us. Did that makes us any better than an angler catching rakes of doubles and low twenties on a club water? Of course not. Commercial puddles overstocked with carp as against large, sparsely populated gravel pits? One angler pulling out loads of fish, the other sitting it out for one run a month if he was lucky. Did that make Mr Onerun superior? In his head as he sneered down at the weekend angler from his lofty point of self-opinionated moral high ground, maybe. Foreign fish against English ones? Foreign fish masquerading as English fish? English fish shoved from pillar to post, sometimes with consent sometimes without? The non-indigenous species argument? Who could unravel the tangled intricacies of the carp catching pecking order and who gave a toss if they could? Not Rambo or myself, I have to admit. The non-level playing field, which constituted the impossible conundrum of who was the best carp angler, was littered with potholes for some and, metaphorically speaking, riddled with performance enhancing drugs for others. But each to their own, let anglers carp fish on their own terms according to their own lives and personal situations. It was a good job different anglers were prepared to fish a wide range of assorted venues and I suspected most fished a variety to satisfy a certain craving for a certain type of carping at any given time. Except when you were in a syndicate as brilliant as ours. But that was another argument.

Away from proceedings at the pit Sophie was looking more and more the mum-to-be daily. Not that I could rigorously verify the statement seeing as I wasn't seeing her on a daily basis. I was away working, in chunks of three or four days, sometimes Monday to Wednesday, sometimes Wednesday to Friday and also on the odd Friday to Monday. I did feel a bit bad about the continual duping I was giving her but I played the doting father-to-be to perfection when I was with her. To be fair that isn't correct, I didn't play it, I genuinely was it. My revelation during the first scan wasn't a five minute wonder, although maybe the sex act that had created the baby might have been, I couldn't really remember, it was a for-life feeling. I felt comfortable with my impending change of circumstances, unlike I had earlier, and I felt shamed by my original thoughts. I was proud of my future contribution to the human race and knew I would cherish her once she was born. Why she might even like to come fishing with me when she grew up!

What with my positive attitude towards the pregnancy and my apparent work ethic, Sophie and I were getting on famously. The large wads of cash Rambo kept insisting on giving me for our 'work' made the scam complete and, in Sophie's eyes at least, financially underlined my commitment. I felt sleazy enough taking the dosh from Rambo but what I'd have felt like should Sophie have ever found out what I was really up to, I shall never know. At least that's the way I wanted it to stay and I prayed it would stay like it forever! Questions like the one asking if I would still have been doing the same thing if it weren't for the ghost were inclined to be tucked away at the bottom of my brain. My one redeeming thought, in my head, was that I was only tricking Sophie to get to the bottom of the ghost and the fish stealing plot and not to go carp fishing *per se*. Hmm?

Sophie would spend hours playing music to Amy, with the portable cassette player pressed against her swollen belly. She claimed she'd read it was very therapeutic for the developing child to be subjected to music and language even when still in the womb. The beneficial developments in terms of speaking and communication, once born, were meant to be outstanding and how could I argue? I mused frequently on the subject of how, just how, I had known the baby inside Sophie was a girl and why she would be called Amy. It was a disconcerting feeling, one that was enhanced one evening when Sophie, having finished subjecting her stomach to Robbie Williams, had started to talk about names. She had previously bought one of those books detailing nearly every name under the sun which also details a brief history of origins and meanings. She'd casually asked if I'd any ideas and I told her I hadn't and feeling intrigued and nervous I'd asked if she had.

"I've spent a few hours looking at the book I bought the other day and I've picked three which I really like, do you want to hear them? If you don't like them I'll have another look, it's got to be a joint decision, after all she is ours," she'd said.

I'd nodded enthusiastically. "She'll be ours when she's good and yours when she's naughty," I'd said trying to play down the moment-of-truth shortly to arrive.

Sophie had gone and picked up the book. "Here we are. The first one I like is Chloe, that's a Greek name meaning 'fresh young blossom'. The second is Bethany, which is Aramaic and the third one is Amy, which is a French name meaning 'beloved friend'."

"They're all nice," I'd said. "I really like them all. You choose, I don't mind either way."

Sophie had given me a rolled eyes look. "Come on, you must like one more than the others. You must have a preference, however slight."

"Have you got a preference?"

Sophie wrinkled her nose. "Sort of."

"Write it down on a piece of paper and then go and get the envelope, the one I sealed with candle wax," I'd said.

Sophie had looked a bit bemused but she'd indulged me and wrote her favourite name on a scrap of paper and had gone and got the envelope.

"Fold up your bit of paper and give it to me," I'd said, like I was some sort of professional stage magician. I'd no doubts but this was the time for reality to authenticate what I'd learnt asleep in the old woods inside a mud stained bivvy. Calling 'girl' was no different than winning the toss of a coin but getting the name correct meant something odd had happened to me. I already knew it had happened but this was the hour of confirmation.

Sophie had handed me her scrap of paper which I hadn't opened. "Sit down and undo the envelope."

"What's this all about, Matthew?" she'd asked and I could tell she really had no idea at all.

"Open it and you'll see."

Sophie had ripped open the envelope like a child tearing at a Christmas present, her face expressing both delight and curiosity until it changed to one of complete stupefaction. Her mouth had fallen wide open as she'd sucked in air and she'd let out a little cry of shock. Her yawning maw had been immediately covered by a trembling left hand. While she had stared at the piece of paper, I, rather superfluously considering her reactions, had looked at hers. On it was written 'Amy'. Yet again a shrill tingle had zoomed up and down my spine like a deranged yo-yo. It was all for real, whatever it was.

I'd felt compelled to tell her when she'd asked how I'd known. I'd wanted to tell her the story of the ghost and the surrounding mystery and to be honest if it hadn't been for Rambo and the work scam, I would have. As it was I'd shrugged and explained that I couldn't explain it. At least I hadn't lied on that occasion. Secretly I'd hoped she'd mark it down as an extreme case of father/child bonding, while I wondered if it was more a case of carp angler/ghost bonding.

"Do you think we'll ever crack this one, boy?" said Rambo, dragging me back into the present.

"Buggered if I know," I said with passion. "If something else doesn't give soon we might have to go to Michael with what we've got, or if he's too ill, I guess we'll have to tell Hollywood instead." Rambo said nothing. I'd told him all the stuff concerning Michael and his implication of Hollywood eventually becoming the proud owner of the syndicate. "What do you think?"

Rambo chucked the dregs of his tea onto the grass. "I'd hold fire for a bit longer, boy. Make sure we know exactly what's what and who's with who before we put our cards on the table. We've got plenty of methods to explore before we're up shit creek, most of them pretty desperate but torturing Rocky is something I'd be prepared to put up with if I thought it was going to help."

"How much do you hate him?" I asked.

"On a scale of one to ten?"

"On a scale of me to Watt," I offered.

Rambo considered. "If it isn't quite Watt, it isn't very far off, I can tell you."

"You've mellowed, though," I said.

"What do you mean?" snapped an indignant Rambo.

"Well, you don't sit there breaking 15lb Big Game line between your bare hands in times of stress, like you used to."

"I'm on Pro Gold now," said Rambo disdainfully.

"Is that a mono or a type of marijuana?"

"Cello haps! Sorry! Hello chaps, how are you?" The pair of us looked up in surprise at the new voice that had snuck up on us, the new voice which simply had to belong to Noel. Elusive Noel, namer of the forty, Flit Spin, he of the occasional spoonerism and possible head of fish stealing activities, had come to us at last. "I'm Noel. Are you Matt and Rambo?

We both nodded. Noel didn't look much like a fish thief as I eyed him up and down but when I came to think it through it occurred to me that Rambo did. Never judge a book by its cover, or so they say. Noel was a small bloke, no more than 5' 8", mid forties at a guess, short-cropped hair which was receding at the front and he wore glasses. He looked… benign but I reminded myself it was often the way with people like him, it was the thugs who did the dirty work while the brains hid discreetly in the background.

Noel continued to explain himself. "I wanted to come and find you because when I was talking to Michael some time ago he mentioned Rambo had caught the pit's first ever fifty. I was so thrilled I thought I must make the effort to come and congratulate you. Michael told me what sort of car the pair of you usually came in and when I saw it in the car park I decided I must pop in. I seem to have been constantly missing you because I've made the point of asking other members about you?"

"Which ones?" I asked. I mentally winced, a bit too brusque and strained.

Noel seemed unflustered. "Darren and Rocky, they fish frequently and have seen you, Grant, I think and one or two others. I've made quite an effort, usually I simply fish and only really bump into people in the car park or clubhouse. I can't remember the last time I nipped into an angler's swim. Not really my style, I'm afraid. Anyway," Noel walked up to Rambo and offered his hand. "Congratulations. Well done! Let's hope that soon there are a few more."

Rambo gave me a quick glance and shook Noel's hand. I stared at the grip wondering if Rambo would scrunch Noel's hand to pulp but either Noel was impervious to pain or Rambo went easy on him because his friendly smile never wavered.

Noel gave a jaunty little step. "Well, chaps. That's it, I won't disturb you any more, I'll go and get myself set up and leave you in peace! Goodbye and good luck!"

Noel turned to go and I stepped forward. "I'll come back to the car park with you, I need to use the toilet before I go back to my swim and cast out again."

Noel looked moderately surprised. "Right-ho. As you wish."

I did that quick little shuffle people do when they walk across a pedestrian crossing after the waiting car driver has ushered them over and caught Noel up. "So how long have you been in the syndicate, then?"

Noel gave me a brief smile. "Oh, ten years now, it must be. I don't know of too many longer standing members apart from Gary and Alan. I know it must sound odd me saying such a thing but in all honesty I'm not familiar with all the members. You don't seem to ever get to meet them all, it's a bit like us, if I hadn't popped by I'd have gone and set up and you wouldn't have even known I was here if you didn't know my car."

"That's right," I said. "It was one of the first things we noticed coming from other syndicates, how disjointed the membership was."

Noel chuckled. "Just between me and you I think Michael quite likes it that way. He's an odd chap, very particular about members, I'm convinced he's always imagining we're all up to something."

"And are we?" I said.

"Lood gord no! Well, I suppose I have to temper that statement by saying not that I'm aware of. Who in their right mind would risk getting expelled from here? Apart from losing a hefty 1st deposit there's the fishing as well. I mean, is there a better carp water in England than this one? I very much doubt it."

"True enough," I said. "And we've got a ghost thrown in for nothing!"

Noel scoffed. "Crap! What a load of codswallop. I've never had a hint of anything remotely ghostly happen to me. The only people who ever mention it are Alan and Gary. Alan believes in it and Gary seems to love mentioning it because it upsets Michael so."

"Why would Gary do that?" I asked. "He's Michael's best friend isn't he? I know he's only mucking around but why do it." Noel went silent and never answered. "Why though?" I asked again.

Noel stopped walking and faced me. "I have my theories but they're not for me to say because they might be wrong."

I decided to go for it. "I bet I know," I said. "You think Gary mentions the ghost because he knows Michael is afraid of it, which means Michael must believe in it too."

Noel gave a smirk. "Of course. What you must ask yourself is why he does it. Does someone with Michael's obvious nervous disorder need to be upset, even if it is in jest, by his best friend? Is it conducive to improving his health or not, and if not, why do it? Why add to his worries even if it is only in fun?"

It suddenly clicked in my head. Hollywood did reckon Michael was going to leave him the syndicate when he pegged out. He was simply trying to speed up the process of it happening, albeit in a very understated manner. Still, if the odd jibe concerning the ghost amounted to knocking six months off poor old Michael's expected life span, it might be worth it from Hollywood's point of view. It suddenly went double click in my head. Noel might be painting Hollywood in a terrible light to smoke screen his own dubious, fish nicking motives. Realistically how potent a weapon was the mention of a ghost in trying to shorten someone's life span? Mind you, it was true. Hollywood had even done it in front of us once! Bloody hell, more sodding questions than answers as usual, the major one being why was Michael so scared of the ghost? He'd definitely got even more jumpy when I'd confronted him.

I turned away from Noel and looked towards the car park and to my discomfort I saw Rocky unloading a large designer camouflage rucksack while in full designer camouflage regalia. Shit! It was time for me to run the gauntlet.

"Rocky's here," I mumbled weakly.

"So I see," said Noel and we started walking again. "What on earth is he doing unloading his tackle in the car park?"

The pair of us marched on side by side in silence until we arrived at the back of Noel's car. Rocky's ever increasing pile of predominantly neo-camo patterned tackle was adjacent to it as was a very agitated Rocky.

"What are you doing, Rocky?" asked Noel.

"Got a fucking flat," said Rocky wrestling with the now exposed carpet of his estate car to get at the spare. "It only happened at the top of the track. Fucking marvellous! You come fishing to get away from agg and you get shit like this happen."

"Hardly life threatening, though," said Noel disinterestedly. "You have to put these little blips into perspective, you see."

Rocky gave Noel an evil glare. From my perspective it looked pretty life threatening but thankfully only for Noel. If these two were in cahoots they were good at acting out denial. I watched Rocky perform in fascination, as it seemed odd to be so close to him in the daylight and for him to be aware of my existence. At least I presumed he was aware of my existence because he'd not so much as glanced at me, let alone acknowledged me. Normally I would have been buried in some clump of foliage in the pitch black, listening to his voice and imagining his movements in his trendy, now you see me, now you don't outfit. Not that I saw him at all at night so maybe that explained my present total absorption. Sweat had made Rocky's forehead glisten as he uncontinuously heaved the spare wheel out from its snug hiding place and he tossed it onto the ground. His head and shoulders plunged back into the estate car's rear and he literally threw out the jack and wheel brace backwards while still stooped under the rear door. Both the jack and brace thumped into the dirt.

From within the car I heard Rocky start to whinge again. "What the fuck's that doing in here?" Rocky's muffled voice turned clear again as he came back up for air. He had black marks on his nose where he had rubbed it after handling the spare. "I don't need that fucking thing either," he said to no one in particular and he tossed aside an old rusty hammer.

Something inside me stirred. "What's that you've just chucked out," I asked, nodding at the rusty tool lying on the ground.

It was my turn for the withering glare. "Do what?" said Rocky.

"That. That hammer," I said as I walked over to it and proceeded to squat down alongside it.

Rocky snorted. "It's a fucking hammer you idiot, what do you think it is?"

I tentatively ran my fingers above the wooden shaft and then above the top of the rusty head. A ballpane hammer. A very rusty ballpane hammer. I touched it and a searing flash of pain shot up my arm. I'd got a poke from a rusty ballpane hammer! My hand pulled back instinctively like it had many times before when I'd accidentally touched a live wire at work and had got a belt of 240 for my carelessness. It sparked my brain as well. Rocky had been watching. He let out a cold laugh.

"Jesus! Are you for real, pal? It won't bite you."

"Where did you get it from?" I said, unperturbed by his clear hostility to me.

"What?"

"Where did you find it? Did you find it here?" I continued.

"I found it in the back of my car," said Rocky smugly, as if he'd cracked the world's funniest joke.

"Before that," I said evenly. "Where did you find it before that?"

"You are one sad bastard," said Rocky picking up the jack and wheel brace.

"Please tell me," I said.

Rocky looked at me as if I was mad. He might have been right, it was hard for me to tell at that precise instant. He started to put the jack into position and said nothing.

"Did you find it in the water?" I said, not giving in.

Rocky's large shoulders were winding the jack furiously. He stopped. "If you must know, saddo, I foul hooked it in the pit about three days ago. I was practising my casting and must have crashed one out nearly two hundred yards and when I wound in the hammer was on the end." Rocky turned around from his car and faced me. "You can keep it if you like. Now, would you be so kind as to fuck off and leave me alone?"

Gingerly I picked up the hammer. Nothing. I walked the short distance back to Noel who had been watching the whole thing. I gave him a dumb little smile. Noel gave me a look of disbelief back. My eye caught a sticker in the back of his car window. On it, it had the words 'Broughton Motors. Quality repairs and servicing'."

On seeing the word 'quality', I was time warped. "See you then, chief," I told Noel and I strode off towards Rambo. I felt his eyes follow me.

When I got back to his swim I could barely contain myself and jabbered and babbled my short story to him like a man possessed, or at least like a man who had been previously possessed. Rambo looked flummoxed throughout and simply stared at me as if I was barking mad. "This is it!" I cried holding out the rusty hammer in both my shaking hands. "This is the murder weapon. This is the blunt instrument of death that beat the ghost to an early grave and was thrown, presumed to be hidden forever, into the pit by the assailant!" I could hardly contain my excitement. "And…

And," I said feverishly. "I know where the grave is! When I got the jolt from…" I waved both my hands above my head as I became lost for words, "… from wherever… I remembered! I fucking remembered! And, this is the real big one, if I'm right, I know who the murderer is." I shook Rambo's shoulder with my non-hammer holding hand. "I don't know why I didn't think of it before. I saw the ghost blast out across the pit but I needed to remember to fit it all together, and now I have!" I paused for effect. "Across the pit to the island! The ghost went across the pit to the island. My island! The one I was casting to when I had the visitation in my swim! And if there's a body on the island, there can only be one murderer! I know who it did it! I can't believe it but it explains everything! I know! I bloody well know! If there's a body there, I know!"

I looked at Rambo in a state of disturbed and distraught demented disorientation. I was more unhinged than a sink estate maisonette's front door after a drugs bust. Genius and madness often go hand in glove, they have a thin dividing line and for a moment I stood astride that line, with a foot in either half, wearing a glove with 'madness' written on it, sheathing a hand with 'geni' tattooed across the knuckles. Things never work out perfectly in the limited world of knuckle tattoos but amazingly away from the world of four letter words all was hunky-dory. I'd finally cracked it.

I looked at Rambo who'd remained silent. I clenched my teeth and expressed my hands emphatically in front of my body. They screamed 'there you are'. Rambo lifted his head and stretched the underside of his chin but stayed mute.

"Well say something," I said in frustration. "Even if it's only 'bollocks'!"

Rambo's face was set in stone but eventually he raised a single, Spock-like eyebrow. I nodded enthusiastically, eyes wide open, in order to draw out his verbal response.

Rambo gave a little shake of his head. "There's no way that bullshitting cunt can cast two hundred yards, you know."

Chapter 16

Despite an hour elapsing since I'd first told Rambo what had happened with Noel and Rocky I was still flabbergasted. "So you don't want to know who the murderer is?" I demanded, my voice strained with incredulity.

"Nope," said Rambo emphatically. "When we find the grave and the body in it, then you can reveal the whole story, but until then, boy, it's zipped lips on the subject."

I was like a dog with a new bone and I couldn't let it lie. I picked the bone up, flicked it in the air, watched it turn somersaults and caught it in my stinky, dog-breath teeth. "Why don't you want to know?" I asked again. "I cannot comprehend the fact you don't want to know. All this time we've been striving for a breakthrough and now we've got one you don't want to know. Why? Eh? Tell me why?" I said feeling miffed.

Rambo was unconcerned. "Don't fret over it. If you're right we'll find the body on the island. If we find the body on the island then you say you'll know who the murderer is and that will be the time for you to inform me of your theory. You see, boy, from where I'm sitting all we have is a rusty hammer that prick-face says he foul hooked from the pit having cast two hundred yards into it. No doubt using an eleven-foot, 1¾TC rod armed with 20lb mono on a centre pin reel. From my perspective, I have no ghost and therefore no murder victim and no tale of a failed friendship, no brutal beatings, no pain and no desperate thirst for revenge and help. I have no hint of the island which you now say you remember as being significant as revealed by a separate source…" I tried to interject but Rambo held out a hand and I stopped. "… What I *do* have is your tale of the ghost and a trail leading into the old wood. And, having looked at the end of that trail and found nothing, I have my own certainties that somebody else went back to look over the same area as I had. I have to admit the person who did go back must have known the area but without your input I'd have no reason to have gone there in the first place and I would also have no reason to suspect any dark dealings whatsoever."

"Don't you believe me?" I asked. I tried not to let it sound sulky but it was mission impossible.

"You definitely don't have to worry about that one," said Rambo flashing me a 'chin up, son', smile. "I have every confidence in you. No! I have total confidence in you and I'm sure what you have worked out in that whirring brain of yours will turn out to be right." Rambo came over to me and put a friendly arm around my shoulder. He knew I was upset by his not wanting to know and this was his way of telling me not to take it personally. "You see, boy, the real reason I don't want to know yet is because I want to have a clear run at solving the fish nicking problem.

If you fill my head with ideas over the murder it might distract or influence me from sorting out Rocky and Co. The two might not be directly linked as such or they may be. Time will tell. I simply need an unclouded view." Rambo gave me a crushing hug that a bear would have been proud of. "I'm glad you've sorted it. We're a team, me and you, stronger together than apart." He took his arm away and gave me one of his friendly jabs to my shoulder. More bruising. "Besides, it's too early to give the game away now. They never give the game away too early in books and films, do they?"

I laughed. "I suppose not."

Rambo gave me a wink. "Get back to your swim and go catch some carp and when we come back next time we'll go take a look on the island. I'll sort out all the gear we'll need and we'll do it and find the truth once and for all. At night. Just so we can have the shit scared out of us!"

I gave a small jerk of the head and a rueful smile. "Do you think the garage sticker fingered Noel?"

"Leave it to me. Rocky and Co. are on borrowed time." Rambo's face changed and turned dark, it was a look I hadn't seen since the first syndicate. "Especially, Rocky. I don't like him at all. Big understatement. He's got it coming!" With perfect synchronicity Rambo punched his fist into his open palm with a loud crack. The camouflage war clouds were rolling in over the horizon, they were black, ominous and doom-laden. I said my goodbyes and turned on my heels and walked back to my swim. Perhaps we'd have a double murder on the water.

I walked back to my swim, aimlessly spinning the rusty hammer, one hand twisting the wooden shaft, the other palm acting as a loose socket, lost in a world of my own thoughts. I had it sussed. I was convinced. Everything now fitted perfectly into place except one thing. Why? Why had it happened? What was the reason? I had no idea but the burden of knowing the rest was enough. Rambo had hit the nail on the head, I stopped spinning the hammer and swung it down to earth to mirror my thoughts, without the ghost we had nothing. But I did have the ghost, it had called for help from me and through a succession of hard work and luck I now had the answer of who had killed it and what weapon had done it. I looked at the mundane tool in my hand. There was something similar to it in virtually every household in the country. How could anyone wield it so cruelly? What on earth could drive a person to such lengths? What could make a person bludgeon another to death in such a deeply personal and intimate manner? A pilot could drop a bomb on a spot on the earth's surface and kill hundreds but it lacked, to my mind anyway, the sickening violence of actually beating someone to death as you stood over them and pounded and pounded and pounded. As you dripped sweat on them, so their blood splashed over you. How fucking gruesome was that? And yet he'd done it! And it made such perfect sense, now I'd remembered the whole thing after the surge of power had untangled my brain when I'd first touched the hammer. Was that the work of the ghost as well? Had I somehow built up a charge of ghostly static, which had discharged itself when I'd touched the murder weapon? Close analysis was a tad overbearing. Much more of this psychic phenomenon shit and I'd end up sitting in a tent gazing into a crystal ball at some freak show. I laughed to myself, from one freak show to another. Syndicates; love them or hate them, I had no chance of denying them.

Looking ahead to our next visit I was filled with dread at the prospect of finding the body and felt I would only cope because Rambo would be with me, if he wasn't elsewhere engaged stringing Rocky up by his bollocks and dropping molten lead up his nostrils. Strange how that idea wasn't quite so sickening. I didn't like Rocky either. Or Darren, the snivelling little shit. The other onerous thing was what were we to do once we had a body, a murder weapon and, legally speaking, a suspect? Suspect my arse, guilty party more like. But what was the ruling on evidence submitted by a third party to a key witness, the third party being dead and even more importantly, the victim? A load more dosh for the ultimate parasites on the human race, namely solicitors and barristers and other learned professions, that's what. The scumbags. Sucking money out of people's misery at a cool £148 an hour, or whatever the going rate happened to be. What a rip-off. The ultimate irony, seeking justice only to get stitched up in court. Legal aid? Got nothing, earned nothing, contributed nothing? You can have it. Got something, earned a bit, contributed lots? You can't. Pay up and look big with the chance of costs taking everything you've ever had away from you. So many arguments but always only one sure winner. To be fair, maybe society got the type of legal people it deserved but what a disaster area. Estate agents? Not in the same league. Rogue builders. Bloody amateurs! The law is an ass. An ass-shaped piggy bank stuffed with fifty-pound notes. Allegedly.

I cast out my three rods but I was the epitome of the phrase 'going through the motions'. I sat and waited for the session to end and it couldn't come quick enough in my eyes. I was transfixed with wanting to do the dirty job on the island to get it over with and yet at the same time not wanting the day to come. At night I struggled to sleep, not because of noisy buzzers, but because my mind was a bait box of heaving, writhing maggots, ones left out in the summer sun. Like so many events in my life before I went over and over the same ground time and time again, only now the conclusions were all exactly the same. When I had mulled over Rebecca at Lac Fumant it had been like plucking petals off a flower and saying: 'She wants to shag me, no she doesn't, she wants to shag me, no she doesn't'. Of course there was a parallel plucking going on at the same time when I asked: 'If she wants to shag me I will, if she wants to shag me I won't'. There were none of those types of quandaries to concern me, the jigsaw was complete and the picture made utter sense, all bar the big question of why? The motive. I squeezed my eyes shut and waited for the release of sleep. No wonder he was the way he was, it was getting to me and I hadn't even done it.

It was a week before we were ready to go back and do the deed. Rambo had organised the operation with his usual military precision and flair putting together all the necessary hardware and the game plan. In the back of my van were two wetsuits, two pairs of flippers, a small inflatable boat, a foot pump, paddles, rope, a shovel, a spade, a band saw, a mattock, lights, various hand tools and a body bag. My contribution was the rusty hammer.

"No petrol generator and Kango?" I'd quipped. "And what the hell have we got a body bag for?"

Rambo gave me a deadpan look. "That's in case you die of fright, boy and I have to bring you back. Or I can always bury you alongside the ghost if you like!"

"Very funny. We're not thinking of exhuming the body there and then are we?" I queried, swallowing deeply.

Rambo hitched up his shoulders. "I wouldn't have thought so. It was more belt and braces thinking than anything else, I like to be fully prepared for every eventuality."

"I know," I said ruefully. "Do you still keep a spare couple of hand grenades in your rucksack?"

"You just try stopping me."

"What colour are the wetsuits?"

Rambo looked puzzled. "Black!"

"Not camo?"

"Not camo," said Rambo categorically. "Come on, let's get the fishing gear in over the top of this lot and get going. The quicker we get it over and done with the better."

The pair of us chucked both our sets of gear into the van, climbed in and headed off to the pit. It was virtually dark by now and spots of rain fell on the windscreen as I drove. By the time we got to the pit from Rambo's place it would be nearly eleven o'clock at night and by the look of the weather, pitch black. The plan was to drive around the pit to my swim at the back of the island, close to the ancient wood where I'd had my visitation, pray it was vacant and unload everything. Then I'd take the van back to the car park while Rambo set up a bivvy and on my return the pair of us would pump up the inflatable, change into the wetsuits, get the gear into the boat and get out to the island as quietly and discreetly as possible. Rambo said the wetsuits might appear over the top but he intended us to swim alongside or holding onto the boat and use the boat solely for transporting equipment, hence the flippers. All the fishing gear was as much for cover as anything else but Rambo did suggest we could fish on for a day or two should we wish to. Apparently he'd drawn out some cash to cover the work we were supposed to be doing. Electrical work that is, not body snatching.

The journey was boring and dull in the dark and yet my sense of trepidation heightened by the mile and I became tense and terribly on edge. I knew what we would find, a body, but what it would look like, what state it would be in, what state I would be in were all imponderables. It's not every day you get to meet a ghost in the flesh, or perhaps it might be more expedient to say 'in the bones'.

I'd turned on the windscreen wipers but they served only to smear the screen, the rain wasn't sufficient to wet it thoroughly and even an intermittent wipe was too frequent. I peered uneasily out into my full beam glare and with a rather macabre mind wondered what anyone would make of what was in the back should we have an accident and both die. I imagined Sophie, heavily pregnant with a now fatherless child, telling the police that as far as she was concerned I was out working at a flat in London doing a re-wire. It was a completely abnormal situation, it had to be said, although I didn't, only to myself and I was curious as to what Rambo might be thinking. I suppose it was run of the mill to him compared to what he'd seen and done and I thanked my lucky stars that he was with me for the umpteenth time since I'd become his unlikely friend all those years ago.

"All right, mate?" I asked.

"Yeah. You, boy?"

"Yeah. I'm all right." And on the whole I could just about shade it and say I was.

Unusually for us the journey carried on in silence because the weight of expectation of the deed we had to carry out was no small burden for either of us. Rambo had been genuinely put out when I'd told him of the ghost and therefore the 'life after death' connotations, which accompanied it. Maybe he felt a little like I did but for differing reasons and as if by magic he asked me a question as I was thinking those very thoughts, his first question in over an hour of sitting alongside me.

"Do you think the ghost will come to us if we disturb its body?"

"I haven't a clue," I said honestly. "If I feel like I did after the last time watch out for the projectile vomiting."

"I didn't think to bring a diving mask and snorkel," said Rambo lugubriously. "Still, maybe you haven't eaten much and I'll get away with a light flecking." Rambo went silent and eventually asked. "I wonder if I'll be able to see the ghost if it comes when you're around?"

"Pass."

"Do you think it rests in the remains of its old body when it's not out chin wagging with partially psychic carp anglers?"

"If it does," I assured Rambo, "it must get bored shitless." I glanced over at Rambo. "Funnily enough I did ask myself the very same question, the one about what it did with itself all the time. It's not as if it's out haunting the crap out of everybody, but then perhaps not everyone can be contacted as we've said before. I do have a theory, it's to do with what you said about Rocky."

"Oh?"

"Yeah. It was when you cast, hah-hah, aspersions on his terminal rig tossing tendencies…"

"His cock tossing tendencies, more like," said Rambo.

"… Whatever, but say he could cast a one-fifty, even at the very limit a true two hundred, would it be reasonable to expect a murder weapon to be dumped within a two hundred yard range of the edge? If you wanted to chuck something in an expanse of water so it was never likely to be found, where would you chuck it?"

"Right in the middle," said Rambo.

"Exactly. And what would your guesstimate be on the spot most furthest from any bank?"

Rambo blew out his cheeks. "Hard to say. We're into the old chestnut of distances over water and every arsehole casting a ton which is really seventy yards." Rambo pondered. "It's got to be two-fifty at least."

"The distance," I said, "is immaterial, the phrase 'out of casting range' is the key. If the hammer was dumped in the approximate middle of the pit it would be out of casting range, right?"

"Right," concurred Rambo.

"So my theory is the ghost has spent all its time using its will power to move the hammer closer to the edge by beyond-the-grave telekinesis in the hope one day it would be found and help bring to justice its assailant. And now it has, only we haven't brought anyone to justice yet."

"Or Rocky's the murderer and kept the hammer in his car in case he wanted to do it again but in a fit of madness gave it to you instead." said Rambo.

"You don't really believe that, do you?" I asked. "That's a bit far fetched."

"Far fetched! And you reckon a ghost who can't connect with 99% of people because they haven't got the gift of medium can nudge a ballpane hammer along the bottom of a fucking gravel pit! Through the weed, up the bars and down the other side, a millimetre here and a millimetre there, taking years and years to move it half a football pitch. I know! Maybe the carp gave it a little nudge as well. They're prone to inspecting unusual objects! I read it in a carp fishing magazine so it must be true."

"I did say it was only a theory," I said trying to defend myself. "Did I ever tell you about the time I woke up and knew the sex of my unborn baby and her name and how, much later, the baby's mother chose the very same name?"

"Yeah!" said Rambo. "On the fucking morning I was with you when you woke up and knew the sex of your unborn baby and her name. And then you fucking well told me again when Sophie had picked three names from a book and, at your insistence, had written down her preference, it being the same one you had earlier put in a sealed envelope!" I grinned from ear to ear in the dark. "But all that doesn't make it any more possible for a fucking ghost to fucking well drag a fucking heavy old hammer along a pit bottom in an average of eight foot of fucking water."

Rambo's rant and tirade at my overstretched imagination had lifted my spirits. It was time for a song. "If there's something strange, in your syndicate pit. Who ya gonna call? Ghostsavers!" I sang.

"I ain't 'fraid of no ghost!" answered Rambo.

Together we chanted the hook. "Derna-nerna-nerna! Derna-nerna-nerna! Derna-nerna-nerna! Ghostsavers!"

Like idiots we shouted our stupid little hearts out until we tired of the joke and a few minutes later we made the turn into the long track down to the pit. At the end of it Rambo jumped out and undid the combination padlock, I drove through the gate and Rambo locked it behind the van. In the car park there were three other cars. I could hardly see them. I put the wipers onto fast speed. Now they weren't smearing but struggling to keep up with the rain. It was pissing down.

"Good job we brought the wetsuits," said Rambo brushing large droplets off his camo coat. "It's hammering down."

"Don't be a pain in the balls keeping on about the hammer," I reminded him.

"Very good, boy," Rambo acknowledged. "But will the jokes last all evening?"

I gripped the steering wheel tight in both hands and went for an eloquent summary. "Fucking hell!"

"Kiss in heaven?" offered Rambo.

"Who can say? Let's go and find out."

I put the van into gear and edged past the other cars. One was Noel's but the other two were vehicles I didn't recognise. It hardly mattered as long as their owners weren't fishing in my swim. I drove slowly and deliberately around the track because the rain was persistent enough to make it slippery and I hadn't ever had cause to negotiate it in the dark. Halfway up the west side the old wood came into view in Rambo's side of the windscreen. It looked tortured and ugly in the van's headlights and for the first time I felt doubts concerning what we were going to do. How would the ghost react to desecration? Had it already tried to show me where its grave was hidden or did my help not extend to wanting me to unearth its old body? No! The hammer had jump-started my memory. It wanted me to find it. It must do. I shut my thoughts off as best I could and inched the Escort around to my swim and stopped. Rambo jumped out and ran quickly down to the water's edge. I saw his large powerful body disappear into the gloom and then re-emerge a short time later.

He opened the passenger door. "We're in luck. Nobody's around. Kill the engine and let's get the stuff off as quick as we can."

I turned off the ignition key and got out of the car and was peppered with heavy raindrops.

"Shit!" I muttered under my breath as I legged it round to the back of the van and grabbed the rear door handle. The back doors were locked. A precaution to a spilled load. "Fuck!" I said through clenched teeth as I went back and plucked the ignition lock free of its key. I unlocked the back doors and the pair of us grabbed the fishing gear and whizzed it down to the swim as fast as we could. We came back for all the other assorted paraphernalia and after five trips each we had successfully unloaded our cargo.

"Go and get shot of the van, boy, while I get a bivvy up to keep some of the gear dry," said Rambo.

I nodded and jogged back to the van, hopped in and, a little faster than before I must admit, picked my way back around the east side of the pit, past the stock pond and back to the car park. I locked up and walked quickly back towards Rambo in the same direction as we'd travelled with the van on first arriving. I'd put on my waterproof coat and held my tiny Maglite torch to shine no more than a few feet in front of me. I had no idea where the others were fishing apart from the obvious and

I hoped they were all asleep and hadn't heard us arrive or, even more importantly, that they couldn't hear me now.

My waterproof coat rustled at high volume and the raindrops exploded on the thin hood like mini thermonuclear devices. Pock-pock-pock they went and when the wind dislodged rainwater from the branches of the trees they went pockapockapockapocka in a drum roll of clatter and commotion. Amazingly nobody heard, or if they did they chose to ignore it and stay snug in their bivvies. Maybe the rain was a blessing in disguise but it's hard to be objective when you're soaked to the crotch.

When I got back to the swim Rambo had already got the Apotheosis up and I nipped inside, glad to get out of the heavy rain. There was a bivvy light on and Rambo was taking off his damp clothes.

"This is the Cowboy's revenge, mate," I told him.

Rambo laughed. "He only had a poncho, though. At least we've got a wetsuit each and flippers. Here, put this on." Rambo handed me my wetsuit. "It should be the right size."

With two of us in the bivvy there was little room so I sat on the floor and stripped all my top garments off and then took off my shoes, socks and tracksuit bottoms. For some reason, embarrassment I guess, I didn't feel inclined to expose my bits to the bivvy so I kept my wet underpants on and plunged one of my damp feet into the appropriate leg of the wetsuit.

"The zip goes up your back you halfwit, not up your front," said Rambo.

I took the offending foot out of the now apparently inappropriate leg and had another go. My sticky foot was reluctant to be forced into the constricting neoprene but I shoved and pulled and eventually my toes broke through at the other end. Rambo was in his suit by now and he pulled on a pair of wetsuit type boots, dropped my pair beside me and went outside saying he would start to pump up the inflatable. I managed to ease my other leg in and forced both my torso and arms into the tacky rubber. I contorted myself to pull the rear zip up about halfway and then had to force my right arm down over my shoulder by pushing up on my right elbow with my left hand. Eventually, now winded by my enthusiastic if misplaced efforts, I managed to grab the tag of material attached to the zip and pull both it and the zip up to the top of the collar. I hauled on both boots and promptly, don't ask why, felt like an eel. Some people had a fetish about wearing stuff similar to this, Christ knows why, because it felt decidedly odd having a second skin of rubber.

I scrambled out of the bivvy into the pouring rain to hear the puffing noises of Rambo pumping up the inflatable. The foot pump was shaped like a football cut in half with an umbilical chord running from just above the cut to the boat. Rambo's foot pummelled the soft rubber top like a drummer's bass pedal on a three minute, race you to the end, punk thrash and because of it the inflatable quickly grew and took shape.

"Start putting all the stuff in the boat, boy," said Rambo in a soft voice. "Go easy with the mattock and hand tools. We don't want a puncture and end up looping the loop over the pit like a untied balloon."

The vision of the boat whooshing over the pit, cartoon style, propelled by a jet stream of Rambo's recently introduced compressed air, spilling tools, lights, hand grenades and me into the water below tickled my hyped-up senses. Giggling like a schoolgirl I carefully loaded the boat, which was almost fully inflated. A fine tribute to the piston-like qualities of Rambo's right calf muscle. The last object I put in was the rusty ballpane hammer.

"What's so funny?" asked Rambo.

I waved a 'disregard it' hand. "Just something you said. It's an over-reaction to how worried I am about what we're going to see later."

Rambo shook his head in non-comprehension, disconnected the pump and placed it back in the bivvy. When he came back he took out a couple of waterproof torches from a bag I'd put in the inflatable, turned his on and gave another one to me.

His torch flicked over the contents of the small boat. "That the lot? It looks like it is."

"I think so," I answered.

"Ok. Let's slide the boat down to the edge and get it in the water. I'll hold it while you take off the boots and put your flippers on, then you put the boots in the boat. You might be glad of them once we get onto the island. After you're done you hold the boat for me. All right?"

"All right."

"Come on, let's go and find out if you've cracked the mystery or not." Rambo bent down to pick up the boat but stopped and straightened. "I wonder if the ghost *will* come?" he said, as much to himself as to me. I didn't answer.

We slid the boat down to the edge and I did as Rambo had told me. If I felt dorky in the wetsuit, once I had the flippers on I felt even more cumbersome.

"Go in backwards," whispered Rambo once his flippers were on. "When you kick, keep your flippers well into the water. If you start flapping them about on the surface some prick will come around and cast a bait at you! Once you're in we'll line the boat up with the island and we'll try and get as close as we can without putting on any lights in case anyone happens to look our way. When we swim, hold the torch in one hand, it can go under the water and hold the boat with the other. You go on the left side so you can hang on with your right hand. "

I murmured acknowledgement and the pair of us edged backwards into the dark water. I felt the coldness of it eek its way up my legs, around my rapidly shrinking nuts and cock and over my torso and shoulders. It was why it was called a wetsuit but the physical feeling of the water becoming an insulating layer between the outside of my skin and the inside of my second rubber one was disconcerting. It was similar to the cold fear of dread washing over my brain.

Having turned one-eighty we lined up the boat as best I could standing up to my neck in water in the deep margin.

"That's it," I said, eyeing the trees of the island against the dark sky.

With both of us hanging onto the rear of the boat we launched ourselves forward. There was no joyous cracking of champagne over the bow, nor any - I name this ship 'Dreadalot' – only a feeling of no turning back. The pair of us started to swim and to push our laden inflatable out towards the island. I clung on grimly in the pitch black listening to the sound of the water lapping against the boat and our bodies as we made our way across the pit. The rain slanted into my face, little rivulets of it ran into my eyes and I was consumed with an eerie feeling. The gusset of my wetsuit was riding up into the crack of my arse but apart from that my whole body felt riddled with anxiety.

It felt as if we were moving pretty fast. I decided seventy yards under dual outboard flipper power shouldn't take too long provided Rambo kept his extra horsepower under control otherwise we'd be going round in circles until daybreak.

"Turn on your torch and see how we're doing," hissed Rambo after a minute or so.

I did as I was told and shone the torch directly in front of me. There, only twenty yards away, loomed the trees of the island. They looked like sinister guardians, ones we would have to breech to complete our challenge.

"Not far to go! We're bang on target," I exclaimed with pride.

"Good!" replied Rambo. "When we get to the edge we'll feel our way along and try to find a gap in the trees to get onto the land. We can tie the boat up with the rope."

"Right," I said.

We swam on a bit further and soon I heard the scratching noise of a branch running over the front of the boat.

"Land ahoy!" I whispered and then suddenly the water in front of me exploded into life and I nearly went down like a dropped anchor from heart seizure coupled with blind panic.

"What the fuck was that?" said Rambo, his voice heavy with concern. The boat had been between him and the splash.

"A carp!" I said feeling mightily relieved.

"Any good?" said Rambo, his tongue plunging out through one of his cheeks.

"I caught the scale pattern, it was the big mirror I had at over forty," I said equally as facetiously.

Rambo's voice came back loaded with sarcasm. "Keep reading the magazines, boy."

Rambo pushed the boat into the island broadside and came around the outer side of it and stood next to me. The water was up to his chest. Feeling foolish I stopped treading it. He turned on his torch and for a short while a mass of tangled, spiteful overhanging branches were fleetingly revealed.

"These trees haven't been cut back in years," he said.

"I know," I replied.

"We'll never get through them here, let's work our way down a bit further."

Both of us moved the boat and ourselves further down the island and although the boat itself only rode a foot or so above the water we constantly had to lift up heavy branches to get it past. Doing it in the dark meant we were both constantly caught by branches and twigs poking us in the face and shoulders. This, coupled with the ungainly effect of trying to walk in over five foot of water with flippers on, made me struggle immensely. Every now and then I'd miss a foot hold and fall forward and usually get gouged by a branch for my troubles. Not only was it one of the most mad things I'd ever done it was actually quite dangerous. I could easily picture one of my eyeballs ending up skewered on a pointy branch.

"The boat's been untouched for a few feet," Rambo said quietly. His voice dragged me away from my pitiful moping. "Let's have a look here."

Rambo flashed his torch and lo and behold, he was right. No branches and a three to four foot gap. Here was our landing spot.

"I'll tie the boat up as tight to the bank as I can and then we'll go and have a look."

I nodded in the dark but said nothing. This was it. We were going over the top. Over the top of the water and up onto dry land to look for dry bones. Only the land was wet and the rain was still pouring down.

Chapter 17

I put my pair of flippers into the boat. Tiny bits of weed writhed in and out of my toes now they were off and the sensation of standing in a small weed bed made me feel squeamish. I pulled out the wetsuit boots and, while hopping on one leg and then the other, managed to get them both on. Fortunately the water had shallowed off slightly and was only waist deep so putting them on and getting up onto the island was easier than I expected. I heaved myself out by grabbing hold of a small bush and beaching myself stomach down. Rambo was already on land and he was unloading some of the inflatable's cargo, namely the lights and the bag of hand tools.

"Have you got your torch?" he asked.

"Yeah."

"Ok, let's go and have a look and see if we can find anything. Try and keep your beam pointing to the ground."

Although I was warm enough due to the insulation value of my suit I was shivering with apprehension. I had a slightly sick feeling in my stomach and my heart was palpitating but I did have a sudden thought to accompany them.

"Just let me get the hammer," I said and I reached back into the boat and picked it up. "Right, I'm ready."

Rambo led off, picking his way under and around branches as he carried the bag of tools and his own torch. "I'm going to try and find the approximate middle," he whispered. "The whole island can only be about sixty yards long and I would think twenty-five yards at its widest point. Not much room to bury a body you would think, but hard enough to find one especially if it's all like this."

I could see what Rambo was driving at. In the light of my narrow beam I saw vegetation and precious little else. Trees, saplings, bushes, tall weeds, nettles, all manner of covering growths and not one bit of neat grass. Certainly not a piece of flat, open grass with a six foot by three foot bump in it. I was struck by the futility of what we were trying to achieve in the middle of the night in such an environment. The island was completely overgrown, there was barely space to stand let alone dig up a body. As we inched forward, under this branch and around that one, circumnavigating this bush, squeezing through another and all the time traipsing through knee-high undergrowth I became more and more distraught. We weren't going to find it. After all this effort we weren't going to be able to prove my theory. My heart sank and the feeling of apprehension drained away into one of utter disappointment. I'd been so scared of what we would find I hadn't even considered not finding it at all. I was sure it was here but this was a needle in a haystack, a tiger nut in a fifty kg sack of mini boilies and literally a body on an overgrown island job. Above all else this was hopeless.

"Rambo!" I called gently. "This is a waste of time, mate. We're never going to find it in amongst this lot."

Rambo stopped and turned back to face me. We both stood in the pouring rain, torches limp at our sides. He let out an audible sigh. "It's not good, boy, I have to admit." Rambo paused and I could tell he was deliberating in his mind. "I'll tell you what, let's get up to the other end and see if it's all like this and if it is we'll think again."

"Is it worth it?" I asked dejectedly.

"Probably not. But now we've made the effort we might as well see it out to the bitter end."

"Fair enough, I …" I stopped. I suddenly felt very cold. Very, very cold. I felt, or heard, I'm not sure which, a wind spring up from somewhere. My mind was numbed by the realisation of what was going to happen. "It's coming!" I said in a dry, shaky voice.

"What is?" said Rambo.

"It's fucking coming! The ghost is fucking coming!"

"The ghost?"

"Can't you feel the cold? Can't you hear the wind? Feel it?" I said in an emotive voice. "It's over the water…" and I span instinctively to face it. Rambo was already facing the right way and he shone his torch back towards my bivvy and into the trees that lined the island. Fleetingly I saw their branches writhe and change into awful, gruesome, hideous shapes before I heard them being bent and swatted aside with seemingly effortless ease. For an instant I heard the shattering sibilant hissing sound of before but then it passed high above my head. Both of us shone our torches into the air directly above our heads and I saw the end of the shimmering haze buffet away thousands of raindrops. The rain stopped. We looked up into the inky sky but no rain fell on us yet I could hear it landing on the leaves around. All was calm.

Kapow! Deluge! Jet-powered rain suddenly flew down at us, the spots feeling like mini-daggers such was their velocity. We both simultaneously turned our heads and shielded our faces from the onslaught of tiny knives. I held my hammer holding arm tight across my face and waited for it to stop and in the instant that it did I felt the shimmering haze hit the hammer. The hammer leapt into life and started to vibrate like a large rotary drill punching into hard concrete. It had become the mother of all dildos. Such was the violence of it I dropped my torch and hung onto the hammer with both hands. Rambo was shining his torch on the hammer and I looked at it juddering and jolting wildly like a demonised bucking bronco. It's edges had become indistinct and blurred, it was one of those paint mixing machines where a whole 5litre can is mixed in less than a minute and I was attached to the end of it. My teeth started to clatter together and my arms felt as if they would be wrenched out of their shoulder sockets at any time. My head was tossed and rolled and I could feel the flesh of my jowls and lips slapping against jawbone and teeth. Saliva started to get flicked from my mouth and my eyeballs rattled in their sockets while my brain was put on a hot wash inside the oscillating washing machine drum called a skull.

The hammer lurched to the right and pulled me forward with such force I nearly toppled over. If this was what Thor had to put up with he could keep it. I staggered forward five steps as I was towed by the possessed hammer and crashed through several branches that scraped themselves across my head and face. I was like a tiny child being taken for a walk by a huge dog, I had no say in direction or speed and I merely attempted to keep up and to hold on. After the short traverse the hammer jerked me down to earth and embedded itself in the undergrowth while I fell winded, still, some might say, heroically hanging on to the wooden handle. The vibration had stopped. The hammer was still.

Rambo was alongside me only a second after I'd hit the deck. "Holy fucking shit!" he said. I'd never heard Rambo sound so put out. "I've seen some things in my time, but boy that takes some beating! That was seriously fucking freaky!"

"You should have been trying to hang onto the end of it," I moaned and spat out a combination of blood and leaf.

I eased myself up onto all fours. I could taste the blood trickling from my mouth and when I touched my forehead it felt sticky as well. It didn't matter.

"I guess we dig here," I told Rambo.

"I'll dig. You sit." Rambo insisted. He shone a torch on my face. "You look a bit of a mess but it's only superficial stuff. You'll live."

Rambo gently but firmly nudged me aside, pulled out the half buried hammer, gave it to me and cut down all the nettles and weeds with a small scythe he'd taken from the tool bag. He cut back any branches that were overhanging with one of the band saws and in a quarter of an hour he had cleared a little plot and scraped all the vegetation a few yards away. I watched him in stunned silence. He went back to the boat and got the bivvy lights, the mattock, the shovel and the spade. With two lights on Rambo used the large flat blade of the mattock to loosen off around nine inches of the topsoil. It was festooned with roots and would have been impossible to dig with a spade but once he'd severed them he could easily bottom out the area with the shovel. After that he started to dig with a spade but the pit wasn't a gravel pit for nothing and most of the time he had to use the mattock again and again because the spade kept on hitting bits of rock and pebbles. He worked like a Trojan, his immensely strong body seemingly impervious to normal human traits such as muscle fatigue and decreasing efficiency. The area of excavation was soon a foot deep; in no time it was eighteen inches and then a couple of foot.

The bivvy lights cast an eerie sheen across the clearing, the wet leaves reflected light back and Rambo's wet face, both from the rain and from sweat, did the same. I gingerly ran my sore tongue around my two fat lips and watched fascinated and mesmerised by the awesome Rambo in full flow. The heavy mattock was wielded like a balsa wood toy and the regular thuds as it bit into the soil were matched by Rambo's equally regular breathing. I flicked my mouth into a smile. It hurt. Didn't he ever get winded and gasp for air like the rest of us? It seemed not. It was perpetual motion by torchlight.

Rambo bottomed out the hole once again. Thirty inches down, two and a half feet. How much deeper? The mattock went in again, into the middle of the hole and it pulled up not just soil and stone but something with it. A thin, whitish-brown, curved, broken stick some twelve inches long sat on top of the last clump of earth Rambo had eased out. Rambo put the mattock down and picked the stick up.

He looked over to me and actually bit his bottom lip before he said ever so calmly and quietly. "It's a rib bone, Matt. We've found it!"

The sight of the bone transfixed me. It was all coming to realisation. "Uncover some more," I heard myself say.

Rambo starting digging again only with much more care and within a matter of minutes he'd uncovered a rounded surface of the whitish-brown material. It was a skull bone. Rambo dug it out with his large bowie knife and carefully extracted it. Like a Shakespearean actor he held it carefully in his hand. On the right hand side of the cranium, just above the temple, was a huge hole where the bone had been imploded by a blunt instrument.

"There's the killer blow, boy," Rambo said in a solemn voice, passing me the skull.

I said nothing but lifted up the hammer and tried to fit it into the horrid opening. The first way round, trying to fit in the square faced end wasn't right, the hammer was too big. When I turned it around and presented the ball-shaped end it matched perfectly. The rounded face sat snugly in the gaping wound.

"And there's the murder weapon. The weapon that Michael used to kill whoever this poor sod is," I said.

Rambo seemed unperturbed or even uninterested in my revelation and was digging again but this time much further away from where he had unearthed the skull.

"Did you know it was Michael?" I asked him as he frantically clawed at the soil. "It was him. It all fits in. It wasn't illness or paranoia or running the syndicate that made him a gibbering wreck, it was trying to live with this horrendous crime he'd committed. The ghost had visited him after he'd killed its body, he must have been receptive, and it'd obviously shit the life out of him. That's why he never night fished. It's also why his condition deteriorated when it did a few months ago. It was just after the time he had visited me and spoken about Watt. I presume he'd seen the broken branch and had gone back into the old woods, to exactly the same spot where you had traced the trail of broken twigs and branches. God knows what had gone through his mind when he saw the whole of the spot had been searched. The very spot where, I'm surmising, the murder act had taken place. He was the one who went back all right and *he* was the one who disturbed what you had disturbed. You'd noticed it on your second visit even if you weren't exactly certain what had been altered. It must have blown him away to have all this happen after such a long time and really shaken him up. Even if he'd struggled to live with the crime I suppose the swine thought he'd at least got away with it. All that must have been thrown into doubt, hence his mysterious illness, when he realised someone was on the trail of the murder. He must have been riddled with fear of getting found out. Serves him right, the bastard." My diatribe ceased for a few seconds but Rambo kept digging. "You know the thing that I couldn't remember? The thing that came back to me in a flash when I first touched the hammer, well, it was something Grant had said to me in the car park. Despite all the work and trimming and shaping which goes into this place Michael had never allowed any boats, nor anyone to cut back the trees on the islands. Grant had told me the island margin was snaggy in casting terms, what with overhanging trees, but I simply didn't remember. Until I touched the hammer. I think the ghost had been moving the hammer, you know," I said, carrying on and not taking much notice of Rambo inspecting something small between his fingers. "I think it knew it must somehow bring the murder weapon to light and it was Rocky of all people who'd happened to hook into it…"

"It's a woman!" said Rambo.

"Eh?" I grunted.

"The ghost is a woman," Rambo re-iterated. "I thought I'd try and find the hands and see if by remote chance there was a ring or bracelet and there was. Look!"

Rambo handed me a small gold ring which had a large emerald stone mounted in a gold clasp. I slipped it onto my little finger but it wouldn't go past my knuckle joint. It was a woman's ring no doubt and the thought of it was a shock to comprehend. Michael slipped down even further in my estimation, two blokes having a ruck and one getting carried away and topping the other was bad enough, but a woman? No wonder the bastard felt bad, so he should. I tilted the top of my left hand towards myself and shone the torch onto the green stone and it seemed to glow. A strange sensation started to creep up my left arm; it was like rising pins and needles. I felt panic rise in me and split second realisation.

"She's in the ring!" I screamed at Rambo. "The ghost is in the ring!" And, into the bargain for free, my ring-piece started to pout.

"Take it off!" said Rambo alarmed. "Take the fucking thing off!"

I went to grab the ring and pull it off but I stopped. My panic eased as I applied a little logic, which was quite a feat considering my circumstances. She hadn't hurt me on purpose, I reasoned. So she'd made me puke and battered me around a little but then she was upset. Frustrated. Who wouldn't be? The tingling was now up to my shoulder. She'd asked for help and I'd given it, I'd nothing to fear. My right hand went slack and I let it fall to my side. I saw Rambo stare in abject horror. The tingling went up my neck and into my head and my hair felt as if it was standing on end.

She was in my head but this time it wasn't crushing emotion that filled my thoughts, it was a voice. It was all vague and watery and slightly sibilant. "Matthew! You've found me! Take me away with you, away from my body and bury me properly. I mustn't stay long. Tell him, Matthew. Tell him you've found me! Justice will come! Tell him! Your baby daughter is well. She wanted to be called Amy. You are my beloved friend. My thanks to you. Thank you! Take the ring off but take it with you. Take *me* with you. Thank you."

The tingling swept back down my left side and was gone. I took the ring off. My head throbbed and ached.

Rambo shook me. "Are you all right, boy?"

I roused myself from my thumping headache. "I'm ok. I'm on message, mate. Let's clear up our stuff and go. Put the bones back and cover her back over." I looked at Rambo's worried face. "It's ok," I assured him. "I know what to do."

Without any fuss or questions Rambo put the skull back and covered the remains of the body with all the earth he'd dug. He slammed the loose dirt down with the back of the shovel, all pretence of a clandestine operation long gone. Next he carried all the tools back to the boat and within half an hour we were ready to set sail and leave the island. While Rambo had been busy doing all the donkey work I'd taken a piece of string from the tool bag, tied the ring on a loop, put it over my neck and forced it inside the collar of the wetsuit. I mustn't lose it; above all else I mustn't lose it. I'd never forgive myself.

We put our flippers on, plopped into the water and headed back to the bivvy. It wasn't hard to know which way to head back to the bivvy because we could see at least three different lights. Whoever was fishing had heard our little get together on the island and had come round to see what was going on and welcome us home with a reception committee. This was going to be great. As we got near to the bank I started to hear voices. Indignant voices.

The pair of us climbed out of the deep margin and Rambo pulled the inflatable, complete with its array of odd cargo, up onto the bank. We said nothing. The three other anglers said nothing. Rambo sat down and pulled off his flippers and I did likewise. Out of the corner of my eye I saw Noel shine his torch into the inflatable while the other two also looked on.

Eventually Noel turned to us. He had both his fists jammed onto his hips and I could tell he was absolutely seething. "Would you mind explaining what the bloody hell you've been up to? Disregarding the fact that you have broken several of the syndicate rules, have you no regard for other anglers? I'm quite sure I don't know what you've been doing but whatever it was you certainly made enough noise doing it." He waited in vain for an answer and when he realised none would be forthcoming he became even more agitated. "Well? Are you going to give an explanation or not?"

"I lost a lead in the branches the other day and a bit of line. I wanted to get it back in case any birds got tangled in it," I said in an off handed a manner as was possible.

"What utter rubbish!" stormed Noel.

"Tell him the truth," said Rambo.

"Ok," I said. "We were rowing some baits out."

"What!" Noel was almost apocalyptic. "With all the stuff you've got in there?"

He waved his torch beam inside the inflatable. "In any case most of the time you were *on* the island!"

"I like to get my baits *real* tight," I said sarcastically.

"Well, I'm afraid Michael is going to have to hear about this," huffed Noel.

"Yeah! And we've got a few things to tell him about *you*," I said as menacingly as my weary body could manage.

Noel's voice stopped dead in his tracks. "I can't possibly imagine what you mean," he said and with a wave of his torched he stomped off. The other two, I had no idea who they were, went with him.

"Fancy staying on for a couple of days?" asked Rambo, once they had all gone.

"God no. Get me home. I feel like a human punch bag," I cried.

"Do you think he'll tell Michael?"

"All depends on what he's got to hide," I answered. " By the way, did you manage to suss out the fish nicking problem without having your ideas prejudiced by me telling you the murderer?"

Rambo shook his head apologetically. "No. I'm afraid I didn't. Rocky and Darren in the field but the person behind it? If there is one? I've no better ideas than I had previously. It could be Noel. Oh, if the worst comes to the worst, I'll find out where Rocky lives and beat it out of him."

We laughed, but on what side of our face it was hard to say. We packed away all our paraphernalia and left.

Three days after that fateful night I received a phone call from Michael summoning Rambo and myself to his house the next day. I asked what it concerned but Michael flatly refused to discuss it on the phone. Despite him not saying anything you didn't need to be Einstein to work out it was most likely to be concerning a complaint from a certain Noel. The bastard.

Michael had sounded awful and I knew he was unlikely to be going into remission when I spilt the beans. Spilling the beans! Telling him someone was nicking his fish would be bad enough but telling him the story of the dead body and ghost was another. I was going to have to be very careful, I wanted to tell him the score but without telling him I knew he'd committed the murder. I wanted us to come across as diligent syndicate members trying to unearth, bad pun, the truth on the ghost and the fish nicking and use Michael's request for us to keep a lookout for him as some sort of justification for our actions. As much as I loathed him for being the ultimate cowardly bully I didn't intend to tell him so. You see I had no idea why the ghost reckoned justice would come when I told Michael I'd found her. He was hardly going to admit it after all the lengths he'd been to conceal it. Or was he. Or was I expected to shop him to the authorities. If I did it was goodbye syndicate, Michael would have ample time to boot us out before he was either convicted or found not guilty in court. If it ever got that far. Oh what a wondrous spider's web we weave, when first we practise to deceive! You see, sad as it might seem, even at this eleventh hour I was still hoping to come out of it with mine and

Rambo's places in the syndicate in tact. There were some very good fish in the place after all.

"Bye, Sophie!" I called.

"Bye. Try not to fall over again!" said the very pregnant love of my life. I'd had to tell her some sort of story to cover the knocks and bruises on my face. I was becoming adept at lying. Good job, seeing as I had a rather tricky situation to resolve.

I picked Rambo up from his place. "Got the ring?" he asked. I nodded. "And the hammer?" I nodded again. "I still think we should have brought all of her back."

"She didn't want us to," I explained. "Her soul, or whatever you want to call it, is in the ring, which we'll bury later in proper consecrated ground."

"If you ever catch a sixty from the island swim then she'd already be on some," said Rambo with a cheeky grin.

"Consecrated in terms of the church, not in terms of carp fishing," I pointed out.

"I don't know," said Rambo thinking aloud. "They've got the bible, we've got 'Carp Fever'. They've got exalted cathedrals; we've got awesome waters. They've got God, we've got... who do you think?"

"I think 'God's gift' to carp fishing would be more appropriate and there'd be plenty of candidates who consider themselves to be legends in their own tackle boxes!"

"Tell me about it. No! On second thoughts don't, I couldn't take the pain!" Rambo's voice turned serious. "So what's the game plan? What are we going to tell our benevolent, female-killing syndicate leader?"

"We tell him everything. Everything we've found out. We show him the hammer and the ring, the only thing we don't tell him is the fact we know he's the murderer. The ghost said to tell him we'd found her. Not to tell the police. Not to tell her family or anybody else. Just him."

"Just him?" repeated Rambo.

"Yep! And we'll see what happens." I put my foot down hard. In a strange way I was looking forward to the showdown with Michael and revealing our hard found knowledge. Part of it was for my mine and Rambo's gratification but the biggest satisfaction was for doing it on behalf of the ghost. Having said that I desperately hoped it wouldn't end in tears and us out of the syndicate.

Once we'd arrived and had a terse greeting the pair of us sat on the two same chairs in the same room where we'd had our original interview some six months ago. An awful lot of water had gone under the bridge since then; pregnancies, jobs for cash, thirties, forties and fifties, ghost visitations, fish nicking, spying, investigating and the odd bit of nocturnal exhumation. The atmosphere was tense for differing reasons from our original interview. Previously it had been to do with getting in, now it was to do with us possibly getting chucked out and the heavy burden I was going to lay on the pitiful looking Michael.

Michael was straight to the point. "I'm afraid I've had a very serious complaint," he said, his skinny chest heaving with the effort like it had when he'd come around to see me after his period of absence.

He looked both of us in the eyes as his opening statement sank in. It was a game of bluff, he must have feared we had found out his terrible secret but he couldn't show it in case we were on the island for some other unknown and unrelated reason. He had the power to out us from the syndicate, it was his big stick but I was the one with the big hammer. Michael's physical appearance was dire. As I'd remarked earlier his close-set eyes lacked their earlier beady characteristics and they looked dull and glassy. Even his pointy nose looked dull and less sharp. He looked ill, very ill but I was willing to bet a pound to a pinch of shit he'd look a whole lot worse when I'd finished with him. I'd been wrong when I'd said I was wrong about him and put his problems down to disease. So very wrong, and yet in another way he was one sick fucker, that was for sure. Sitting looking at him I was traumatised by the vision of him clubbing to death a defenceless woman with the hammer I had in my small kit bag. It was a West Ham United kit bag. A delicious irony that would probably be lost on him but it so pleased my sensibilities when I thought of it, I simply had to go out and buy the claret and blue item.

"Noel, supported by two other witnesses, has informed me you were seen using a boat on the pit. That you were wearing wetsuits, flippers and had all manner of tools with you and that you spent at least two hours on the large island. Doing what, he wasn't sure, but he did say you made a lot of noise doing it. Is it true?" demanded Michael.

"Sure is," I said breezily.

"You don't deny it?"

My eyes rolled around the top of their sockets and looked at the ceiling. "No," I said sarcastically. "Does it sound like it?"

Michael seemed unflustered. "I'd like to hear why you were doing what you were doing and then I'm afraid I'm going to have to rule you in breach of contract. Quite frankly I can't think of a single reason you can come up with which will defer me from doing so. I'm disappointed. I expected better from the two of you."

Michael's words hung in the air but he was trying to front us out. After all, he was the one who had most to lose if by any chance we'd discovered the secret of the island. He must have been dreading the possibility.

"What you don't understand, Michael, is we were doing it for you!" I pointed out to him firmly. I tempered my tone slightly. "Possibly that is my fault because I, we, haven't told you what we've discovered so far. We never informed you because we wanted to clear the whole thing up before we came forward. Unfortunately things have moved on at a pace we couldn't control, we have all the jigsaw pieces apart from two and now circumstances have forced us to reveal what we know. We'd have preferred to have had everything all signed and sealed but unfortunately we haven't, not all of it. Most of it. But not all of it." This time my words hung in the air, but not for long, they were too heavy. "Firstly, I have to admit I lied to you regarding the ghost. I was visited on my very first night on the water and it was no night breeze or temperature drop from coming out of a sleeping bag, I can tell you. It was a unique and frightening experience but it left me with a tale, a story, if you like, of a friendship turned sour which led to death. Not a natural death but murder." I paused and saw Michael grappling with his emotions, trying to keep a lid on his festering guilt. He sat rigid yet shivering slightly in his chair.

"Go on," he said in a low voice.

"I was so convinced I'd been contacted by someone beyond the grave that I told Rambo and we agreed to try to find out more about this unique manifestation. Rambo traced the ghost's route back into the old woods and searched in amongst the trees and leaves but found nothing." I watched Michael crumple a little more into his chair. "This had been the direction the ghost had come from and it had disappeared over the pit towards the large island. As time passed I finally thought we should look on the large island regardless of the rules we would undoubtedly break. To be honest I thought you would be only too pleased for us to clear up the mystery of the ghost once and for all, but as I said earlier we wanted the whole story before we bothered you with it. Coincidentally I had a massive stroke of luck when Rocky, I'll tell you more about Rocky later, foul hooked something from the pit. I happened to be with him when it came out of his car and I persuaded him to give it to me. I believed, at the time, it was the murder weapon and I now know I was right." I bent down to the kit bag and took out the hammer and held it out to Michael. He squirmed in pain and shook his head and turned his face away from it. He wouldn't touch it. His eyes started to well with tears, his body shook and juddered. She had the same effect on me, I thought, almost relishing his discomfort. I leaned forward in my chair so I was closer to him. It was my turn to look him in the yes. I spoke slowly and emphatically. "We went to the island, Michael, and we found her. We found her body. And we found this." I took the piece of string, which hadn't left my person since the night of the wetsuits, only when I'd hid it from Sophie, and showed him the gold item by offering it forward. He could barely bring himself to look. He wiped away his flowing tears, his bottom lip pushed up and out, quivering like a distressed child. I sat back in my chair. "This was her ring, the poor girl," I said evenly. "It's all that's left of her apart from her bones." I went matter-of-fact. "We found her skull, it had a massive hole in it where somebody had smashed her head with the ball end of the hammer. I even tried the hammer in the hole to make sure we were right. We were. I mean, how could anyone do something so hideous?"

Michael was curled up on the chair like a foetus, sobbing, his eyes now closed I wondered if he was replaying his terrible deed in his head. I pressed ahead in full-on lie mode. "The only missing part is the motive and who was the murderer, that's jigsaw piece number one. Now the other thing which we haven't got quite so sussed, and I know you're upset about having something so terrible happen on your property and in a way this is almost as bad, is the fish nicking." Michael stopped blubbing and sat upright, wiping away his tears. It was difficult to assess what was more important to him, being confronted with his murderous act or someone pinching his beloved carp. I carried on with the story. "Now, me and Rambo here, actually saw Darren and Rocky stealing fish, it's as open and shut and as straightforward as that. We went to an awful amount of trouble to catch them at it, believe me, but catch them at it we did. We used to bivvy up in the old wood after walking there via the north end, one hell of a trek that was, so no one knew we were around and once it was dark we'd go and spy on them. It was hard graft and we did it at many times but we only caught them once, a little while after you were first taken poorly. Darren was lay-lining the stock pond all the time they were alone on the water and Rocky was taking out what he caught from the pit itself. Like I say, it only happened the once, well, once as far as we were around to see it happen and on that occasion he called up a bloke called Alan to collect the fish. We heard Rocky make a phone call from his mobile to this Alan but it also seemed, by the way Rocky spoke, as if someone else from the syndicate was the ringleader. When Alan, not syndicate Alan the artist by the way, turned up to take the fish away, Rambo was all set to deck him plus Rocky and Darren, but he didn't because something odd happened."

Michael was sitting bolt upright by now and was paying full attention. Old habits die hard. "What was it?" he asked.

"The vehicle Alan came in was your pick-up. If you can remember this was the reason why I asked you about it and you said it'd been in the garage for ages, at Broughton Motors garage. Rambo was so thrown by your pick-up being used to steal fish from your water he was a bit nonplussed to say the least. Making a decision on the spot he let things play themselves out because he couldn't work out what the fuck was going on. Unfortunately this one incident turned out to be our only success because on all the other times we went through the procedure it never happened. Sometimes they never caught anything, other times other anglers turned up, and we just didn't get lucky again. Rambo did visit the garage but no Alan worked there and we've not managed to get any further with it. We were reluctant to tell you until we had more proof but as I explained earlier things had moved on with the finding of the body and of course Noel's complaint. I'm afraid we're a bit stuffed as to who the ringleader Rocky spoke to might be. We did notice Noel's got a Broughton Motors sticker in his car so it might be him. Perhaps his moaning about us is a bit of a smokescreen to hide what he's been up to. You see, another thing is that after he spoke to you about his new forty and you informed him of Rambo's new fifty, Rocky knew all about it. The idiot actually mentioned it to Rambo so perhaps that links the two of them together."

"It's not him," said Rambo to my surprise, uttering his first words of the session.

I shrugged my shoulders. "So there you have it, or rather most of it, the ringleader is the second jigsaw piece which we are missing." I continued. "Who killed the girl and for what reason? And why was your pick-up used without your consent and crucially who is the ringleader of the fish nickers?"

Michael's demeanour had changed completely. His face was full of anger and his nervous traits seemed to have miraculously disappeared. Rather strangely he looked a lot healthier. "I have the two pieces of the jigsaw you're missing," he said grimly. "I'll see to it that both matters are put right. I promise you I will do the right thing, I should have done it years ago. What you two have done is highly irregular but I understand why you did it."

I bided my time and looked over at Rambo and nodded. "So, are we still both in the syndicate?" I asked in a perky voice.

"Very much so," said Michael. "Provided you don't mention this to anyone else."

Chapter 18

When I returned home that evening after confronting Michael with the bane of his guilt-ridden life, I told Sophie. I told her the whole rambling affair, showed her the hammer, showed her the ring and only managed to forget one bit of the last epic six months. The bit about working on non-existent jobs for Rambo's carp fishing cash. It somehow seemed to sour the flavour of an otherwise staggering tale. She had sat on the chair, her hands clasped across her full belly no doubt feeling the wriggling movements of baby Amy's feet, arms and head, absolutely smitten and engrossed. She stared in frightful horror at the hammer and gently held the ring by its gold band as if it were an instrument of mass destruction which could explode at any second, wiping out the entire northern hemisphere. She bit her lower lip as even the mighty Rambo had. She looked confused, overwhelmed, flummoxed, perplexed and puzzled as she vainly tried to grapple with the myriad of implications and questions my story had caused to form in her head. Her eyes were wide, her jaw was slack and although I could tell some large part of her doubted the validity of what I was saying, I could also tell, deep inside her heart, despite what her brain might say, she knew it was all true. During the whole time she never said a single word as she hung onto every one of mine.

When I'd finished she asked all the questions I'd asked myself. Could we now say with all certainty there was life after death? Could we now say there was conscious life before birth? And if we did, could we say the two were operating in a twilight zone that was neither life nor death but something in between? How did the ghost talk to Amy even if this twilight zone existed? How did Amy tell the ghost she wanted to be called Amy? Why did Amy say she wanted to be called Amy? How did the ghost talk to me when I had the ring on, yet couldn't form words, only emotions, when I hadn't? Why had the ghost come into being in the first place? Why didn't every dead person become one? What significance did this all mean in terms of there being a God, a heaven or a hell, or meeting dead relations when you yourself died? Why had the trees morphed? Why couldn't the ghost get Michael herself, if she could make a hammer move around so viciously when I was on the end of it why didn't she simply hit him over the head with it? And why couldn't she get it out of the pit in the first place? What was the relationship between her and Michael? When had he killed her? Why had he killed her? Why had I been chosen to help or was I the living, receptive, slightly psychic embodiment of 'any port in a storm'? Who were her next of kin? Why had she only said to tell Michael I'd found her? Why not the police? Why not her family? Why had she asked me to take her away while her soul/lifeforce/deathforce/whatever you wanted to call it was in the ring? Why did she want to leave her body behind? Where was I going to bury her 'properly'? What was Michael going to do? Who was the fish-stealing ringleader who Michael clearly knew? Why had his pick-up been used? The list of why's, what's, how's and when's went on and on and on, and neither of us could answer any of them with any certainty. It was outside of our sphere of reference and beyond our knowledge and understanding. All in all it was singularly the most baffling and bemusing thing we'd ever heard of, let alone have happened to us.

The only thing Sophie took me to task on was my duplicity regarding Michael. I was, she said: 'A bit of a two faced bastard', because although I'd acquitted myself pretty well in nearly every other aspect she felt as if I should have made it perfectly clear to Michael that I knew he was the murderer.

"Why didn't you tell the horrid man you knew?" she demanded. I said nothing. She already had the answer. "You didn't tell him because you thought he might kick you out of the syndicate in an act of retribution. Never mind a woman has been murdered, never mind she's dead and he's never paid for his crime just so long as you can go carp fishing on his water!" She was cross.

"Honest, Soph, she only told me to tell *him*," I said trying to both defend myself and placate her. "Like I said, she never told me to go to the police or tell her family. She told me to tell Michael and then she said justice would be done. I think he'll turn himself in, to be honest," I said, not being very honest at all because I had no idea what he would do. "Then Hollywood will take over. Michael's become ill because of the stress he's been living under, he even hinted he might peg out fairly soon. Whichever way it works out it'll end up the same only the time scale will be substantially different. Michael will be out of the equation at one time or another and Hollywood will end up running the syndicate. I suppose all of us will have to take our chances with him when that happens. You know, Michael did say he'd do the right thing, perhaps he thinks I'll shop him if he doesn't. He must have considered I'd sussed it was him. But what if I did shop him? Could it be proven? I don't know." I gave Sophie a hangdog look. "Ok, so I'm not being totally upfront but at least I did risk getting chucked out in order to find her body and I've done everything she's asked of me. Nobody else had managed to help until I came along."

Sophie let out a long sigh. The carp angling side of things held little interest to her. "Are we really having this conversation? Or am I dreaming?" she asked and stared into space, trying to get her head around what I'd told her. "It's all a bit scary isn't it? Your whole concept of life and death being turned on its head. Our lives will never be the same again, I mean, how could you possibly think of things in the same light after all this?"

She was right in one respect, it was scary when I stopped and really thought about it. So many deep meaningful questions with only shallow, superficial theorised answers. Still, life and death had to go on and so did carp angling, especially as Rambo and I had provisionally booked in a three day session in a week's time on the way back from visiting Michael. As I explained to Sophie what with all the work I'd been doing I hadn't really been so much. What a scheming ratbag I was.

She agreed. "You go, Matt," she said giving me a hug. "You've done really well, I didn't mean to sound angry. I'm proud you've helped the poor woman; lesser men would have been scared away. Let's hope she's right and true justice does come her way."

I gave Sophie a hug back and again felt her bulge push into my lower abdomen. A tiny wave of guilt washed up on the shores of my conscience but it soon disappeared into the sand. What the head doesn't know the heart can't grieve over. I mean it wasn't as if I'd killed anyone. It had only been a tiny white lie to give me a chance to help the ghost and, I grudgingly admitted to myself, help me catch a few more of those lunkers. I'd let it run its course until Amy was born. You see the thing was it'd soon be September and all the carp would be stacking on weight, a bit like Sophie come to think of it.

The week soon passed and when it had Rambo and I were speeding back to the pit. In the van we had a very similar conversation to the one I'd had with Sophie. Even Rambo admitted to losing some sleep over all the tricky questions a genuine, no smoke or mirrors ghost caused your average individual to consider.

"I'll tell you what, boy," said Rambo sincerely. "It's going to be highly embarrassing meeting up with a load of people I've bumped off, if and when I get to the same place as them."

I laughed. "There's no 'if' about it, death is a dead cert for us all. Whether the ghost actually means there's anywhere we all go to is another matter. Besides all your ex-enemies might be downstairs in the hot department and you might be upstairs shagging Cleopatra and Marilyn Monroe, amongst others." I shot him a glance as I took my eyes off the road. "While all your ancestors watch you and shout words of encouragement. Well, all your good ancestors, anyway."

"Or I might be downstairs in the hot department," conceded Rambo.

"It'll only be for eternity," I reminded him.

"Do you think there'll be a lake?" asked Rambo.

"Full up with brimstone, for the naughty stroke-pulling, deceased carp anglers, that's ninety-eight percent of them and then they'll be a few fishing upstairs at a venue that's a cross between Hamworthy and Lac Fumant. Syndicate heaven and syndicate hell!"

It was Rambo's turn to laugh. "We've already had a dollop of both in this world!" The van's engine took the place of silence. After a while Rambo spoke in a serious voice. "We'll find out one day."

I nodded. "I'm quite happy to wait as long as I've got to find out," I assured him.

"Me too," he agreed and the moment of sobriety had gone. "There's so much left for me to do, I mean, I've got to punch that twat, Rocky, on the nose yet!"

I grinned. "Here! That reminds me! I forgot to ask you why you said to Michael it wasn't Noel who was the ringleader of the fish nicking arm of our syndicate."

"Another hunch," said Rambo. "Just another hunch. I'm catching all this psycho mumbo-jumbo off you, you know," he added sarcastically.

"I tried it on the gee-gees the other week," I told him.

"And?"

"Fucking useless! Not a single winner!"

"What a waste of time! You'd be better off trying some mind-melding with my fifty, my *English* fifty and having a go at trying to catch it," teased Rambo.

"Don't start all that again," I warned him.

"Do you think Michael will turn himself in?" said Rambo changing the subject.

"I don't know," I said. "What do we do if he doesn't? He must know we would consider him to be the culprit but he might try and brazen it out. I suppose we'll have to wait and see... anyway, bollocks to all of it, let's go and enjoy this session for what it is. Christ we've hardly had any where we've only gone to fish. So, which swim are you going to go in?"

As it turned out we both ended up fishing in swims we hadn't previously occupied. This was due to me not wanting to fish the usual island swim and the knock on effect of that decision. Accordingly Rambo persuaded me to fish in his favourite swim, the south-east point while he, also looking for a fresh challenge, popped himself into the south-west point. Noel's car, complete with its Broughton Motor sticker was in the car park as was Rocky's and two others, which I never recognised. It seemed as if the other four were further up the pit towards the old wood as no one was in between our two swims and as such it suited us fine to have it that way. Rambo gave me a few pointers on where he'd picked up most of his carp and then left me to set up so he could have a little dabble with a marker float and lead to suss out some depths in his unfamiliar swim.

By five in the evening I was all sorted and had my three rods on the money, my bivvy was all set up and the obligatory kettle was on the boil. I looked up from behind the butts of my three rods towards the opposite side of the island Rambo and I had excavated and contemplated the meaning of life. And the meaning of death, which due to recent experience, didn't seem quite so cut and dried as it had half a year earlier. How could an electrician and fanatical carp angler hope to fathom out the depths of existence, non-existence and all the shades between them? The greatest minds in history hadn't so what hope had I? I'd thought all this before and couldn't ignore what had happened but I seemed unable or unwilling to change my life viewpoint in any significant way because of it. Although Sophie seemed to think she could never view life the same again I begged to differ. Ultimately all the things I'd learnt were of little use, they couldn't change my day-to-day perspective in a lasting manner. It was as I'd reflected at Rambo's bogus burial. Petty issues would still cloud my judgement and I would forget the fundamentals of a happy life because of them. Petty issues were a part of life. A big part of life and when occurring seemed anything but petty at all, quite the opposite, they often seemed the most important thing in the universe. Your telly broken and England playing in the World Cup? A

PB carp coming off at the net? What could be more petty and yet equally, at the precise moment, more important? I doubted if many could live a 'big picture' existence, dismissing the everyday stuff with a shrug and living on a diet of altruism, thanks for good health and family bonding. A few devout monks and other religious nutters could probably pull it off and maybe the truly wicked might reflect on their actions if they had experienced what I had, but reflecting on them and then changing because of them were totally different things. Did afterlife judgement and all the other big themes exist? I couldn't prove it any more than I could before my visitation from the ghost. All I could be certain of was there was something. What the something constituted I couldn't say. Good to know? Uplifting? Disturbing? Fuck knows. I could see the whole episode would remain a tantalising enigma much like fluoro-coloured pop-ups, anti-eject rigs and watching a carp's response to bait in a clear margin.

As if to prove my own 'petty issues' point I suddenly wondered if I would catch a carp to match the one of Rambo's and it took over completely from my previous mental ruminating. Hamworthy's second fifty... or was there a sixty swimming around in the clear water? Not for the first time I tried to look with my mind under the water, but I was pissing in the wind on a dark night. I fell back on something I was capable of and made myself a cup of tea. I bullied the teabag in slight agitation at my own limitations. I couldn't do it on my own, something else, whether drugs or ghosts, had to help me. Being an alarm induced adrenalin junkie was fine, but I'd no intentions of becoming a real one despite the odd chance of miraculous insight. It had never worked with my odd dalliance with lager and I wasn't trying anything stronger, not on purpose anyway.

Having made the tea, for no reason I looked up from my mug towards the track running around the pit and out of the corner of my eye saw a thin figure. It was no more than thirty yards away and coming towards me. My first gulp of piping hot tea nearly choked me. It was Michael!

"Good evening, Matthew," he called as soon as he saw I'd noticed him.

I felt awkward not knowing how this little scene was going to scan. "All right, Michael?" was my opening move.

"Yes, fine thank you," he replied, now virtually upon me. "Any luck?"

"No, we've only just got here. I've only been set up for an hour or so."

Michael lifted his head in understanding. "It's usually a good time of year for catching, good weights as well. We've had loads of new forties come out in September, probably more than any other month," he said. "I think I'm right in saying the last two..." Michael's words faded out of my head and I became bewitched by the stranger in front of me. Michael looked well. In fact he looked so well he might even have put on a few pounds. Closer examination showed he looked positively chunky compared to his previous 'stand sideways and poke your tongue out, there's a zip' physical appearance. His complexion looked rude and healthy and, most startling of all, his nervous traits had altogether disappeared. Usually his face had more tic(k)s on it than a dog working in a flea circus or a Mensa candidate schoolboy had on his homework but not now. His face, like a broken mechanical watch, had stopped tic(k)ing. His previous humming-bird wings eyelids were normal and not a single vein so much as throbbed or pulsed nor even hinted at a conciliatory palpitation. I dropped my gaze. His fingers had stopped their St Vitus's dance. I upped my gaze. His eyes looked beady again, and with hindsight a touch cruel, and his nose looked sharp and rodent-like. *Rattus norvegicus,* the brown rat. What was going on? I'd expected him to be in an even worse condition than he was when we were summoned to him. "… Matthew? Don't you think so, Matthew?"

"Sorry… yeah, that's right," I blagged, coming out of my trance with a bump.

"It's a beautiful place, isn't it?" said Michael, looking around himself. "It's probably the best carp fishery in England, you know," he added.

"It is lovely," I admitted.

Michael seemed serene. "Yes, you'll get a lot of satisfaction fishing here over the years. You never can tell but one day you may even catch the British record from here."

I nodded and gave a weak smile. What was I meant to say? The last time I had spoken to this bloke I'd showed him the nuts and bolts of a grisly murder he'd committed and he'd cowered and cried like a baby. Now, a week later, he seemed to have banished all his ills and was waxing lyrical regards the British Carp Record and the scenic glory of his current environment.

"You out for an evening stroll, then?" I said, trying to get on more stable ground.

"No. I'm fishing. I'm set up two swims clockwise from Rambo, I popped in to see him and thought I'd nip and see you before I went back and cast out for the night."

"For the night!" I blurted, unable to contain my astonishment.

"Why yes!" said Michael as if him doing a night was the most unexceptional thing in the world. "I do night fish sometimes." My stunned air must have forced his hand because he did eventually tack on the words. "Although not too frequently, it must be said." He unclipped something from his belt. "Look, I've even bought myself some micro transmitter upgrades for my set of Delkims and a new receiver box." He thrust the Rx receiver box under my nose. It was a four way one.

"The 2004. I hope you're not going to be fishing a snide," I said jokingly.

"I've spent what seems a lifetime trying to stop that sort of thing so I'm hardly going to do it myself am I?"

You tell me, mate, I thought. If you can smash a woman's head in with a ballpane hammer I think you could run to chucking an extra rod out in the dark. "Of course not," were the weasel words on my lips. Sophie did have a point, after all I hadn't the gumption to ask him what he intended to do about the fish stealing or the murdered body we had found.

Michael seemed to have made up his mind and glanced at his watch. "Ok, Matthew, I won't hold you up any longer. I hope you enjoy all this. Goodbye." And he held out his hand for me to shake.

"Right, thanks," I said, taken aback. I rather self-consciously and a little belatedly put out my hand to shake his. His grip was weak and clammy. "I'll see you later."

Michael gave me a hint of a smile. "Goodbye, Matthew," he said simply and turned and left.

Once Michael had gone I drifted into the familiar routine of preparing for a night's fishing. I taped my torch to my landing net handle with electrical tape after checking it still worked and the batteries were ok. I positioned my small Maglite at the bottom of one of my bedchair legs, unzipped the sleeping bag and corrected the pillows and positioned unhooking and weighing equipment on the outer side of my mosquito door. The unhooking mat was staked out in a nice clear area of the swim and the baitrunner conversions on my Daiwa Emblems were checked at least three times on each rod, as were the alarms and receiver box. By nightfall I was tucked up inside the sleeping bag listening to Radio 5 Live at very low volume wondering when the buzzers would crackle into life. By ten the radio had crackled its last words for the evening when I prodded its off button and I lay on the bedchair all snuggled up in my bag, eyes shut, feeling warm, expectant but sleepy. I forced myself to get up and have one last piss and returned to how I was before. With the outer door rolled up I zipped the mozzie door around to within a foot of completely closed as this was the location it needed to be. I was fully conditioned to waking up and instantly groping for the zip in that position. Years of fishing meant I'd be out of the bag, out of the bivvy and on my rods in a matter of seconds. I had no fear of Michael getting me on the twenty-second rule and, come to think of it, seemingly Michael had no fear full stop. What had happened in his head? It could only have been in there where the goalposts had been shifted. I gave it some thought but it couldn't have been for long because I was soon sound asleep.

A buzzer awoke me. Not a loud one, not my one, but a buzzer none the less. I looked out of my opaque door and to my surprise it was light, I'd slept through the whole night. I could still make out the sound of a one-noter so I dragged myself off my bedchair, undid the mozzie door zip and stepped outside. The buzzer was a little louder. I frowned. I'd never noticed hearing anybody else's alarm on the pit before, unlike some waters I'd fished where every moron and his mate seemed to revel in setting indicators with their alarms cranked to full volume. I tried to make out where the sound was coming from. It seemed to be from a westerly direction, around to where Rambo was fishing. Why was it still going? I strained my ears. Yes, it was definitely still going. I stood in limbo by my rods, intrigued by the reason a take should be unattended for such a time but also loathe to wind in my rods to go and look. The alarm continued. Bollocks! What was I going to do? If I pulled in I'd possibly foul up a good chance of a run. I'd had several fish early morning which had fallen to baits cast the previous afternoon. I could chance it. I could leave the rods out and go and look but with Michael on site that would have been bordering Kamikaze. The buzzer went on and on. It must have been a good minute by now. Reluctantly I wound in all three rods and legged it off around the track towards the sound.

As I ran around the track the noise of the buzzer became louder very quickly and by the time I was nearly to Rambo's swim it was virtually full volume. Confused I stopped and in the undergrowth by the side of the track I homed in on the noise and spotted Michael's receiver box, its red led flashing away, belting out the decibels. I picked it up and turned the volume down to zero. I shook it. The red led kept on flashing. I continued on to Rambo's south-west point swim only to discover he wasn't there. Now I could hear another buzzer going! Completely at sea I ran towards the latest take but as I pumped my arms and legs as fast as they could go, I realised I was more than likely running towards the same take the receiver box was telling me about. The buzzer sound became louder as I sprinted but it had stopped being a one-noter, it was now a sporadic run. I stopped. Breathing heavily I looked at the receiver box and listened intently. No sound. No red led. Dedededede! Flashflashflashflashflash! It was the same take. Michael's take! I sprinted on again around to Michael's swim, two up, count them, from Rambo. I scrambled off the track and down to the swim where Michael was fishing. It was one of the furthest from the track at around thirty yards distance. When I got there I could see Rambo standing next to Michael's bivvy, an Apotheosis like mine, and Michael's middle buzzer intermittently sounding off.

"What's going on?" I asked breathlessly.

Rambo turned towards me. "I wondered if you'd hear it. It seemed to be coming from either side of me."

I held up the receiver box. "I found this on the edge of the track. He must have dropped it last night. Where the fuck is he? Why hasn't he hit the run?"

"I don't know," said Rambo. "The fish must be on its fourth lap of the island now."

I walked down to Michael's rods and looked back at the bivvy. His front door was down and zipped. At that moment Noel arrived.

"You two!" he exclaimed frostily. "I'm surprised you're still allowed to be fishing here."

"Look, mate, it's all been squared..." I began but Noel cut me off.

"Michael's already told me you were there on his behalf. He must like you two for some reason, letting a pair in the syndicate *and* letting you use a boat for..."

It was Noel's turn to be cut off. "Shut the fuck up," said Rambo striding a few paces towards him. Noel shut up. The buzzer ran a staccato five-second tune. "Where, the fucking hell, is fucking, Michael?" snarled Rambo.

All three of us looked at the zipped-up tight bivvy and then at each other. "You're so worried about being left out of everything, *you* fucking well look... in there," Rambo growled at Noel whilst nodding at the bivvy.

Noel was losing colour fast but he did what he was told. He unzipped both sides of the angled front door and carefully rolled it up and secured it with the two toggles at the top. The inner door section, the one in two halves was fully zipped as well. Noel swallowed deeply and looked back, almost pleadingly, to Rambo and me.

"Go on," said Rambo coldly.

Noel knelt down and unzipped the inner door. As it fell away it revealed the mosquito door. It too was fully zipped. Noel turned back to look at both of us again but said nothing. He started to unzip the mozzie screen and instinctively both Rambo and myself edged forward to get a better look. The screen fell away and the first thing I saw was a butane/propane gas cooker and then set back in the gloomy recess of the bivvy was Michael lying on his bedchair all wrapped up in his sleeping bag, his eyes tightly closed.

"Michael?" said Noel quietly. "Michael?" There was no response. Noel crawled into the bivvy and put his hand on the sleeping bag roughly in the position where Michael's bony shoulder would be. He shook it. "Michael?" There was rising alarm and slight panic in Noel's voice. He shook Michael's prostrate body even more violently. "Michael! Michael!" screamed Noel hysterically. Noel frantically put his palm onto Michael's forehead and seemed to recoil in horror at what he felt and he scrambled out of the bivvy as fast as he could screeching and hollering. "Hucking fell! Hucking fell! He's ducking fead! He's only ducking fead!"

I looked over to Rambo who was watching Noel wiping the hand with which he'd touched Michael down the front of his jacket like he was trying to rid it of a dirty stain. In a way he was, it was the stain of death. Noel ran up towards the track shouting he'd tell the others. "Justice," I informed Rambo, "has been done."

"And seen to be done," said Rambo softly, dragging his frowning stare away from the deranged Noel. "It was rather nicely staged managed, as well, all it needed was a carp picking up a bait to draw our attention to it."

"What was?" I asked.

"Michael's suicide," said Rambo as he strode over to the bivvy, went in, did a cursory check on Michael's stone cold forehead and picked up the gas cooker. He held it up to his ear and waved it around. "Empty!" he declared. "Flue!"

"Flu?" I said.

"Severe lack of it," said Rambo. "Carbon monoxide poisoning. Michael killed himself by zipping himself up and lighting the cooker. It's like the candle in a glass bell experiment, instead of a flame being extinguished by a lack of oxygen you get a life being extinguished by a lack of ventilation and carbon monoxide poisoning. It's happened to other anglers in the past, through ignorance, this happened through knowledge. He knew exactly what he was doing."

"What now?" I asked.

"We wait for the others." Rambo scratched his chin. "I don't think we should say anything concerning suicide or the other stuff that's been going on."

"Death by misadventure?" I offered.

"Much better," confirmed Rambo.

A few minutes later Noel returned with two other anglers and Rocky. Rocky strutted down the grass path in his designer camo jacket, designer camo trousers, designer camo hat and expensive sunglasses. Completely ignoring both of us he zipped up the mozzie screen and inner door, unfurled a skull and crossbones flag and hung it across the bivvy's entrance.

"Just so everyone knows the score," he said to no one in particular.

"Do you always keep one of those handy?" I asked caustically. Rocky ignored me.

Noel was wringing his hands and seemed extremely upset. "What's going to happen to the syndicate now poor Michael's gone?" he asked anxiously. "What's it going to mean?"

"I don't know about you tossers," said Rocky smugly, "but the only thing it means to me is I'll be using four rods from now on and sacking fish to get some nice photos in daylight until someone else tells me different. Shall I phone for an ambulance? He'll start smelling if we leave him in there too long." Rocky finally turned his attention on me. "You can have his boilies if you want, hammer-nerd, he won't want them any more."

I expected Rambo to wade in and help me but he was far too busy trying to wind in three hundred yards of line and a carp.

Chapter 19

Michael was no more. The ambulance crew had carted him away later that fateful day once the emergency doctor had certified him dead. A few hours after, a suitably sombre Hollywood had arrived and carted all Michael's tackle away. All this took place after Rambo had amazingly landed the carp, which had, in its own strange way, signalled Michael's death to the rest of the world. Despite the probability of Michael being taken by the Grim Reaper a good seven hours before the carp had taken his boilie it seemed a fitting epitaph for his life. Especially as the carp was a new forty.

"Photograph him with it," Rambo had suggested. "It's what he would have wanted."

And sick as it might seem to an outsider all the carp anglers present had agreed, even the belligerent Rocky. It was what he would have wanted. His final night aptly spent on his water, the one great achievement of his life, and his final carp. And what a carp. Forty-five pounds plus of fully scaled delight. The detail of Rambo landing it after Michael had died seemed, in this instance, of little consequence. It was Michael's rod, his bait, his rig, his cast and magnanimously we awarded him its capture posthumously.

Getting Michael to hold this brand new forty had been a little tricky but eventually with a little cute thinking a suitable pose had been struck. Rambo had dragged him out of his bedchair, all cold and stiff - a bit like we've all been at times - and sat him up. He then stretched Michael's legs straight out in front of him and by the judicious use of a couple of banksticks had managed to prop his upper body at right angles to his legs. The weight of the carp had successfully pinned both Michael's hands to his legs and consequently arms to his side. He looked fine apart from a rather ungainly lolling head. To remedy this Rambo had laid on the ground behind Michael, on his side, so the camera couldn't see him, and held his head straight by grabbing a scruff of his hair. I was ready with the camera and the new forty, fortunately knackered from its marathon swim, had kept still long enough for me to take a few decent snaps.

"I had to hold his head," Rambo had explained, kicking away the banksticks so that Michael's body had slumped back onto the dirt with a thud, "because I wanted to preserve his dignity."

"But what's the new forty going to be called?" Noel, who was clearly a traditionalist, had asked.

We'd all stopped and thought. Ideas had been bounced around and rejected until I'd cracked it. "I've got!" I'd said. "Swansong!" And I had.

Covered in slime Michael had gone back into the bivvy and covered in slightly less than it had to begin with, Swansong had gone back into the pit. Rocky had put his flag back across the bivvy's entrance and as he'd correctly prophesised, Michael had soon started to smell. Only of rotten fish rather than rotten flesh.

That was all over a month ago and I was encouraged by how neatly all the loose ends had been tied up apart from one. The coroner had recorded a 'death by misadventure' decision, going to great lengths to point out the inherent dangers of using gas fired cooking or lighting in confined, unventilated conditions. He'd hoped that if any good came of Michael's sad accident it would be the publicity the incident raised therefore bringing it to the attention of others to hopefully stop a repetition of this tragedy. Hollywood had asked for a publicity ban on where the incident took place and it had duly been reported as 'a gravel pit in Kent', for which we were all grateful. There was absolutely no evidence of any foul play, he'd said, and due to the clear nature of the accident both his and the police's investigations had been nominal. Rambo was especially grateful for that as well.

On a different level I was happy to think the ghost had got what she'd wanted, the ultimate revenge, an eye for an eye and a life for a life. Going to any authority would have been far less conclusive. Somehow she had known the final straw that would break Michael's mental back would be the revelation of another human finding her remains, her ring and the murder weapon. Yet finally, at the death, so to speak, Michael had found release in the decision 'to do the right thing' as he'd put it and it was why, once having made the decision, he'd lost all his debilitating nervousness. 'Goodbye, Matthew', he'd said and he'd meant it. He had however, died an innocent man. Only myself, Rambo and Sophie knew of his terrible crime but it would have been churlish for me to worry over something the victim hadn't even concerned herself. She'd just wanted the bastard dead and at least Michael had redeemed himself, although forced, in a tiny way. I was fretting more over somebody like Noel wondering what we were really doing on the island and not whatever it was that Michael had told him. He might uncover the remains of the ghost again. Then the balloon would go up. I hoped not but the possibility existed. The only other problem was what of Michael doing the right thing over the fish stealing? How could it possibly be resolved now? It was the one loose end and I felt as if I could do little about it for things had changed rapidly at the pit since Michael's demise.

Rambo and I had buried the ghost's ring in the graveyard and therefore her soul, in the very grave where he himself was buried, if you see what I mean. In the middle of the night, again, we had sneaked in and with a small garden trowel I'd dug a tiny hole to the depth of my arm a couple of feet down from Rambo's headstone and popped her in. I was tempted to try the ring on to see if she was still there but I'd decided against it. It was time for her to rest peacefully forever.

Sophie was getting larger than ever but had kept her figure well, she had the bump and bigger boobs, but that was all. It hadn't spread to her arse and thighs, which pleased both of us in equal amounts, although possibly for different reasons. I was quite happy for her bust dimensions to stay the same now her bosoms had blossomed to 'D' cups. Our nights of passion, lit by her different body and raging hormones had long passed and the discomfort of sleeping, being awake and effectively feeding and nourishing the growing baby inside her had sapped her energy somewhat. Although Sophie was obviously apprehensive about giving birth for the first time and with still six weeks to go, I sensed she'd be happy when it was all over. Amy, though, seemed to be doing fine and every check up went without a hitch and all seemed normal. Everything else was really inconsequential when put alongside this.

As my fatherhood approached I felt no rising panic. I'd truly cured myself of my earlier terrible attitude, but I still felt the urge to go fishing. It was tempered with a desire to help Sophie get by the last most difficult few weeks, from a physical point of view, and also because the ghost and Michael had been laid to rest. Michael had been cremated and his ashes scattered on the margins of Hamworthy Fisheries. Only Hollywood had been invited to the funeral, apparently there had been a Will left by Michael which was in the hands of his solicitor, who was the executor, and this desire had been expressly stated. It seemed all too clear who was going to be the syndicate leader and I wondered how Rambo and myself would fair under the new regime or if we would fair in it at all. In moments of weakness I wondered, in spite of the heinous crime Michael had committed, whether it would have been a case of 'better the devil you know'.

The principal reasons for these bouts of weakness were the changes I'd mentioned at the pit. Attitudes had changed and become much more lax amongst some of the members now the fear of a Michael-instigated expulsion were gone. For those who didn't blatantly flout the rules there was the sense of being in limbo and of course many were still in shock. Speculation on how someone as experienced as Michael could possibly die in such a manner was rife. Some mentioned the possibility of suicide because Michael had a life threatening disease and only a short, painful time left to live but the autopsy, by all accounts, had only revealed carbon monoxide poisoning. Apparently it forms a stable compound with haemoglobin in the blood stopping it from transporting oxygen to the body tissues. Not a lot of people know that, or need to know that. Of all the other rumour and gossip only Alan surmised that it was the ghost who had separated Michael from his breath. I'd told him ghosts were notoriously hopeless when it came to using cigarette lighters or matches and he'd walked off in a huff. I mean, what bollocks! If we were talking third parties then if anyone was the killer it was me, with, it had to be said, a bit of help from the ghost, Rambo and that foliage-festooned pig, Rocky, for his Rocky horror hammer hooking show.

Since Michael's death Rocky had become insufferable, strutting and swaggering around the pit, all dolled up in his high specification designer outfits, like he owned it. The Goretex Muppet. He'd become even more obnoxious and he intimidated nearly everyone he spoke to, apart from you know who. Rambo continued to turn the other cheek, he was biding his time for the climax I felt sure, whenever it was likely to be. Darren was now openly photographing fish with a bait company's hat on or wearing another bait company's sweatshirt or having some other tackle brand name emblazoned somewhere upon on his person. And sometimes all with the same fish! I waited for the first crop of pictures to turn up in a magazine advert or, even worse, an article. Generally speaking members wandered about more, left their rods out and, not unsurprisingly, started to mix more than they'd ever done now all the constraints were gone. Hence rumour, gossip and opinion were voiced more readily than at any other time in the syndicate's history. Alan moaned and Noel moaned, both were annoyed at how standards were slipping but both were careful to avoid doing so while Hollywood was around. Yes, even Hollywood turned up to fish and brought his two stunning looking, lap dancing, ex-international gymnasts, who were also bisexual nymphomaniacs. And Christ on a bike, or on a dyke if you like, were they! No one complained about that either. Guests were supposedly not permitted but sycophancy was the name of the game, as everyone now knew the score. Hollywood was the man in waiting.

Mind you, only a nutter or a raving homosexual would have complained or been uninterested in the girls. It was hard not to gawp at them such was their stunning, I hesitate to use the word 'beauty', 'allure' is better. One of them was blonde and the other was a raven-headed brunette. Brunette in the sense of dark-skinned, not exactly black, but more a dark coffee colour. Even in the midst of visualising the frantic, lust-charged bedroom scenes from what Michael had told me I hadn't, for some reason, thought of them as one being white and the other black. Somehow it gave them more enticement than they had in the first place and they had plenty of it even then. They both possessed feline grace and silky motion with even the most elementary of movements such as walking, bending over, especially bending over, seemingly supercharged with sexual promise. (It was funny how anglers were always passing by Hollywood's swim, wherever it was). Even from a distance, ok so it was from a distance through binoculars, I was smitten. Both girls oozed, absolutely oozed, sex. If I hadn't known they were two stunning looking, lap dancing, ex-international gymnasts, who were also bisexual nymphomaniacs I'd have probably guessed it. When all three disappeared into the bivvy it left a dry sensation in the mouth and a yearning to be Hollywood for just one day. No wonder he gave up fishing! And now he didn't even need to do that because he could bring them to the pit! And he was going to get the best carp syndicate in England given to him! The moon on a stick? A pantechnicon of gold? A lifetime's supply of boilies? Crap. BBC quiz prizes. Hollywood had it all, or at least he would soon.

In early October I received a letter from the amusingly named solicitors Farrington, Farrington and Furlington. It was from Mr Furlington (senior partner) in fact, requesting my attendance at a meeting, at the syndicate clubhouse on the 16th October, 7:30 pm (bring bird and bottle) where the final Will and Testament of Michael Edward Brown would be read to all parties invited.

"It should be a fun evening," I said to Rambo when I phoned to see if he'd got a letter as well. He had.

"Wouldn't miss it for the world," he said. "Hollywood might bring those couple of tarts along."

"I like tarts," I said. "Especially burnt ones. I could eat them all up."

"You're not getting any are you?" came the reply down the phone.

"She's nearly eight months gone and looks like she's going to burst!" I explained. "I don't like to ask in case it's me who bursts her!"

"Pin-prick!" said Rambo and hung up.

On the night of the 16th Rambo and I travelled to the pit. I was under explicit instructions not to leave my fully charged mobile unattended for a second in case Sophie rather inconveniently went into labour. I promised not to. On the way we chewed over what we should do, if anything, about Rocky and Darren and the fish stealing. Rambo thought it would be prudent not do anything until we knew for certain who the new leader would be.

"But it's going to be Hollywood!" I exclaimed.

"Aren't you forgetting something?" said Rambo.

"Like what?"

"Like Michael saying he'd do the right thing about the fish stealing. Maybe he's sorted it and Hollywood's first act as leader will be to chuck the pair of them out and possibly the other one we don't know about. It's why I haven't flattened Rocky, I don't want to jeopardise our fishing if I don't need to."

Rambo was right. We'd keep it buttoned up tight and go with the flow.

When we arrived the clubhouse was packed and everyone appeared to be there. It was just like another work party, the whole syndicate had been invited and if there was going to be any dirty washing done it was going to be in public. The room thronged with tiny conversations. I caught snippets of them as we walked into the room.

"… I'm not saying she's ugly but she looks like she's been set on fire and then put out with a shovel…"

"… Twenty notes I paid for it, I didn't think that was too bad…"

"… Anyway he was putting out freebies in the dark tied with pva to a bankstick so they landed spot on. Clipped up boiles! Neat!…"

Rambo and I made our way through the seats, which had been split into two banks of ten, a line of four, three and three again with a corridor gap between them. I recognised Darren, Rocky, Alan, Grant, Noel, a smug looking Hollywood, on his own disappointingly, and a few other faces I could now put names to, Jim, Gary and Jez. We parked our arses in the last empty pair of seats, which were on the left side, second row, looking into the room. This put us directly adjacent to Rocky and Darren and it was Rambo who elected to sit in the outer chair, the one next to the corridor to mirror Rocky who was also perched on an outer seat. On the one hand traditional camouflage, on the other neo-designer camouflage. A thin, balding man wearing a dull grey suit sat at a table at the head of the room, peering at papers through a pair of glasses that looked to be sitting too far down his nose. He looked over the top of the glasses at the motley selection of individuals in front of him and eventually spoke in a Radio 4 announcer's voice with extra plums.

"Good evening, gentlemen. If I may have your undivided attention." The room went quiet. "Thank you. Let me introduce myself if I may. I am Justin Furlington, senior partner in Farrington, Farrington and Furlington solicitors…"

"F-f-f-fucking hell," whispered Rambo.

"… And I am here this evening in my capacity as executor of the late Michael Edward Brown's Will and Testament. Now firstly I need to ascertain that everyone is present. The correct number of people seem to be here but I'd like to read out from this list," he held up a sheet of paper, "the names of all the present members of the syndicate and for you to individually indicate your presence. Similar to a school register if you like. So. Gary James,"

"Here!" said Hollywood, a little over-enthusiastically.

"Grant Curtis."

"Yes!"

"Darren Armstrong."

"Here."

Mr Furlington, I couldn't bring myself to think of him as Justin, worked his way around the room carrying out his first mundane task, no doubt being charged out at £148 an hour, until he announced the name Tobias Simpkins-Smythe.

"Yep," answered Rocky.

Rambo let out a huge guffaw but never so much as glanced at Rocky when he did. Rocky's head ripped to his left and he glowered at Rambo with a look of pure malice. He saw I was looking at him and turned his withering glare on me so I looked at Mr Furlington who completed the full set of names without further ado.

"Ok, gentlemen, thank you. Now what I'm about to read to you are Mr Brown's wishes for the disposal of Hamworthy Fisheries." Mr Furlington stopped and took off his glasses and held them by an arm, swinging them between a thumb and finger. "For those of you who aren't aware, Hamworthy Fisheries, or perhaps more pertinently, what you perceive to be the syndicate you are in comprises an area of land around sixty acres. This obviously includes the pit and all the fish resident within it, this clubhouse," he twirled the glasses as if they were a pointer, "and the access track from the main road." He put the glasses back on again halfway up his nose and peered at us over the top of them. "The Will is very straightforward and leaves no ambiguity. Other assets which have nothing to do with you have already been dealt with so the section of the Will dealing directly with this estate can be read to you verbatim." Mr Furlington looked down at a piece of paper and then looked up. "There is, however, another matter to be dealt with which isn't to do with the disposal of the estate but once again this is very straightforward and self-explanatory."

My heart bumped. Had Rambo called it right?

Mr Furlington held up the piece of paper. "This is the part of the Will, as we received it, that concerns you all. I read as follows." Mr Furlington cleared his throat and read aloud. "Dear fellow members of the syndicate. As you listen to this you are no doubt wondering what is going to happen to the syndicate now I am dead. Most of you will be aware that building up the syndicate from scratch has been the most important thing in my life. Years of effort and hard work have gone into making it the finest carp water in England and, despite the fact I'm no longer around, I still want my legacy to live on and improve. Over the years I have run the syndicate in virtual solitude, taking and making decisions on my own and, it is my belief, this autocratic rule has lead to the eminence of the water. As an individual I could make hard, clear, fast judgements without having to go through the fudging and compromise which sometimes arises as a result of too many people having a say. Consequently I envisage and therefore insist on a similar arrangement taking place in the future. The syndicate, post Michael Brown, will be run by one person. Clearly the person who takes over the running of the syndicate will have to be someone I can trust to carry on my life's work in a manner I would approve. How he runs the syndicate on a day-to-day basis will differ from how I did but I hope the individual concerned will adhere to the standards I have set and try to improve on them. A full list of details will be given to that person tonight appertaining to legal and financial matters but as such this is not information the rest of the members need to be privy to. Running the syndicate will not be easy and it may be an onerous task to take my place but nevertheless, I have every confidence in the individual concerned. I'm sure he will be more than capable of the task. I have also decided to allot a percentage of the yearly syndicate fees as part of my Will to the creation of a paid position within the syndicate. This position will be something akin to being the syndicate leader's right hand man, a lieutenant, if you like, to help carry out the more mundane tasks involved in running the syndicate. The person who commands this position will report directly to the new leader and it will be up to him to enforce syndicate rules on the ground. Again a full list of details will be given to that person tonight. Hopefully this new position will help assist the new leader as he comes to terms with his new job and stop any future unsavoury activities. With hindsight it is perhaps something I should have considered in my time, as a partner to help share the burden of day-to-day events would have eased my pressures considerably. So, fellow members, that is my legacy and how things will be in the future. As you can appreciate, no sweeping changes, no radical upheaval and the ship sails on to bigger and more numerous carp. I hope you will all give your very best support to the new Hamworthy Fisheries regime and that you will all act correctly and subsequently make his life easier. Therefore I need only say that I wish the very best of luck to the new owner of the entire Hamworthy Fisheries estate, Matthew Williams, and his new lieutenant, Rambo." Mr Furlington looked up over his glasses. "It is signed Michael Brown and dated."

I looked at Rambo and he looked back at me. I was in a state of complete and utter, numb, knock me down with a feather, can't believe my ears, shock. Had we both really heard what we thought we'd just heard? The way everyone in the room was rubbernecking the pair of us, their faces contorted with stupefaction, I guessed we had. The words 'hit', 'fan', 'shit's' and 'the', sprang to mind. Mr Furlington cantered on.

"I have also in my possession three expulsion letters which came to light during our work on Michael's Will and these must be implemented as decreed in his list of unusual circumstances. Therefore the following people will be expelled from the syndicate in breach of contract, with loss of 1st deposit on the grounds of fish stealing; Darren Armstrong, Tobias Simpkins-Smythe and Gary James."

Holy fucking mega-pandemonium. There was the mass screeching of chair legs dragging across the floor, powered by the backs of the members' legs standing to attention. It was like Old Trafford with Giggs homing in on goal.

"What the fuck's all this about," roared Rocky squaring up to Rambo.

"Go to it, lieutenant," I said into the back of Rambo's ear. "'Enforce the rules of the syndicate on the ground', the man said."

"Gladly," said Rambo in a low growl.

"Sit down, Simpkins," snarled Rambo. "Before I put you down."

"Oh, yeah?" said Rocky.

"Yeah!" said Rambo.

"All right," said Rocky mildly and sat down.

His arse had been barely parked a nano-second when Rocky bolted out of the chair from his sitting position and rugby tackled Rambo in the midriff. The pair of them careered into me and three other members knocking them and chairs asunder like a bowling ball ploughing through skittles.

I heard Mr Furlington shout. "I say, would you mind stopping, please. We are all civilised human beings after all."

Wrong species I thought as I removed a chair leg from my ear, we're carp anglers. I looked up from my prostrate position of being flat on my back to see Rocky hit Rambo across the back and shoulders with one of the wooden chairs. It went kit form on impact and shards of wood fell to the floor but Rambo remained standing. Rambo dived over the strewn chairs and bodies and clattered into Rocky like a piledriver. Suddenly my vision of the camouflaged contenders' combat contest was interrupted by a hysterical Hollywood.

"What have you fucking done? You conniving little fuck! This place is mine! Mine!" Hollywood hollered.

"Piss off!" I told him. "If it was so important to you why did you help nick fish from it?"

Hollywood's handsome face was distorted with anger and rage but his mind seemed to be grappling with the consequences of his foolish actions. As we stood, well, as he stood and I lay flat on my back, eyes locked like rutting stag's antlers, with no words spoken, I could tell he knew he'd blown it. For whatever the reasons were for him to help pinch fish from the best carp water in England, only now, on the day when it should have been all his, could he see how ridiculously inappropriate they were. If it was greed or arrogance, jealousy or because of some slight, whether real or imagined by Michael, I'd never know. All I was sure of was this was Hollywood's moment of reckoning. I wondered how hard he'd hit me. Our eyes still held and then Hollywood wrenched his away, dropped his gorgeous face into his two open hands and started to cry like a baby. His shoulders heaved and despite the Rocky and Rambo show crashing around in the background like a couple of bulls in a china shop, I could hear him sob. He was crying like his mother had died. His rich mother, who had written him out of her will at the last moment and left it all to a virtual stranger who she'd meet eight months ago.

My mobile rang and my heart leapt into my mouth. My home number was showing on the display. Forgetting Rambo, Rocky, Hollywood and the distraught Mr Furlington who was dabbing at his bald head with a hanky crying for order, I answered it. It was Sophie.

"Matthew! Come quickly! I think it's started!" said the nervy voice on the other end.

"I'm on my way," I heard myself say. FAB. Thunderbirds are go. I needed Thunderbird 1 but the van was more like the fucking Mole in terms of speed, not digging ability of course.

I turned round to see Rambo spinning Rocky around horizontally on his shoulders like they were a pair of satellite TV wrestlers.

"Put him down! She's started to have the baby," I shouted.

"Don't panic, boy, first one's never pop out quick," said Rambo effortlessly, while completing a full three-sixty. "As you wish."

Rambo walked out from underneath Rocky who fell with an almighty crash to the floor. Gamely he staggered to his feet but Rambo took hold of his right arm by the wrist and elbow with both of his hands and shoved down hard while bringing up his right knee. There was a sickening noise. Think; big wind up on 13ft broom handles, 5-ounce lead and a shut bail arm.

"You won't be holding a rod for a long time, mister," said Rambo evilly.

Rocky's face was twisted in agony and as I looked at the compound fracture of his right arm, the bone poking out through the skin like a jagged piece of metal, my stomach turned and I felt faint.

*   *   *

Sophie's face was twisted in agony and as I looked at her hand squeezing mine so tight it had turned white, what with the heat and smell of the hospital my stomach turned and I felt faint.

"One more push, love. Nearly there, one more push," said the midwife.

If Sophie wasn't near to the end of her limit, I was. It'd been nine hours. An hour and a half's mad drive from the clubhouse, all alarm and consternation, half an hour to get to the hospital and then seven slow-motion hours of me sitting around being there. Being there. That's all I was and all the good I was. I could contribute, had contributed, absolutely nothing apart from my being there. It was out of my hands and the feeling of helplessness and inadequacy was awful. Everyone else knew better and was more equipped to help and the pain and suffering that Sophie was being subjected to made it all the worse. I was nothing. I was the dad. End of story. I'd done my bit and now I felt as if I was in the way and a waste of space. I was waiting for the wonder of childbirth but all I saw was the suffering of my partner. It wasn't a joyous occasion and despite whatever I might feel when eventually Amy did get forced out it would be mightily tempered by what Sophie had gone through to get her there. First births are often difficult. I'd read it in a book, now I could see it was true.

"That's it! That's it! Here she comes! Here she comes!" encouraged the midwife.

I stared down past Sophie's pulled up knees to watch in fascination as the midwife took a tiny body from her and lifted it up and after a while put it onto Sophie's chest.

"Here you are, love, here's your daughter. She's perfect."

Amy started to cry and Sophie, forgetting her pain, cuddled her. The midwife clamped the chord and asked me if I wanted to cut it. Dimly I nodded and did my one party piece of the whole rigmarole. The midwife wrapped Amy in a small blanket and asked if I'd like to hold her while she attended to Sophie and the other end of the chord. Feeling cumbersome and inexpert I self-consciously cradled my little daughter. She was so tiny. I gently kissed her little head and felt all my pent-up frustration and emotion spill out of my body. I cried like Hollywood had, not over loss but over my gain. The wonder of birth and life, at last, despite trauma and worry, finally hit me. A mass of thoughts and feelings rampaged through my body. Death, life and something in the middle, I'd been witness to them all over the last three-quarters of a year. I'd ended up with two new avenues in my life, a daughter and a syndicate and the two seemed strangely and inextricably linked.

* * *

Amy was fast asleep in her cot alongside Sophie who was fast asleep in our bed and I was downstairs with Lieutenant Rambo. All the papers I'd hastily grabbed from Mr Furlington were sprawled on the floor and the pair of us perused them. I was a rich man, it appeared, what with the fishery and the associated finances. The top and bottom of all the legal papers were, in a nutshell, that Hamworthy Fisheries belonged to me. I had to run it for five years before I could sell it, should I want to, but apart from that I was free to do with it as I pleased. Rambo, as my right hand man, was entitled to draw 10% of the members' fees as wages, plus his ticket was gratis. I looked at the deeds of ownership with bemusement for all the necessary documents had my name on them. It was almost as amazing as little baby Amy upstairs in the cot. What with my commitments to her and to the syndicate I could see life would be one hell of a juggling act but at least I was interested in what I was juggling. What a life and all because of a couple of deaths.

The final letter was still to be opened. It was marked for my attention and had 'Strictly Confidential' in bold letters. A wax seal was on the rear. Even Mr Furlington hadn't read this one. I opened it up and read it to Rambo. It was a long rambling account of why it was me who turned out to be the beneficiary of Michael's Will and, fascinatingly, a small insight into Michael's relationship with the ghost. Basically the unknown Alan was the fish farmer Michael had dealt with during the original stocking of Hamworthy. Apparently he had become a firm friend of Hollywood's over the years and it was because of this Michael had the notion of Hollywood's involvement. The pick-up *had* been in the garage during the general period of the fish raid but Broughton Motors had confirmed to Michael it had been ready way before the time he eventually collected it. They also confirmed that Hollywood had borrowed it on the pretence of making sure it was all right, during the precise time of the fish raid. When Michael had subsequently asked Hollywood about this he, unwittingly, sealed his own fate by saying he'd used it to shift some rubbish but hadn't wanted to bother the unwell Michael with such details. Hollywood was unaware of Michael's new information that I'd given him and so my facts were confirmed and Hollywood, Rocky and Darren's treachery was exposed. Why Hollywood had betrayed Michael was still a mystery. Perhaps it was for the old evil of money. Michael knew too well its siren-like temptation.

Michael and the ghost had been lovers; intent on marriage and buying a house together but unexpectedly the pit had come on the market, put up for sale by the old gravel working company. Obsessed with his fledgling idea of a carp fishery Michael had used both his and the ghost's, or I should say young woman's, money to buy it. When she'd found out he'd tricked her to meet him on the grounds of reconciliation and in the old woods he'd bludgeoned her to death. And then buried her on the island. Riddled with guilt Michael began his physical deterioration but the drive to make the fishery was stronger than the one to admit his crime and lose it. Even when he himself was visited by the ghost he simply stopped night fishing and pressed on until Rambo and I discovered the truth. Faced with fresh investigation, Rambo's sortie into the woods, and finally with hard evidence, the hammer, ring and our finding the body Michael could take no more. The double blow of being betrayed by his one best friend over the thing he held most dear finally persuaded Michael to take his life, as the ghost had foreseen. Justice, at last was done.

At the end of his letter Michael wondered if I would reveal the truth to the rest of the world about his accidental death being suicide and the grim reasons behind it. He knew that Mr Furlington would keep his own doubts concerning the late alteration to the Will and his own sudden demise to himself but would I? He also answered why Hollywood had been the only member in attendance at the scattering of his ashes. It was simply to make him think he was still going to get Hamworthy and therefore it would be more of a knife in his ribs when he found out he wouldn't even be fishing it let alone owning it! The thin line between love and hate!

"Well, I guess it clears up a few questions," I said quietly to Rambo.

"And leaves a few hundred more," he replied. "Will you tell the world?"

I thought hard. "What good would it do? The pit would be splashed all over the press, there'd be a major upheaval, and the fishing would be disturbed. I can't see any reason to do it to be honest."

"What about her relatives? At least they'd know?" said Rambo.

"She never mentioned them. Maybe there aren't any, weren't any and that's why there didn't appear to be any outrage when she originally went missing. 'Tell him', she'd said and she'd asked to be buried elsewhere, that was all. There was definitely no mention of anybody else."

"What about her bones?"

"They'll have to go. We'll have to dispose of them somehow and it must be our first job. All it'll take is one inquisitive member like Noel or Alan to find them and it would be a complete disaster." I said adamantly.

"It's your decision. It'll always be your decision from now, boy."

"I know," I said meaningfully. "I bloody well know."

After Rambo had gone I gently kissed Amy in her cot and then kissed Sophie. Both of them were blissfully asleep but Amy would be crying for her milk fairly soon. I decided to wait up until she did so I could feed her and let her mum get some well-earned sleep. To pass the time I went and cleaned my teeth and then looked at the photo of the dead Michael holding Swansong. It was all right as trophy shots go, maybe a bit of an unusual pose I had to admit and certainly not a standard number one. And as for the expression on Michael's face? Well, loads of us had shut our eyes at the wrong time when being snapped. For all anyone might know, who wasn't party to the bizarre truth, the sun might have been shining in his eyes. Idly I wondered how many anglers had caught a fish after they'd died? Surely there weren't many? I could only think of two, Michael and Rambo.